Single Black Female

Also by Tracy Brown

Criminal Minded

White Lines

Twisted

Snapped

Aftermath

White Lines II: Sunny

White Lines III: All Falls Down

Boss

ANTHOLOGIES

Flirt

Single Black Female

TRACY BROWN

ST. MARTIN'S GRIFFIN
NEW YORK

This is a work of fiction. All of the characters, organizations, and events portrayed in this novel are either products of the author's imagination or are used fictitiously.

First published in the United States by St. Martin's Griffin, an imprint of St. Martin's Publishing Group

For information, address St. Martin's Publishing Group, 120 Broadway, New York, NY 10271.

www.stmartins.com

Library of Congress Cataloging-in-Publication Data

Names: Brown, Tracy, 1974– author.
Title: Single black female / Tracy Brown.
Description: First Edition. | New York : St. Martin's Griffin, 2021.
Identifiers: LCCN 2021021933 | ISBN 9781250043016 (trade paperback) | ISBN 9781466841000 (ebook)
Classification: LCC PS3602.R723 S56 2021 | DDC 813/.6—dc23
LC record available at https://lccn.loc.gov/2021021933

First Edition: 2021

10 9 8 7 6 5 4 3 2 1

This is dedicated to Black women.
The world wants our rhythm, but not our blues.
May we continue to wear our crowns with grace,
ever mindful that we are royalty.

Part One

Fool's Gold

Ivy sat at the table in the drafty visiting room at Elmira Correctional Facility, staring down at her hands. The place looked like a castle from the outside, but felt like a cold fortress within its steely walls. It was a setting that was sadly familiar to her. In the years since Michael had gone to prison, Ivy had soldiered on, raising their two sons, Noah and Kingston, single-handedly. She brought them to visit him often, no matter how far up north the state of New York moved him. The demeaning routine of traveling to prisons in the wee hours of the morning, storing their valuables in lockers, and being searched invasively by aggressive guards had become a regular part of their lives. To say it had taken its toll on all of them was putting it mildly.

She had come to visit her man on a Thursday morning. It was a deliberate choice. Her work as a salon owner and top-tier stylist had her busier than ever. She had scheduled her clients carefully this week to leave this day open. The upcoming weekend would be a hectic one, and this was the only day she could get here. Her sons—sixteen and twenty-two years old—were usually with her on these visits. But she had allowed them to sit this one out, much to their relief.

As she waited for Michael to come down for his visit, she thought about what she had come to tell him. She knew that it wouldn't be easy. She glanced around the room at other visitors sitting happily with the inmates they had come to see. She looked at the grimacing guards at the front of the room watching everything closely and doing nothing at the same time.

Finally, the door in the corner opened and a guard escorted Michael out. He smiled the moment he spotted Ivy and walked smoothly in her direction.

Ivy stood and hugged him warmly and briefly, aware the guards were quick to issue a stern verbal warning whenever there was too much contact. Michael had been confined at this facility for the past several years and had built a contentious relationship with most of the guards. For that reason, they cut him no slack in the visiting room. She held on to his hand as he sat down across from her, still as handsome as ever after all these years.

"Hey, beautiful," he said. "You looking good. All thick and shit. I like it."

Ivy was tall and statuesque with a gorgeous sepia complexion, a set of dimples that made every woman jealous, and *style* dripping from every pore. She was big boned, but not fat.

The very definition of thick, with an enviable wardrobe to accommodate those curves.

Ivy smiled, grateful for the compliment, but aware he was being generous with his praise. She'd packed on about fifteen pounds over the past few months and she wasn't happy about that shit at all.

"Thank you. You look good, too."

"I thought all night about what you said on the phone yesterday," he said. He looked her in the eyes, searching for what she wasn't yet saying. "You said you had something you wanted to talk about. Wouldn't tell me what it was. Had me thinking all types of shit. So, let's talk."

She nodded, slowly let go of his hand. This was it. No foreplay. Just straight to the point. She told herself she shouldn't be surprised. Michael was always the type to get right down to business.

"This is gonna be my last time coming up here for a while, Mikey."

Her voice was light and far less confident than she felt. She cleared her throat and spoke with more authority this time. "I need a break. Noah and King do, too."

She rubbed her arms as if she were cold. But really, she was attempting to comfort herself and push herself to say what she came to say.

"I've been telling you for a while how I feel. When you were eight years in, we talked about it for the first time. I sat in this same room and told you how tired I am. How hard it is to get up here all the time. I keep talking about it. But it's time for me to make a move. I can't keep doing this, Mikey."

He shifted in his seat, glaring at her.

She continued. "Things are different now. Noah and King aren't kids anymore. I'm getting older, too. This is getting harder. I've been taking care of everything for a long time now. I'm at the point where I need to start taking care of myself more. Recognize when I need a break. And I need one now, Mikey. Just for a little while."

Michael stared at her in silence for a time, then he nodded slowly.

"That's why the boys didn't come here with you today?" he asked. "They need a break?"

Ivy could hear the anger beneath his words. The hurt. She stared at him, wishing she could make him understand how hard it had been for her to come here today and have this conversation. How incredibly hard it had been for all of them for the past sixteen years of his incarceration.

She nodded. "King had school today."

"And Noah?" Michael was smirking, but he wasn't amused at all. "He dropped out of college and moved out to Staten Island with you. So, what's his excuse?"

Ivy sighed. "They're *tired,* Mikey. We just moved, still getting used to everything. After King gets out of school today, they're gonna go to Coco's place. She needs their help doing a few things around her apartment. I'll pick them up from there."

Michael let out a laugh, though she could tell he found nothing funny.

"Wow. *Coco.* I haven't seen her in a while, either. I guess my little sister—who I spoiled rotten and put through college—is tired, too, huh?"

"She is," Ivy said, nodding. "All of us are. Coming up here as often as we do is taking a toll on everybody. Every two weeks without fail, one of us or all of us comes to visit you. That's not easy, Mikey. We have to reschedule and cancel appointments, wake up in the middle of the night and drive four hours. It's not like we're all sitting around scratching our asses. Every one of us is working hard."

"And what you think I'm doing, Ivy? You think this shit ain't hard?"

She watched him closely as he glanced around at the other inmates in the room. She knew from their conversations over the years that some of the inmates were Mikey's friends, some of them foes. Ivy knew that she and the rest of his family had no idea what he was dealing with on a daily basis. She assumed that he shielded them from most of it, the constant fight he was in to remain dominant in a climate that epitomized the notion of survival of the fittest.

In comparison to many other inmates, he wasn't having the worst experience behind bars. His commissary was at capacity, his locker stocked with everything he needed and more. He called home daily and received biweekly visits from his lady, his kids, and his extended family. He got mail all the time from his family and friends. He had "friends" inside and was feared and revered by many. But what he didn't have was the constant presence of the people he loved. He didn't have the freedom to come and go as he pleased, or the ability to progress in life the way everyone else was. He was stuck in a cage, cornered and stagnant, while the whole world was going on without him.

"You know I don't need this shit. They got me in here doing life, Ivy. Y'all trying to leave a nigga now?"

"First of all, stop saying that. Nobody's leaving you. We never left you. Not once. And stop saying you're in here for life. You can still get out."

"Pfft," he scoffed. "I pled guilty in exchange for fifteen years. Every time I turn around, they charge me with some other bull-shit and add more time to my sentence. I went before the parole board and them muthafuckas couldn't wait to deny me. What you think is gonna happen the next time I go in there? They gonna change their mind?"

Ivy hated the hopelessness she saw in his eyes. Hated herself even more for feeling that same hopelessness inside.

"When I was home, I always took care of you."

"Mikey—"

"Never told you 'no.' If I had it, you had it. Now I'm down and out and you wanna stop coming up here. You wanna take a break. Does that shit sound right to you?"

"I'm not saying it's right. I'm just saying we've been coming up here every month for sixteen years."

The expression on Michael's face made it clear he didn't see the problem with that.

"You were going with me to the car dealerships and all the stores for ten years before that. I didn't hear you complain. So now that it's the downside of the game, you can't take it no more?"

He sucked his teeth in disgust.

"When I was out there making moves, everybody was good. I made sure of that. I bought my mother a house before she died—the same house my sister Patsy lives in now. I put Coco through college. I gave you the world. Left you with everything I had. Enough for you to start your business and take care of you and the boys. And now that Patsy got the house and Coco got her degrees and you got your career, y'all gonna leave a nigga behind. I see how it is."

Ivy threw up her hands. "You've been locked up for King's whole life, Mikey. Noah hardly remembers a time when you were home with us. I've been bringing them on these visits for *sixteen* years. Since they were kids. They're grown-ass men now. They love you. They know it's not easy for you being in here. But this is hard on them, too. It's hard on all of us."

"What's hard? Driving your new car up here and then going back to your new house? It's hard for Coco to live in her high-rise apartment in Manhattan and play dress-up all day? For Patsy and her kids to be living in the house I paid for?"

Ivy frowned. "That's what you think we do all day?"

"Yup," he said defiantly. "Every one of you is living off the work I put in."

"You make it sound like we didn't put in work, too."

"You did?" Michael folded his arms across his chest and sat back, waiting for her to explain that one.

Ivy was hurt and it showed. She thought of all the years she spent taking risks in the name of love. Michael sounded like those risks meant nothing to him.

"You were the one who paid for it, but Coco worked hard to finish college and get her master's degree. And, yeah, you set me up. Made sure me and the boys had enough to get by."

"More than enough," Michael corrected her.

"But I took what you gave me and quadrupled that shit. I've been running my business for ten years now. By myself. All while holding you down and making sure that our sons are on the right track."

He shook his head, still defiant. "You're trying to make them into something they're not. I keep telling you that. You sent Noah off to college, wasting money. I told you he was never the type of kid that's cut out for college."

"And what was the alternative? Let him get in the game?"

Michael smirked. "And end up like me? Just say it."

Ivy didn't deny it.

"You changed. I noticed it years ago. Pushing for Noah to go to college instead of letting him get out there and put in work like a man. Selling the house in Brooklyn so you could move out to Staten Island. Out there with Deja and her trifling ass. Supposedly because the schools out there are better for King. But we both know you're just trying to get them away from Patsy and her kids and the truth of who we are and where we come from."

"And what do you want for them, Mikey? This?"

Ivy looked around the room questioningly.

"I want them to be men!" he said. "Not some sucker niggas who can't hold their own when the time comes."

"And being a man means what? Looking over their shoulders all the time? Getting so powerful that they start to feel untouchable like you did?"

"So now you're blaming me for being in here, knowing that I did what I had to do to protect all of us."

"I'm not blaming you."

"Sure fuckin' sounds like it!"

"I knew who you were from the beginning. I knew the life you were living. But call me crazy. I thought you knew that shit couldn't go on forever. I thought you would find a way out of that life eventually. The businesses I helped you set up. The investments. I never wanted you to be in the streets long-term."

Michael shrugged. "The streets is all I know. My father was a hustler till he got killed. My uncle died in jail. I did what I was taught to do. Maybe you saw a future where I wasn't hustling. But I never saw that shit. The grind is in me. The streets is who I am. And you used to love it. Or you acted like you did. Now you got a little freedom, and you think you get to walk away. With my sons? You must be crazy."

The look he gave her sent chills down her spine. So cold and threatening.

"Those are *my* sons. Not just yours."

"Whether you think so or not, I'm doing a great job with Noah and Kingston. They're on the right track. I'm trying to keep it that way."

Ivy felt a headache coming on and sighed.

"I just want to spend some time getting settled in. We just moved in a few months ago, and there's still boxes everywhere. I need to stand still for a minute. Just stand still and take a fuckin' breath and unpack . . . all of it."

She was talking about much more than the boxes piled up in her new house.

Michael looked around the visiting room at others like him, dressed in their prison uniforms but mentally transported somewhere else while they enjoyed their visits. As long as they were seated at these benches smiling at their loved ones, they could pretend they were someplace else, that things weren't as hopeless as they seemed when they were locked away inside the toxic prison walls that housed them. He thought about how excited he got whenever a visitor was coming. He would lay his clothes out the night before, wake up early that morning and wait for them to call his name. Each visit was an opportunity to break out of jail for a while. Now the privilege of escaping reality—at least mentally during the duration of their visit—was being snatched from him. Instead of bringing him a few hours of happiness, Ivy had brought him another painful reason to go back to his dorm and sulk.

He looked at her, long and hard. There were so many things he wanted to say in that moment. None of them nice, but he kept his mouth shut until he had his emotions somewhat under control.

"You should have just left in the beginning the way that Deja did with Rashid," he ultimately said, as calmly as he could. "At least he knew from the start that he had to do his time alone."

Ivy's eyes narrowed. Deja and Rashid's relationship had always been a sensitive subject for them to discuss. When Michael had gotten arrested in connection with a drug-related murder, his boy Rashid had gone down with him. Ivy had been by her man's side in the years since then.

Rashid's girl Deja had jumped ship immediately. Ivy didn't appreciate the comparison Michael was making one bit.

She took a breath. "Listen. I know this ain't what you want to hear right now. You feel like you're being abandoned in here. But you know I would never do that to you. None of us would. We just can't keep coming up here all the time. But you can still call. We'll still write, still keep the packages coming."

Michael glared at her. He wanted to go off, but the corrections officers in the room guaranteed that wouldn't end well.

"What's his name?"

She frowned. "Who?"

"You tell me. Who you with? What's his name? It must be some nigga you met that got you switching up all of a sudden. You sold the apartment in Brooklyn, moved out to Staten Island with the kids. Away from my family. Away from yours. Got you a new car. Now you can't come and see me as often. All of a sudden, your grind got you tired. Shit ain't adding up. So, just keep it one hundred. What's the nigga's name?"

This time Ivy had to restrain herself. She wanted to spit in his face.

She leaned in toward him across the table. "You know how fuckin' insulting that is?"

He laughed, convinced his assumptions had to be right. He couldn't think of any other reason for her desertion.

"I'm sitting here telling you how I feel, how hard it's been for me all these years to hold you down, and you think I'm leaving you over some dick?"

Ivy waited for a response and got none.

"Ain't no nigga. But there probably should be. All the bitches you had on the side! Calling the house asking for you, showing up at our door looking for you, trying to fight me at parties. I put up with all that shit. So, yeah. You're right. I probably should go and get me a new nigga. Let you see what it feels like."

He stared at her and she stared back with equal rage. Finally, she looked down at her hands, staring at the expensive wedding ring that was entirely symbolic. They had never gotten married, never had the joy of a ceremony. Michael had gotten locked up three months before the big day. Ivy had been wearing the ring for years as a symbol of her loyalty to him. It was fool's gold, just like their relationship had been starting to appear lately.

She looked at him again wearily. "When you and Rashid first got locked up, I thought Deja was wrong for abandoning him like that. She never looked back; got married and moved on with her life. I thought it was foul. But she's my friend, so I didn't make a big deal about it.

"In the back of my mind, though, I thought I was better than her. Or at least that our relationship was stronger than theirs—because I stayed, and she ran. And here you are comparing me to her."

"You're doing the same thing she did. It just took you longer to walk away. That's the only difference."

"Nah," Ivy said, all of her sympathy for Michael finally drained. "There's another difference. Rashid wasn't guilty."

Michael was so furious that the vein in his neck visibly throbbed.

"He just rode it out for you," Ivy continued. "Wouldn't turn on you. He got sent away with you. *All of us* have been locked up with you, Mikey. Some of us physically, some of us mentally. And all you care about is whether or not these crackers call your name for a visit every two weeks."

"Fuck you, Ivy!"

She jerked as the harshness of his words and tone hit her in the face like a fist. As rough and ruthless as he was in the streets, Michael had never spoken to her this way.

Ivy opened her mouth to respond but no words came out. Michael wasn't done yet anyway.

"You must have forgot who the fuck you're talking to!"

"SETTLE DOWN!" a guard shouted in their direction.

Michael's chest heaved as he glared at Ivy. "I know you think I don't have any more power now that I'm in here. That's why you're trying to walk away from me now. But I'll show you. Ain't nothing changed."

Ivy felt a shiver go down her spine as she stared into his eyes. Michael looked like a man with his back against the wall.

She leaned forward in her seat, desperate. "Mikey, I need you to let me go. Please."

He watched tears fill Ivy's eyes.

"Please," she repeated. "I looked around one day and noticed that all of my friends are people I met through you. All of my family is your family. I don't have a life that doesn't include you and I know it sounds selfish. Maybe it is. But I want to see what it feels like to have a life that's my own. Just for a little while."

His hands fisted involuntarily. There it was. He had sensed it for a while now. Ivy was leaving him slowly but surely. It enraged him.

"You remember what you said to me the day I got sentenced?"

His words hung there for several moments before they hit their mark. Ivy's heart sank.

Her mouth went dry and she stared at him blankly.

From the expression on her face, Michael knew the blow had landed. He smirked.

"You said that they had just sentenced *you* to life, too. That you would do every day of this bid with me and you would never walk away. No matter what."

He started counting with his fingers.

"No matter how tired you might get. No matter how busy or lonely or whatever. No matter how old the kids get or how much shit you gotta do. That's what I *thought* you meant, but now I see it for what it is."

He stood and motioned until he got the attention of the guards.

Ivy's pulse raced. She looked at him anxiously. "What are you doing?" He looked at her like she was a stranger. Like she hadn't been by his side from the start.

"Take your tired ass home and get some rest."

Ivy watched, stunned, as Michael announced to the officer he was ending the visit.

"Michael, seriously?"

He looked down at her. "Be back here next week and make sure you bring my sons with you."

He didn't bother to look back as the guard led him away.

Ivy sat there fighting back tears, shocked and embarrassed. She took the ring off her finger, struggling a bit to get it off with all the weight she had gained. When the guard motioned for her, she stood and followed him as he led her out. She was hurt beyond her ability to express it. But as she retrieved her belongings from the locker, she knew she would never allow Michael to make her feel this small again. This was the final straw.

She tossed the ring in the trash can near the locker and stepped out into the sunshine. As tears streamed down her face, she decided that she was walking out of that prison for the last time.

Quiet Storm

Coco tossed the phone down angrily. Her brother had called her right after terminating his visit with Ivy. Normally, she tried her best to sympathize with Mikey. Tried to understand he was dealing with more than any of them could possibly imagine while he served his sentence up north. But Coco had watched her sister-in-law work hard over the years to keep things afloat in Michael's absence. She had done a tremendous job of it, as far as Coco was concerned.

Coco—whose real name was Cara—had been given the nickname as a kid. Like her siblings, she had beautiful deep brown skin. Along with her impossibly long legs, toned body, and infectious smile, she had a charming personality that magnetized everyone around her. She stretched those long legs out in front of her now as she sat on her sofa thinking about her brother and the heated conversation she had just had with him.

Mikey had been indignant.

"She came all the way up here just to tell me she's not coming back again anytime soon. What type of shit is that?"

"You sound crazy," Coco said. "Ivy's out here busting her ass to keep Noah and King on track. She's running her business, making sure you have what you need. She's human. She's allowed to get tired and need—"

"Fuck that!" Michael said. "I'm the muthafucka who's tired!"

Coco sucked her teeth. "You're my brother. I love you. I tell you that all the time and it's not just because you spoiled me. You know I always loved you and appreciated how you looked out for me. For all of us. But you're wrong here, Mikey. Ivy's not the bad guy for feeling how she feels. She's human. She's probably lonely."

"I don't care," he admitted. "Let her figure it out. But if she's not back up here next week with my kids, it's gonna be a problem, Coco. Make sure she knows that."

Coco sighed. She hated when her brother flexed his figurative muscles. It often had disastrous consequences.

"Ivy loves you. This ain't about her abandoning you. Ivy and the boys are settling into their new place. Noah just took a semester off from college and he's trying to figure out what he wants to do with his life. Ivy's doing everything she can to help him pick a career path. Not just a job, but a career he'll love and enjoy."

"Noah is like me. He just wants to get money."

Coco agreed. "And Ivy's worried that can lead him in the wrong direction if he's not careful."

"Noah's smarter than I was," Michael said. "Ivy worries too much about him."

Coco disagreed. "Maybe she's worrying for no reason. Maybe not, but she's his mother and she loves him. So, regardless, she's doing the right thing. With you being away, the responsibility of keeping him on track falls on her. And not just Noah. King, too."

"King needs to man up," Michael insisted.

"He's only sixteen," Coco said. "Just because he's taller than all of us doesn't mean he's grown. King is a kid in a man's body. Ivy knows what she's doing, brother. Those boys are on the right track. Both of them."

Michael didn't respond right away, thinking about everything his little sister was saying.

"I don't understand why she moved out to Staten Island," he said at last. "In Brooklyn, at least, she had Patsy around the corner. Now they're out there in Staten Island by themselves. That's what I'm not understanding. It don't make sense. Must be some other nigga she's fucking with out there."

For a moment, Coco thought she heard him wrong, but then her brother doubled down.

"That's the only way I could see her disrupting everything. And I would respect her a lot more if she just told me that."

"Mikey, you can't be serious right now."

"So, all of a sudden she's too busy to come and see me? The boys are too busy?"

"Nigga, *yes*!"

Coco rarely resorted to using the N-word. She preferred to get her point across without it, but this time, there was no suitable substitute for what she needed to say to her brother.

"You act like it's strange that a person would need a timeout from running up north every month, dragging packages up there, going through searches, putting her *kids* through that shit! That's not unusual, Mikey. I bet you the other inmates in there know what it's like to go without a visit every twenty to thirty days. Instead of appreciating what Ivy's doing, you have the nerve to accuse her of cheating on you? After all these years?"

Coco couldn't recall a time when she had been more tempted to hang up on her brother.

Hearing Coco's reaction, Michael felt like a fool. He knew

being locked up for so long had made him paranoid, anticipating the abandonment he believed was inevitable.

"Would you tell me if it was true?" he asked.

He hated the doubt he felt, wished he didn't struggle to believe people meant what they said to him. But the truth was he doubted everything lately.

"I wouldn't have to," Coco replied. "Ivy would tell you herself. She's a real one, and I shouldn't have to tell you that."

Michael felt a pang of guilt. "I been in here sixteen years, Coco. Everything I thought I knew I don't know anymore."

She felt sorry for him. Michael had been locked up for half her life. She hated that fact, but it didn't change reality.

"Well, know this. You got people out here who love you. People who think about you every day. We would never abandon you. None of us. Especially not Ivy and the boys. And definitely not me and Patsy. You're not by yourself. But you're acting real silly right now."

"*Silly?*" Michael had been going along with what she was saying until he heard that word. "I'm acting silly, Coco? For wanting my wife to stick to her word and stand by my side? For wanting to see my kids, and wondering what the fuck is going on while I'm not around? You the one that sounds fuckin' silly!"

The recording came on, notifying them that their call was coming to an end. Coco was grateful for it. If they had gone on much longer, she knew she would have let him have it.

"Mikey, you're upset, so, I'm gonna give you some time to calm down. Then, I'm coming to see you face-to-face."

He sighed. "Ivy and the boys are coming next week. So, you can come with them."

Coco shook her head. "I can't come next week, Mikey. I have—"

"See? That's the bullshit I'm talking about."

Coco sat up, gripping the phone, prepared to light into him, but the call dropped. She threw the phone on the coffee table angrily and closed her eyes. She took a deep breath and told herself to relax.

Of course, she sympathized with her big brother. Michael had always been protective of her, and he was telling the truth when he bragged about spoiling her. Since she could remember, he had always taken care of her. That was just how he was. "Mikey," as his family and friends called him, took care of everyone he loved. When he started getting money, he assumed responsibility for all the major expenses in the family. Just like their father had before him. They came from a family of hustlers. Michael was no different. He'd taken care of her tuition. Coco had been afforded the best education, traveled, and enjoyed the best wardrobe and cars a girl could ask for.

However, she often reminded herself that she had personally done the hard work it took to earn her MBA. She knew she and her family owed Mikey their loyalty and their time, but she agreed with Ivy that he was asking for too much. He wanted everyone to drop everything and atone for the decisions he alone had made. And, in Coco's eyes, that wasn't fair.

She put on a fake smile as her nephews Noah and Kingston finally emerged from the video game marathon they had been having in her spare bedroom. Noah came and sat in the recliner across from Coco, and Kingston headed straight for the kitchen.

"I'm telling you," Noah said. "I didn't realize your place is this nice. We need to come over here more often."

"Word," Kingston agreed from the kitchen. "We always spend the night over Aunt Patsy's house because our cousins are there, and we hang out and all that. But you got it made over here.

PlayStation, sound system, big-screen TV. Why you still single, Aunt Coco?"

Coco laughed louder than she meant to.

"You know what, King? That's a good question."

She thought about Derek and the roller-coaster relationship they were riding. There was a lot of activity between them sexually. But there was no doubt. He was definitely not her man. The PlayStation was his, a toy he'd installed in her apartment for the time he spent there. Lately, though, she hardly saw him.

"She's single because she ain't settling for no suckas. That's why."

Noah winked at his aunt when he said it.

"Aunt Coco got high standards. She ain't like them hos on Instagram."

Coco felt flattered and offended at the same time. "Don't call them hos."

Noah frowned. "Why not?"

"Because it's degrading."

"He's right, though," Kingston said. He walked into the living room, chewing on a granola bar. He sat on the sofa. "They dress like it and act like it. So, if the shoe fits . . ."

Coco shook her head. "So, you think Nikki Diamond is a ho?"

Both boys reacted loudly.

"Naaah. Not Nikki."

"Nikki's different."

"How?" Coco challenged them.

Kingston sat back, chewing as he spoke. "We know her."

Coco nodded. "And you know that she's just playing a part so that she can make money. So are a lot of those other girls. Don't believe everything you see. Just because you don't know them like you know Nikki doesn't mean they're all the same."

Noah shrugged. "You might be right."

Coco sat cross-legged in her seat. She decided to switch topics. "How do you guys like Staten Island so far?"

Kingston seemed to consider it before answering. "I like it."

Noah shrugged again. "It's different."

Coco waited for them to elaborate, but neither of them did. She pressed further. "What about your mom? You think she likes it?"

Kingston smiled. "She seems happy so far. She gives me more freedom now that we're out there. I like that."

Coco's eyes narrowed. "Freedom to do what?"

Kingston played innocent. "Just normal teenage stuff."

"She wasn't letting you have as much freedom when you were in Brooklyn?"

Noah chuckled. "She kept us busy all the time, so we don't end up like Dad."

Kingston agreed. "Aunt Patsy . . . she lets us hang out for real over there. Mom don't like that."

Coco knew exactly what her nephews were alluding to. Her sister Patsy—older than Michael by two years—always took pride in the family business. She loved the street life and all that it entailed. It was a world Patsy understood completely and could navigate easily. She saw Ivy and Coco as bourgeois benefactors of the grimy work Michael had done to keep the family afloat. Patsy's own sons were deep in the drug game, and she was aware of it. In some ways, she even encouraged it. Coco wasn't surprised that Patsy would allow her nephews unlimited freedom in her home. Patsy had never really grown up. She had aged, but not matured. Patsy partied, drank, and smoked weed with her kids. And when Noah and Kingston came over, she urged them to join in the fun. Patsy didn't think of herself as a bad influence. She thought she was playing the role of the cool aunt. She wanted Noah and Kingston to become miniature versions of their father, while Ivy was doing her best to prevent that at all costs.

"You remember the big fight Mom had with Aunt Patsy that time?"

Coco groaned and nodded.

"How could I forget?"

Months ago, Ivy had gone out of town to work on a movie set in her role as a hairstylist. It was a great opportunity in LA that would give her more exposure and help expand her brand. She was still living in Brooklyn at the time, around the corner from Patsy and her kids. Ivy left Noah and Kingston in Patsy's care while she flew out of town for the three-day shoot. Patsy had assured Ivy that everything would be fine. Instead, all hell had broken loose.

Patsy's oldest son, Dashawn, had gotten into some street beef over money. Unbeknownst to Ivy, in the days leading up to her trip, that beef had reached a fever pitch. Returning home one night while Ivy was away, Dashawn had been involved in a shoot-out right outside Patsy's brownstone. Noah and Kingston were inside and had witnessed it all, including the moment Dashawn rushed in with a smoking gun still clutched tightly in his hand. Patsy had helped her son stash the weapon and pack a bag. She had made several frantic phone calls and gotten Dashawn out of town before the police arrived to ask questions.

The moment Ivy heard about it, she had dropped everything and rushed home. She arrived at Patsy's house the morning after the shoot-out, saw the tree outside still adorned with crime scene tape, and hurried inside. She found her sons sitting with Patsy as she schooled them on the rules of survival in their world. How the next step for Dashawn was to lay low until the time came for him to retaliate against the man who shot at him.

Ivy had been outraged.

"You can't be fuckin' serious right now! That's the shit that got Mikey locked up! Don't sit here and talk to my sons about killing somebody like that shit is an everyday part of life. THIS is not normal. Living like this. Knowing that your kids are in that life, risking everything for a dollar. Dashawn getting shot at in front of your house . . . the fuckin' crime tape is still outside. And you're in here talking about retaliating? Talk that shit to your kids if you want, Patsy. Walk them right into the jail cell or the morgue if you want. But keep that shit away from my sons!"

Ivy had snatched Noah and Kingston and all of their belongings and gotten them out of there quickly. That was the last time she asked Patsy to babysit, and it wasn't long afterward that Ivy made the decision to leave Brooklyn altogether.

"Now that we moved to Staten Island, she loosened up a little," Kingston continued. "So, I'm cool with the move so far."

Coco looked at Noah for his take on it.

He shook his head.

"I miss Brooklyn. Where we're at now is mad white."

Coco laughed. "What about Bree? She's Black."

Noah smirked. "That's King's girl."

Kingston sucked his teeth. "Shut up. Ain't nobody thinking about little Bree."

Coco watched them, smiling. She wished her brother were there to guide his sons into adulthood. To help them navigate relationships and big moves. She knew firsthand the void that was left in a father's absence. Hers had died when she was in elementary school. Michael had risen in his wake and taken the reins, but he couldn't replace their father.

Coco had been in the fifth grade when their father—a

hustler also—had been killed. Mikey was in high school, and he picked up the baton he felt their father had passed to him. It happened almost immediately after their father died. Mikey hit the streets and ran headlong into the crack game, as if he felt that the responsibility to provide for the family fell squarely on his shoulders. He had driven Coco to her fifth-grade dance while the family was still in mourning. He had listened when she spoke to him about her crush on a boy she liked and had lavished her with all the material things she desired in an effort to fill their father's shoes. He had financed her education, had given her advice when she needed it. Still, Coco missed her dad. She missed his presence in the house, his laughter, and his voice. She recognized that in stepping into their father's shoes, Mikey had forfeited what remained of his own childhood. It was a sacrifice that had cost him much more than he bargained for.

"How's everything with you guys and your dad?" she asked.

"Good," Noah answered quickly. "He said he understands me dropping out of college and coming home. Told me to keep an eye on everything. So, that's what I've been doing."

Coco shuddered a little inside. She hated the burden her brother often placed on Noah's shoulders as his older son. Too much pressure, in Coco's opinion.

"Keep an eye on what?" she nudged.

Noah looked at his aunt. "Mom, mostly."

Coco shook her head. "Ivy is grown. You don't need to keep an eye on her. She's your parent. Not the other way around."

"Not like that," Kingston defended his brother. "Just saying that Dad wants us to hold it down, you know?"

Coco frowned. "I don't know. What do you think your father expects of you, King?"

Kingston took a sip of his Gatorade and thought about it. "He wants us to be like him. Only better. I think he likes that I play ball. He was cool with Noah going to college, but he wants to make sure we're thorough, too."

"Thorough?"

"Yeah. Like Aunt Patsy. And like you." Kingston flashed his million-dollar smile.

Coco laughed. "You got your father's charm. That's for sure. Don't worry about keeping an eye on your mother. Focus on figuring out what you want to be. Your father's expectations are one thing. But you gotta expect a lot from yourself first."

"I just want to get money," Noah said firmly. "Period."

"How, though?"

He sat forward. "It don't matter. School wasn't putting no cash in my pocket. Now that I'm home, I'm just trying to figure out where it's at."

Coco groaned. "You need more than that. The love of money is the root of all evil. You need a purpose. That's what your mother keeps trying to tell you."

Noah stared at her blankly.

"I'm gonna get you an internship at my job," she said. "Maybe in the mailroom or something like that."

Noah frowned. "The mailroom? Ain't you like a top executive or something over there?"

She nodded proudly.

"Let me work for you then."

She smirked. "Baby steps, kid."

He smiled. "You mean 'young man.'"

"Boy, bye!" Coco stood. "Come in here and let me make you some lunch."

Ivy drove home with her mind in a fog. It felt surreal each time she replayed her visit with Michael in her mind. It didn't seem possible that the man she knew would speak to her like that—would walk away from her without breaking stride.

For the first hour of her drive back to the city, she thought about the early days with him. They had met in high school back in Brooklyn during the early 1990s when he was cute, cocky, and paid. Michael and his boys were getting money hustling for some older dudes around the way. All the girls liked him. He was handsome, well built, and charming. That he wore all the latest fashions only added to his appeal. He was in Ivy's history class, and they got paired up for an assignment. She'd quickly realized that he'd expected her to do all the work. So, she let him know in no uncertain terms that she wasn't about that life.

"You think 'cause you cute that I'm gonna let you get away with doing nothing, but I'm not like these other girls. All captivated by you. I'm only doing *my* part of the project. You go 'head and stand up there looking stupid when it's your turn if you want."

She'd expected him to go off on her. Dudes like him let their egos get the best of them when they felt challenged. But, to her surprise, Michael had smiled, sitting back and staring at her for a while. Then he'd nodded.

"Okay, shorty. What you need me to do?"

Later, he'd told her he'd gone home that night and looked up the word "captivated" in the dictionary. He was intrigued by her, and he agreed with what she said. She was definitely not like the other girls. She had confidence and intelligence. And she was cute. So, Michael pursued her full throttle from that day forward. They'd gotten an A on their assignment, and Michael dropped out of high school soon after. He'd taken to the streets full-time, leaving academics behind to pursue the big money that came with high stakes.

Nevertheless, he continued to romance Ivy. He picked her up from school each day, took her to shops, restaurants, and the movies. They became a couple, despite her focus on school and his immersion in street life. They became inseparable, even meeting each other's families. The only time he wasn't with her was when he was out there getting money. He was there when she graduated from high school. She went to college while he went back and forth to jail. Never for long, though. He was always bailed out quickly, never facing any serious time.

Instead of the close calls chastening Michael, they emboldened him. Michael became more daring, expanding his empire. Ivy watched as he bagged up drugs, stashing them from time to time in the apartment he'd provided for her. Guns, too. He provided excitement and a life full of lavish spending and extravagance. It was a life that she grew to love.

Ivy had grown up differently than Michael. Her parents had met and married when they were nearing their forties. She was their only child and had been doted on from the start. She used to be embarrassed when her parents came up to school for assemblies or conferences. They were so much older than everyone else's parents, so much more boring in her opinion. She loved them, but wished she had younger, cooler parents who shared her natural flair for fashion and style. At home she was lonely and often longed for siblings. She spent hours in her room alone, listening to music while she practiced doing her hair and makeup. On weekends, she went to the movies with her friends and tried to catch the eye of cute boys. Then she would go home and spend the night alone in her room longing for some excitement. Meeting Michael and his family had been a thrill. She had bonded quickly with Coco and had hit it off with Patsy in the beginning, too. Michael's mother was much more laid-back than her own, never complaining if Ivy stayed too late, never objecting to the hours Ivy and Michael spent in his bedroom with the door locked. In the early days of their relationship, Ivy thought she had found what she longed for at last. Excitement, fun, and a sense of family unlike anything she had experienced before.

Eventually, though, the charm wore off. She began to see more of Michael's friends going to jail, more of them dying in the streets. She worried for him and began thinking about better uses for all the money he was making. Michael drove the hottest cars and bought one for Ivy, too. She accepted it, reluctantly, insisting that she didn't really need it. They had everything they wanted, and Michael was still spending exorbitant amounts of cash on things that would depreciate in no time.

Ivy applied the things she was learning in her business courses in college and urged Michael to purchase property. He listened, buying his mother a beautiful Brooklyn brownstone. Then he invested in a strip mall in Queens. Soon, his money was working for him, and he had a legitimate stream of income if the feds came calling.

She got pregnant with Noah before she could complete her bachelor's degree. Both of their families were ecstatic. Noah would be the first grandchild for both sets of grandparents. She reflected on those early days when Noah was small, and Michael spent more time at home with them than he did in the streets. He had been a doting father, often beating Ivy to Noah's crib when he cried in the middle of the night. Their family was the sweetest joy of her life in those days. However, it wasn't long before Michael got lured back to the money, the adrenaline rush, and the thrill of breaking the law.

Ivy got back to work, too. Noah's adoring grandmothers alternated as his babysitters while Ivy returned to college part-time. She completed her degree and thought she might enter the workforce, but Michael had other plans.

Now that Ivy had taught him the value of owning property and businesses, his family members were urging him to invest in them. His younger sister, Coco, was attending college down in Atlanta on his dime. His mother was having fun furnishing her new home. Ivy and Noah were driving around in a new Mercedes and wearing the latest designers. Now his sister Patsy wanted her piece of the pie.

Patsy convinced him to give her one of the spaces in his strip mall in Queens to use as a beauty salon she would run. After much persuasion, he agreed. She insisted on having the best of everything—state-of-the-art equipment, chairs, and sinks; mirrors and lighting everywhere—all the supplies she would need. Patsy hired a few stylists she knew from around the neighborhood and hosted a grand opening. Business was decent at first, but soon the clients started going elsewhere. Patsy's ghetto fabulous (emphasis on the "ghetto" part) made it tough for her to keep good stylists on board. Loud, nearly violent arguments between her and the stylists resulted in them leaving one by one, taking dozens of clients with them each time.

Michael wanted Ivy to come in and help his sister out. Patsy needed someone to handle the clients and the stylists, to balance the bills, and to keep Patsy's spending in check. It was no easy task. Ivy hadn't been enthusiastic about it, but she set her career plans aside and got busy helping Patsy keep the salon afloat. After a while, things began to turn around. Patsy, at first resentful of her "sister-in-law's" presence, came to appreciate the fact Ivy did have a keen business sense. The place became profitable and they began to enjoy a steady clientele.

While working with Patsy, Ivy started watching the stylists and learning their techniques. She had always loved doing her own hair and makeup and was quite good at it. But watching the professionals do their thing made her want to step her game up. She went to school part-time to learn the trade and became a certified cosmetologist. For the first time, Ivy began to see how she could play a more direct role in their growing family's success.

Ivy became not only the salon's manager but one of the top stylists as well. Michael proposed to her on her birthday, and things seemed like they couldn't get any better. Then Patsy started feeling like Ivy was taking over what was supposed to be her business. They argued constantly until Ivy finally quit. It was for the best, she'd reasoned. She had just found out that she was pregnant, expecting a baby in the fall of 2003. She started planning for a wedding and a new baby and left Patsy to run her business into the ground.

A month after Ivy quit, Michael was locked up and charged with first-degree murder. It had all happened suddenly. One minute, they were living the good life. The next minute, the police were kicking down their door and dragging Michael out. He was charged in connection with a shootout in Bed-Stuy. Witnesses and surveillance cameras placed him at the scene. Michael—unmasked—had jumped into the passenger seat of a black car after gunning down a rival. The driver had worn a black hoodie, and no one could say for sure who it was. At the time, Michael and his friend Rashid were together all the time. Police assumed Rashid was the mystery man driving the getaway car. They fixated on him, locking him up on other minor offenses while building a case against him as Michael's accomplice. They badgered him to turn on his friend and take a deal, but Rashid had maintained his innocence and refused to betray his friend.

From the beginning, Michael had been honest with Ivy about his role in the murder. He was guilty, although he insisted he had only done what he had to do. He was unapologetic about what the streets required of him. Much of it was ugly, and this was just one of those things. But Michael told Ivy Rashid had not been the driver. It was a coward named Lamont, who let Rashid take the fall instead. The police charged Rashid as an accomplice to murder. He took it to trial and lost. At his attorney's urging, Michael took a deal and pled guilty to manslaughter and got fifteen years. In the years since then, Michael had been involved in a number of altercations with inmates and corrections officers, and had years added to his sentence. His parole had recently been denied, forcing him to spend at least another three years locked up before he would see the parole board again.

Ivy thought about all the things she and Michael had said to each other during their brief visit today. It was true. Ivy had changed over the years. She had grown and evolved. Michael had remained the same. Both of them blamed each other for it. He resented her growth while she felt suffocated by his immobility.

Michael was guilty of his crime and was not being punished unjustly, the way Rashid was. During his incarceration, Ivy had stood dutifully by his side even as she fell out of love with him. She was lonely. His insistence that she continue to do that made her more determined to break free. Now more than ever her mind was made up. She would live the rest of her life on her own terms. Michael be damned.

He had reminded her of her promise to do each day of his sentence with him. Until now, she had been doing just that despite finding out about all the other women he'd had throughout their relationship. Women who'd made themselves known to her one by one in various ways over the years. She'd tucked the pain away and convinced herself those women were just part of the game; a downside of being a hustler's "wife" was the cheating. That was what she told herself. She and Michael had argued over the women each time, but she got past each infidelity, determined to keep her family intact.

She shook her head at the thought of it. So many foolish years spent playing a role that wasn't real. Michael wanted to marry her, of course. But having some ceremony in a jail cell with no family and friends, no celebration, felt cheap to her. She'd told Michael she didn't need a ring to be his wife, but the truth was she'd always suspected Michael's incarceration right before their wedding was some type of omen. She had never given voice to it—not even to herself—but Ivy had been second-guessing the life she'd chosen for a long time now.

Watching her sons growing up as part of Michael's family had presented major challenges for Ivy. She wanted her sons to have structure and normalcy. Those things were lacking in Michael's world, especially once he went to prison and Patsy became the family matriarch.

During the years of his incarceration, Michael's mother had passed away, his sister Patsy had been forced to shutter her business and was now living with her three grown children in the house Michael had bought for his mother.

Ivy had picked up the torch and ran with it. She gave birth to their son Kingston alone, raised both boys on her own, and put everything she had learned over the years to good use. She opened her own salon in Brooklyn in 2009 and hired the top stylists in the borough. Noah and Kingston were eleven and six years old, and they watched their mother build her business from the ground up. Constantly upping her game and taking courses on the latest techniques, she soon became one of the most sought-after stylists in the city. She leveraged the relationships she'd made with Michael's powerful and well-connected friends and began working behind the scenes on the sets of modeling shoots and video productions. After a while, her clientele expanded to include VIPs, and the rest was history. The name Ivy Donovan began to ring bells in all the right circles, and she achieved success in her own right.

Through it all, she had gathered her children in the wee hours of the morning, loading the boys, their necessities, and Michael's commissary packages into her car on cold winter mornings and hot summer ones alike. For sixteen years, she had trekked up north without complaining. Had put clients on hold so she could take Michael's calls, dropping everything no matter what she was doing at the moment. Had come in late from work at the salon or on some set so many nights, exhausted, and still sat up yawning as she wrote a letter to her so-called husband.

Michael's words today were violent. Despite the fact he was playing the victim, Ivy was done sympathizing with him. She felt she was the one who had been abandoned. He had literally left her sitting alone in a room full of strangers after everything they had been through. He had belittled her contributions to the family's success. Had accused her of creeping with someone else. Worse, in fact—he had suggested hooking up with another man was the only thing that would give her the strength to do what she had been contemplating in secret for years.

Now she felt like a fool for waiting this long to take a stand. It had been years since the boys started complaining about their grueling biweekly visits to the maximum-security prison where Michael was confined. When he got into fights and got moved to prisons farther and farther north, Ivy pressed on and made the trip each time.

She'd told herself she was doing it for her kids. Her sons needed their father. Even under his grim circumstances, she'd believed Michael could offer his sons some much-needed guidance and wisdom as they grew older. Kingston had never known his father outside the prison system. Unlike Noah, he had no memories of running in the park with his dad or even waking up with his father in the house with them. It was through those monthly visits that Kingston formed a relationship with his dad. As unfortunate as the circumstances were, they managed to create a bond that wouldn't have been likely without Ivy's dedication.

She finally found herself back in the thick of New York City traffic and welcomed the familiar chaos. She was back on her turf, and she pushed thoughts of what happened with Michael to the back of her mind. By the time she arrived at her sister-in-law's high-rise building in Battery Park City, she was thinking about her friend Nikki's upcoming party, and all the things she still had to do in preparation for the big event.

She parked her car and headed into the building, greeting Coco's doorman as she passed him. After a short elevator trip up to Coco's floor, she walked down the long hallway to Coco's door. She could already hear the music blaring from the apartment before she reached it. She frowned, knowing her boys were behind the heavy bassline shaking the floor beneath her feet. She rang the doorbell several times, sure they wouldn't hear it over the noise. Thankfully, after a few moments, Coco opened the door. She smiled and held the door wide for Ivy as she entered.

Ivy was one of the most beautiful, confident women Coco knew. Even as what some might derogatorily call a "big girl," Ivy was a bad bitch. She had success, a strong moral and spiritual center, and talent to match. Coco wanted so badly to see her happy again.

Ivy walked in and saw both of her sons standing in the middle of Coco's living room, breathless and smiling. It looked like she had walked in on a full-blown party in progress. Coco was laughing as she turned the music down.

Kingston plopped down on his aunt's sofa to catch his breath. He saw the confused expression on his mother's face and decided to explain. "We were doing a TikTok with Aunt Coco."

Ivy wasn't sure what that was but decided not to question

it. She put her bag down on the coffee table and sat down in a chair nearby.

Noah frowned. "You're back early. What happened?"

Coco looked at Ivy. She hadn't told her nephews about the details of her conversation with Mikey earlier. She thought it would be best to leave it up to Ivy to let them know how upset their father was.

"Your father said to tell you he loves you. He's gonna call you soon."

Ivy didn't make eye contact with any of them as she said it.

Noah and Kingston exchanged glances. They knew visits up north took the whole day. The drive alone was eight hours roundtrip. So, seeing her back while the sun was still shining had them confused. But they knew her well enough not to press the issue.

Coco offered Ivy something to drink.

"What you got?"

"Water, juice, or wine."

"Wine. A big glass, too."

Coco nodded. She looked at her nephews before heading to the kitchen.

"I thought y'all wanted to go down to the ball courts to show these Manhattan kids what you got."

Kingston sucked his teeth. He stood up and stretched his six-foot-five frame. His long legs and arms seemed to span the entirety of the large room when he did so.

He smiled. "These rich boys out here can't play no ball."

His deep baritone voice, and his tall and toned physique, made Kingston appear to be a grown-ass man. But when he grinned, it was clear that a boyishness existed beneath the surface.

Coco laughed. "Go prove it. Come back soon, though. I'm sure your mother wants to get home and relax."

Noah and Kingston took their cue. They grabbed Kingston's basketball and headed outside. Once they were alone, Coco returned from the kitchen and handed Ivy a tall wine glass full of pinot grigio. She sat down across from her on the sofa with a glass of her own.

"Mikey called. He told me what happened."

Ivy took a long sip. She closed her eyes and sighed. Opening them again, she locked eyes with Coco.

"I love him, Coco. You already know. But I'm done. I made up my mind. The way Mikey talked to me today . . . I didn't deserve that."

"I told him he's acting like a spoiled brat," Coco said. "And I don't blame you. He's my brother and I love him. But there comes a point where you have to do what's best for you."

Ivy was relieved to hear Coco say that. She was sure Patsy wouldn't feel the same way.

"He told me to take my tired ass home and be back up there next week. Ordered me to do it like I'm one of his workers."

Coco wasn't sure what to say. Everybody knew her brother had a hot temper, but this was a new low.

Ivy shrugged. "He's used to having his way all the time. It's our fault. Every one of us has been doing whatever he says, catering to him. It started when he was a kid."

Coco thought about all the ways their mother coddled him as her only son. His success as a hustler only added to her perception of her son as a savior. Having his mother's adoration meant always getting his way. In Coco's view, that was why he was having a tantrum now. Things had changed and his reign at the top of the pyramid was coming to an end.

"Let me guess. He brought up the tuition he paid for me, didn't he?"

Ivy laughed and nodded. "That and the money he left me

with. He said we play dress up all day and drive around in our fancy cars all because of him."

Coco chuckled. "I love my brother. But he's ridiculous sometimes." She shook her head again. "He knows that's not true. He knows that I bust my ass and so do you. He's just in his feelings right now, Ivy. That's all it is."

Ivy nodded. She took another long sip of her wine and savored it. "I'm done."

She said it so calmly that Coco thought she heard wrong. But then Ivy repeated herself.

"Done." She looked Coco in the eyes. "I mean it this time. I know that I've said it before. Whenever I found out about the other women he was fuckin' and the kids that might be his. I said I was walking away, but I kept going back. But not this time. I'm moving on with my life. I'll always make sure he has what he needs. The boys will keep in touch with him. But the way that man talked to me today . . . turned his back and walked away from me without looking back . . ."

Her gaze sharpened, her expression sincere.

"He can kiss my ass."

Hours later, after Ivy and the boys left, Coco sat alone in her apartment and thought about it all. Truth be told, she understood both sides of the situation. By the end of the day, she was overwhelmed by everything. The thought of Mikey and what he was going through behind bars gave her anxiety. The idea of Ivy ending her relationship and moving on made Coco anxious. She hated to think of what it would mean for their family going forward.

Family had always been important to them. When their mother was alive, Sunday dinners were the norm. Even as Mikey grew bigger in the streets, he made time to attend those weekly gatherings with his family. When the money poured in, he spread it among them. When Mikey went away and their mother died, Ivy did the best she could to keep the family connected. Coco was always caught up in her own life and career, and Patsy was notoriously messy and resistant to harmony. So, she stirred up drama with Ivy every chance she got. Still, Ivy had stayed the course. Until now.

Sipping her wine, Coco turned on her high-end stereo system and let the music wash over her. Relationships had always been complicated for her. It was tough to find men who measured up to her brother, her father, and the men she had experienced growing up. The men in Coco's family were larger than life. Masculine, tough, fearless, sometimes ruthless. As much as she loved them, she realized very early in life that their choices came with dire consequences. Being hustlers meant dying young—whether behind bars or in the streets. So, she did her best to avoid dating those types of men. She dated men who filed legitimate tax returns each year. Ones who didn't live in her brother's world. And she'd convinced herself she was somehow breaking the cycle. But her nephew's question was still haunting her all these hours later.

"Why you don't have a man, Aunt Coco?"

It was one of those things that she told herself didn't really matter. She had a great career, a nice apartment, a loving family. But she didn't have a man. The closest she had to that was Derek. So, she texted him.

Months had passed since the last time they were together. That was how it had always been between them. One moment they would be spending time together constantly. The next, he would be off on one of his disappearing acts. Then he would reemerge without explanation. Coco told herself she was fine with their arrangement. Things had never been that deep between the two of them. No whispered "I love you's" or breathless proposals of marriage during their hot sessions together. Their relationship was simultaneously casual and deeply intimate. He touched her tenderly, fucked her perfectly, and built her up verbally. He took her out on her birthday, sent her flowers from time to time, but, Coco had no delusions that they were exclusive. She had come to terms with that long ago.

Their relationship was easy and without any boundaries. That was what she told herself. But, deep down inside, she knew she hungered for more. Maybe she wasn't dating men involved in criminal activity like those she'd grown up around, but she was certainly drawn to the ones who were emotionally unavailable and reluctant to settle down. And she knew it.

When Derek responded to her text that he was on his way over, she hated herself for the excitement she felt. The moment he walked through the door, it was on. They devoured each other as if they had both been starved for months.

Hours later, she was naked and nestled in the crook of his arm as he slept, her head on his chest and her eyes wide open.

Glancing at the clock, she groaned at the fact that it was almost four o'clock in the morning. Restless, she turned left and right, doing her best to ignore Derek snoring deeply beside her. She was happy he was there. Nights like this were rarer than ever these days.

She climbed out of her bed gently, not wanting to wake him any sooner than necessary. She knew once he woke up, he would make some excuse to leave. *Right away.* It was always urgent. Always some important photography assignment to get to or some subject to shoot. Or his mother needed him to take her to run errands. Or something. She knew the routine all too well by now and was fully aware of the fact that she was settling. Even if she didn't say it out loud.

She tiptoed into her living room, reached inside her keepsake box on the end table, and retrieved a perfectly rolled blunt. It had become her nightly ritual to smoke a fat one to help her relax and sleep. Tonight, though, she'd hoped being fucked for the first time in months would be the only lullaby she would need. She had been wrong about that, and she sparked up the weed now so she could get some much-needed rest.

As she puffed away naked in her darkened living room, she caught a glimpse of her reflection in the mirror on the far wall and did a double take. She hated to admit it, but she looked so sad. So *lonely,* even with a man snoring feet away in the comfort of her king-sized bed.

She smoked, easing herself into contentment, reassuring herself that it wasn't all bad. Derek was fun to be around, affectionate and generous. He was as familiar to her as her heartbeat. She knew the scent of him, the taste of his skin, the sound of his laughter. Had memorized those things over many years filled with the sweet and tender moments they had shared. The walks through the park discussing the milestones they had reached in their careers, both together and as individuals. The occasional dates at late-night venues filled with brown liquor, local bands, and the faint scent of incense and weed smoke. The countless nights she spent wrapped in his arms with the pressures of life in the grown-up world laid aside for a blissful while. Derek was her safety net in a life that was quite a whirlwind.

She looked again at her reflection in the mirror, staring this time, and had a silent conversation with herself. She reminded herself that she was a bad bitch. That she deserved to have it all.

She finished smoking and walked back into her bedroom. She looked at him sleeping in a deep and oblivious slumber. From the looks of it, he didn't have a care in the world. He snored softly through his parted lips, his chest rising and falling with each breath. She watched him for a while as he slept. He was a beautiful man. There was no question about it. Deep brown skin stretched tautly across a body crafted like a sculpture of an African warrior. His full lips left her breathless each time they touched her body. Derek was the total package: sexy, cultured, and woke with just the right amount of "hood" sprinkled in. If only he could love her right.

She crawled into bed next to him and he stirred at the motion of her arrival. He opened his eyes and smiled at her, a sexy grin that made her melt in an instant. He stretched out his arms and pulled her close, wrapping her firmly in his embrace. Within seconds, he was snoring again.

She leaned in and kissed his lips, stirring him awake once more. He opened his eyes slowly, looked at her, and grinned as she climbed out from beneath the sheets and straddled him.

"Round three?"

She nodded and punctuated her answer with her hips, grinding into him. He leaned over and reached eagerly for a condom.

Before she realized she was doing it, she grabbed his hand, meshing her fingers with his. She let out a soft giggle and nuzzled his neck with her lips.

"Mmm-mmm. We don't need that."

Derek looked at her oddly. In the darkness of the room, he tried to focus his gaze. Surely, she had lost her mind.

"Nah." He laughed it off and tried to pull his hand free, but her fingers locked with his own. Suddenly, their hands were in a tug of war.

He frowned now. "What's going on?"

She snapped out of it then. What the fuck *was* she doing?

The mood broken now, Coco sighed and climbed off him. She sat naked on the side of the bed and looked at him in the moonlight.

"You ever think about settling down, Derek? Like . . . get married? Have a baby?"

His eyes widened. Even in the darkness, she could see them.

"Really? You serious right now?"

Coco sighed slightly and absently lifted her hand to stroke her belly. She caught herself and ran her hand through her hair instead. For the thousandth time, she heard the deafening tick of her biological clock. She wanted a child so badly. The urge was stronger than ever lately, to the point of obsession. It was one of those things she never gave voice to, not even to her closest friends. It was taboo to admit that she longed for a family, that the green-eyed monster within her reared its ugly head whenever she watched Ivy and Deja mothering their children. Women who "had it all" weren't supposed to feel unfulfilled like she did.

"You said you didn't want kids, Coco."

"I said that I didn't want kids without being married," she clarified.

He groaned, ever so slightly, but Coco heard it. Her heart sank.

"Listen . . ." Derek looked at her. "So, what you saying?"

She stared back at him in silence. He was smart enough to figure it out.

This time, he was the one who sighed. He stared up at the ceiling, realizing this was it. No more procrastinating. He searched his thoughts for the best way to say this to her. The last thing he wanted was to hurt her feelings.

He cleared his throat. "What I always like about me and you was that we never put any shackles on each other. You know what I mean? We go out, eat, party, and do our thing. And we come in here and it's just me and you. No work, no pressures or responsibilities. It's light."

She nodded. She could tell he was setting her up for the letdown. She already felt like she had made a fool of herself.

"I need that," he went on. "I thought you needed that, too."

"I do. But lately, I'm thinking about my life as a whole. What legacy am I leaving behind?"

Derek propped himself up on one elbow and faced her. "You have your career. Your family. You're a star, Coco. Everybody knows that."

She appreciated how generous he always was with his praise of her. It was one of the things she craved from him. But this time, it felt condescending. Like he knew she was right on the verge of falling. After all, she wasn't *in love* with Derek. Not yet. But that was only because he had been so unavailable, keeping himself always at a safe, emotional distance. She had fought hard to do the same, keeping her emotions under control as much as possible. She wouldn't let herself fall for him completely, and that was only because she knew it wasn't safe to do so. But all he needed to do was say the word, and she would fall headlong. It wouldn't be hard at all.

"I want a family of my own. Not one like the one I grew up in. I had love, but it was dysfunctional as hell. I don't want that type of environment for my kids."

"I can understand that," Derek said softly.

"And you're right. We always keep it light between us. But I'm getting older, Derek. I'm starting to see that it's not easy finding somebody who fits the description."

Derek chuckled. "The description?"

"Yeah," she said. "Of what I want in a husband and father of my children. I'm not saying that you fit the description completely. But I think you would be a great father. And maybe we could be happy together if we tried. I want to start a family with you."

She shrugged. There. She'd said it. For the first time, she had admitted it out loud—both to Derek and to herself.

"And you never answered my question," she continued. "Do you ever think about it, too?"

Derek let out a longer, deeper sigh this time. He sat up in the bed, rubbed his hands across his face, and sat with his eyes closed for several moments. Finally, he swung his legs over the side of the bed and reached for his clothes.

Coco frowned. This was not the reaction she had expected. Her question hadn't been that tough. But seeing him preparing to leave in the wee hours of the morning had her second-guessing herself.

He stood and pulled on his boxers, finally facing her. He looked like a kid standing before his parent with a bad report card.

"I didn't want kids, either. Until a few months ago."

His voice was barely audible in the otherwise silent room.

"I met somebody recently . . . someone I work with. Probably about a year ago. I never mentioned it because at first, it wasn't nothing serious."

She stared at him in silence.

He could hardly look at her as he continued dressing. "I was going to tell you when the time was right. But I haven't been seeing you. When you texted me tonight, I had plans to tell you when I got here. But then . . ."

He gestured toward the rumpled sheets and shook his head. He looked at her, obviously trying to read the expression on her face, her body language, something. But she kept staring at him, her expression blank.

"I didn't plan it. The baby thing. I told you I never saw myself as a father. I never had one to show me how it's done. This shit just . . . happened."

Coco stood on her feet and glared at him. She told herself she must have heard him wrong.

"A baby? Wait!"

"That's what I'm saying. It happened so fast."

She watched him get dressed, a dull and palpable ache building in her chest.

"It's not . . . Listen, I never thought about it, to answer your question. I didn't want kids until . . . until now. When she told me, I was shocked."

"Who is she?" Coco hated herself for asking it, but she needed to know.

"You don't know her."

"What's her name?"

"Jordan," he said.

"You got a bitch pregnant, Derek?"

"I know. It still feels . . . I mean . . . I'm excited . . ." He looked at her, guilt written all over his face. "But you know me. I never pictured myself settling down, having a family, being a father. That's what I always loved about me and you. We just . . . we just have what he have and . . ."

He stood there for a few moments, speechless. His eyes searched her eagerly. She continued staring at him in silence.

"Coco, I should have told you before."

"You should go," she said at last.

Her tone was flat, but her heart was slowly shattering in her chest. She looked over every flawless inch of him. Surely he would make the most beautiful baby on earth.

"I'm sorry."

"GET THE FUCK OUT, DEREK! You could have texted me this shit. You could have called and told me on the phone. Doing it this way, after everything we did tonight . . ." She shook her head. "You're a piece of shit."

Derek grabbed the rest of his things in a rush.

"I'm all fucked up," he said. It was the most honest thing he had said all night.

Coco watched him gather his things. She tried to memorize the moment, knowing it would be the last time he ever set foot in her home again. She watched him put his cell phone in the pocket of his jeans and grab his wallet. This was it. So many years wasted.

He turned to face her again. "I'm sorry I hurt you."

He looked at her sincerely as he said it, which only made it hurt more.

He clearly wanted to say something more, but he did them both a favor and just walked out.

She shut the door behind him. Only then did she allow the waterfall of tears to cascade down her cheeks.

Mask Off

Coco drove to Ivy's salon in Brooklyn the next day for some much-needed self-care. From the moment the door swung open, the energy within the place felt warm and familiar. She strode in and greeted the receptionist and all the stylists one by one. It was a Friday morning, and she had arrived to a packed house. Ivy got right to work, washing and conditioning Coco's short hair and seating her under the dryer. Coco settled in next to Deja. The women had a long history together and greeted each other warmly.

"What's up, girl?"

Deja smiled. Her dryer was reaching the end of its cycle and the temperature was slightly less excruciating now. "Ugh! Ivy's trying to kill me with this heat. If I didn't love her, I would trip her ass the next time she walks past."

Both women laughed and only got louder when Ivy shot a suspicious glance in their direction.

"I know y'all are over there talking about me," Ivy called out. "It's all good." She clicked the scissors in her hand suggestively.

Deja and Coco leaned into each other, still laughing. Coco straightened up after a moment.

"I better be nice before she gets too scissor happy." She fingered the nape of her tapered haircut.

Deja nodded. "True."

"How's the family?" Coco asked.

Deja was a real estate power broker with the Maddox Firm, or simply "The Firm" as it was known in the city's most elite real estate circles. Her husband, Bobby, was a police sergeant with the NYPD. Together, they were raising Deja's daughter, Bree.

"They're fine." Deja took a sip of her wine. "Bobby took Bree to her dance class today. Normally, I don't have enough free time to get in here on a Friday. There's usually a million things on my schedule. But I cleared my calendar for this weekend. Nikki's party is gonna be packed with potential clients. Gotta look my best." She winked.

Deja had been working in real estate for close to twenty years. Much of her success was due to her constant presence at the hottest events throughout the city. Networking was her forte. So, she made sure her name remained on all of the most exclusive guest lists in town.

"You always look good. Never a hair out of place," Coco said.

It was true. Deja was notoriously vain, fixated on always appearing perfect and polished. It used to irritate Coco. Back in high school, Deja had been the girl all the guys had wanted to get with: light skinned, pretty, and long haired with a nice body and a brain to match. She was stuck up, though. At least that was what all the boys thought who never had a chance with her. She'd become part of Coco and Ivy's world when her man at the time, Rashid, was getting money in the streets. Once their paths had crossed, Mikey and Rashid became a dynamic duo. Deja, in turn, became part of Coco's circle.

Deja had been prissy, in Coco's opinion. At times when they'd hung out with Ivy, their playful banter had turned a bit sinister. But, overall, they loved each other. Their friendship had been through its share of trials, and they had weathered the storm.

Deja's younger sister Nicole—better known in her social media career as Nikki Diamond—was more to Coco's liking. The sisters couldn't be more opposite in both appearance and personality. Nikki was a brown-skinned beauty with curves that made men drool unapologetically. She was loud and boisterous with a penchant for playing it up for the camera. Deja was the opposite—lighter skinned, softer spoken, and demure—at least on the surface.

Coco thought Deja was a study in contrasts—bourgeoisie and ghetto at the same time. Depending on her audience, Deja could play either part. She could slide some slang into a conversation and even let the N-word fly a time or two. Or she could silently endure the political views of her husband's conservative friends at a cocktail party. Ivy referred to Deja as "the plug." She knew someone for everything. If you needed an event planner, stylist, or publicist, Deja had someone on call. If you needed a lawyer, plastic surgeon, or an insurance agent, she had those, too.

Shrewd in business and blessed with incredible instincts, Deja was a silent investor in Ivy's salon. She also had her hands in a few other successful businesses. It all added up to Deja having the ear of all the tastemakers in the city.

"Bobby even got the night off so he can come with me," Deja added.

"Damn," Coco said. "If Bobby's coming, it must be a full moon."

It was common knowledge Bobby hated Deja's sister Nikki.

Deja nodded. "Tell me about it." She gave a slight eye roll and sipped her wine. "You know I love him, but he's boring the shit out of me lately."

Coco's eyes widened. This was a rare glimpse at the cracks in Deja's carefully crafted public image.

"Bobby has always been boring, though. That's nothing new," Coco said.

Deja chuckled. It was true.

"I know. And I used to like it. But now he's so predictable that it's a turnoff. He falls asleep at the same time every night; has the same routine. Nothing new. Ever."

Coco crossed her legs. "How's your sex life, then?"

"Dry," Deja deadpanned and looked sidelong at Coco. "That's why I need you to cover for me."

Coco frowned. "Cover for you how?'

"I've been secretly meeting up with Sterling. He's the guy—"

"I know who Sterling is," Coco said. Her gaze narrowed, making her look even more exotic with the dark cat-eye mascara she was rocking today. "The guy you sold the townhouse to on the Upper East Side a few months ago. You can't stop talking about him lately. I knew something was up."

Deja blushed a little. "We've been hanging out a lot. It's nice. I need a little excitement in my life. I love Bobby. More than that, I love the life we built for Bree. But I'm starting to feel a little . . . bored."

Coco stared at Deja in silence. This was a whole new woman. Deja had never been this candid before. Gone was the sulking, sarcastic person she usually was. In her place was a woman who looked happy and genuinely excited for the first time in years.

"What does Bobby know about it?"

"He doesn't know anything really. He might be starting to suspect something, though. I started slipping a little. The other night I didn't get home until six in the morning. Lost track of time."

Coco's eyes widened. "What did Bobby say when you came home?"

"He was pissed! But I told him that I was with you. That's why I need you to cover for me."

Coco was stunned. "What?"

"I told him that me and Nikki were hanging out at your house after one of her events and that we started having drinks and girl talk, and I lost track of time." She batted her lashes at Coco sweetly. "If he asks you, just stick with the story."

Coco shook her head slowly. "It sounds like you're playing with fire, Deja. Now you're dragging me into it."

"I know. I shouldn't have said your name. But Bobby hardly sees you. I thought you were the least likely to be questioned by Mr. Officer."

"I really don't mind covering for you. That's what friends do. But you should be careful. Sounds like you're getting in too deep with Sterling. If you're getting so messy that you're coming home with the sun, what is that telling you?"

"That I need to do a better job keeping track of time." Deja smiled. "It was one time. Won't happen again. I promise. From now on, I'll be more careful."

Coco looked skeptical.

"You're the only one who knows," Deja said. "So, don't mention it to Ivy or Nikki. To be honest, I'm only telling you in case Bobby checks my alibi. He goes over our E-ZPass bill with a magnifying glass. So, I said I was with you to back up my trips to Manhattan."

"Mmm-hmm."

Eager to shift the subject, Deja went back to talking about her sister's upcoming party.

"I was hoping Bobby would stay home with Bree and let me have some fun. But now he's stuck to me like glue. So, fuck it. I'm just gonna go and try to have a good time with him. Maybe it'll put some spark back in our marriage."

Coco tried to get excited about Nikki's party, too, but thoughts of Derek kept creeping into her mind. She shrugged them off and told herself to snap out of it. She looked at Deja and put on a brave face.

"What big surprise does Nikki have planned for her party this year? She always does something wild."

Deja rolled her eyes. "Who knows? Hopefully, I won't have to break up another fight. That's all I'm worried about."

Coco side-eyed Deja. Nikki was a handful, but she was a whole lot of fun, too. Nikki was single, beautiful, and making the most of it. Unlike Deja, Nikki didn't marry young or have any kids. Instead, she used her looks and charm to gain access to the right circles. She moved to Miami, then to LA, and got "chose" by one of the mumble rappers on the West Coast. Soon, Nikki became a staple in all of the sensational blogs. She was smart like her sister and parlayed her social media popularity into a lucrative business. Nikki was bringing in *bank* lately, thanks to a ton of endorsements and sponsorship deals.

To say Deja disapproved was an understatement, but she still took advantage of the access her sister's lifestyle afforded her. Deja often accompanied her to red-carpet events, award-show after-parties, and movie premieres. She networked and made connections to help her stay plugged in, all while acting as Nikki's "assistant." Meanwhile, she added big industry names to her growing list of real estate clients, thanks to her sister's popularity.

Even Coco had to admit *some* of Deja's disdain for Nikki's lifestyle was warranted. Nikki often took her antics much further than average. Nikki had been linked to wealthy nineties-era hip-hop moguls and hot young rappers with new money alike. Whoever had the bag, Nikki could be found by his side wearing as little as possible and doing the absolute most. But she was charming, funny, and had an innocence about her that was unexpected. It was hard not to like her. But Deja somehow managed.

"Nikki's not that bad," Coco said.

Deja scoffed. "You must be high."

"Sounds to me like you're the one we need to keep an eye on."

Deja grinned. "Just remember snitches get stitches, bitch."

They both laughed.

The door swung open moments later, and Deja's sister Nikki stepped inside. Loud and boisterous as ever, she greeted all the women.

"Heeeeeeyyyy, bitches!"

Several of the women laughed loudly, and Ivy egged her on. Deja rolled her eyes and looked at Coco.

"Look who's here. You spoke her into existence."

Coco laughed.

Ivy yelled, "Ayyy!" as Nikki started twerking. The whole mood in the salon instantly turned up. Giggling, Ivy fought to catch her breath and looked at Nikki confused.

"I thought I was meeting you at the photo shoot."

Nikki shook her head. "They canceled it, so, I came in to get a quick updo before I head out to my sister's house in Staten Island."

Ivy nodded toward the dryer. "Deja's back there under the dryer with Coco."

Nikki smiled and sauntered off in their direction. Deja groaned as her sister approached.

"Cut it out," Coco chastised her.

"Wassup, y'all?" Nikki rushed over, beaming.

They greeted her, Deja forcing a convincing smile onto her face.

"Did I hear you say that you're planning on coming to my house?" She ducked her head out from beneath the dryer and looked up at her sister.

"Yes. I need to see Bree."

Deja frowned. "See her for what?"

Nikki chuckled. "Mind your business. We have some shit to chat about. That's all."

Deja rolled her eyes. She could only imagine what that might be.

"Plus, I need to raid your closet for my party tomorrow," Nikki admitted.

"See?" Deja looked at Coco. "I knew you had ulterior motives."

Nikki waved her off. "I just need a necklace or something to set off my outfit. Everybody knows you have all the cute accessories."

"With all the money you're making, you can buy your own."

"Shut the fuck up and get back under the dryer before I tell Ivy to turn the heat up."

Coco laughed loudly.

"I just need Ivy to freshen up my hair a little bit," Nikki added, glancing at her reflection in the mirror. "Then I'm coming with you. So, suck it up."

Deja drained her glass and scowled.

Ivy walked over to retrieve Deja from the dryer.

"After Ivy finishes up here, let's go around the corner for a drink," Coco said to the group. "I need some advice."

Nikki's eyes narrowed. "Advice? Okay. I got time."

Ivy nodded. "Me, too. In fact, I could use some advice, too. Let's do it."

• • •

Later, the ladies sat together at a table in a Mexican barbecue spot, sipping drinks and eating nachos.

"You're telling me that nigga has a baby on the way with some chick he works with? And he came over there and blew your back out anyway?" Nikki chewed her food and shook her head in disgust. "That nigga ain't shit. You should consider yourself lucky. At least you're not the one who's pregnant by his trifling ass."

Coco nodded.

Deja rarely agreed with her sister. But this was one of those times. "Yeah. I used to like Derek. I thought you two had potential. But this is some unforgivable shit right here."

Ivy sipped her drink. "I always told you Derek was a bum."

Coco laughed. They all knew that Ivy never liked him.

"I could see right through him. He's cute, has a good job, a nice car. On the surface, he seems like he's something special. But the way he's been stringing you along all these years was a dead giveaway. He never committed, never stepped all the way up. And now that you're ready for those things, he's giving it to someone else. Didn't even have the decency to tell you until you practically dragged it out of him. That's some snake shit."

Coco agreed. "The only problem is that now that it's over, I think I love his trifling ass."

Nikki groaned. "Damn. I know how that is. Soon as it hits you that it's really a wrap, that shit cuts deep!"

"You gotta pivot immediately," Ivy said.

"Pivot?" Coco repeated, confused.

"Yup. You're young, single, ready for love. Get back out there. Time to meet somebody new and start fresh."

Deja agreed. "She's right. You need to get your mind off

Derek. Start seeing other people so you can occupy your time and your thoughts with something besides him."

Coco shrugged. "So, what you suggesting? A matchmaking service?"

Ivy laughed. "You're not that desperate."

"That's not desperate," Deja defended. "Online dating is the new wave, bitch. A lot of my clients met that way."

Coco grimaced. "I don't think so."

"You don't have to date some stranger," Nikki said. "You meet men all the time at your job. You're in media. There's men all over the place."

Coco shook her head. "I've been the marketing director at Live Nation for three years now. All the men I meet are either married and looking for a side chick or gay and looking for a beard."

Deja scoffed. It was times like these that she was glad she was married and not in the dating game.

"Then you should let me hook you up on a blind date," Nikki said.

There was a twinkle in her eye as she said it, and it both intrigued and scared Coco.

"With who?"

Nikki shrugged. "Let me think about it. My party is tomorrow night, so let me go over the guest list in my head. I'll pick out the single men that are coming."

She sipped her drink and mulled it over.

"You trust her?" Deja asked.

Coco shrugged. "How bad can it be? I'm doing a terrible job picking out my own men, apparently."

Ivy laughed.

A light bulb seemed to go off in Nikki's head. Her eyes widened and a grin spread across her pretty face.

"I know exactly who you should go out with!"

"Who?" Coco demanded.

"This guy named Ziggy."

Deja snickered. Coco's eyes narrowed.

"What kind of name is Ziggy, bitch?"

Nikki was beaming. "He's such a nice guy. He works in the music industry. He's some kind of big producer or whatever. Successful, athletic, cute. Perfect for you. I can't believe I didn't think of it sooner."

Coco was still skeptical.

"So, why don't you go out with him?"

"Because, silly. He's friends with Big Baby. So, I can't double-dip. You know what I'm saying?"

Ivy laughed, and Deja rolled her eyes in disapproval.

"I can't imagine being in a relationship with a nigga who calls himself 'Big Baby.'"

Coco laughed. "That's why I'm nervous about this Ziggy guy."

Deja shook her head. "I don't know what makes me sadder. Hearing the bad news about you and Derek or knowing that you're about to let Nikki set you up."

Nikki sneered. "You're just mad 'cause you're stuck with Bobby's boring ass for a husband." She smirked. "Don't hate. Just say the word, sis, and I'll hook you up, too."

Deja drove home afterward with Nikki riding shotgun. Both of them did their best to keep the conversation light between them. When there was no one else around to play referee, they tended to hit below the belt with their digs at each other. Remarks that would normally be shrugged off turned into full-blown arguments when they were alone. So, to keep the peace, they talked about Nikki's upcoming party, about her plans to return to LA in a few weeks, and how Deja's daughter Bree was growing up before their eyes. Deja was careful not to mention anything about her indiscretions with Sterling. If Nikki knew she was stepping out on her marriage, she would have a field day with that information. Bobby and Nikki had a contentious relationship, to say the least.

"Bree said she needed some advice about something," Nikki said. "I bet it's about a boy." She stroked her long ponytail absently. "I just hope it's not one of them corny white boys you got her going to school with out here in Staten Island."

Deja frowned. "Why would she call you for advice about a boy? She has me."

"Exactly," Nikki said, looking at her sister like she was dumb.

"Oh, please! Bree knows that she can talk to me about anything."

Deja secretly wondered if she had missed anything lately while she had been preoccupied with Sterling. She looked at Nikki defensively.

"Okay," Nikki mumbled. "Whatever you say."

Deja sucked her teeth as she pulled into her driveway. She parked the car, still bantering with her sister as they climbed out and walked up the steps and into the house.

Across the street, someone sat in his car watching them. Watching and waiting for just the right time to make his move.

"Hey, Aunt Nikki!"

Bree sprang up off the sofa the second Nikki and Deja stepped through the door. She ran to her aunt and hugged her tightly. Nikki hugged her back just as tightly.

"Hey, sweet pea!"

Deja cut her eyes in their direction. "Hello to you, too, daughter."

Bree finally broke free from her aunt and gave her mother some love in the form of a quick kiss on the cheek.

"Hey, Mom." She turned her attention quickly back to Nikki. "I didn't know you were coming over today."

"I need to raid your mama's jewelry box real quick. Then me and you can chat."

Deja folded her arms across her chest. "Right, because Nikki said you needed some advice—"

"Not *advice*!" Bree protested. She glared at Nikki, her eyes pleading. "It's just something . . . random." She fidgeted with her bracelet. "Anyway, Daddy just got home. He's upstairs taking a shower. I think he wants to go out for dinner."

Deja set her keys down on the table in the foyer and watched her daughter squirm. It was clear Bree wanted to confide in Nikki about something, and now she wanted to shut the topic down.

"We can order something. I ate already. Tell me more about this random thing."

Bree sucked her teeth, and Nikki giggled.

"Stop being nosy," Nikki said. "Bree and I talk about a lot of things without you. We just don't tell you 'cause we don't want to hurt your little feelings."

Deja frowned and opened her mouth to respond, but Bobby walked in before she could utter a word.

"What took you so long to get home?" he asked.

She sized him up, still frowning. "Hello to you, too."

He softened. "Hey, babe." He walked over and kissed her. He waved half-heartedly at Nikki, then turned to Deja again. "You didn't get my calls and texts?"

She chuckled and held up her phone in defense. "Battery's dead," she lied. She had turned her phone off after Bobby's third text.

He nodded and headed toward the kitchen, calling out to her over his shoulder as he walked. "I wanna try out that new spot on Hylan Boulevard. The Mexican spot."

Nikki laughed. "Too late! We just came from a Mexican spot. Food was good, too."

She kicked her shoes off and stepped into her sister's sunken living room, heading for the couch. Bree giggled and followed closely behind her.

In the kitchen, Bobby took a deep breath.

"How long are you staying, Nikki? Shouldn't you be getting ready for your party tomorrow night?"

"Don't worry, Officer. I'll be on my way real soon."

"Sergeant," he corrected her.

She rolled her eyes. Deja did, too, though she was careful to make sure no one noticed.

Bobby looked at his wife. "What are you wearing to this party tomorrow night? I want to make sure our colors don't clash."

Deja laughed. "Who are we, Beyoncé and JAY-Z?"

Nikki laughed, too. "More like Cliff and Clair Huxtable."

Deja stopped laughing and scowled at her sister.

Bree looked at Nikki and smiled, admiring the skimpy, curve-hugging dress she wore. "If I was old enough to go to your party, I would wear *that*!"

Bobby's heart sank. He looked at Nikki's dress disapprovingly. Deja was frowning, too. The garment left nothing to the imagination, drawing attention to Nikki's tiny waist, perky, bite-sized breasts—braless today—and her natural, round-and-ripe ass. The "dress," if one could call it that, was figure hugging and bright yellow, popping brilliantly against her brown skin.

"Fix your face!" Nikki said to Deja, laughing. "You're just mad 'cause you're married and you can't wear clothes like this anymore."

Bobby sucked his teeth. "Deja always had too much class to walk around dressed like that, even when she was single."

Nikki laughed a little too loudly for Bobby's liking. "Okay! If that's what helps you sleep at night. Believe that."

Deja knew what was coming. Every time Nikki hung around too long, Bobby had to make some slick remark to piss her off. Inevitably, Nikki would respond with a verbal takedown, and the two would go at it for hours.

Nikki glared at Bobby. She knew he didn't like it when she came around. She had overheard him saying she was a bad influence on Bree. As if she wasn't the one keeping her young niece from losing herself while growing up in this household. Bree confided in Nikki often, and Nikki kept her secrets. She gave her advice the only way she knew how—raw and uncut. Whether Deja and Bobby appreciated it or not, Nikki's relationship with Bree was special.

Bobby tried to stifle his disdain for Nikki. He hated she was so unapologetically hood. That she sold her body, and seemingly her soul, to the highest bidder. True, it had made her hood rich, but he wished Nikki would figure out a path in life that didn't involve cozying up to some man or putting her ass on display for a dollar. He worried about what Nikki's lifestyle was demonstrating to Bree. She loved seeing her aunt in all the blogs chasing ballers, throwing drinks, arguing, and going shopping. She admired the number of followers Nikki had on social media and the way people reacted to her on the street. But in Bobby's opinion, Nikki's lifestyle was a bad example for his baby girl.

Deja gave her sister a hard time about her life choices, but she often envied Nikki's unapologetic way of navigating life. Nikki grew up being footloose and fancy-free. Popular, loud, and outspoken, after high school, she'd set out into the world like a leaf on a breeze, blowing wherever the wind carried her.

Then, in the blink of an eye, Nikki was on a reality TV show arguing with the wife of some hip-hop mogul—a woman who'd found out Nikki had been her husband's side piece. Instead of being embarrassed by her behavior, Nikki had built a brand around it. Today, she had over a million Twitter and Instagram followers and was often on the same red carpets as celebrities with actual talent.

The difference, Bobby enjoyed pointing out, was that those celebrities had earned their fame through years of hard work in a reputable field. Nikki had taken a shortcut, using nothing more than her looks and her infectious personality. And she was winning! He hated to see it.

Bobby rifled through the drawers in the kitchen looking for menus. He ignored his disappointment that Deja had eaten dinner without bringing anything home for him and Bree.

As if on cue, she entered the kitchen. She wrapped her arms around his waist and kissed his cheek.

"She followed me home from the hair salon," she whispered. "I'll get rid of her soon. I promise."

Bobby smiled and kissed her on the forehead.

The doorbell rang, snapping them out of their stolen moment.

"I'll get it," Bree called out.

"You expecting company?" Bobby asked.

Deja shook her head. Both of them headed for the front door. They found Bree standing frozen in the open doorway. Deja noticed the odd expression on her daughter's face and rushed forward.

"Who is it?" she demanded.

She stepped to the door and came face to face with her past. A gasp escaped her throat.

"Hey, Deja," Rashid said. "Long time no see."

Daddy Issues

Deja froze, just like Bree. Bobby was right behind them, the whole family staring back at Rashid, speechless.

He looked at Deja, drinking in all of her. They were both older now and she looked incredible as always. Still had that long hair he used to play in, that smooth skin. Right now, though, she stared like she saw a ghost. He looked at Bree, who also looked shocked to see him.

Rashid smiled down at her. "Hey, baby girl. Do you know who I am?"

She nodded, and relief washed over him. At least she knew. His smile widened. She was beautiful. The perfect combination of him and Deja.

"You're my father," Bree said.

It sounded like music to him, those words spoken in her sweet voice. He wanted to cry.

Instead, he nodded. "Yes, I am."

He stepped forward, opening up his arms, and Bree rushed in. She began to cry for reasons she couldn't understand as she hugged him, and he fought back tears of his own. In the environment he had been in for the past fifteen years, crying was the ultimate sign of weakness. Prison had hardened him to the point that he wouldn't allow himself to shed tears. Not with people watching. He hugged his daughter tightly and closed his eyes, reveling in the moment. It was one that he would never forget.

Bobby looked on, a whirlwind of emotions stirring up inside him at once. He stepped closer to Deja and placed his hands on her shoulders. She winced a little, feeling it was suddenly inappropriate for Bobby to touch her in front of Rashid. She chided herself, and reached for Bobby's hand reassuringly. She wasn't sure what to feel or what to say. She watched the tearful emotion between father and daughter and wondered what the fuck she should do next.

Finally, Bree stepped back and looked up at Rashid. He wiped her tears and smiled at her.

"You're beautiful. Even prettier than all the pictures your grandmother sent me over the years."

Bree smiled shyly.

"You have my nose," he said giddily. His eyes scanned all the details of her face, taking in all of her features, every freckle.

"Well, who is it?" Nikki demanded as she approached the front door. She saw Deja and Bobby standing frozen like zombies and stepped past them to peer outside.

Just as her sister had, Nikki gasped at the sight of him.

"RASHID! OH MY GOD! WHAT THE FUCK?"

Nikki rushed past her sister and ran toward Rashid. He laughed as she barreled toward him and he scooped her up in his arms, swinging her around.

"Nikki, damn! You're still a wild one!"

He put her down and she could barely contain herself. She hugged him tightly, then stepped back to get a good look at him.

"Oh, my goodness, Rashid! When did you get out?"

"Few months ago. I had to get myself together. Get on my feet; get established. Then as soon as I got that done, I came to see my baby."

He looked at Bree and smiled. She hadn't taken her eyes off him for a moment. He looked at Nikki again.

"Look at you! All grown up. Last time I saw you, you were a skinny little brat that used to follow us around all the time."

She laughed. "I'm still a brat, but I got the followers now!"

"I heard! You got a lot of fans up north, trust me."

Nikki shook her head in amazement. "I can't believe you're here. Oh my God."

She looked at Bree and could see how happy her niece was. She looked at Deja and Bobby still standing frozen in the doorway like mannequins.

"Well, invite the man inside!" she shouted.

Deja seemed to literally snap out of her trance. "Oh! Yeah, come in." She stepped aside, but Bobby didn't move. He looked down at Deja and cleared his throat. His voice was low when he spoke.

"You think that's a good idea?"

Deja looked back at him, unsure what to say.

Nikki read the situation and walked over to them. "This is Bree's *father.* Step aside, let that man in the house, and have a conversation. You owe him that shit at least!"

Bobby glared at Nikki. He had never despised her more than he did right then.

Deja stepped between them. "Everybody come inside." She looked at Bobby. "We don't want to make a scene in front of the neighbors."

Nikki sucked her teeth. "Y'all so full of shit."

Nikki gestured for Rashid to come in, and he followed her and Bree inside the house.

Deja was having an out of body experience as she walked into her home and led Rashid into her living room. She gestured toward the sofa and he sat down. Bobby sat across from him in the recliner, perched like a king laying claim to his throne. Nikki seemed to notice, too, and glared at him, sitting on the loveseat beside her sister.

Bree stood awkwardly near the TV, uncertain what to say or do. She couldn't remember a time when she'd been in the same room as her father. For her entire life, he had been a phantom, an image in a faded photograph she kept in her diary. Her mother rarely spoke of him. She only had a handful of stories to go on. Now, here he was. She wasn't sure how to feel.

Rashid looked at her, held her gaze. "Come sit next to me. Please."

She walked over and sat beside him, wanting to hug him and hold on to him for dear life. But she sensed that urge would betray the man sitting across from her whom she had been calling "Daddy" all of her life. She looked at Bobby now and found him looking back at her. She smiled at him weakly.

"You okay?" Bobby asked.

Bree nodded.

Deja searched her mind for what to say. She had known someday this day would come. That she would be face to face with him again. That he and Bree would confront her with their questions and criticisms about how she had handled things in Rashid's absence. But even though she had known it was inevitable, she wasn't ready. She was unprepared for what would likely be a trial by jury.

"I don't know where to start," she said honestly, looking at Rashid.

He stared at her for a while, thinking of all the things he'd rehearsed saying to her over the years. All the names he'd wanted to call her; all the rage he'd wanted to unleash on her. But now, it all seemed secondary. The most important person in the world was seated beside him.

He looked at Bree. "Let's start with what you know about me."

She glanced at her mother. "Mommy said that you two fell in love in high school. That you were . . ." She looked at her parents, unsure.

"You can say it," Rashid said. "Don't be embarrassed."

She nodded. "That you were committing crimes. Selling drugs and stuff. And somebody got hurt."

Rashid nodded. "That's all true," he admitted. "I was hustling and making some bad decisions. But I didn't kill anybody. I didn't do the crime they sent me to jail for."

Bobby scoffed. Rashid glared in his direction.

Bree cleared her throat and Rashid turned back to her.

"Why did you go to jail if you didn't do it?" she asked gently.

"The cops set me up," Rashid said firmly. "Simple as that. I was nowhere near the scene at the time the man was killed. Your mother testified to that in court. I was with her when they said that I was driving a getaway car. But we couldn't prove it. And the jury didn't believe her."

Bree was surprised by that information. Deja avoided looking in her direction, wringing her hands in her lap.

"You never told me that."

Deja shrugged slightly, shifting in her seat. "It was hard for me to talk about it. I was under a lot of pressure at that time."

Bobby shook his head, doing all he could to hold his tongue. In his opinion, the jury hadn't believed it because it hadn't been true. He'd made up his mind that Deja had been pressured to be Rashid's alibi and had testified under duress. Hearing this criminal defending his drug dealing, murderous past sickened him.

Rashid pretended not to notice Deja's husband as he postured across the room. He concentrated on his daughter.

"There's probably a lot that your mother never told you. She's gonna have to explain that to you. But she knows that I'm not guilty. And I know it. God knows it. I want you to know it, too. I'm a lot of things. Some good, some bad. But I'm not a killer. You don't have to be afraid of me."

Bree nodded. She felt so torn. So grateful to her stepfather on one hand, but so eager to know more about her biological father.

She turned his question back on him. "What do you know about me?"

Rashid's eyes widened. He thought about it, tried to come up with an answer that wasn't as bitter as he felt right now.

"Not much," he admitted. "Your mother did a good job making sure of that."

"That's not necessary," Bobby said defensively.

"This don't have nothing to do with you." Rashid glared at Bobby as he said it. "With all due respect."

"It does, though." Bobby sat forward in his chair. "Deja's my wife and Bree—"

"Nah, Bobby," Nikki interjected, "Rashid is right. This ain't got nothing to do with you. Rashid has been a part of our family long before you came along." She looked at her niece and narrated the story from her point of view. "When your mother was with Rashid, he used to hit us off all the time. Money, clothes, jewelry, whatever. Then he got locked up, and Deja morphed into Michelle Obama. Forgot all about him. She met Bobby, got married, and moved on. Now, he's back, and he deserves the chance to talk to his child without y'all interrupting him."

Bobby scowled at Nikki. "This is my house. If anybody doesn't like the way I—"

"It's *my* fault," Deja said quickly.

This was about to turn ugly, and she wanted to shine the spotlight where it belonged. On herself and the decisions she alone had made.

She looked at Bobby. "She's right."

"Mmm-hmm," Nikki muttered.

Deja ignored her and looked at Rashid. "I'll explain it all. I swear. But first, I need to know when you came home. Where are you staying now? How did you find us?"

He sneered a little, annoyed she thought she could demand answers after years of silence on her part. Still, he decided to humor her. For their daughter's sake.

"I came home eight months ago on parole. While I was away, I learned a trade. Came home and got a job. Got on my feet. I got in touch with your mother. She kept in contact with me over the years. Sending me pictures of Bree, that type of thing. So, when I came home, I reached out to her. She said I should call you, set something up so we could meet. I had your number for a while now. But you don't have a good track record of taking my calls. So, I decided I would just stop by instead."

Deja stared back at him.

"So, Ruthie gave you our address?" Bobby asked.

"No, she didn't give it to me. I found that out on my own, Officer."

"Ha!" Nikki laughed sardonically. "Sergeant, boo. He just corrected me a little while ago on that shit." She rolled her eyes.

Rashid smirked, reminded why he loved Nikki. At least she hadn't code switched the way her sister had.

"You seem to know a lot about us. Where we live, what I do for a living," Bobby said.

Rashid looked him in the eye. "It's my job to know where my daughter is living, who she's living with. So, yeah. I did my homework. Like I said before, this don't have nothing to do with you. I came here to see my daughter."

Bobby huffed.

Bree looked at her fathers—the one who had raised her and the one whose DNA she shared. She could sense they weren't going to get along, and already she could tell she would end up being caught in the middle.

Rashid looked at Deja. "I have some questions for you," he said. "Why did you disappear with my daughter like that?"

"I didn't disappear." Deja's voice was barely audible.

"You ran. With no warning. Stopped writing to me, stopped taking my calls, stopped coming to see me. Even though you knew I wasn't guilty. After all the shit we talked about. Six months after Bree was born, you packed up and moved out of your mother's house. Left her to tell me that you changed your mind. And you never looked back. Now Bree's a teenager and I'm laying eyes on her for the first time. So, if that ain't disappearing, you tell me what it is."

"I think we should have this conversation without Bree," Bobby said. "She doesn't need to—"

"Yo, I'm trying real hard to be respectful in your house, nigga. But you don't get to talk to me about what my daughter needs."

Bobby started to stand. Nikki edged forward in her seat.

"LISTEN!" she shouted.

Bobby froze. Both men looked at her.

"Y'all have to understand where Rashid is coming from. Deja did walk away with Bree." Nikki looked at her sister. "If it was the other way around, you would want answers, too. So, you need to explain to him why you did that. And maybe Bree needs to hear that, too. I'm sure she has a lot of questions, too."

Bree nodded.

"I do. I'm not mad at you, Mom. You told me before that you were young when you had me, and you were scared. I just want to know why you never let me write to him or visit him the way King and Noah visit their dad."

Deja sighed. She looked helplessly at Bobby. She wished he weren't there. He didn't need to be present for this conversation. Then she reminded herself that Bobby had been the only father Bree had known. And, for that reason, she didn't protest when he settled back in his chair.

"When Rashid went away, I had no idea what to do. I never expected it and I wasn't ready for it. On top of that, I was a young mother. I just couldn't do it."

She looked at Rashid apologetically. "I knew you didn't do it. I knew that the cops were setting you up. When I testified, I was scared to death. The DA tore me apart on the witness stand. I was so nervous that I started contradicting myself, but I was telling the truth. I was dumb enough to think the jury would see that. I thought they would understand that I was just nervous, and I was being yelled at with everybody looking at me. I kept thinking it was all gonna go away. That your situation was temporary and that you would come home. But they found you guilty."

She thought about the heartbreak she suffered at that time, losing Rashid to a prison system designed to eat men alive.

"I visited you on Rikers, and it was horrible. I was twenty years old, pregnant, and scared to death. That wasn't the life I was used to or the one that I signed up for. When I gave birth, I was by myself. When I brought her home, I had to figure out how to take care of her, and you weren't there to help me. I brought Bree up there to see you when she was six months old, and it was the worst experience of my life. She was crying, I was struggling, and I felt alone. I was crying because it wasn't the way I'd pictured it. I couldn't imagine a life where I would have to bring my daughter to a dirty, cold prison with guards who treated us like shit. We didn't belong there."

"But I did?"

Deja didn't respond.

Bobby was tempted to. He wanted to remind Rashid he had been the one who'd decided to sell drugs. Not Deja. But he kept his mouth shut and let Deja speak for herself.

"You knew me, Rashid."

"I thought I did."

"You knew that I wasn't built for that life. You knew who I was when we got together. I was never comfortable in situations like that. I was . . ."

Deja glanced at her husband. She wanted to tell Rashid how in love with him she had been back then. How her love for him had made her willing to turn a blind eye to the ways he got money so she could continue to be with him. But saying that now in front of Bobby seemed wrong. Again, she wished that he would go away.

She shook her head, frustrated. "I was never impressed by your money or the life you lived. At the time, I just wanted to be with you. Then it hit me that you were not coming home. I was on my own with Bree. And I could do what Ivy chose to do—stick around and commit to a lifetime of visits upstate and heartache. Or I could live my life and give our daughter the best possible life. That's what I chose to do."

Rashid stared at her for a while, then finally nodded.

"I get all of that," he said. "Fine. You decided you weren't built for a life with me. But why did that mean that you had to take my daughter away from me completely? You could have kept in touch with my family, let them bring her to see me. But you just skated on everybody. Even your mother."

"Hmm!" Nikki said, nodding. "That's a fact."

Deja side-eyed her sister. Rashid kept going.

"And you got a point when you said that I knew who you were when we got together. You was always the diva with high standards. But after I broke through all that and we got together, don't act like you didn't know about the grimy shit I was out there doing. You knew who I was, too. And you said you was down for that. Then you got scared and ran when the shit got real."

"I did get scared."

"You could have told me that. But you just took off. And you took my daughter. I need you to explain that part to me."

Deja sighed. "I didn't know what else to do, Rashid. That's all that I can say."

Silence hung in the air for several minutes, everyone lost in their own thoughts.

Bree spoke up. "I . . . umm . . . I feel excited to meet you finally. But I feel a little confused at the same time. I have a lot of questions to ask you."

She looked at Bobby, saw he was hanging on her every word. Saw a glint of fear in his eyes.

She looked at Rashid again. "Could we go somewhere and talk. Just me and you?"

Bobby shook his head. "It's a little soon for that." He looked at Deja, desperate.

Rashid called on all the things he had learned in the violence awareness program he had taken in prison. Because at the moment, every molecule in his body wanted to charge across the room and fuck Deja's husband up.

"Yo—"

Nikki and Deja both tensed when Rashid inched forward in his seat.

"Hold up!" Nikki said anxiously. "I think everybody should

take a fuckin' deep breath and chill for a minute. I know nobody asked for my opinion, but I think I'm probably the most impartial one here."

She looked at her sister. "You and Rashid need to have a conversation separate from all of us. All of this started with the two of you. Before Bree came along and before you married Bobby, it was y'all two. There's a lot of unresolved shit that you need to iron out before you bring Bree into it. Get on the same page as her parents now that Rashid is home."

She pleaded with her eyes, hoping Deja would listen to reason for once in her life.

"Me, Bobby, and Bree will stay here. You go take a ride somewhere with Rashid and talk this shit out first."

Bobby balked. "You're right, Nikki. Nobody asked for your opinion. You should stay out of this."

"*We* should stay out of this," she corrected. "I know she's your wife and you've been helping her raise Bree. But Bree is not your daughter. Rashid is her father. And he has a right to want to be in her life. Bree has a right to have a relationship with him. Whether you and Deja like it or not. I don't have fancy college degrees like you two do. But I have common sense. If you're all trying to do the right thing for Bree, the only place to start is at the beginning."

Deja was staring at the floor, unsure how to feel. On one hand, she did want to talk to Rashid alone. She had a lot she needed to say to him after all these years. On the other hand, she dreaded his wrath, fully aware he had every right to be pissed about her handling of things.

Rashid nodded. "We can take a walk real quick."

Deja looked at her daughter. Bree looked so hopeful sitting there beside Rashid. Seeing them seated together for the first time since Bree's infancy, Deja could see the resemblance between them. For the first time since walking away from her relationship with Rashid, she began to feel the full weight of her guilt for how she had handled things.

She looked at Bobby and saw he wasn't comfortable with any of this. But Bree was the important factor now. Whether they liked it or not, reckoning day had come.

"Okay," she said, softly. "Let's go."

Atonement

Bobby watched from the living room window as his wife walked down the driveway side by side with Rashid. His blood was boiling, most of his rage directed at his sister-in-law. He turned to her, his face and voice full of fury.

"You have a real hard time staying out of other people's business!"

Nikki sucked her teeth and plopped back down on the sofa. She crossed her legs and stroked her long ponytail.

"Oh, hush. You're just scared that your wife is gonna hang around with Rashid long enough to snap out of the trance you've had her in all these years. Maybe she'll come back here like the old Deja. The one who was in love with a trap nigga and not this Stepford wife married to Five-O that you turned her into."

"Shut up, Nikki."

"Make me."

Bree watched her parents walk off into the distance and thought about what they had been like as a young couple in love.

She watched the way Rashid walked with his hands in his pockets, his shoulders squared, a swagger with each step. Her mother walked with her head hung low and Bree wondered what they were talking about. Wondered what life would be like now that her father was home. She was so focused on her parents as they faded from view and on her thoughts that her aunt and stepfather's arguing was barely audible.

"You know this is the right thing to do," Nikki was saying. "Deja owes him an explanation after all these years. And she's a grown-ass woman. She don't need you there to speak for her or defend her. She needs to handle this shit all by herself. And you need to stay the fuck out of it."

"None of us owes that man shit!" Bobby was fuming. "You got her out there alone with some thug who's been pissed off at her for fifteen years. And I'm supposed to just sit here and be comfortable with that shit?" He walked over and retrieved his car keys from the hook on the wall. "I'm going to follow them."

"You a bitch!" Nikki laughed.

"Nikki, watch your fuckin' mouth!" Bobby shouted.

"Nope!" she yelled back. "If you go follow them, it's because you're insecure. You don't trust your wife. Period. And that shit is corny as fuck."

Bobby's chest heaved with all his anger and frustration. Not just at Nikki, but at the entire situation. Who the fuck did Rashid think he was showing up at their home unannounced? He angrily paced the floor and decided he would use all his NYPD resources to find out everything there was to know about Rashid.

He was unaware Bree was watching him now. As he pulled out his phone and began feverishly texting his cronies, she stared at him.

"Dad."

Bobby froze, looking up at her, and his heart melted. He hadn't realized it until then, but part of him had been wondering if Bree would still call him "dad" now that her real father was back on the scene. Hearing her address him that way made him smile.

"Mommy loves you," she said. "So do I. You don't have to worry. That's not gonna change."

Bobby choked up. He put his phone away and opened his arms. Bree walked over and hugged him, and he told himself that she was right. Nothing had changed.

Then he glanced at Nikki, saw the snide grin on her face, and knew the opposite was true. Nothing would ever be the same again.

Rashid looked around at Deja's suburban neighborhood full of sprawling lawns and wraparound porches. She watched him, noticing he still walked the same way. His stride was confident and controlled; his facial expression was serious. He looked ahead as he spoke to her, avoiding eye contact.

"I thought about you every single day while I was in there. Some days—especially in the beginning—I thought about all the fun we had. All the good times. But then when you bounced on me, I hated you for a long time. I spent years plotting how I was gonna get back at you. I still had friends on the street. They couldn't find you for a while 'cause you got low. Seemed like you disappeared. I would call your mother's house and she wouldn't tell me much. But at least she took my calls. She apologized for you. Told me there was no excuse for the way you were acting, and she felt sorry that I had no contact with Bree. For a while, it was hard to find you. Then my family found you on Facebook a few years ago. I put some people on it and found out you got married to some nigga out here in Staten Island. A fuckin' cop!"

Deja stopped walking. For the first time, it dawned on her that Rashid might have the wrong idea.

"He wasn't a cop when I met him. It's not like I went running to the cops after I took Bree and started over."

Rashid looked at her blankly. "That's exactly what you did. Maybe not intentionally, but you went and married a man as different from me as possible. Tried to make him Bree's father instead of me."

"That's not true."

"Yes, it is. Got her calling that nigga 'Daddy' when I've been right here the whole time."

"That's the part you don't get, Rashid. You weren't right here. You were all the way up north doing fifteen years. I was by myself."

"Until you met ole boy, right? Then you lived happily ever after?"

Deja looked away, searching for the right way to explain what she'd been up against back then.

"The most fucked up part is that you knew I was innocent."

She nodded. "Yes, I did. And you knew it, too. So, I couldn't understand why you wouldn't just tell them everything you knew. You knew who was actually driving Mikey around that night. All you had to do was tell the truth. I was on that witness stand trying to defend you and you wouldn't even defend yourself."

Rashid sucked his teeth. "What was I supposed to do, Deja? Stand up there and point him out in the courtroom, then go back to the hood with my head held high?"

"You were supposed to do what you had to do to come home to me. To Bree."

"That's not reality. Not in the world I was operating in at the time. So, I did what I had to do to survive. I thought you would do what you could to hold me down. I was wrong."

"We were kids, Rashid. I became a stereotype overnight. So did you. I was a single Black mother whose man was locked up. I had to figure out what the future would look like for us if you never came home. So, I moved out of my mother's house and got a place of my own. I went to school part-time and started working on my real estate license. Then I met Bobby when Bree was a year old. He was fresh out of college and had just applied for the police academy. And, yeah, he seemed like a safe bet. He loved me and he loved Bree and he took care of us."

"And I didn't. That's what you're saying, right?" Rashid asked.

Deja stared at him, unable to refute it.

"While you were figuring out how to move on and start a new life, I was fighting for mine. In there going through hell for some shit I didn't even do. I knew a lot of people had doubts about it. Whether I was guilty or not. But you knew for sure. And you still left me. That shit almost broke me. But I thought about this day, when I would finally see my daughter face to face, and I could tell her my story out of my own mouth. Tell her the truth."

Rashid looked Deja up and down.

"I thought about what I would say to you when we finally stood face to face too," he said. "I thought I wanted to say some really foul shit to you. Make you feel as small as you made me feel when I was locked up and you left me."

He looked at her with contempt.

"I wanted to tell you that I really loved you back then. I trusted you and I thought you would have my back and ride it out with me the way Ivy did with Mikey. But, nah. You left me when I was at my lowest point. And then all that love I had for you turned into hate. And there were times when I was in there going through hell, and I wanted you to suffer the way that I was. I even considered making it happen. Even from where I was, I knew how to get it done."

Deja shuddered a little. Rashid kept walking and she followed suit.

"That shit you did—taking my daughter away from me when she was all that I had to hold on to in there—was evil. It was fucked up. And now I don't even want to say all that foul shit to you anymore. I'm glad I didn't make nothing bad happen to you. Because you're not the person I thought I loved. The person I thought loved me. You're a phony. You and your bitch-ass husband. Y'all deserve each other. I really just want to see my daughter. Get to know her. And me and you never have to talk again as far as I'm concerned."

Deja's heart sank. She wasn't sure why his words cut so deeply, but she suddenly felt like crying.

"Rashid . . . I'm sorry."

"Save that," he said bluntly. "All I want to hear from you is that you and RoboCop won't try to get in the way of me connecting with my daughter. I'm not trying to break your little marriage up or none of that shit. You can tell ole boy to relax. All I want to do is see Bree. I want to take her out, bring her to meet her family. I want to talk to my daughter and get to know her. Let her get to know me. So, let's set that up."

Deja wasn't sure what she had expected from him, but she'd never wanted things to be this cold between them. She'd push thoughts of Rashid to the back of her mind whenever they surfaced, reminding herself that she had a new life with Bobby. Now that he was standing before her, as handsome and familiar as he had been years ago, she wanted to hug him. She wanted to apologize and plead for his understanding. But the look in his eyes said it was hopeless. Rashid's gaze was cold and emotionless as he looked back at her.

"Where are you living?" she asked.

"Brooklyn," he said. "I paroled to my mother's house when

I first got out. Like I told you, I learned electrical work while I was up north. Took some training in carpentry, masonry, that type of shit. I was locked up with a white boy. Italian guy with connections in construction. So, when I came home, I got a job working that. I'm still getting on my feet. But you know me. I'm resourceful."

Rashid was indeed that. She imagined he had probably connected with some of his old Brooklyn street cronies also.

"I got a place of my own now. Got a curfew I gotta adhere to and a parole officer I gotta check in with every week. But, otherwise, I'm doing all right. The only thing missing is my baby."

Deja nodded. She wanted to tell Rashid she was proud of him. But, somehow, she suspected he didn't want to hear that.

"Okay," she said. "I won't stand in the way of you having a relationship with her. For the record, I am sorry, Rashid. At the time, I told myself that I was doing the right thing for us. I didn't think about the fact that I was depriving you and Bree of having a relationship with each other. I told myself it was all in the name of survival."

She shook her head, ashamed now of how selfish she sounded.

"When can I come and get her?" he asked, ignoring her explanation.

She sighed. "Bree has a busy schedule—school, plus she takes dance class four days a week. But we can work it out. Maybe you can pick her up from dance class sometimes and drop her off at home. Or maybe you can see her on weekends."

She looked at him apprehensively.

He nodded, then started walking back toward her house. She trotted to catch up.

"What does she like to do?" he asked. "She into movies and music and all the typical teenage shit?"

Deja nodded. "Yeah. She likes all those things. She's close with Ivy's kids, Noah and Kingston. They hang out a lot."

Rashid nodded. "I heard Ivy moved out here last year. I figured you and her were still tight. No other reason for her to move all the way out here to Staten Island."

Deja wondered what else he had heard since his release.

"How long have you been watching us?" she asked.

Rashid stopped walking and looked at her. "You know me well enough to know the answer to that question."

She felt her pulse quicken. She did know. Back when they were a couple, Rashid had been eagle-eyed and shrewd, determined and covert. He would stake things out for weeks before making his move. Deja remembered the way he always kept an eye on her. In the early days of their relationship, it had excited her. He would text her while she was at a McDonald's counter at the mall with her friends and tell her to get him a cheeseburger. She would turn around and find him lurking at a table nearby watching her. It was like he always had her under surveillance. Back then, it had made her feel secure. He'd explained it was his job to make sure she was protected. So, he'd kept an eye on her at all times. She looked at him now and knew he hadn't changed. Surely, he'd had her in his sights for months. It made her nervous and excited at the same time.

"I know that RoboCop has a very close relationship with my daughter. I know that she takes her dance class very seriously. That she goes to a fancy private school with a bunch of white kids. And I know that you step outside with a coffee in your hand every morning at eight forty-five sharp. Usually wearing some heels and a pair of shades."

She hated herself for feeling aroused by the thought of him watching her.

He kept walking toward her house. This time, she had no problem keeping up.

"You still look good," he said flippantly. "Still got them sexy legs I used to spread open." He looked her up and down. "But you changed. You're not the Deja I used to know. That Deja was fun. She was smart and she was tough. She's gone now, though. You turned back into the prissy bitch I met in high school. The kinda chick who needs a man to hold life together for her because she's too weak to hold it together on her own. So, you got what you wanted. RoboCop is your trophy husband. With him, you have the nice house, picket fence, and shit."

Rashid laughed. "I'm happy for you."

She felt like he'd slapped her. Would have actually preferred a physical assault over the verbal one he had just unleashed on her. She fought back tears, aware that what made it hurt even worse was everything he said was true.

"I'll come and pick her up on Sunday. Take her for breakfast then I'll bring her to meet her family. After that, I'll bring her back home. We'll start there."

She nodded.

They arrived back at her front door and she led the way inside, still too choked up to speak.

Bree, Nikki, and Bobby were all seated in the living room with the TV on. None of them were watching it, though. All three of them were focused on their cell phones. When Deja and Rashid entered, they all snapped to attention.

"How was it?" Nikki asked anxiously. "Y'all good?"

Deja nodded and swallowed past the lump in her throat. "Rashid is gonna come and take Bree out on Sunday." She looked at Bree. "Is that okay with you?"

Bree nodded quickly. "Yes! I can't wait."

Rashid smiled. "Me, either."

Bree walked over to him and he hugged her tightly.

"Today was something I was looking forward to for a long time," he said. "I'm glad we're gonna spend some time together now. I promise there will never be a time from this day forward that I'm not in your life."

Bree felt tears spring forth and squeezed him even tighter. He kissed her on the top of her head and rubbed her back.

"I'll see you on Sunday, baby girl."

She nodded. "Okay."

He smiled down at her and wiped her tears away. He looked at Nikki and winked.

"Thank you," he said. "If you weren't here, this might have gone a lot different."

She hugged him goodbye and insisted they exchange phone numbers. Deja and Bobby watched as the two of them traded information. Then Rashid looked at them and offered a weak smile.

"Nice to meet you, Sergeant. Deja . . . peace."

As he walked away, he looked at her again. This time, when their eyes met, he thought he caught a glimpse of the girl he once knew. He told himself it was just his imagination and left her home quietly.

Deja watched the door shut behind him and felt the magnitude of her worlds colliding.

Background Noise

Ivy stepped out of the gym still sweating from her workout. She felt better than ever, like a weight had been lifted off her shoulders. Since deciding her relationship with Michael was officially over, she had stopped taking his calls. She ignored the threatening messages he sent to her through Noah and Kingston, warning if she didn't get back in line quickly, he would be forced to do something horrible. She no longer feared him, no longer cared what he might do or say to hurt her. She was determined to stop ignoring her needs. The first step was getting her health in order. She had joined a local gym and started eating healthier. She was feeling on top of the world.

She thought about her conversations with her sons recently, and how different they were from each other. Noah, who still had fond memories of the days when his father was a part of their lives, was anxious to keep an eye on Ivy. He questioned her comings and goings, and she was sure he was reporting back to Michael faithfully.

Kingston, on the other hand, seemed happy for his mother. He loved his father—as much as he could love a man he'd only connected with during prison visits. But he sensed his mother deserved to live her life. Kingston was adapting well to living in a new borough, going to a new school, and becoming a basketball sensation in the making. Ivy worried less about him than she did about Noah.

While Kingston was making friends in Staten Island, Noah was constantly drawn back to Brooklyn. Back to his aunt Patsy's house and her loose rules. Patsy's boys were hustling unapologetically with a slew of baby mamas to boot. That wasn't the life Ivy desired for her sons. She wanted more for them and was willing to uproot them from Brooklyn to accomplish that. Her recent decisions had been strategic ones. She had encouraged Noah to go to college to keep him off a harrowing path. When that failed, she moved to Staten Island, getting them away from Patsy and her toxicity. She was doing all she could to keep her boys from falling into the same trap she had watched Michael fall into.

As she approached her car, a man walked swiftly toward her. He had a hoodie pulled low over his face, and his hands tucked in the pockets. Years of being Michael's wifey had taught her well. Instinctively, she reached for the blade in her fanny pack, but froze as he got closer and she realized who it was.

"Rashid?"

He slid his hood off and walked toward her, smiling.

"Hey, Ivy. I should have known I couldn't sneak up on you. Always on point."

Her heart was racing. She thought about all the threats Michael had been making toward her lately, how he kept warning her that she never knew where or when something might happen to her if she tried to leave him. Now here Rashid was, out of jail and looming over her. She was breathless, and it had nothing to do with her workout.

"What are you doing here?" she asked. "When did you get home?"

"I came out here to see Bree. Thought I would stop by and see you at your new house. Mikey told me where you're living now."

Ivy nodded, though she was still confused. "But I'm not home. So how did you find me here?" She gestured toward the gym.

Rashid grinned. "I was on my way back to Brooklyn, but I got a call from Mikey. He asked me to stop by and see you. Told me you might be here. Noah said you been coming here a few times a week."

Ivy's heart sank. "So, you've been following me."

"Not for long. Mikey just has some concerns, that's all. Wanted me to find out what's going on with you. After what I went through with your girl Deja, I understand how he's feeling."

Ivy sighed. "Rashid, ain't you tired of doing Mikey's dirty work? Getting caught up in his bullshit cost you years of your life."

"We were both in the same game. We knew the rules."

"Mikey is in there doing time for something he actually did. You two are not the same."

"It hurts the same, though." Rashid's expression was blank, but his words were impactful. "When you go away, whether you're guilty or not, you go through the same shit. You feel alone. The only thing that makes it survivable is knowing that people love you. That they're thinking about you. I'm not saying that you're in the same category as Deja. What she did was fucked up on every level. But you've been doing right by Mikey. Making sure his kids see him, making sure he knows he's not forgotten. I don't think you should stop now."

Ivy looked off in the distance, thinking about what Rashid was saying. Finally, she looked back at him.

"I'm sure Mikey made sure that you came home to a whole bunch of money. You've been loyal to him for years, and I know he rewarded you for it. You still gave up fifteen years of your life being loyal to him. Now he sends you here to talk me out of leaving him. It's time for you to let him fight his own battles."

"He didn't send me here. I was already coming to see Bree, like I told you."

She nodded skeptically.

"And I'm not trying to talk you out of anything. I just want you to know that he loves you. That's it."

She scoffed. "Love is not supposed to be something people just say. Deja said she loved you, but she didn't have the decency to say goodbye to you. Michael says he loved me, but he can't find it in himself to let me be happy. Even for a little while. You of all people should understand where I'm coming from."

She shook her head.

"I'm trying to keep my sons out of jail, Rashid. I'm trying to keep myself from letting life pass me by. I love Michael. Always will. But I gotta love myself now."

Rashid felt sorry for her. He could see the torment she was going through, and her decision to leave Mikey hadn't been an easy one.

"I do understand," he said honestly. "And I hear what you're saying. I know it had to be hard all these years out here by yourself. But you're doing your thing. Mikey is proud of you. I am, too, for what it's worth."

She smiled and hugged him. "I'm proud of you, too. And I'm glad you're home." she said. "If you need anything, you know how to find me, apparently."

He chuckled.

"But I would appreciate it if you stopped delivering messages from Michael to me. I don't want to hear it. And you can tell him I said that."

She squeezed Rashid's hand, then walked off toward her car.

Michael was relieved when the guard called his name early on Saturday morning for a visit. He had worried Ivy had meant what she said, that she wouldn't be here to see him today. Now, he got dressed excitedly, praying she'd brought the boys with her this time. He hadn't seen his sons in a month, and that felt like an eternity in prison.

His days were regimented according to the rules of the facility that housed him. Now that he had been denied parole, this would be his reality for the foreseeable future. It would be years before he was up for parole again. In the meantime, his daily routine consisted of working in the mess hall—a privilege up north because of the access it gave him to food, weapons, and all types of other essentials—count times, yard time, and then lights out at eleven o'clock each night. Each day organized. Despite the privileges he enjoyed on the strength of his status among the inmates, prison was still not easy for him. He could never relax, never let his guard down. Happy moments were fleeting, always followed by some drama among inmates, and sometimes from the corrections officers themselves. Michael looked forward to visits and phone calls like oxygen.

Once dressed, he was patted down and thoroughly searched before the visit. Then he waited for his number to be called. When he finally heard it, he stepped forward and waited. The doors opened and he entered the visiting room, scanning it in search of his family. His jaw clenched when he spotted his little sister Coco seated at one of the tables in the back of the room. Alone.

He tried to hide his disappointment as he walked in her direction. She stood and hugged him tightly.

"Hey, big brother. I dropped everything and came to see you today. So, before we get started, I'm letting you know that if you get up and walk out on me the way you did to Ivy, I will fuck you up."

He smirked, shook his head, and held his hands up defensively. "I don't want no smoke."

"Good." Coco sat back in her chair. "So, let me get right to it. Obviously, Ivy's not here."

"Obviously." Michael's tone was sarcastic.

"She has a big event tonight. Nikki is having a party. Lots of sponsors, some celebrities—a lot of potential clients for Ivy. A lot of good press. Ivy is styling Nikki for the party, and that's an all-day thing. There was no way she could make it up here and get back to the city in time to get herself together for the party *and* get Nikki right. The boys are helping her get shit ready and everyone is busy with that. So, here I am. I moved mountains to get here because I could tell when I spoke to you on the phone the other day that you needed this visit. I could hear it in your voice."

Michael sighed. He looked at his little sister and decided to be honest about his feelings for once.

"Feels like I'm losing control of everything, sis. To keep it real, I'm fucked up off the fact that the parole board denied me. I'm tired of being in here, Coco. I'm starting to feel hopeless."

Coco looked at him, his words sinking in. She thought about the thing they never spoke about. About the life Mikey had taken over a drug debt. Mikey had never denied he'd committed the murder. Not to his loved ones, anyway. They all knew he was guilty of the crime he had been sentenced to prison for, though none of them spoke that truth out loud.

Still, they loved him. He was and had always been sweet Mikey to them, the provider and protector of the family. None of them wanted to see him locked up, certainly not for life.

However, the reality was he was guilty. He had taken a life. As much as Coco hated to admit it, her brother was reaping the crushing result of that decision.

She held onto his strong hands. Covered in jailhouse tattoos now, he looked so tough on the outside despite the inner turmoil he was obviously experiencing.

"They asked me if I was remorseful at the parole hearing," he said. "I told them I acted in self-defense and that I regret being put in that position. I could tell from the start that they had no intention of granting me parole, but I played along anyway. I got my hopes up just a little. Then they brought up all the incidents I got in trouble for since I've been locked up. They said they thought I needed more education. That I should have completed my GED while I was in here. Learned a trade or something. So, they wanted me to stay in, make better use of my time."

He laughed.

"I'm in here fighting for survival every day. Fighting the COs and the inmates, listening to fights happening in the next cell, watching fights in the mess hall and the yard. It's all day, every day. And I don't want you to think I'm in here losing. I'm on top. But I gotta fight to stay there. Every day. I don't bring that shit to Ivy or the boys. I don't even talk to Patsy about it. The only one I've told this to is you. Because I know you can handle it. You're tough. Just like me."

She smiled, flattered he knew that.

"All day long, I'm thinking about fighting. Stealing weapons out the mess hall. Pieces of metal, utensils and shit, so I have shit ready when it hits the fan. This is how I was on the streets, too. Except then, I got a break every now and then. When I came home, I had y'all. Had my family. Each night, I got to put away my weapons and just be Mikey. In here, I don't ever get to put that shit away, Coco. The only time I can breathe a little easier is when I step in this visiting room for a few hours. Talk to my wife, to my kids. Hear the stories about what y'all are out there doing. Watch y'all laugh and all that shit. I go back to my cell and that shit holds me."

As tough as he said she was, Coco was fighting back tears hearing her brother describe what life was like for him now.

"Ivy reminded me that I've been locked up for King's whole life. That Noah doesn't remember me being home with them. That shit hit me hard because it's true. The only thing they remember about me is this place. Seeing me in a prison uniform, herded around by some overseers. This is all they know about me. The only chance I have to bond with them is in here. I get to see them face to face, give them advice, hear the bass in their voices, see how much they've grown. And now she's taking that away from me."

Coco shook her head. "You said a lot just now. I heard every word. Now hear me out."

He gave a slow nod.

"When you first got locked up, I came with Mommy to see you in Rikers and I remember what you said to her. You said that you played the game knowing the rules. And the rules said that you had to stand strong and take the heat, no matter what. So, when they were offering you all types of snitch deals, you turned them down. You copped to your crime and didn't implicate anybody else for anything. I didn't know how to feel about it at the time, but now I respect it."

He nodded.

"When the boys were little and they needed to get to know

you, Ivy broke her neck to get up here as often as possible. When she opened her shop, I watched her work her schedule around her visits up north. When King started playing basketball, she would miss games so that she didn't miss a visit with you. But now it's all gotten bigger, Mikey. The boys are bigger. They have friends and social lives. Girls they wanna link up with on the weekends. Ivy is doing hair for some VIP clients now. It's not just a storefront shop in a strip mall. She's Ivy Donovan, and that shit means something in the industry now. So, she can't schedule a whole photo shoot around her visits up here anymore, Mikey. There's no easy way to say that. She's growing in her career. And she earned that shit. She deserves it. If you love her, you should understand that and cut her some slack. That's all she's asking for."

"That's not all it is. Trust me. I have eyes on the street still. I know she's been working out, shopping and shit. She's leaving me. I can feel it."

"Let's say she does. Is it gonna break you?"

Michael wasn't sure. He shook his head, though.

"Exactly! You're Mikey fuckin' Norris! Stop acting like you're losing. No matter how it might look, you're still on top. You still have me. You're not by yourself."

Coco was right. He sighed, forcing himself to man up. "You said Nikki's party is tonight, huh?"

"Yeah. Nikki's parties are always wild."

He nodded. "That shit's gonna be a movie! All the little young niggas in here love her. She's dating Big Baby, right?"

"I think they're taking a break right now. I'm not sure. She's supposed to be setting me up with some guy tonight. Some dude named Ziggy."

Michael frowned. "Ziggy? What kind of name is that?"

She shrugged. "Guess I'll find out tonight."

He shook his head. "Tell Nikki not to have you out there fucking around with no lame niggas. Find you a nice CEO. One of them corporate dudes you work with. Nice and safe."

Coco laughed. "Now, what would I do with a guy like that? All the men in my life are gangstas, big brother! And so am I."

He laughed. "Yeah. You a gangsta all right. Patsy is, too. Both of my sisters are thorough."

"That's right. Let me demonstrate that by whooping yo' ass at some Uno." She grabbed a deck of cards off the table nearby and grinned.

He rubbed his hands together. "Let's go," he said. "I'm about to make you mad you drove up here today."

Coco laughed and began to deal the cards.

"In two weeks, Patsy's coming to see you. Two weeks after that, I'll be back." She looked at him. "Ivy is taking a break. That's not up for debate. Patsy and I will bring the boys up if they want to come, but it's up to them, Mikey. If they're busy or they don't want to come, you gotta understand that."

He didn't respond right away, just picked up the hand that he was dealt and stared at it. Finally, he met her gaze.

"I hear you," he said. "Loud and clear."

Bobby was torn. Part of him was tempted to skip Nikki's party so he could stay home with Bree. Deja had been crazy enough to suggest they let Bree spend the night with Rashid while they went to the party. But Bobby had shut that down immediately.

"We don't even know this guy, Deja. You're basing your decisions off the guy you grew up with. He's been locked up for fifteen years now. You don't know what type of shit he went through in there, what type of man he is now or what he's into.

We're not leaving Bree with him overnight within twenty-four hours of him popping back in her life."

He was starting to wonder if he knew Deja at all. Even before Rashid showed up, he had felt her drifting. Working longer hours at The Firm, partying more with her sister and her friends. She was slipping from his grasp. Now he had to worry about losing Bree as well.

He considered offering to sit tonight out and stay home with her, but he wanted to keep an eye on Deja, too. Her sister and mother still had affection for Rashid. Nikki had fawned all over him, and Rashid had said Deja's mother kept in contact with him over the years. Bobby knew Rashid was under a strict curfew. And, for good measure, he had a couple of his guys watching his movements. There was no chance of Rashid being at Nikki's party tonight. But in the back of his mind, he wondered if Deja might be tempted to go and see him. To reconnect with the first man she had ever loved.

So, reluctantly, Bobby had agreed to let Bree hang out at Ivy's house while he and Deja went to Nikki's party. Ivy's sons were close with Bree, and he hoped the teens would be responsible enough to enjoy some freedom while the adults danced the night away.

He looked at Deja as she emerged from her walk-in closet in her bra and panties.

"We might not make it to the party if you keep walking around like that."

She was distracted and didn't hear him. He cleared his throat.

She looked at him, bewildered. "I'm sorry, baby. Did you say something?"

He wondered what she was thinking about that had her so

distracted. Then he decided he probably didn't want to know the answer to that question.

"No," he lied. "You almost ready?"

Ivy checked herself out in the mirror and gathered up the last of her things. Satisfied she had everything she needed, she made her way downstairs. She found her sons in the kitchen.

"Make sure that y'all order something to eat and then just keep your asses in the house for the night."

"We know, Ma. We got it."

Noah kissed her on the cheek reassuringly. "You look nice."

Ivy smiled. He always knew how to melt her heart. Compliments were the best way.

"Thank you," she said.

Kingston glanced out the window. "Deja and Bobby just got here."

Ivy kissed her sons goodbye and thanked them as they wished her well at her party. She was already heading down the driveway by the time Bree climbed out of the car.

"Hi, Miss Ivy."

Ivy gave her a big hug and gestured toward the house. "The boys are in there. I told them to order food, so make sure they feed you. And let me know if they do any dumb shit while I'm gone."

Bree laughed. "Don't worry. I will."

She walked into the house while the adults headed to Manhattan. The moment she stepped through the door, Kingston and Noah turned in her direction.

"All right," Kingston said, smiling. "Let's call everybody and get the party started."

Bree took her shoes off and got comfortable. "Is your friend Kevin coming? The one I met at your game that time."

Kingston's smile faded. "Yeah. Kev's coming through. You like him or something?"

"He's cute," she admitted.

Kingston was texting, lying across the sofa with his long legs stretched out before him. "I don't think I like the thought of you hooking up with one of my friends."

Bree laughed. "Why not?"

"'Cause what if he plays you? Then I gotta fuck him up."

She laughed again. "I'm a big girl. I think I can handle myself."

Truthfully, Kevin was the last thing on Bree's mind. She had a crush on Kingston. That had been the "random thing" Bree confided to her aunt Nikki about. She wanted to do something that would make King notice her as more than just a family friend. But she had no experience with boys whatsoever. She wasn't sure how to act or what to say around him. Nikki had advised her to play it cool. Act interested in someone else to see what his reaction was. That was exactly what Bree intended to do tonight.

Kingston thought about it and then shook his head. "Nah. I'm shutting that shit down in advance. I don't want you getting close to Kevin."

Bree frowned at him. "Why not?"

"You're too young for him."

"I'm about to turn sixteen. How old is Kevin?"

"Seventeen. Too old for you."

"Shut up, King!" Bree tossed a throw pillow and hit him in his head.

Noah looked at his brother warningly. "You better have them niggas outta here long before Ma gets back. You know she goes through this place with her magnifying glass like a detective. She finds everything."

Bree laughed. Ivy was notoriously no joke.

"What you 'bout to get into?" Kingston asked.

Noah grinned. "Brittany, hopefully. My shorty's coming over. I'm gonna be on 'do not disturb' mode tonight. You know what I'm saying? So, keep your little friends downstairs."

King laughed. "We're all coming upstairs and busting into your room soon as you get her little panties off."

Noah laughed and playfully hit his brother.

Bree chuckled. "Noah ain't getting no panties tonight," she teased. "Game ain't tight enough yet."

"Ooooooh!" Kingston fell back against the sofa cushions, dramatically.

Noah looked at Bree, surprised. Then he laughed. "Oh, word? It's like that?"

She shrugged. "I'm just saying."

"You ain't even seen me lay my game down on these girls, though. So, I don't know what you're talking about."

She giggled and winked. It was true. She was just talking shit. "Just testing your confidence, that's all."

Noah shrugged it off.

Kingston looked at him.

"She said your game ain't tight."

Noah sucked his teeth and walked out of the room. "We'll see!"

He couldn't wait for Brittany to get there. He would show them.

Kingston and Bree looked at each other and cracked up laughing.

"What you been up to, Bree? I haven't seen you in a while."

She tucked her feet beneath her on the sofa and turned to him. "My father came home from jail."

Kingston's eyes grew wider. "What? When?"

She shrugged. "A few months ago, I think. He just showed

up at my house yesterday. Freaked my parents out. Aunt Nikki was there. It was wild."

"Did you talk to him?"

"A little. But he talked to my mom the most. He's upset that she left him when he was locked up. That she took me away from him and kept us from knowing each other."

Kingston recalled all the conversations he and Bree had had over the years about their fathers. Kingston and Noah complained sometimes about how tiring the visits were. By contrast, Bree often complained her mother refused to give up many details about her father.

"How do you feel about it?" he asked.

She shrugged again.

"I want to get to know him. I always had questions about my father. I want to have a relationship with him and everything. But Bobby is my dad. He's been there for me my whole life. So, I don't want him to feel pushed aside. I just feel kinda mad at my mom. I don't understand why she never thought about how everybody would be affected by what she did. It's like she did the thing that was best for her, whether it was fair to me and my father or not."

Kingston nodded. "I think I would feel the same way if I was you. It's not easy to go see my dad all the time. Wait by the phone for his calls, send him packages, write him letters, and all that. But my mother does it. And I appreciate her for it."

She smiled at him. "I knew you would understand."

He nodded. "No doubt. You know I always got your back."

She swooned a little. "Good," she said. "So, let's talk about Kevin."

Kingston hit her with a pillow. "Stop playing with me, Bree!"

She laughed and set off a pillow fight of epic proportions.

• • •

Coco parked her Mercedes at the garage across the street from the venue and stepped out onto the streets of Midtown Manhattan in her Valentino pumps. Nikki's party was on the top floor of the iconic Decoration and Design building on the Upper East Side. Coco could barely contain her excitement as she stepped across Third Avenue.

She walked into the venue and headed for the elevators, her heels click-clacking across the tiles as she stepped. She was pleasantly surprised to find Deja and Bobby standing there waiting for the elevator, too, looking like an ad in a magazine. Bobby wore a fitted gray suit, and Deja looked incredible in a short and sexy white romper that showed off her long legs.

"You two look like a Black Ken and Barbie." Coco greeted them with hugs and kisses. "Is Nikki here yet?"

Deja rolled her eyes. "You know the diva has to make a grand entrance. Ivy went to meet her at the hotel so that she can style her hair for tonight. They'll be here soon, hopefully."

Coco nodded and gripped her clutch bag as they boarded the elevator. As it rose, they could hear the music from the party growing louder and louder.

"This should be fun. Just when you think Nikki won't be able to top herself, she does exactly that," Coco said.

She hadn't realized how excited she was until now. She was the first one to step off the elevator when it reached the top.

The place was jam packed. Beautiful people of every color, shape, and size filled the room, spilling out onto the terrace and moving on the dance floor.

Coco spotted a few familiar faces in the crowd and got lost within moments, greeting one colleague after another. Deja and Bobby headed for the bar. They ordered their drinks and stood there looking around at all the party people.

Normally, Deja would be working the room while he watched. But tonight, she sipped her drink in silence and didn't budge from her spot at the bar. Bobby had been watching her closely ever since her rendezvous with Rashid, taking notice of how zoned out she seemed lately.

"You okay?" he asked. "You seem distant."

She frowned. "I've been calling my mother, but she won't answer. I think Nikki told her that Rashid's home, and now she's ducking me."

Bobby waited for her to say more. It took a while, but she finally spoke again.

"Why would she go behind my back and send him pictures, write him letters, take his calls?"

Bobby waited again.

"It has to be because she knows I'm a fucked-up person. Bree thinks so, too. I can tell. She hardly talks to me since he came back."

Bobby sucked his teeth. "You know that's not true, Deja. It's only been one day. Everybody is just trying to process this shit."

"Bree is pissed. And she has every right to be. Nikki said—"

"Fuck Nikki!" He set his drink down on the bar. "I'm sick of her always saying something about how we handle things. She doesn't know what it was like for you all by yourself before we met."

Deja cringed a little, thinking back to what Rashid had said about her looking for a safe man to hide behind instead of finding the strength to stand on her own two feet.

"It wasn't that hard," she said.

Bobby frowned at her. "When I met you, you were living in a one-bedroom apartment in the Bronx with a one-year-old baby. You were on your own working part-time jobs so you could pay the rent, getting government assistance. Your family was in

Brooklyn and you were by yourself. You can't tell me that wasn't hard."

She frowned as he described the state he had found her in so grimly.

"I didn't have to do that. Maybe that's the part I never told you. My family had money. Rashid's family could have taken me in. I didn't have to do it on my own. That was my choice. I ran. From my family in Brooklyn, from Rashid, and from the person I used to be. Because that's what I needed to do. I didn't worry about what anybody else needed, and that was selfish. I gotta own that shit."

She took a good swig of her drink and set the glass down.

Bobby opened his mouth to speak but was literally drowned out by the crowd erupting into cheers. It sounded like Beyoncé herself had stepped into the room. Instead, as Deja and Bobby craned their necks to see over the crowd that formed around them, they discovered Nikki had entered the party.

The whole atmosphere had changed. The deejay switched to Cardi B, and the crowd parted as Nikki strutted through the center of the dance floor wearing a skintight red latex bodysuit, thigh-high boots, and the biggest, most fabulous Afro wig anyone had ever seen. It towered above the crowd in gigantic perfection as Ivy smiled proudly nearby. She had been working with Nikki in secret on this wig for weeks. Nikki wanted to look like a Black superhero with an Afro that would break records. This one came damned close.

Nikki danced provocatively in the crowd, everyone surrounding her now. She twerked and bounced her body to the beat. The party went ballistic. Deja looked around; Bobby had gotten lost in the press of the crowd. She looked again at Nikki, who was eating up all the attention and dancing with Ivy in the middle of the party.

Envy tugged Deja's chest as Nikki danced happily in the center of the room. Everyone was admiring her, cheering for her, adoring her.

Deja realized the last thing she felt like doing tonight was partying.

Bobby came up behind her, his arms encircling her waist. She tensed a little.

"Your sister always does the most," he said in her ear.

She smiled, painting on her poker face. "Right?"

She faced him, flipped her hair, and took his hand. "I think I had enough fun for tonight. Let's go home."

Bobby smiled. "I'm with you. Let's go."

Black Effect

The party was in full swing, and everyone was having a great time. Nikki gasped suddenly and gripped Coco's hand tightly.

"I see him," she whispered urgently. "Ziggy. He's here. Come on. I want to introduce you to him."

Coco's eyes widened. She wasn't expecting to meet this guy so soon.

"Damn, bitch! Let me pull myself together first."

Coco smoothed her dress and looked at her face in her cell phone camera.

Nikki swatted the phone down and led Coco away by the hand. Coco followed her nervously, glancing ahead to try and get a peek at whomever she was about to meet. She prayed for the hundredth time that he was cute at least. She knew Nikki had her best interests at heart, but the last thing she wanted was another disappointment.

Finally, they arrived at a group of people who were deep in conversation. Upon seeing Nikki, though, the crowd instantly parted and they all welcomed her with hugs and love.

"Nikki!" one older Black gentleman said.

He had salt-and-pepper hair and a very nice build for a man his age, but the man was old enough to be her father. Coco glanced at Nikki anxiously, praying this wasn't her mystery man.

"Oh, my goodness!" Nikki gushed. "Thank you so much for tonight. This is beyond all my expectations."

Nikki looked around as she said it. Waitresses were circulating hors d'oeuvres, ice sculptures were dotting the room, and free top-shelf alcohol was flowing freely. Nikki could see all her guests were enjoying themselves.

Radiating with joy and pride, she looked at Coco, who was still gripping her hand tightly.

"Coco, this is Mr. Edwards, the new eastern district brand ambassador for Mercedes-Benz. He helped sponsor tonight's event."

Coco shook his hand, her stomach doing flip-flops. His hand felt clammy in hers. She shuddered at the thought of it touching her body. She plastered a smile on her face, though, and greeted him warmly. She shot a look of quiet desperation at her friend.

Nikki had to resist the urge to laugh. Coco was probably cursing her out in her mind.

"Coco," Mr. Edwards was saying. "My wife has the same Cartier bracelet you're wearing, so, I can already tell you have great taste."

Coco smiled wider, relaxing a little at the mention of his wife. So, he couldn't be the "Ziggy" she was supposed to meet. Her eyes darted to the other people in the group. An Indian man, a blond white woman, two polished and well-dressed Black guys, and one tall—and rather handsome—white man. *None* of them looked the way she had pictured this "Ziggy" guy Nikki wanted her to meet. She was expecting a tall, dreadlocked Black man with a thick West Indian accent. Coco scanned them all again before Nikki finally stopped toying with her.

"Coco, I want you to meet Zachary Bauer." She gestured toward the white man, who Coco noticed was smiling at her brightly. "But all of his friends call him Ziggy."

Coco, stunned, drank him in. He *was* a good-looking man. Smoldering eyes, well groomed, cute. He looked like he might be in his forties, and it was clear he was fit from the way his suit hugged his body. He wore a dark-blue suit with an icy-gray shirt underneath. It was unbuttoned at the collar, revealing the slightest hint of dark chest hair. He had a sexy five o'clock shadow with a light mustache. His eyes were deep, dark blue and there was something about them that drew her in. He was intoxicating.

She looked at Nikki, her eyes wide.

"Ziggy?" Coco repeated in amazement.

Nikki nodded, smiling. She could tell Coco was absolutely floored and prayed this had been a good move. She wasn't sure whether Coco's reaction was because Ziggy was white or his undeniable good looks.

Finally, Coco pulled herself together and faced him again. "Ziggy." She chastised herself silently for repeating his name over and over like a fool. "Wow. It's very nice to meet you." She offered her hand to him in greeting.

He smiled, and the whole room lit up.

"The pleasure is mine, Coco. I've heard a lot about you."

He took her hand and held on to it. His voice was smooth.

Coco swooned a little.

Nikki beamed.

"I met Ziggy when I was a plus one at a big party he hosted at his house in the Hamptons. He works at Sony Music, and he's the coolest white guy I ever met."

Ziggy laughed.

"For real!" Nikki was smiling brightly. "And I remembered what you said to me by the pool that night."

"I remember, too," he said.

Nikki looked at Coco. "Ziggy was celebrating his fortieth birthday that night. He said he was sick of having all that house and nobody to share it with, and I should hook him up with a nice girl like me."

Coco chuckled. Nikki was a lot of things, but a "nice girl" wasn't necessarily one of them.

"So, here she is!" Nikki continued. "This is Coco Norris. She works in marketing at Live Nation, and she's a badass bitch!"

Coco smiled humbly.

"Coco has been my friend for years. We're practically family. So, don't embarrass me, Ziggy. Show her a good time."

Ziggy nodded. "You got it."

Coco looked at Nikki, her eyes still wide with amazement. This was unexpected. But with a friend like Nikki, Coco reminded herself there was never a dull moment.

Nikki disappeared into her crowd of adoring friends and fans, and together, Ziggy and Coco walked over to the bar. They jockeyed for position among the crowd. Finally, someone vacated a stool and Coco scampered onto it. Ziggy stood beside her, leaning against the bar. He gestured for the bartender and asked what Coco was drinking.

"Vodka and cranberry." She watched him order it and a glass of Jack Daniels for himself. Her eyes scanned his body. It was clear that he was toned and muscular underneath his tailored suit. He wore a simple gray pocket square in the suit jacket and no other embellishments. Coco was intrigued.

So was he, apparently. "So, you work in marketing. You like it?"

She nodded. "I do. I'm into seeing a project take shape from start to finish. Determining what will sell and what won't. I'm analytical, so it works for me."

He looked impressed.

"What do you do at Sony?" she asked.

"I'm a producer. That's how I met Nikki. I was working with Big Baby on his last album, and he brought her to my birthday party. She dared all the women by the pool to jump in naked. And she led by example—stripped her bikini off and jumped off the diving board. The other ladies followed suit. I loved her right away!"

Coco laughed. "That's my girl! Nikki knows how to get the party started."

Their drinks arrived, and he took a sip of his. "She knows how to end it, too. She got in a fight with one of my neighbors and kicked her ass on the front lawn."

Coco looked horrified. "Oh, my God."

"I didn't care. I can't stand the bitch. She's a racist Trump supporter who wasn't even invited to the party. She came to complain about the music and on her way out, she walked past Nikki. Made the mistake of saying the N-word within her earshot. The next thing I knew, Nikki had that lady sliding across the petunias!"

Coco laughed so hard she nearly spat out her drink. Ziggy laughed, too, still tickled by the memory.

"Anyway, I'm sure you understand why we've been friends ever since." He moved a little closer as the crowd swelled.

"So, you've known Nikki for a long time."

She nodded. "Feels like I've known her forever."

"How did you meet?" he asked.

"Our families used to be in business together. When the company folded, we remained friends."

He nodded. "What kind of business was it?"

Coco smiled. Normally, she would tell the truth about her family's history to any guy she dated. She wasn't sure why she was hesitant to do so now. She decided to keep it real.

"Pharmaceuticals."

He looked at her, and a slow grin graced his lips. "I see. Risky business."

She nodded. "Yes, it is."

"Is Coco your real name?" He sipped his drink, intrigued.

She smiled. "Wow, you start right in with the probing questions, huh?"

He held up his hands, apologetically. "Too personal?"

She chuckled. "No, it's good. You're direct. I like that. My name is Cara. 'Coco' is a nickname my mother gave me when I was a baby."

"Cara is a beautiful name."

She thanked him. "Did you always want to be a music producer?"

He shook his head. "No. Growing up, my mother wanted me to be a doctor. I went to college pre-med and all that. But I hated it. I was only in college for the parties. I started deejaying and learning the engineering side of music. My grades were terrible. I dropped out eventually and got a job interning at Def Jam. Broke my mother's heart."

"But look at you now," she said. "She must be happy that you turned out successful."

He nodded. "She lives in Florida now. And she's very happy that I made it. But she still tells me that she'd rather brag to her friends that her son was a doctor than a music producer."

He laughed.

"What kind of doctor would you have been?" she asked.

"A pediatrician." He took another sip of his whiskey.

Her eyes widened. "You like kids?"

"Love them. Nikki told you I turned forty last year. I thought that I would have a whole bunch of kids by now. But I've been so career driven. Makes it hard to settle down. Lately, I split my time between New York and LA. I prefer New York most of the time. But in the winter, you can keep it."

She laughed. Knowing how brutal New York City winters could be, she didn't blame him one bit.

"You should let me take you out some time. Get to know me a little better."

Coco giggled. As cute as Ziggy was, something just didn't feel right about it.

"Slow down, Ziggy. I gotta see if you can dance first."

He laughed, peeled out of his jacket, and gestured toward the dance floor.

"Let's go!"

Coco laughed, slid off the barstool, and led the way.

Kevin looked around at his teammate's spacious multilevel home on the richer side of Staten Island. When Kingston had invited them over to hang out, this was definitely not what he'd expected. The neighborhood where Kevin lived was nothing like this. He had grown up in the projects, where he and his family remained until about three years ago when his mother had saved up enough money to get them out. Now they lived in a modest apartment on the first floor of a home on the North Shore that was kind of rundown, but still had character. But for all the charm and comfort of his home, the place was nothing like Kingston's house out here on the predominantly white South Shore. As Kevin stared at the high ceilings, winding staircase, and plush carpeting, he realized for the first time that his new teammate was wealthy.

Kingston plopped down on the sofa, kicked his feet up on

the coffee table, took a pick to his Afro, and smiled. He couldn't stop smiling, actually, thanks to the effects of the weed he and his friends had just finished smoking. He watched as Mariah sprawled herself across the chaise facedown. He admired her ass, which was like a work of art. She groaned and rolled over on her side.

"I'm so high!" She exhaled deeply after she said it, twirling her long coils of hair with her fingers. "Kevin, where did you get that weed from?"

Mariah's friend Danielle and a few of Kingston's teammates from his high school basketball team scattered the room. Kevin plopped down in a recliner. He cracked open a bottle of Heineken from the six-pack they had brought over and took a swig.

"That's some purple I got from New Brighton yesterday. My man D be having that fire!"

"For real!" Mariah pulled herself upright and looked at her friend. "Danielle, no wonder you've been so mellow and calm lately. Ever since you and Kevin started going out, you been getting that *good* weed!"

Danielle laughed. "You act like we do this all the time. We ain't potheads!"

Kevin nodded. "Can't smoke during basketball season. Coach ain't having that shit. But now that the season is over, and we're just doing workouts here and there, we can get a little loose." He pulled Danielle closer and she leaned into him.

Kingston was their classmate at Curtis High School, a school with a good reputation for both sports and academics. The Warriors was both the name of their team and the spirit of their bond. Kingston had transferred there from Midwood High School in Brooklyn during his sophomore year and was welcomed to the team and the school with open arms.

Mariah nodded. She turned her head in Kingston's direction

and smiled. He was so cute to her as he sat there picking out his Afro with his eyes low. "I love your hair, King," she said, emboldened by the weed. "Can I braid it?"

Every molecule in his body wanted to jump off the couch and leap for joy. He had been crushing on Mariah since the moment he saw her in the hallway at his new high school months ago. Now, here she was hanging out in his living room asking permission to play in his hair. He forced himself to remain calm, cool, and collected.

"You can."

She smiled. "You gotta come over here, though. I'm kinda stuck." She giggled, clearly feeling a buzz.

Just as he was about to stand, Bree walked into the room.

"You better not let nobody do your hair, King. Miss Ivy will kick your ass."

He looked at Bree, surprised. He sat back, realizing she was right. His mother was protective of his crown.

"Where you been?" Kingston asked. "I forgot you were here for a second."

Mariah laughed, and Bree shot her a death glare.

"I was upstairs in your room going through your stuff," she said.

"You better not have been in my shit," he said, searching his mind for what she might have found there. "Why were you in my room?"

"Because I don't want my clothes smelling like *weed*. Y'all smoked like four blunts back to back in the garage. It smells like the projects out there."

Kevin laughed. "How you know what the projects smell like, shorty?"

She smiled and winked, pretending to be infatuated with him, according to her plan. "I might know more than you think."

Kingston frowned. He hated seeing Bree flirt with Kevin.

"Come sit down," he said, gesturing next to him. "I gotta keep an eye on you."

She tried to hide her excitement as she scampered onto the sofa beside him.

Kevin sipped his beer, his eyes still scanning the room and settling on the little details.

"So, how you like it out here in Staten Island so far, King?" He sat back, tempted to tuck his feet beneath the table. King had instructed them all to take their shoes off at the door, and Kevin was a little self-conscious about his socks as he sat in this spotless, fancy house.

Kingston shrugged. "I like it. Y'all been teaching me what I need to know about the different neighborhoods. Where to shop and eat and all that. So far from what I've seen, it ain't too different from Brooklyn. Just a lot quieter at night."

He laughed, and so did his new friends. One thing he had learned since his arrival in the city's "fifth borough" was that the island was a close-knit community. It was easy for promiscuous girls to develop reputations here. It made Mariah even more of a catch because none of his friends had been with her before him. Even at their young age, that was rare in a place like Staten Island.

Another teammate, Hezzy, gestured toward the TV that took up an entire wall on the far side of the huge room they were sitting in. He said the words they'd all been thinking since they'd gotten there.

"Niggas from Crown Heights living like *this?* You never told us you were rich, my dude."

Kevin and another teammate, Brian, laughed.

"Word!" Kevin bellowed, relieved someone else had spoken about it. He pointed toward a large and expensive-looking carving of an elephant hanging on the far wall near a large ficus tree. "I'm sitting here trying not to act all surprised. But, I'm like . . . I've never even been this far out on this side of the island before." He shook his head. "And this house is like a mansion or some shit."

Kingston chuckled a little and nodded. "My family in Brooklyn gets money. You know what I'm saying. Pops is locked up north doing time. He's been away since before I was born. My aunts and all my cousins are still in that life. My mother wasn't feeling it. She moved us out here to get me and my brother away from all that."

Kevin looked impressed. "Your pops been locked up your whole life? Damn!"

Kingston shrugged, looked at Bree, and patted her playfully on the knee, sending shivers down her spine.

"Mom's holding it down, though. She's friends with Bree's mother, who's a real estate agent. So, the next thing I knew, we were moving to Staten Island. My moms fell in love with this house the moment she saw it."

Mariah nodded. "I can see why."

Hezzy looked at Kingston. "What about you? You feeling it out here or nah?"

Kingston shrugged. "It's different. I'll say that much. Shit is divided. It's been like ten months now since we moved out here. So *now* when I go to school and then come back home every day, I can see the difference. Over where y'all live and where we go to school, that shit is like Brooklyn and the rest of the city. But over here, it feels like we living upstate somewhere. This is the suburbs for real!"

Kevin laughed. "You ain't lying. I've never seen this part of the island before, and I've lived on Staten Island all my life!"

"Word," Hezzy agreed.

Kevin swigged his beer again. "Cops don't fuck with you out here, King?"

"Nah. Cops don't patrol out here like that. I hardly ever see a patrol car over on this side. Only time I see cops is when I'm coming out of school. Over here, the worst part is the neighbors staring at me. Especially when I wear my hair out. They stare *hard*! I'm telling you, they act like they never seen Black people before."

He noticed his friends still looking around, admiring his home, and it made him feel uncomfortable. He hadn't invited them here to flex.

"Cops *stay* fucking with me," Hezzy said, staring at Kingston knowingly. "It's like they can't wait to see a nigga locked up. Like last week after I left my shorty's birthday party. It was a sweet sixteen, my nigga. I had a suit on! Cops still stopped me. Fucking with me. Asking me for ID. Wanting to know where I live. Talking 'bout '*Whose party was it? Are you selling drugs?*' Yo! I can't stand the cops, word to everything!"

"Especially out here," Kevin said, looking at Kingston. "Staten Island cops are different. They're all white, and all of them mu'fuckas is racist."

Bree sucked her teeth, thinking of her dad. "Not *all* of them."

Kevin shrugged. "All the ones I met out here are racist."

Kingston noticed the mood in the room changing. The difference between how he was living versus his friends was sucking the life out of the party.

"Come on, y'all. Let's turn up before my moms gets back!" He grabbed the remote for the stereo system and pressed the power button. Music filled the space. "Roll that weed up, Kev!"

An hour later, trap music still blared at full volume from Ivy's expensive sound system so loudly the floors quaked with the bassline. Noah had locked himself in his bedroom with his girlfriend long ago. They showed no signs of emerging anytime soon. Kingston's friends filled the lower level of the house while a few more of them were hanging out with him in the back of the house.

The garage had been designated the smoking area because Ivy never parked there when it was warm outside, opting for the driveway instead. So that was where Kingston was holding court now. He leaned against the wall, watching his friend Rickie rolling up some weed in a gutted Backwoods cigar. A few of their friends made amateur attempts at freestyle rapping in a cypher, Kevin among them. Bree stood nearby watching, a slight smirk on her face as she watched Kingston hyping up his friends.

He looked up and caught her staring. A smile crept across his lips, and he motioned her over. She smiled back and was just about to walk over to him and his friends when Mariah suddenly appeared at her side.

"Hey," she said. "Bree, right?"

Bree's smile faded involuntarily. She couldn't put her finger on it, but there was something she didn't like about this Mariah chick. She nodded. "Yeah."

"I think your parents just pulled up. There's a pretty lady in a cute short set with some corny dude looking for their kid out front. It's probably time for you to go." Her tone was antagonistic, her expression smug.

Bree stared at the girl, momentarily stunned. First of all, it was way too early for her parents to be there. Nikki's parties always went on well into the wee hours of the morning. Second of all, she didn't like Mariah's tone. She wanted to slap the bitch in her face.

Bree glanced at Kingston, who was laughing obliviously with one of his friends. She turned her attention back to Mariah.

"My father's not corny. And I ain't no kid, bitch. So, watch how you talk to me."

Mariah's face registered momentary shock. Then she laughed as Bree rushed past her into the house in search of her parents.

Bree cringed at how much louder the music was inside the house, and she cursed under her breath that Kingston and his friends had ignored her earlier warnings to turn it down. She walked through the dining room and found her parents standing in the adjacent living room surrounded by a bunch of Kingston's friends. Her mother looked uncomfortable, standing half-dressed in a room full of teenage boys. Her father's expression was one of pure fury.

"Where's King?" he barked. "And Noah? Where are they?"

Even over the loud music, Bobby's voice resonated. One of the girls closest to the stereo fumbled to turn the music down, and several of the teens nearby started gathering up their belongings, suddenly aware there was a situation at hand. A few of the kids wondered aloud whether these were Kingston's parents.

Bree held her hands up defensively. "Calm down. King is outside. I'm not sure where Noah is."

"What the hell is this, Bree? This is why you wanted to come over here tonight? For a party?"

Bobby was angry and hurt at the same time. His vision of his daughter as just an innocent ballerina was being shattered right before his eyes. The cop in him had already scanned the house and seen the blunt wrappers and liquor bottles strewn about. He was furious.

"No," she said. "But what was I gonna do? Leave?"

"Show me where Kingston is," Bobby demanded, looking around at every kid present.

One of the kids nearby led the way to the backyard, and Bobby was hot on his heels.

Deja chuckled despite herself. She pulled out her cell phone. "I'm calling Ivy."

Bree put her hand over her mother's and squeezed it gently. "Don't do that, Ma. Please. Don't tell on them. They're just having a little fun."

Deja sucked her teeth. "Are you crazy, Bree? We heard the music from down the block. Ivy would lose her mind if she knew all these kids were in her house, drinking and God knows what else. Everybody in here needs to go home right now."

The doorbell rang, and Deja and Bree looked at each other.

"Probably the neighbors complaining about the music," Deja fumed.

She walked over to the door while several of the boys nearby watched her booty jiggling in her tiny shorts with each stride. She opened it and was surprised to find several police officers staring back at her. The kids behind her started yelling loudly and rushing toward the back of the house to warn the others.

"It's the cops!"

"The police are here!"

"Told y'all niggas the music was too loud."

Deja stepped just outside the door, leaving it slightly ajar behind her.

Four cops stared back at her. Nobody smiled.

"We got a complaint about the noise, ma'am. Are you the owner of this house?"

Deja shook her head. She could see some of Ivy's neighbors across the street coming outside to see what was happening. The police had kept their flashing lights going when they exited their vehicles. The whole cul-de-sac was lit up in NYPD blue.

"It's my friend's house. She's at a party in Manhattan tonight, and her sons decided to do the same thing while she was away. I just got here, and I'm shutting it down. We're sorry for having you guys come out here."

The officer looked her up and down skeptically. "It's your friend's house?"

Deja frowned. "Yes."

"What is your friend's name?"

"Ivy Donovan."

"And she's not available to speak with us?"

Deja shook her head, growing irritated by the officer's tone. "I just told you. She's at an event tonight in Manhattan. Me and my husband just got here. We found out that the kids were having a little party that got out of hand. We're shutting it down."

"We got a report that some of the kids are doing drugs. Is it all right if we come in and look around?"

Deja frowned. "Nobody's doing drugs. It's just a bunch of kids sitting around listening to music and trying to have a little fun. It's not that serious, Officer."

Deja looked at him and his colleagues and saw no signs of empathy. All of them stared back at her in silence, one with his walkie-talkie blaring loudly at his hip.

The cop in charge kept talking. "It's serious enough that we got several calls tonight, ma'am."

Deja frowned as two more police cars pulled up. "This is crazy. Why are all these cops here for a noise complaint?"

"Do you mind if we come inside? Take a look around? Like I said, the neighbors are saying that—"

"Is there a problem?" Bobby asked as he stepped outside. He could sense the tension in the air.

The officer seemed irritated by Bobby's presence. "Yes, there's a problem. Are you aware that this is a residential neighborhood?"

Bobby scoffed at the audacity of this smug rookie. He took out his badge and flashed it at them.

"I'm aware," he said.

Instantly, the young officer's facial expression and body language changed.

"Sorry, Sergeant. We got a bunch of calls and it sounded like something crazy was going on in there."

Suddenly, the cop was all smiles as he addressed his superior officer.

Bobby grinned at how quickly the rookie's tone changed when he saw his badge. He was glad Deja got to see how powerful he was in his job. Already, two of the cops who had just arrived on the scene retreated to their cars and slowly drove away.

Instead of being impressed, Deja was annoyed. She wondered how things might have gone differently if Bobby didn't have a badge of his own to show the officers. Scowling, she addressed the cop again.

"Like I said, we were just sending all of the kids home. It's a house party that got out of hand. That's it."

"My apologies, ma'am. Thank you, Sergeant. You all have a good night."

Bobby watched as each one of them turned and walked back to their police cars, seemingly dejected. His joy was short lived, quickly giving way to anger. Kingston and Noah—and Bree by default—had crossed the line tonight. If he hadn't been there, the police had been prepared to confront those kids with unnecessary aggression.

Deja seemed to read his mind. She tiptoed and kissed him on the cheek.

"Thank you, baby." She watched the cops drive away slowly. "Fuckin' assholes."

"Fuckin' *rookies,*" he corrected her.

They went back inside the house where the mood had shifted drastically. The music was off, and girls scampered around picking up trash and doing their best to straighten up the place. They all looked at Deja and Bobby expectantly.

"Everybody needs to go home now," Deja said.

Immediately, the kids all began scurrying for their shoes, heading for the door, calling cabs, and asking each other for rides. She found Noah and Kingston in the crowd and looked at both of them, shaking her head in disappointment.

Noah walked over first. "I'm sorry, Deja. We know better than this."

Deja fought the urge to laugh. "Spare me, Noah. You and King played yourselves. What if your mother came home early instead of me? If Ivy saw this, she would lose her mind."

She looked over at King, who was walking toward them now.

"Your mother works too hard for you two to be doing dumb shit like this. What if Bobby wasn't here when the cops came?"

She waited for an answer but got none.

"*Four* police cars pulled up here just now. What if we weren't here, King? These are your friends, right? Noah? This is your house, your responsibility!"

Kingston did his best to avoid making eye contact with Deja, but she sensed something was off with him. She stared at him, her eyes searching his, and finally narrowed her eyes in disgust.

"Are you *high,* King? Were y'all getting high in here?"

She turned around wildly, looking for Bree.

Bree's eyes went wide. "Not me, Ma!"

King shook his head. "Deja, tonight got out of hand. I'm not gonna make excuses. I'm just being honest. It's the end of the school year; tonight was Nikki's big party. We had the house to ourselves for the first time. We were just trying to have a little fun. But it went too far. Please don't tell on us, though. We're gonna clean up the house and make it like nothing ever happened. I swear. And we won't ever do this again."

"Yeah," Noah said under his breath. "Now that we know these snitches out here will call the cops on us."

Bobby glared at him. "They called the cops because the volume was turned all the way up like this was Summer Jam. You had a bunch of underage kids in here with no adult supervision, and you guys are in here smoking weed, drinking, and . . . who knows what else!"

"Dad . . . please!" Bree pleaded.

She hated he was proving Mariah right, sounding more like the cornball she'd said he was.

"'Dad' nothing! Get your stuff and let's go."

Bree did as told. Kingston walked his friends out. Noah approached Deja and Bobby.

Deja still shook her head at him, disappointment etched all over her face.

"I'm sorry," Noah said. "This was a bad idea."

Bree returned. She looked at her mother.

"Ma, don't tell Ivy, please. For me?"

Deja thought about how upset Bree had been with her for the past couple of days. Then, she looked at Ivy's boys and sighed.

"Get this place cleaned up. I mean it! Y'all better get this house in top shape before your mother gets home. If she sees *one* thing out of place, you know she's smart enough to figure it out. Or one of your neighbors might rat you out. Either way, if she asks me whether or not y'all had a party, I'm *not* gonna lie to her."

"*Come on!*" King protested.

"Nope. I'm not gonna volunteer the information. But if she suspects it herself and asks me to verify it, I'm not about to lie to my friend. So, get your shit together in here. She's having a good time tonight, and I don't want y'all to upset her with this bullshit when she gets home."

Noah nodded, and Kingston resigned himself to there being no guarantee of Deja keeping her mouth shut.

"Why are you guys home so early?" Bree asked. Her curiosity couldn't stand the suspense any longer. "Aunt Nikki's parties never end until the sun comes up."

Deja frowned. She had almost forgotten how pissed she was about Nikki's grand entrance.

"I wasn't feeling well," she lied.

Deja hugged Noah and Kingston goodbye, mushing them both in the head for good measure. They both shook Bobby's hand and thanked them both for their silence and their help with the police.

As they left, Bree glanced back at Kingston. He winked at her and smiled, his eyes still low after smoking so much weed. Bree smiled back. She waved at him, followed her parents out, and promised herself that one day soon she would make her move.

Part Two

Consequences

Kingston approached the house, dribbling his basketball as he walked. He saw his neighbor from across the street, a blond girl with pretty blue eyes and no ass at all. Michelle, he thought her name was. He waved at her. She waved back and crossed the street in his direction. He didn't know her well. Although she was about his age, they didn't go to the same high school. They only saw each other in passing. Her mother, Teresa, was a constant annoyance to Ivy, always stopping by unannounced for some reason or another.

As he watched the girl approach him, he forced a smile, deciding to find out if her mother had been the one who called the cops on them the night before.

"Hey, Kingston."

"Wassup, Michelle?"

She frowned. "Damn. You've been living across the street for almost a year and you didn't even bother to learn my name. It's Michaela."

He sucked his teeth and resisted the urge to say, "Same difference."

"My bad. I'm not good with names."

She smirked. "You're not good with inviting me to parties, either. Heard you had a big one last night and got the neighbors all pissed off."

Kingston's head snapped toward the house, praying his mother wasn't within earshot.

"Shh!" he hissed. "You heard about that?"

Michaela shrugged since that much was obvious.

"Do you know who called the cops on us?" Kingston asked. "Was it your mother?"

Offended, she shook her head.

"No. My mom is a pain in the ass, but she wouldn't call the cops on you guys. She wanted to call *your* mom, though. My mom loves to get in good with the parents in the neighborhood by telling on the kids. I talked her out of it. My sister Emma had tennis practice this morning, so she had to be in bed early. But your music was so loud that Emma kept getting up out of bed, complaining that she couldn't sleep. My parents were both pretty pissed. My mom was planning on going over there this morning and telling your mom what happened." Michaela giggled at the thought. "But I reminded her that I did the same thing last summer when my parents went to the Hamptons for the weekend. Nobody ratted me out."

Kingston nodded. "Thank you. I still can't believe one of the neighbors called the cops on us."

"It's because you're Black," she said flatly. "They never do that shit when the other kids in the neighborhood have loud parties or race their cars and motorcycles through here. It's all political around here. Everybody's part of some club and you guys moved in and never gave a shit about that club. Your mom doesn't play the game. She doesn't make phony conversation or invite everybody over to get in her business. So, you guys are different. Around here, different means weird."

She shrugged. "Not to me, though. I think you seem kinda cool."

Kingston nodded. "So do you."

She smiled. "Anyway, we saw the cops pull up, and then after a few minutes, they drove away. It got quiet after that, so I guess the party was over." She shrugged again.

"Make sure your mother doesn't mention it to mine. That's the last thing I need," he said.

Michaela smirked. "My mother is a chatterbox, in case you haven't noticed. You better hope something else interesting happens to make her forget about it. That's the only way she'll keep her mouth shut."

King groaned, dreading the thought of his mother hearing about last night.

"Anyway, the next time you have a party, you could at least invite me. I'm not as uptight as some of the other people in this neighborhood." She smiled. "Especially if you and your friends smoke pot and pop pills like me and my friends do."

Kingston laughed. "I like you. You're a real one.

She nodded. "Good. Remember my name next time, then."

"Yup. Michaela."

She turned and headed back toward her house. Kingston entered his own, bouncing the basketball absentmindedly.

Ivy, chatting on the phone with Coco, was distracted by the sound of her son noisily entering the house. She heard him bounce his basketball in her foyer and her blood pressure soared instantly.

"Hold on, Coco," she muttered into the phone.

"Hey, Ma!" King entered the kitchen and smiled at her broadly, momentarily disarming her. His smile had always had that effect on her. On everyone, really.

"Don't you 'Hey, Ma' me! How many times do I have to tell you not to bounce that damn ball in this house, King?" Ivy was pissed. "I spent a lot of money on these floors for you to fuck them up with that basketball."

He headed for the fridge, stifling a laugh. For all her boisterousness, he knew she was harmless. Kingston flashed her another irresistible smile.

"Sorry, Ma. It won't happen again." He nodded toward the phone in her hand. "Who's on the phone?"

"Coco," she answered, her tone clipped. "Don't try to change the subject. If I have to tell you about bouncing that ball again, I'm gonna knock that smile off your face."

He chuckled, though he did his best to mask it, relieved the only thing she was beefing about was a basketball. If she knew half the shit of what he and his brother had gotten themselves into, she would self-destruct. Still smiling, he walked over to her and planted a big old kiss on her pretty, chubby cheek.

"I apologize."

"Ivy, leave that boy alone."

Coco put the phone on speaker and she spread herself wide and flat across her mattress like a starfish.

"King is a good boy. Noah is, too. Lighten up."

Ivy sucked her teeth. "You say that so sincerely, Coco, from your immaculate, child-free penthouse apartment in Manhattan. If I sent King over there for a weekend, you would send his ass back by Saturday morning."

Coco laughed. "First of all, this damn sure ain't the penthouse. And King is welcome here anytime. He knows that."

"Whatever. I'm gonna tell him about your new *boyfriend* that Nikki hooked you up with," Ivy teased.

Coco gasped. "Calm down, 'cause I don't like him like that. I don't know what it is."

"Maybe that he's white?"

"No," Coco protested. "It's not *just* that. I was surprised when Nikki introduced us. I thought 'Ziggy' would be some Rasta with sexy locs and a Caribbean accent. The man I met the other night was not that."

Ivy chuckled. "He might turn out to be exactly what you need. Give him a chance."

"I don't know. For now, I'm just thinking about how I can add some of the artists he works with to our roster. Live Nation is always looking to partner with the hottest talent. Ziggy's a popular producer from what I hear."

Ivy sighed. "You're just like your brother. Always focused on the money."

Coco laughed. "Is that a bad thing?"

"I watched you and Ziggy dancing. Y'all looked cute together. I think you should try to think of him as more than just a business connection. He might be just the type of man you need after dealing with Derek for so long."

Ivy recalled standing at the bar wistfully watching all the couples two-stepping on the dance floor at Nikki's party. While her friends were dating, vacationing, and being intimate with their men, Ivy was barely allowed to touch hers. All the simple things regular couples took for granted were fantasies for Ivy. Instead of leaving the party and enjoying a passionate night with her man, Ivy had come home and gotten busy with her vibrator.

She glanced out the window and frowned at her older son walking slowly up her tree-lined block. "Anyway, girl, let me get off this phone. Noah is just coming home from . . . God knows where."

"Lay off those boys, Ivy."

"I'll try! You just make sure to keep an open mind about Ziggy. I want to see where this goes."

Coco agreed, and they hung up just as Noah walked into the kitchen.

"Hey, King. What's up, Mama?"

Kingston greeted his brother while pouring himself a bowl of cereal. Ivy's frown deepened as she looked at Noah.

"What's up with you? Where's your car? Why'd I see you walking up the block?"

Noah wondered which of her questions she wanted to be answered first. He loved her, but his mother was always raining down on him. Today, he was hardly in the mood.

"The car is at a mechanic over by the ferry terminal. Last night we—"

"What happened?" Ivy interrupted in typical fashion.

Noah continued. "While you were at Nikki's party, I drove King to his friend Kevin's house to pick up a homework sheet."

Ivy smelled bullshit immediately. The expression on her face illustrated that fact.

"What *homework* did Kevin have that you needed?"

The truth was Noah's car had broken down on the way back home after they'd dropped off a few of Kingston's friends after their party ended.

Noah and Kingston had sat up all night coming up with a good story to explain how Noah's car had ended up in a mechanic's shop on the other side of the island.

King chimed in. "You remember I had that doctor's appointment last week. I missed a quiz. Mr. Carter gave Kevin a take-home test to give to me for my history class."

Lying was becoming such a habit that he was getting damned good at it. He only prayed Ivy didn't ask to see it. She had been known to call his bluff before.

Noah continued quickly. "On the way back home, the car broke down right at a light on Bay Street. I thought I ran out of gas at first, but eventually, I got it to start back up. I drove a block or two, and it shut off again. It kept doing that, and somehow, I made it all the way to the gas station near Hannah Street. This man named James works there fixing cars. It was late, and the mechanic shop was closed for the night, but he took a quick look under the hood for me."

"That was nice of him." Ivy made a mental note to tip this mechanic when she retrieved the car.

"Yeah," Noah agreed. "So, he said he thinks it's a problem with the starter. He couldn't fix it for me right there. So, he told me to come back this morning to pick up the car. I woke up today and took the train over there to get it."

He laughed. "They got a tiny little train station out here. Only goes around Staten Island, though."

Noah went to the fridge and poured himself some juice.

Ivy was annoyed that he had left her hanging. "So, where is the car now, Noah?"

"The guy James changed the alternator, and it still ain't running right. So, now he's trying to figure out what's up. He told me to come back later this afternoon."

Ivy groaned now. Maybe this "James" wasn't getting a tip after all. It sounded like he was trying to hustle her son out of more money. She would definitely be going with him to pick up his car that afternoon.

"Why didn't you call and tell me what was going on?"

"Ma, you were in the middle of Nikki's party. I wasn't trying to mess up your night with our little problem. So, I handled it."

Ivy felt proud of him. Maybe he was truly over his irresponsible phase.

"How did you and King get home last night?"

"James gave us a ride."

Ivy sucked her teeth, her gaze alternating between Noah and Kingston. So much for feeling proud.

"You let a *stranger* drive you to this house?"

Noah laughed. "You underestimate me, Ma. I'm from Brooklyn."

"So? People from Brooklyn get kidnapped and robbed every day."

She walked over and poured herself some coffee. It smelled divine. She took a whiff and then a long sip before addressing her son again.

"You should have called me and told me what was happening, Noah."

"I didn't need to call and bother you. He dropped us off and went on his merry way. Me and King ordered pizza. Everything was fine." He winked at his mom and watched her soften.

"Did you have fun?" Kingston asked. "I heard you talking to Miss Coco when I came in."

Ivy smiled. "It was amazing. Everybody had a great time." She turned her attention back to Noah. "What time are you going back down to the mechanic to see about your car?"

"He said to come back around three."

She nodded. "I'm coming, too."

She poured a little more coffee into her cup, filling it to the rim. "I want to meet this James."

The moment Deja walked into her mother Ruthie's house, she heard voices coming from the kitchen. Nikki's laughter mingled with their mother's. She walked through the home she had grown up in, looking around at all the old, familiar furniture and pictures on the walls. The place felt warm and cold at the same time. She rarely came here these days. Nikki always gave her hell about that, and she had to admit she deserved it. This place was full of too many memories for her, some of them more pleasant than others.

She found them in the kitchen sitting at the table with a bunch of old photos spread out in front of them. Her mother looked up and smiled at her as she entered.

"Look who's here!" she shouted. She stood up and hugged her daughter tightly.

Nikki forced a smile. "Hey, Deja."

Deja waved at her. "Hey," she managed as she sat down at the table.

"What a surprise!" Ruthie gushed.

"I've been calling you," Deja said. "No answer."

Ruthie's smile softened. "I figured if I didn't answer, you would come over eventually. This was a conversation I knew we needed to have in person."

Deja glanced at Nikki and found her staring back at her.

"You left my party early and didn't even say goodnight. What happened to you?"

"I wasn't feeling well," Deja said, sticking with the same excuse she had given Bree. "Then me and Bobby had to get in the middle of Ivy's kids and some cops that got called to her house while Bree was over there."

Nikki frowned, deeply. "The cops? What happened?"

Deja shook her head. "I promised Noah and King that I wouldn't tell Ivy. But when we went by there to pick up Bree, there was a full party happening. Some of Ivy's neighbors called the cops, but Bobby handled it."

Deja picked up a photo of her father that was lying on the table. "I never saw this one before. Is that me he's holding?"

Her mother looked at the Polaroid. "Sure is. You were just a few days old there."

Deja stared at the picture, trying to summon memories of her father. The few she had of him were fleeting. She could recall his voice. The way his gray eyes lit up when he smiled. The way he spent his final months coughing all the time, growing thinner by the day. The way he disappeared into a hospital ward she was too little to be allowed inside. The way he was gone. The cancer had ravaged his body in ways none of the doctors had been equipped to tackle. Through it all, his wife had been by his side. Faithful till the end.

"So, I heard you've been talking to Rashid."

Deja looked her mother in the eye as she said it, eager to hear her response.

Ruthie smiled weakly. "Yes, I have."

"For how long?"

Ruthie sat back. "Since you snatched Bree up like a thief in the night and moved out of here and never looked back. I never thought that shit was fair to Rashid."

Deja shook her head. "I never said it was fair. But it was my life. My daughter's life. So, it was my decision to make."

Nikki scoffed, but Ruthie looked at Deja compassionately. "When Rashid got sent away, I was right here with you when you cried. Every court date, every hearing you were there. When you gave birth to Bree, I was there timing the contractions. You brought her home from the hospital, and we spent all those months talking for hours every day. About Rashid, and about you and Bree and what the future would look like for all of you. You loved him, as much as a young girl can love a man for the first time. But you weren't ready for a life like the one he got sentenced to."

"I tried to be," Deja said. "I really tried. I testified in court. I went to visit him, took his calls, wrote him letters. I just couldn't deal with it. I felt like I was suffocating."

"I understood that," Ruthie said. "You were grieving. Facing any amount of time in prison feels like a death sentence. So, you were grieving the death of your relationship just like I was after your father died. I got depressed. I didn't know it was depression then. In those days, we didn't go to doctors to talk about our feelings and all that. I thought what I was going through was normal. My hair started falling out. I lost weight. Gave up on life, really. If it wasn't for you, Deja, I might have laid down and died right next to your father.

"That's how you were acting after Rashid took the plea deal. You started losing yourself. Started falling into depression. When you told me that you were moving out, I wasn't happy. But I understood that you needed to shake things up to get your control back again."

Deja nodded, grateful her mother had understood.

"I felt guilty about it," she admitted. "When I left, I told you not to give Rashid my phone number or my address."

"That was fucked up," Nikki said.

"I needed to breathe," Deja answered flatly.

"I was that way, too," Ruthie said. "You were four years old when your father died. It took me months to get up out of bed and go outside. But one day, I got up and went and got my hair cut, bought some new clothes since I had lost so much weight. And before I knew it, I met Frank."

Nikki smiled. Even though she knew her father wasn't shit, she still loved him. He had been in and out of her life—mostly out—for as long as she could recall. Never consistent, never faithful to his words or his women. And he had a lot of them. Nikki had a bunch of siblings on her daddy's side.

"Frank was tall, Black, and beautiful. He had a way with words. Swept me off my feet. I should've known his ass was too good to be true."

Ruthie laughed. Nikki did, too. Deja wasn't in on the punchline.

"He left you alone with two kids to raise on your own," she mumbled.

Nikki stopped laughing and looked at her sister with disdain. Deja never failed to take a jab at her, even if she did it in the roundabout way of criticizing her father.

"Your pops left her alone, too, sis. Ain't neither one of them here now."

Ruthie chuckled a bit at the irony in that. "My point is that the same thing happened with you, Deja. You moved out, took Bree, and started over. Then you met Bobby."

"Hmm!" Nikki said, connecting the dots for the first time.

Deja was realizing the parallels, too.

"Sometimes we think we're taking flight when we're really just looking for a soft place to land."

"WHEEEWW! That's deep!" Nikki fanned herself dramatically.

"I always admired Bobby for the way that he loves and takes care of Bree," Ruthie said. "But I know that every child needs and wants to know their own father. And I knew back when you made your decision that someday Bree would want answers for the choices you made."

Deja thought about that, guilt creeping back into her heart once more.

"So, when Rashid called here, sometimes I answered. I felt sorry for him. It didn't seem right for him to lose his freedom, lose you, and lose his child all at the same time. Every now and then, I sent him packages, pictures, and things like that. Just so he didn't feel completely cut off."

She looked at Deja.

"I knew you wouldn't like it, so I didn't tell you."

"It makes me wonder whose side you're on," Deja muttered.

Ruthie smiled wryly.

"When your father died and left me this house, I struggled to hold on to it. Working two and three jobs to pay the mortgage, clipping coupons, getting free food at pantries and all that. For years, it was tough! It even got to the point that this house was about to get foreclosed on."

Ruthie looked at Deja.

"You remember that?"

Deja nodded. "I remember."

"Rashid saved us. Gave me the money to pay the bank. Took us grocery shopping, got us back on track. I can never forget that."

Deja stared at her hands, racked with shame. She remembered how relieved her mother had been when Rashid had gotten them out of the hole they had been in.

Ruthie watched her, waiting for her to respond. Instead, Deja kept staring blankly, her eyes cast downward.

"Then he got locked up, and Deja forgot all about him." Nikki's tone was matter of fact.

"I never forgot him," she said softly. "I just had to move on.

"From a nigga that literally saved us from homelessness. Wow!"

"You don't know what it's like to be a mother, so, you wouldn't understand. I had to do what was best for my daughter."

"And depriving her of her father was the best thing?"

Deja stared at her sister, silent.

"You know," Ruthie said, "being a mother is tough. The hardest job I ever had in my life was raising you two side by side."

She sounded weary as she said it. Even now after all these years, it was clear playing referee between these two had been no easy task. She looked at both of her daughters intently.

"That's the thing I wish we could work on."

Nikki sat back and looked at her mother. "Ma, let me ask you this. And be honest, please?"

Nikki waited for confirmation. Reluctantly, Ruthie nodded.

"Did Deja change after she met Bobby?"

Thick silence hung in the air. Deja watched her mother struggling to find the words to answer, words that would appease both of her warring daughters.

Deja didn't wait for the response. "How did I change? I settled down, got married, bought a house. I got my real estate license and got on my grind. How is that negative?"

"Nobody said it was negative, Deja." Ruthie's tone was soothing.

"It *was* negative," Nikki insisted. "It's not like you just got successful and now I'm mad about it. *You* changed. You abandoned your first love and the father of your child so you could switch lanes. That shit is corny."

Deja groaned, sick of her sister's mouth. "Nikki, what the hell do you know about it? You act like Rashid was your Prince Charming riding on some white horse to save us. You were like thirteen years old when that shit went down. A kid! You don't know what you're talking about."

Nikki shook her head. "He wasn't my Prince Charming, bitch. He was yours. You spent his money, took all the perks of being his girl, rode around with him in his car and all that. But once he got locked up, you chose to disappear. You got with Bobby and all of a sudden, me, my friends, and people like Rashid are 'gutter garbage,' as you put it. Your ass is phony."

"Nikki, first of all, watch your mouth," Ruthie checked her.

"Sorry, Ma." Nikki sipped her water.

"Deja's right," Ruthie continued. "You were too young to understand all of it. He's the one who did the time. But it was hard for her, too."

Nikki shrugged.

"What does he say about me?" Deja asked. She had been dying to know.

"Mostly, he wanted to talk about Bree."

Deja's heart sank a little.

"We talked a little about old times. He asked about you at one point. He wanted to know if I gave you all the letters he sent you over the years. I told him that I did and reminded him that you've been married for fifteen years. He reminded me that he was locked up for sixteen years."

Deja closed her eyes against the magnitude of that. She opened them again and her mother was looking at her sadly.

"We talked about how it was for him. How it's been since he came home."

Deja nodded.

"I'm glad he's home now," Ruthie said. "Sixteen years is a long time."

"Has Bree seen him since the other day?" Nikki asked.

"She's with him now. They're spending the day together."

"How does Bobby feel about it?" Ruthie asked.

"He's not excited. Keeps telling me that I should go through the courts and do some kind of legal custody arrangement."

Nikki rolled her eyes. "Of course, he wants to put that man back in front of a judge again. Bobby's a dick."

Deja ignored her. "I'm just focused on Bree. Like you said, Ma, it all comes down to me and my child. And I have to make this right for her."

Ruthie smiled at her reassuringly. "You'll do the right thing this time. I believe that with all my heart."

An hour later, Deja sat in her parked car on a tree-lined block in Brooklyn. The engine was off, and she sat in silence, watching joggers go by and kids running through a nearby playground. She stared at her cell phone for a long while, then finally pressed the dial button.

"Hello?"

His voice in her ear sent her pulse racing.

"Hey, Rashid. It's Deja. I just wanted to check in. Is everything going okay?"

"Yeah," he said. "We're at my mother's house. Deja's meeting her cousins for the first time. She's having fun. You want to talk to her?"

"No . . . thank you."

Deja had been texting Bree all afternoon, so she knew she was fine. She summoned the courage to tell Rashid the real reason for her call.

"I was wondering . . . do you think we could meet somewhere and talk? Just us."

He was silent so long she looked at the phone to make sure the call hadn't dropped. Finally, his voice came through the speaker like music.

"Yeah. Where and when?"

She pressed the button and started her engine, putting her car in drive. "I'm in Brooklyn now. Meet me at our spot."

Rashid grinned, pleasantly surprised she still remembered it. "I'm on my way."

Restart

Rashid approached the oddly shaped elm tree near the boathouse in Prospect Park and saw Deja standing there. She was leaning on a fence that surrounded the historic tree, staring at it as if she were seeing it for the first time. He grinned as he watched her crane her neck to stare at the twisted branches growing parallel to the ground. The tree had always fascinated her. They had discovered it together while walking through the park during her senior year of high school. She'd fallen in love with the tree, declared it their spot, and the two of them had spent many blissful afternoons there doing things young lovers do.

He looked at her as he approached her from behind. Today she had her long hair pulled back in a ponytail and wore jeans and a simple T-shirt. He checked out her butt, impressed it still looked good after so many years. But then he reminded himself that he'd spent the past few hours asking his daughter questions every father should already know the answers to because Deja had come between them. No matter how good she looked, what she had done was unforgivable.

"What's up?" he asked as he neared, startling her.

She turned and looked at him, composing herself quickly. "Hey, Rashid. Thank you for coming."

He nodded. "What's up?" he asked again.

She could sense the hostility in his voice, felt the tension in his body even from a couple of feet away.

"You remember the day we found this tree?" she asked.

He looked at it, slowly nodding. "Yeah. You saw it and lost your mind. Said it was the prettiest tree you ever saw in your life."

She smiled. "It was. I loved it because it was so different, so special and weird. I said that it looked like it didn't belong here. Like it was too fancy for Brooklyn."

He nodded again. "I remember that."

"And you said I was just like this tree. That I didn't belong in Brooklyn, and you were gonna get me up out of here. Said we would go and live somewhere fancy, live a good life."

He looked at her. "So, you mad that I didn't keep my promise?"

She shook her head. "No. If things had been different, I know you would have made good on it."

She took one step in his direction.

"But you were right. I didn't belong here. I didn't belong in that life. I was pretending to be *that* girl so that I could be *your* girl. As long as I was with you and you were with me, I could continue to play that part. But when I realized you were gone and that you might not ever be the same when you came back, I couldn't keep it up. I know that you may never understand. But the only way I could imagine surviving without you was to start over."

A warm breeze rustled the leaves of the tree.

"You're right," Rashid said. "I'll never understand it."

She stared at him as he looked ahead, avoiding eye contact with her again.

"You ever try to put yourself in my shoes?" she asked.

He laughed and looked at her again, his expression incredulous. "Yeah! Plenty of times. I thought about how scared you must have been, how alone you probably felt. I thought about the fact that I was doing fifteen years and you probably couldn't handle what went along with that."

He shook his head.

"But you knew that I didn't do it. You knew that, and you still left me to deal with that shit alone. That's the part that I'll never understand. Even if you didn't love me anymore, you were still supposed to be my friend. As your friend, there's no way I could have walked away from you when you were at your lowest point. Without a conversation, a letter, a phone call, or something. You just went ghost on a nigga."

He chuckled a little.

"When you're locked up, every day you sit around hoping for something to look forward to. A letter, a visit, a package, something. Anything to keep you connected to the outside world, to your sanity. I sat around for months wondering if today would be the day you finally wrote to me or came to see me. I called your mother's house, sent letters to her house for you, letters for Bree. I waited for a response. Never came. That shit was like torture."

The thought of it made him feel that loneliness all over again. He looked at the elm tree in all its twisted glory.

"You never belonged in Brooklyn. I was right about that. You were always bigger than this place. You belong in a fancy life. If that's what you went out there and found, I couldn't be mad at that. But you didn't go nowhere really. You only made it as far as Staten Island. And ain't shit fancy about that."

He scoffed.

"Married to a cop, going to PTA meetings, selling real estate. That's your reality now. And you look bored out of your mind. You don't seem happy."

The weight of his words crushed Deja. Tears formed in her eyes. It was true. She had been unhappy for a while, long before Rashid reentered her life. She had numbed her pain by sleeping with Sterling, creeping behind Bobby's back and living a double life.

Rashid kept going.

"Nikki is living a big life, but yours seems average, and I think that's why you don't like her. She's being herself and the world loves her for it. You're a fraud and nobody's buying it."

He shrugged. "I think you got it wrong. I don't believe you were pretending when you were with me back in the day. That's not when you started playing make believe. That happened when you got with RoboCop, 'cause none of this shit looks like it fits you."

He looked her up and down appraisingly. She felt like she had been stripped naked and read for filth.

She shook her head, fighting back tears. "I can't expect you to understand."

He felt sorry for her despite the pain she had caused him. Standing there, she looked so sad. Like despite all her best efforts, she still wasn't living the life she always dreamed of.

"I understand more than you think," he said.

"Do you hate me?" Her voice cracked as she asked it.

He gave it some thought before responding. "Not anymore," he answered honestly.

"I thought I only had two choices. Stay and struggle or go and have a chance at happiness. If I could do it over again, I would have told you. I would have been brave enough to come and have a conversation with you and tell you what my plans were. I would have let your family have a relationship with Bree, and I would have sent her with them to visit you. I just wasn't strong enough to do the right thing. And by the time I felt guilty enough to reach out to you, it just seemed like so much time had passed that I wasn't sure where to start." She shook her head again. "I was a coward. And you're right. I ran. I'll always regret it. I just wanted to tell you that."

He looked at her, saw the sincerity in her eyes, and nodded slowly. "Thanks."

He reached out his hand to give her five like old friends. She stared at his hand, then grabbed it and held on to it tightly. She leaned in and hugged him, inhaling his scent.

He didn't hug her back, just stood there as she clung to him. He thought about Bree, about the beautiful and intelligent young lady Deja had raised so far. He felt his heart soften just a little.

He stepped back, releasing himself from her embrace. He looked down at her, gave her a weak smile, then turned and walked away.

"I'll bring Bree home in an hour," he called out over his shoulder. "You should get back home to RoboCop."

Deja watched him walk away before picking up her pride and leaving Brooklyn.

"It's hot as all hell out here!" Ivy complained as she hurried toward her car. She slid into the driver's seat, started the car, and turned the air conditioning up full blast. She fanned herself while she waited for her sons to get in. She turned all the vents in her direction as sweat dripped mercilessly down her face.

"Come *on*!" she shouted, already irritated.

She checked herself then, reminding herself she was working

on her disposition—especially regarding her sons. She thought back to her conversation with Coco that morning. More and more, her girlfriends were urging her to "ease up off those boys," telling her she had "good kids" who stayed out of trouble for the most part. She knew she was hard on them and she didn't want her sons to resent her toughness. She took a deep breath and reminded herself to be nice.

Kingston climbed into the back seat, and Noah rode shotgun. The first thing Noah did was change the radio station. Trap music filled the speakers and a rapper Ivy couldn't identify mumbled and muttered his way through the laziest verse she had ever heard. He kept repeating the same phrase over and over. She fought the urge to complain even as Noah turned the volume up and he and Kingston danced wildly in their seats. She clenched her teeth, forced the fakest smile, and drove as quickly as possible to the mechanic Noah had told her about.

A song came on and Noah cranked up the volume even louder. Ivy frowned and groaned. Some fool was yelling, "I got them keys, keys, keys . . ." nonstop on the track. She turned the radio off after hearing him say the same thing for the fifth time.

"Uh-uh!" she protested. "Don't nobody want to hear that shit!"

Kingston laughed. "Ma, you're buggin'! That song is fire."

Noah turned the radio back on but lowered the volume. It didn't matter, though. Kingston began singing and rapping along so loudly that Ivy felt surrounded. Grateful for the sparse traffic, she sped down the highway and tried not to be annoyed by the aggressive music pumping through her car stereo.

When they stopped at a red light, Kingston sat forward in his seat and started talking. Noah turned the volume down, much to Ivy's relief.

"What did you say, King? I couldn't hear you over all the noise!" Ivy glared at Noah.

"I said it's a lot different out here than it is in Brooklyn. Feels segregated. All my Black friends live on the other side of the island."

"Deja said Staten Island is the most racist borough in the city. White people out here are used to an old-school way of thinking," she said. "They keep the Black people on the North Shore and when they try to move to the South Shore with the whites, they won't rent to them."

"Why didn't they give us a problem when we moved in?" Kingston asked.

"They must know who not to fuck with!" Ivy said, laughing.

"Maybe we should move back to Brooklyn," Noah said. "Staten Island is wack."

Ivy frowned at him and shook her head. "There's racism everywhere you go. Even in Brooklyn."

Noah nodded. He knew that. "This feels different, though. White folks out here are different. They walk around wearing MAGA hats. Trump signs on their lawns. Why we wanna live around people like that?"

"Because their time is up. This borough is full of white people who haven't had to integrate like the rest of the country has, and they gotta get the hell over it."

King smiled at that. "You think you're tough."

Ivy rolled her eyes and Noah laughed as they pulled up at the mechanic shop. They all climbed out of the car. Ivy was surprised when King rushed ahead of them, walking fast to greet the Black man heading in their direction.

"What's up, James? I texted my coach to ask him about what you said yesterday, and he said you're right!"

James laughed heartily. "I told you, King! You thought I was playing?"

Ivy was frowning now, wondering what all this was about. She forgot all about the oppressive heat, her gaze bouncing back and forth between them. This *James* was smiling at her son with the intensity of a proud dad and calling him by his nickname like they were old friends. He was cute, though. She couldn't help noticing. He was about her age, with a salt-and-pepper goatee and mustache. His muscles pressed against his work shirt. She cleared her throat.

King looked at her. "My bad. Ma, this is the guy James that helped us out last night." Kingston looked at James and smiled. "This is my mother."

James stepped forward, wiping his greasy hand on a towel he pulled from his back pocket. He extended his hand toward her apologetically, aware it was covered in dirt and grime.

She shook it and smiled. "I'm Ivy."

"Nice to meet you, Ivy. You have two very nice young men here."

She lit up hearing that. It always thrilled her when people let her know her boys had presented themselves well when she wasn't with them. It was one thing to act right when Mama was breathing down their necks and another thing to know they were still behaving in her absence.

"I'm sorry that my sons bothered you last night."

"I wasn't bothered at all. I'm glad I was still here when they came in. I was happy to help. King was telling me that he plays basketball at Curtis High School. I used to go to school there. Played point guard for the Warriors back in the nineties." James smiled proudly.

Kingston nodded. "James said he held the school record for

most points scored in a game. I thought he was lying, but I checked with Coach and he confirmed it."

Kingston was beaming with excitement, like he was talking to Magic Johnson or something.

Ivy looked James up and down. He was tall, but not quite as tall as Kingston. She wondered how he ended up working as a mechanic at the neighborhood shop after such a promising sports career in his heyday.

"Nice." She plastered on her phony smile again, convinced she was getting better at it. "Did you figure out what was wrong with the car?" She looked around, hoping to spot it parked nearby.

James immediately led the way to the back of the shop. She spotted Noah's black BMW and walked over to it. James watched her, admiring the way her booty quaked with each step.

"Noah said that you thought it was the starter," she said. "Since you were wrong, we don't need to pay for that, right?"

James smiled. Ivy was already trying to protect her coins.

"I ran a diagnostic scan and I found a faulty sensor. I had to replace the sensor to get it working again. But I think you should probably change the starter, too. It's an expensive part for this car, but you'll be better off replacing it now."

Ivy sucked her teeth. It sounded like James was running the typical mechanic's hustle on her.

"Is the car running now that you replaced the sensor?"

James nodded. "Yes, but that might only last for a little while. Then you'll have to replace the starter like I told you. Might as well do it now if you—"

"The car is running. That's all I wanted. How much do I owe you?" She fumbled around in her purse for her wallet.

James stood with a look of obvious surprise on his face. He

recovered quickly, and his expression softened. He smiled at Ivy. She noticed how handsome he was when he smiled. His eyes crinkled up at the corners, and she suddenly felt even hotter than before.

"Just pay for the sensor. No charge for the labor," he said.

Ivy looked at him questioningly. "Why no charge?"

"'Cause you're gonna need to change that starter soon. You'll be back. I'll charge you for the labor then." He winked at her.

She grinned. "If that happens, I'll just bring it to my regular mechanic, so, just let me know what I owe you."

James looked her over, his gaze lingering on her curves in such an unapologetic way that Noah and King exchanged glances. Ivy pretended not to notice, but she was very aware of the way his eyes swept her body from head to toe and back again. She didn't mind it one bit.

James led Ivy over to the counter and this time she watched him. Broad shoulders; clean, bald head; confident walk. He stepped behind the counter and gave her the bill for the sensor. She looked it over and then paid it, her hands trembling slightly from nerves she couldn't explain.

While he processed the payment on Ivy's credit card, James cleared his throat and made eye contact with her.

"Your sons were telling me that you're new out here. What part of Brooklyn are you from?"

"Crown Heights."

He nodded. "How you like it out here so far?"

She shrugged. "It's okay. We were just talking about it on the way over here." She glanced warily at his white colleagues nearby. "It's different."

He laughed, nodding again. "Takes some getting used to. It helps if you have friends out here to show you around."

She blushed a little. "I do. My friend Deja's been living out here for years."

"Nothing wrong with making new friends, is it?" He handed her back her credit card and gave her the receipt to sign. "You should let me take you out sometime." He was smiling, but he was also dead serious.

Ivy signed the receipt and handed it back to him, grinning shyly. She was sweating profusely now from the heat of both the atmosphere and the moment. Men flirted with her all the time, but there was something about the way this James was undressing her with his eyes that made her blush.

Suddenly, both Noah and Kingston were on either side of her. She looked at them questioningly.

"She's good," Noah said to James. His facial expression was serious, his tone flat.

Ivy looked at him like he had lost his mind.

James looked at Noah. "My bad," he said. "I didn't see a ring."

Kingston looked at his mother's hand and noticed for the first time that she wasn't wearing her ring anymore.

He repeated his brother's assertion. "Nah, she's good."

James nodded and handed Ivy the car keys.

"No disrespect."

She sucked her teeth, thoroughly annoyed.

"First of all," she said to Noah, "stay out of grown folks' business. Second of all, unless you got some money to put toward getting *your* car fixed, I suggest you back up." She handed Noah the keys and shooed them both away. "Y'all can go now."

Neither of her sons moved, looking at her like she had lost her mind.

"BYE!" she said.

Reluctantly, they walked off to Noah's car, both glancing

back as they slowly retreated. They mumbled to each other, clearly not pleased.

She looked at James, embarrassed. "They must be having some type of heatstroke. Excuse them."

He smiled. "They're protective. And they should be. You're a beautiful woman. I would be protective, too."

Her panties moistened. "Okay, James. Take my number so you can take me out."

James quickly pulled out his phone. "I'm ready."

New Normal

Michael had gotten up early in the morning in anticipation of his sister's visit. As the time approached for visiting hours to begin and his name had not been called, he dialed her house number frantically. As he listened to the phone ring, Michael silently prayed no one answered. An answer would mean his worst fears were confirmed and Patsy wasn't coming. It took at least four hours to get to the prison from NYC. If she was still at home at this hour, it meant no visit for him today.

On the fourth ring, she picked up the phone and his heart sank.

"Yo, what happened, Patsy? You're supposed to be here today!" Michael barked into the phone.

"Mikey, calm the fuck down!" Patsy shouted back. "I tried to get up there today to see you, but these fuckin' kids of mine! I was up late babysitting for Dashawn so him and Keisha could go out for her birthday. I overslept. My bad."

Patsy's excuses fell on deaf ears. He was furious. "That's fucked up, Patsy. I never let you down like that."

She groaned. "Don't start all that feeling sorry for yourself shit with me. Coco told me how mopey you been lately. Cut that shit out. That ain't you."

Michael closed his eyes and let out a deep sigh. Patsy was right. She was one of the few people who could snap him out of his bullshit.

"I'm just saying. If I knew you were looking for me to come through, I'd never leave you hanging."

She sat on the edge of her bed and lit a cigarette.

"You right," she said, exhaling. "And I'm sorry. I should have made sure I woke up on time. But that bus up north leaves Brooklyn at four o'clock in the morning. I was up late with the baby and I overslept. Once I miss the bus, that's it. I don't have a fancy car to drive like Ivy does."

Patsy took another puff. She hadn't always resented Ivy. In the beginning, they had been friends. But Patsy grew to resent the access Ivy had to Michael and his cash.

"Coco has a car," Michael pointed out. "Why you ain't call her?"

Patsy sucked her teeth. "Coco said she had to work this weekend. I can't remember if it was tonight or last night. I don't keep track of her like that."

"Why you ain't call her and find out?"

"Yo, you sound real thirsty right now. Do you really think everybody is sitting around doing nothing? People can't just drop everything and drive up to Elmira."

Patsy pulled the phone away from her ear long enough to yell at her son. "WATCH THE BABY BEFORE HE FALLS OFF THE CHAIR!"

Michael listened to the chaos going on in the background and imagined his nieces, nephews, and extended family fucking up his mother's house. When she was alive, she kept everything neat and in order. She had loved that house, loved the neighborhood as a whole. Buying that brownstone for his mother was one of the proudest moments of Michael's life. Since her death seven years ago, he knew Patsy and her kids had allowed the place to fall apart. Ivy and Coco both disapproved of her and her kids living there rent-free, but Michael had a weak spot for Patsy. He reasoned their mother would want him to look out for the family.

Now that she'd missed today's visit, though, he decided to fuck with her a little.

"I'm thinking about selling that house, Patsy. Ivy told me that Deja sold a brownstone in that area for $3.5 million."

Patsy froze with the cigarette in midair, rage surging through her. "You keep letting Ivy get in your fuckin' head if you want! Sell this house for what, Mikey? To put even more money in her bank account?"

"This ain't got nothing to do with Ivy."

"She's the one telling you to sell the house!"

"No, she's not. All she said was that Deja made a big sale out there. I'm the one saying it might be time to sell it. What you doing with it, Patsy?"

"I'm living in the bitch! What the fuck!"

"You and all them kids. Their girlfriends, their kids. All them niggas should be out there getting money instead of laying up under you all day."

As true as it all was, Patsy hated hearing it from her brother. It was bad enough he had been the apple of their mother's eye. Then he became the man of the family financially and protectively. Even after he went to jail, he never stopped being their mother's favorite. She had died of a broken heart. They all knew it. Life without her beloved son was no life at all. Now, hearing him preach to her about her failure to raise sons who had even an ounce of the drive Michael had at their age crushed her.

"I'm gonna tell Ivy to let Deja send her appraisers over there," he said. "Just to see what I could get for it."

Patsy fumed. "Coco said you walked off a visit with Ivy a couple weeks ago. Now all of a sudden, she got you ready to sell Mama's house."

"At least she shows up for the visit. Unlike you."

Patsy scoffed, taking a final drag of her cigarette, then crushed it out in the ashtray.

"Okay, Mikey. I'll be there next week."

"We'll see," he said. He hung the phone up and sulked back to his cell.

Once he got there, he sat fuming silently for close to an hour. They all had him fucked up. Ivy, his sisters, the other inmates. Everybody. He needed to make a move. He used his next phone time to call his cousin Bam.

Bam earned his name for his reputation as a trigger-happy member of Michael's crew. He always answered when Michael called and today was no different.

"Yo," Michael said. "I need you to do me a favor."

Ziggy waited anxiously at the bar in his friend's restaurant in Manhattan's Meatpacking District. Tonight was his first official date with Coco after several weeks filled with a flurry of mixed messages.

On one hand, Coco seemed to enjoy their conversations. She spoke freely about her work, friendships, and future plans. On the other hand, she pumped the brakes whenever he suggested that they go out and connect face to face.

During their many phone conversations, they discussed the prospect of Big Baby developing a tour with Live Nation. On the day the deal was sealed, Ziggy had surprised Coco at her office with flowers and chocolate-covered strawberries. She'd seemed pleasantly caught off guard and had reluctantly agreed to this date. Now he waited, glancing occasionally at the door.

Coco arrived at the trendy bar that took up an entire corner of the long block. It was clear from the loud music, raised voices, and patrons scattered outside smoking cigarettes and joints that the place was very popular. The crowd was a multicultural mix of young New Yorkers sipping assorted drinks and chattering endlessly.

She finally stepped through the door and spotted Ziggy at the bar. The smile on his face left no doubt that he was happy to see her.

Coco smiled, too, strutting toward him with her heart beating rapidly. He took her all in, every inch of her, delighted with what he saw. She was dressed casually tonight in deconstructed jeans that exposed a nice bit of leg and a simple black tank top with some crisscross details in the back. Her short hair was styled to perfection, and she wore very little makeup.

The heat hadn't let up despite the sunset. Ziggy was grateful for the warm weather as he studied Coco's lovely brown skin peeking through her skimpy top and the rips in her jeans. He would be thanking Nikki for this introduction for a very long time.

She reached his side, and he felt butterflies.

"Hi," she whispered as they embraced.

She had been looking forward to seeing him again. Their phone conversations had been frequent, each of them about an hour long.

Derek had been calling, too—quite often, in fact. Coco had been fighting the urge to see him again. Just one more time. Part of her enjoyed seeing him grovel, happy to know that he realized that he had fucked up a good thing. Still, she held her ground. She decided that she loved herself too much to take him back. Not this time.

She focused instead on getting to know Ziggy. She found that they had a considerable amount in common. They enjoyed the same food, types of books, and movies. They had traveled to similar places, indulged in many of the same exotic delicacies. They had a bunch of differences, too, which they discussed unabashedly. He introduced her to music she hadn't heard and taught her a few phrases in Italian. Their conversations had been interesting and devoid of awkward silences. Tonight was no different as they fell into an easy banter.

"I'm so hungry," he said. "I was so excited about seeing you tonight that I skipped lunch."

Coco smiled. It was a relief hearing that. She hadn't had a bite since breakfast, either.

Ziggy held her gently at the small of her back, ushering her through the tight crowd. It wasn't long before a tall blonde barreled in their direction, smiling from ear to ear. She greeted them, pulling Ziggy into a warm embrace. He smiled and introduced them.

"This is Emilia. She's my friend Jason's wife and co-owner of this place."

Coco extended her hand to Emilia, but the woman pulled her into a tight hug instead, catching her off guard. Coco smiled anyway and told her what a nice place it was. Soon, they were joined by a man who was almost as pretty as Emilia was. He had dark hair, thick eyebrows, and intoxicating brown eyes that seemed to size Coco up and welcome her all at the same time.

"And this is Jason," Ziggy said. He stepped back and watched Jason hug Coco.

Jason beamed. "Nice to meet you!"

Coco giggled as Jason took her by the hand and led her toward the back of the bar. Ziggy and Emilia followed close behind them. The bar was full of sounds—music blaring through the speaker system, people yelling to one another from across the room, others standing side by side and bellowing to be heard over all the other noises. Still, there was something about this place that made Coco feel like she was right at home.

They reached a set of stairs that led down to a cozy Prohibition-era cellar. The walls were exposed brick, the lighting warm and amber toned. The vibe was completely different from the one upstairs. An indie band played their hearts out in the front of the room, and the audience was so enraptured that they barely noticed Coco and the gang as they made their way through the crowd. Jason never let go of Coco's hand as he ushered her past several patrons nestled together at modest round tables. Each table had a flickering red candle on top of it. One was set aside in the back, a RESERVED sign sitting on top of it. Jason tossed it aside and motioned for Coco and Ziggy to sit. They did, their seats just inches apart because of the limited space. Coco got a whiff of Ziggy's cologne and approved. He smelled divine.

"Make yourselves at home," Emilia said. "We're sending over some food for you to nibble on. But, if you want to order anything special, just let us know. Everything is delicious. But, obviously, I'm biased."

She laughed, revealing brilliant white teeth. She was a lovely woman, and her personality was equally endearing.

"We'll be around if you need us. Ziggy knows his way around here pretty well, so you're in good hands." She gave them a wink as she and her husband retreated.

A server arrived with a generous platter of all sorts of appetizers. Ziggy dug right in. He grabbed a slice of wild mushroom flatbread and took a healthy bite.

"Mmm." He closed his eyes, relishing the taste of the mushrooms and cheese. "Taste this."

He hovered the food at her lips, watching them part as he fed her. She opened wide and tasted the food, and he felt the deepest desire to kiss her.

Coco nodded. "It's delicious."

She smiled, enticed by the way he looked at her. She wiped her mouth, feeling a bit shy under his gaze.

The band's lead singer—a freckled redhead—stepped up to the mic and began singing "Killing Me Softly" in the deepest, most sultry voice Coco had ever heard come out of a white girl.

A server brought some drinks to their table, and Coco marveled that Ziggy had remembered what she liked.

"Vodka and cranberry, right?"

She nodded. "Good memory," she observed. "I like that."

He gave a humble nod.

"What kind of women do you usually date, Ziggy?"

He thought about that. "I don't have a type, really. I've always been attracted to smart women. I like to be challenged. And I do a lot of challenging in return."

She raised an eyebrow. Derek had been a challenge. The emotionally unavailable kind.

He noticed her reaction and wondered what he'd said wrong.

"Challenges," she repeated. "What kind of challenges do you like?"

He grinned. "I like to be around people who make me think. People who teach me new things. I like a woman who isn't afraid to debate me when she disagrees. Someone willing to try anything once. I like to walk on the wild side every now and then. I love not knowing what to expect."

"So, you're spontaneous?"

"Very!" His eyes were wide with mischief. "To me, the worst thing in the world is boredom. Routine. That shit ages you. Before you know it, you've been living the same day, same year, over and over your whole life."

He shuddered at the thought.

"That's not for me. I like adventure and fun. And I can tell we'll have fun together. Any lady who's friends with Nikki knows how to have a good time."

She laughed. "Well, don't get your hopes up too high. I'm not as exciting as she is."

He waved her off. "That's not true. The Coco I've been talking to and texting every day is very exciting. I like talking to you. You don't hold back."

She grinned, so intrigued by this man that she could barely stand it. She could sense that, at the very least, Ziggy could help get her mind off Derek for a while.

"I'm glad you like that about me," she said. "I like to speak my mind. That's how I was raised. My whole family is assertive."

She thought about Patsy and chuckled a little, realizing that she would probably be better described as "aggressive."

"Not everyone can handle that," she said. "Especially a clean-cut white guy like you."

Ziggy laughed. "Clean-cut? God, I wish my mother heard you say that. I'm the rebel in the family. At least that's how they see it."

Coco sipped her drink. "Why? Because you dropped out of college and followed your real dreams?"

He nodded. "In my family, that's unheard of. Leaving a carefully plotted career path for the music industry? To them, I walked away from stability for a world full of sex, drugs, and rock and roll. For years, they thought I was crazy. My mother was at church lighting candles, praying all the time. She thought I was gonna get lost in that life, never find peace. The only one who really had my back was my sister."

"Penny, right?" Coco recalled hearing him mention her during their countless conversations over the past few days.

"Yeah. She's two years older than me, so she knew how hard it was to live up to the expectations our family had of us. When I was struggling to make ends meet but too proud to go ask my parents for money, Penny paid my rent. The first thing I did when I got my first decent royalty check was pay her back. She wouldn't take the money. So, I bought her a car instead."

Coco smiled. "Sounds like the kind of relationship I have with my brother, Mikey. He always looked out for me like that. But there's no way I could pay him back. Even if I tried."

He saw a flash of sadness in her eyes as she said it.

"I hope I get to meet him."

She looked at him skeptically. "He's in jail," she said. "Serving time for murder. He's been in there for sixteen years so far. Just got denied by the parole board. So, unfortunately, I doubt you'll get to meet him."

Ziggy tried his best to hide his shock but failed. "Wow. That must be hard for you."

She shrugged. "It's harder for him. He put in all the work, took all the risks. Now he's paying the price while the rest of our family reaps the benefits of his sacrifice. Mikey put me through school, financed my sister's business, bought my mother's house, and left a nice nest egg for his wife and kids. But what was the point of all of that if he can't enjoy it, too?"

Ziggy thought about that.

"I bet he takes solace in the fact that you're successful because of his help. That the family is established because of the risks he took. Really, it's no different than the sacrifice John

Gotti made for his family. Or the Wall Street investment bankers who get locked up for insider trading. They pay a hefty price, going to jail. But you could argue that the price was worth it for the way their families benefited from what they did."

Coco nodded, pleased by Ziggy's outlook on the situation. "That's true."

"Your brother sounds like a solid man."

Coco grinned. She certainly agreed.

They sat together in silence for a while, listening to the band playing and sharing the delicious food Jason and Emilia had sent over to their table.

Coco looked at him. "I'm glad you're so open minded. One of the things I was worried about when Nikki introduced us was that we might be too different."

He smirked. "That's what makes life interesting," he said. "We may come from different backgrounds, but that'll give us more to talk about and explore. More to understand. I'm open minded. So are you. So this will be easy."

She liked his optimism.

"What else worried you about dating me?"

She shrugged, pretending not to have any other reservations.

Still smirking, he leaned in close to her. "You can say it. I already know what you're thinking."

She chuckled. "I don't know what you're talking about."

He nodded. "Yes, you do. I'll say it for you. You're worried that all the things they say about white guys are true and the sex will be wack."

Coco laughed so hard she nearly spat out her drink.

Ziggy laughed, too.

"Let me put your mind at ease. I can handle you."

"You think so?" she asked, grinning.

He nodded. "I like a challenge."

"I hear that," she said, smiling.

They sat for hours in the darkened basement of the restaurant as other patrons began to make their exit. Coco and Ziggy remained there, talking, laughing, sipping drinks, and breaking bread together.

It was nearly two o'clock in the morning by the time they reluctantly agreed to call it a night. Ziggy led her out of the dark basement and up the stairs to the main bar. She felt his hands brush her ass as she passed him, and it thrilled her. She locked eyes with him and bit her lip.

When they found Jason and Emilia, they could barely stand the formalities. They rushed through the obligatory "goodbyes" and the promises to get together again soon. All they wanted was to get somewhere alone, away from the prying eyes of everyone around them.

They stepped out of the bar and onto Ninth Avenue, and Coco gasped when Ziggy gripped her tightly around the waist and drew her closer to him. He kissed her intensely, his tongue dancing with hers in such an erotic way that a moan escaped her lips. He held her tighter, kissed her deeply, hungrily. People walked by, some smiling at the couple lost in their own universe. A faint breeze blew, nudging them back to the reality that they were not alone. Slowly, Ziggy eased up, kissing her softer, brushing his lips tenderly across hers. Then, he reluctantly stepped back, smiling down at her.

"See? Told you I can handle you."

Coco gripped her bamboo clutch bag tightly with both hands. Her panties were wet enough to feel them. She knew that if she didn't leave right now, she was gonna fuck the shit out of this white boy tonight.

She smiled at him. "Good night, Ziggy."

He smiled back.

"Goodnight, Cara. I hope to see you again soon."

She turned and sauntered off, exhaling deeply.

"You will," she said over her shoulder.

Deja sat in her car listening to old love songs on the radio. It was a Saturday night and Bobby was working. Bree was at home in her room watching YouTube makeup tutorials and music videos. For no good reason, Deja was parked outside Rashid's apartment building, staring up at his window. Rashid's apartment was on Flatbush Avenue near Beverley Road, walking distance from several shops and cafés. She scanned the neighborhood, imagining him existing among the people there. Living his life as a newly freed man. She saw a light on in one window and wondered if he were alone. She prayed he was as she dialed his number.

"Hey," he answered. "What's up?"

"Hey," Deja said. "I'm in your neighborhood. I was wondering if you felt like having some company."

He hesitated. "You're in Brooklyn? On a Saturday night?"

She laughed uneasily. "Yeah."

"Where's your husband?"

"Working."

Silence again.

"Where in Brooklyn are you?"

"I'm downstairs. Parked outside your building." She paused, aware that she sounded crazy. "Can I come up?"

Rashid sat up on his sofa, looked around at his modest apartment, and suddenly felt embarrassed by it. It was definitely an upgrade from the prison accommodations he had endured for the past fifteen years, but now it felt insignificant in contrast to Deja's home.

"I'll come down." He hung up the phone before she could respond.

Deja waited uneasily in her car. She second-guessed herself for coming here. Wasn't even sure what she wanted to say. She slid the driver's seat back and unlocked her car doors as Rashid emerged from the building and scanned the block for her car. He spotted her and walked in her direction as she watched him. He wore a gray hoodie and jeans with a pair of sneakers and still somehow looked like a million bucks.

He climbed into the passenger seat of her car and shut the door.

"You're out here parked in front of my building acting like you're not married to a police sergeant. I don't need that nigga fucking with me because of you. He's already been calling my probation officer, making sure I'm meeting my curfew. She told me about it. I don't need that shit. What's up, Deja? What do you want to say to me?"

She was surprised by his greeting. "Hello to you, too," she said sarcastically.

He huffed.

"I miss you," she said softly.

Rashid looked at her like she had lost her mind. "Did you miss me for the past fifteen years while I was locked up?"

"I did."

"Then where the fuck were you?"

"I was being a fraud, like you said. Playing a role. Trying to have a perfect life on the surface, but I haven't been happy for years."

Rashid shook his head. "That's between you and your husband. That's got nothing to do with me."

"I know. I don't expect anything from you, Rashid. I just want you to understand that I didn't get away scot-free like you think I did. I was affected by what happened, too. I just didn't realize how. Then I built this life with Bobby, tried to give this perfect life to Bree. All because I was running from the mistakes I made with you. But since you've been back, I understand what it is. I miss you. I miss us. And I miss who I used to be."

Rashid watched her as she spoke. He wasn't sure what to say.

"I don't have a right to ask you for anything, but I just want to be your friend, Rashid. I want you to know that I'm sorry for what I did. And I miss what we had. How you knew parts of me that I tried to keep tucked away. And how you let me see you for who you really were."

"And what did you do with it, Deja? With all that access I gave you to my heart?"

She looked away, convicted.

"You knew about the shit I went through as a kid. I told you about it. Watching my mother get her ass whooped by my stepfather. Me and my brother acting up in school, getting sent to group homes and juvenile detention centers. Preparing us for jail. Institutionalizing us at an early age. I didn't choose the streets. The streets chose me. I told you that and you acted like you understood."

"I did understand. I loved you anyway."

"So, you should have stood by my side when I did what I had to do."

"I was too weak to do it then."

"And what? You're strong now?"

His smirk was condescending, and she hated it.

"I'm trying to be, and I'm gonna start by apologizing to you. Asking for your forgiveness. And for your friendship."

He looked in her eyes and saw the old Deja he used to know. She was still there, just buried deep beneath the façade she had constructed for herself. He sighed.

"Apology accepted. As long as you keep RoboCop from fucking with me, we can try being friends again."

She nodded.

He opened his car door and put one foot out. He turned to her before climbing out.

"Next time call first. I might have company."

She felt a twinge of jealousy.

"Next time invite me upstairs," she said. "I won't bite."

He laughed as he got out of the car. "Then you really have changed."

He heard her laugh as he shut the car door and walked back to his building.

Heart of the Matter

Grinning, Kingston drove his brother's car away from Hezzy's house. He had been chilling with Mariah. Today, she had finally made it clear how much she was feeling him: kissing him, rubbing on him, grinding on him. For a minute, he thought they might go all the way, but then his phone went off and interrupted their heated make-out session. It was Bree.

She was calling to tell him that she was stranded at her dance studio. The whole thing was a lie, part of a carefully crafted plan Bree had devised to get his attention. She and Kingston had been texting each other more often. They were still in the friend zone. But he was beginning to open up to her more. He told her that he was planning to hang out with Mariah that afternoon, and Bree started thinking of a way to interrupt that.

Today, Rashid was supposed to pick Bree up from her dance class, but she had called and told him that her class was canceled.

"You don't have to pick me up after all," she had told her father.

Rashid, toiling on a worksite in Queens, had said okay and hadn't questioned it further.

Satisfied, Bree had called Kingston instead. "I'm stuck here. My mother's showing a property, and Dad's on assignment," she'd explained. "I can get an Uber if it's too much trouble."

But Bree was his homegirl. Kingston couldn't leave her out there like that. So, he'd told her he was on his way, wrapped up his wonderful afternoon with Mariah, and was now headed to Bree's dance school in New Dorp. He merged into traffic on the highway and thought back to a few nights ago at his house when Bree had met Mariah for the first time. As promised, she'd sized her up, offering Kingston her opinion of his love interest after their little party was over.

"She's pretty," Bree had said. "She just doesn't have any depth."

King had laughed it off. Bree was the same age he was, but she was definitely not as experienced. She didn't smoke weed, didn't drink. Still, despite her reputation as a good girl, there was something about Bree that had him seeing her in a different light lately.

He pulled up in front of the dance studio and found her standing outside talking to a Hispanic girl and a white lady. When Bree saw him pull up, she smiled. She said goodbye to her friend and the older woman, and walked toward the car, gripping a pink Nike duffle bag in her hand. She got in the car and greeted him with a fist bump.

"I would hug you like usual, but I smell kinda funky right now," she said. "Miss Linda rode us hard today."

"Pause." He laughed as he put the car in drive and pulled off. "'Rode us hard'? I bet your parents don't know that's the type of shit that's going on at your dance school."

She laughed so hard that her abs hurt even more than they already did. She winced, still laughing, and punched him playfully on the arm.

"You're nasty. Get your mind out the gutter." She shook her

head and looked away so that he wouldn't see how hard she was smiling. "What took you so long?"

He sucked his teeth and looked at her sidelong. "You're lucky I came to get you at all. I was about to get the panties today. Mariah couldn't keep her hands off me!" King looked out the window wistfully.

Bree's eyes narrowed. "Mmm-hmm. Good thing I called you when I did."

He looked at her, surprised. "What type of shit is that? Don't be a hater."

Bree shook her head. "You're so *stupid,* King. What did I tell you about that girl? She has no depth. You gonna mess around and get some silly dumb girl pregnant. Messing up all that melanin in your bloodline with her pale ass."

His reaction was priceless. King didn't know whether to laugh or be pissed. The result was a frustrated flutter of his lips, followed by a smirk and then a frown. Bree had to resist the urge to giggle.

"First of all," he said, "I'm tired of you talking about me getting somebody pregnant. Like I ain't smart enough to put a condom on before I slide up in something. I ain't stupid, Bree. Just 'cause I play sports don't mean I'm dumb."

She allowed him that and chose not to respond.

"Second of all," he continued, "why you worried about it?"

She shrugged. "Hate to see you fuck up a good thing. That's all. You're going somewhere in life, with or without getting in Mariah's panties. Just don't let her get you trapped. You have way too much to lose." Bree looked at him as she said it, daring him to disagree.

Again, he looked at her sidelong. "Okay. You have a point."

Bree looked out the passenger window, done arguing for now.

"What's up with you and your father?" he asked. "Rashid, I mean. How's that going, getting to know him?"

She sighed. "It's weird, you know? It's nice. We talk all the time. He texts me every morning, every night before bed, all through the day. He's really trying to make up for lost time. And I love talking to him. He's so cool, mad down to earth."

Bree was smiling as she said all this. Then her smile slowly began to fade.

"He wants me to call him 'Dad.' I do when it's just me and him. But I don't know what to do or say in front of my parents. I don't know how my mother feels about the situation, honestly. Since he came back, she walks around like she's in some kinda fog. But my dad—Bobby—he raised me. Until a few weeks ago, he was the only father I knew. So, as happy as I am that I'm getting to know my biological father, I feel like I'm betraying the man who raised me."

Kingston nodded. "All that shit sounds wild to me," he admitted. "Both of our fathers have been locked up our whole lives. But your mother got married, and mine stayed single. Until now. All of a sudden, she's dating again. I don't like that shit at all."

He shook his head, thinking of the mechanic he and Noah had unwittingly introduced her to.

Bree frowned. "Why don't you like it? What's wrong with Miss Ivy dating? She still looks good."

Kingston scoffed. "She's been riding it out with my dad all this time. Why stop now?"

"Because life is short," Bree said. "She should be happy, too."

"My dad was making her happy all this time. Shit don't need to change now."

Bree looked at him oddly. "Your mother is a grown woman. She can make her own decisions."

"What if she makes the wrong one? We don't know this man from Adam. He could be a serial killer for all I know."

"He's Black, ain't he?" Bree scoffed, an outraged expression on her face. "Black people don't do that."

Kingston laughed.

"How did she meet him?"

He told her the story about meeting him at the mechanic shop the night of their impromptu party.

"He used to play ball at my school. Coach told me all about him," Kingston said.

Bree threw up her arms. "So, he's not a stranger at all. If your coach says he's all right, you should trust him."

Kingston shrugged. "I think I don't like it because it makes me feel kinda the same way you feel. If she gets serious with a new nigga and I accept it, that's like I'm betraying my father."

She thought about it. "See? I knew you would understand. You're the only one I can talk to about things like this. And the little silly girls you like can't get this deep with you. So, you should stop wasting your time with them."

He looked at her while they were stopped at a red light. Saw her with new eyes, really. She was pretty. He had always thought so. But this was his "little sis." Wasn't she? Beyoncé's voice came on the airwaves singing about taking the top off a Maybach. Bree sang along, and he grinned, thinking maybe it was time to take shorty out of the friend zone.

The light turned green, and he drove on. He glanced at her again.

"You got a boyfriend at your little private school?"

Bree stopped singing and looked at him.

"Nope," she said firmly. "I'm still waiting for your friend Kevin to ask me out."

He sucked his teeth. "I told you, that shit ain't happening."

"Why not? It's not like *you're* gonna ask me out."

Bree's heart was beating so fast that she gripped the car door for strength.

King's eyes were wide with surprise. "I'm wasting my time?"

They arrived at her house, and he almost wished she lived farther away. The conversation was just getting good.

"Okay, so, what's up?" he said, smirking and licking his lips in his best mack daddy impersonation. "Shoot your shot, Bree."

She laughed, thinking he was teasing her, and started to get out of the car. But he protested.

"Nah! Come on. It sounds like you got something to say. Let me hear it."

She sighed, nervous energy coursing through every molecule in her body.

Bobby stood at the window and called Deja's name. She joined him, and they peered through the glass, watching Bree sitting in the passenger seat of Noah's BMW and talking to Kingston.

"What's this about?" Bobby asked, looking at Deja like she held the answers. "I thought Rashid was picking her up."

Deja shrugged her shoulders. "I don't know," she said. "I thought so, too."

"So, he's already letting her down?" He walked away from the window, disgusted. "It's his third time picking her up from dance class and he dropped the ball. Just like I told you he would."

Bobby wanted Rashid gone. Wanted his life with Deja and Bree to go back to normal. He had always known, of course, that Bree's father was a convict. He had never felt sympathy for those types. His own father had gone to jail, abandoning him and his brother as kids. It made him crave the stability and structure of a normal family. Made him develop a love for law and order. It had shaped him into the man Deja had fallen in love with, one who would protect her and provide for her and her child. Lately, though, it felt like Deja and Bree no longer needed him. He blamed Rashid for it. But the truth was, he had felt it all slipping from his grasp long ago.

Deja rolled her eyes. Rashid was all Bobby could talk about the past few days. He kept stressing how opposed he was to Rashid spending time alone with Bree, bringing her around his family. He was like a man obsessed.

"I'll call Rashid and find out what happened," she offered weakly.

Bobby leaned on the counter. "What about her hanging around with this kid?"

Deja frowned, glancing out the window to be sure she was understanding him right. "'This kid'? You mean King?"

Bobby nodded.

"You act like you don't know him. We watched King grow up. Ivy's our friend. What's the problem?"

Bobby scoffed. "You approve of Bree hanging out with him?"

Deja felt like she was in an alternate universe. "Bobby . . . why wouldn't I approve? Kingston is a good kid."

"Is he?" Bobby scoffed. "We just pulled up on him having a house party with a bunch of druggies and gang members the other night, and he's a good kid?"

Deja laughed maniacally, sure now that her husband had lost his mind. "They're kids! That's normal teenage shit. You're overreacting."

He stared at Deja, disappointed by her passivity. "Kingston's father is a drug dealer," he said. "Doing time in prison for killing somebody. Kingston himself is hanging around with a questionable crowd. I don't want Bree hanging out with him."

Deja's blood was boiling. She glared at him defiantly. "I don't really care what you want. Leave Bree alone about it."

"You're starting to act real strange, Deja. All of a sudden, it's like I don't know you anymore."

"What's this really about, Bobby? You've been walking around here with an attitude ever since Rashid came back."

Bobby's instinct was to react defensively. His body language showed it when he looked away in disgust. Then, he thought about the tension in the house since Rashid had set foot in there days ago. Even after he'd left, his presence seemed to linger. Deja, Bobby, and Bree were walking on eggshells around one another. Even he had to admit it.

He looked at her. "I don't like this shit," he said truthfully. "None of it. I don't like Rashid stepping back on the scene like he has a right to disrupt her life—*our* lives—without warning. I don't like Bree spending time with this kid who seems like he's headed down the same path as his father—same path as Rashid—while you sit by like nothing's wrong with that shit."

Deja breathed deeply as Bobby continued his rant.

"And I don't like the way you seem distant since Rashid came back. Since before he came back, really. When's the last time we had sex?"

She laughed. "Bobby, seriously. That's what's on your mind right now?"

"A lot of shit is on my mind. Mainly the fact that you've been distant lately. Like you're starting to question every decision you made over the past sixteen years. Including being with me."

She walked to the refrigerator and opened it, unable to face him. She pulled out a juice container, her hands trembling.

"I hear you," was all she could manage.

"That's it?"

"I don't know what you want me to say." She was weary. "I think you're blowing this out of proportion. If I've been distant lately, it's because I'm worried about Bree. Let's just wait for her to come in the house and find out what happened. How's that?"

"Not good enough," he pressed her. "I want to know what's going on with you, Deja. Speak up! I know you've been calling him. I get the phone logs. Ten minutes here. Thirty minutes there. The other day, you talked to him for an hour. I'm walking around here waiting for you to stop bullshitting. What the fuck is going on?"

She lost it then. "You know what, Bobby? I'm calling Rashid and sneaking around and shit because I'm *bored*! With you, with my life, with all of this. And it has nothing to do with Rashid. Or maybe it does. Maybe I'm starting to feel like the fraud he keeps saying I am."

Bobby was pissed. "You are a fraud! Wasting my time all these years pretending to be in love with me. All the while you just loved the stability I provided. Now you resent me for it. You're bored. Get the fuck out of here."

"It's the reason I keep arguing with my sister. Criticizing her all the time. It's because I'm jealous of her."

"What are you talking about?"

"This person I've become . . . it's not the real me. Nikki's right."

Bobby groaned. Not Nikki again.

"She been saying for years that I've been faking it. Living a lie. And she's right. I'm not in love anymore. Not with you or with this house, this life. I need a break."

She looked at her husband and saw the stunned look on his face.

"You asked why I've been in a funk lately. Well, that's why."

Bree shifted her weight in the passenger seat of the car and faced Kingston bravely.

"I like you, King," she admitted. "You're dope. So am I. It's a no-brainer. You should be spending more time with me than with them silly girls you like." She shrugged. "That's me shooting my shot."

He laughed, his mind reeling. This was all so unexpected, and he felt so flattered. His smile wide, he saw that Bree was staring back at him deadpanned.

He tried to get serious. "Okay," he said, smiling. "You wanna pull up with me to my basketball team's awards dinner in two weeks?"

Until this moment, he'd had every intention of asking Mariah to go with him. But there was something about the way the light was catching Bree as the sun set over their neighborhood, the way her lip gloss sparkled in that light and how her eyes twinkled when she smiled. Maybe she was right, and he had been missing out on a good thing right under his nose.

She smiled, wide and unashamed. She nodded. "Yeah. I'll go with you. Text me the details." She opened the car door and paused. "Thanks for picking me up. Good talk."

She winked at him and climbed out of the car, her heart pounding like a racehorse's hooves. She prayed that he didn't notice her nervousness as she shut the car door.

Kingston watched her walk to her door and waved to her as she went into the house. She waved back, her heart pounding.

Beaming, Bree was immediately greeted by her stepdad.

Bobby was frowning. "What's Kingston doing dropping you off? What happened to Rashid?"

Deja emerged from the kitchen, looking concerned.

Bree looked at both of her parents and shrugged. "He got stuck at work and couldn't make it," she lied. "So, I called King."

Bobby's frown deepened. "Why didn't you call me? Or your mother?"

"I was going to," Bree lied. "But then King called me and asked what I was doing. I told him where I was, and he came and got me."

"*Rashid* was supposed to come and get you," Bobby countered angrily.

"Bobby, calm down."

Deja's voice was low and steady. She looked at Bree, smiled weakly, then returned her attention to her husband. "Let her explain. She just got in the door."

Bree sensed the tension in the air. "Like I said. He called and said that he was stuck at a construction site and he couldn't make it in time to pick me up. So, I was about to call one of you. But then King called me. So, he picked me up instead. It was no big deal."

"It's a big deal because Rashid didn't call to tell us that the plans changed. He shouldn't be calling you directly."

Deja scoffed. "Why not? He's her father, Bobby!"

The words were out of her mouth before she had time to think about it. It hadn't occurred to her that they would cut so deeply.

Bobby looked like he had been slapped.

Bree stood, helplessly, immediately regretting her decision to involve her parents in her lie. All she'd wanted was to get King's attention. This was going too far.

"And what am I, Deja?"

"He has a right to talk to her. That's all I'm saying."

Deja walked away. She stepped down into their living room and sat on the couch. She wasn't surprised when Bobby followed her, but she groaned anyway.

"Call him right now," Bobby demanded. "I want to talk to him. He's a grown-ass man. He should have called us like a grown man instead of calling a child to say that he couldn't handle his responsibility."

"You're blowing this out of proportion."

"No, you're not giving the situation enough energy. That's the problem. He's been locked up so long he doesn't know how to interact with people. I see it all the time. But this shit don't fly. He needs to explain himself. Call him."

Deja opened her mouth, but Bree cut her off.

"I lied," she admitted flatly. She sadly shook her head. "Okay? I'm sorry. I just wanted to spend time with King. I called Dad—"

Her eyes went wide, and she looked at Bobby, horrified.

Bobby stared blankly at her.

"I called him and told him that my dance class was canceled. He was on a worksite, so he didn't stay on the phone long. But he asked me if I was sure. And I told him that I was. Then King came and picked me up and dropped me off here."

Deja breathed a sigh of relief. She had been hoping that Rashid hadn't disappointed them already.

"So, you lied about all this just so you could see Kingston?" Deja asked.

Bree nodded.

Bobby stood with his hands on his hips, visibly pissed. "Bree, that's not cool. We don't want you hanging out with Kingston anymore."

Bree balked. "Why not?"

"Because he's a bad influence. That's why."

Bree looked at her mother pleadingly. "Ma! That's not fair."

Deja sat forward in her seat and looked at her husband. "Bobby, we didn't agree on that."

"Fuck that, Deja!" Bobby was done playing softball with them. "I'm putting my foot down on this one." He looked at Bree. "You're lying, sneaking around with him. I'm not gonna watch you mess your life up for some wannabe thug."

Deja stood. She felt like Bobby was inadvertently talking about Rashid rather than Kingston.

"Bobby, you lost your fuckin' mind! That's Ivy's son! We know Kingston."

"Every savage I lock up on those streets is somebody's son," he said.

"King ain't no *savage,*" Bree said defiantly.

Bobby sucked his teeth. "That's just what we call the idiots we lock up," he explained. The NYPD officers he worked with referred to the perps that way.

"Savages?" Bree asked, incredulous.

Bobby felt guilty. He had heard the term thrown around so much on the job that the severity of its meaning had gotten lost on him. The irony of calling Black men savages while working for a largely white police force had never occurred to him.

Deja shook her head. "You're standing there comparing King to the guys you lock up every day? Bobby, you're not making sense. Like I said before, you need to calm down. We all need to talk."

"Talk about what?" he demanded.

"About Rashid being home, and how it's making all of us feel. About Bree and the lie she told, and how it caused more trouble than it was worth."

She shot a stern look at her daughter for good measure.

"And about Kingston. He's harmless, and I don't have a problem with Bree seeing him."

Bree was relieved. She smiled at her mother.

Bobby stared at them, aware that he had already lost this fight.

"Cool," he said sarcastically. "Y'all talk about it. Maybe you can call Rashid. Let him weigh in." He grabbed his car keys off the hook on the wall. "I'm going out."

He walked out the door while Deja and Bree looked on in silence.

Ivy arrived home from work exhausted. Her salon manager had run things at the shop today while Ivy worked on the set of a magazine photo shoot. She had been styling elaborate hairdos all day, standing on her feet. Her hands were sore, her back hurt, and all she wanted was a shower and her bed.

She stepped into her living room expecting to see Noah and Kingston. Instead, she found Mikey's cousin Bam and two of his cronies sprawled out across her living room furniture. They had their muddiest Timberlands on, and Bam had the nerve to have his feet up on her coffee table. He smiled at her as she entered.

"Nice place you got here, Ivy. Mikey said you had leveled up. I didn't know you was living this large, though."

Ivy was enraged. "Why are you in my house, Bam? Where are my sons?"

"They're upstairs. We asked them to give us some privacy. Mikey called and talked to them. Explained what was happening. We just want to talk to you. That's all. You should sit down."

Ivy glared at him, pissed that he had the audacity to invite her to a seat in her own home.

"I'll stand," she insisted. "What do you want?"

"Mikey wants to see you. He needs you to come visit him."

"I'm not doing that."

Bam took his feet off the table and sat up. "That's gonna be a problem," he said bluntly.

One of his cronies leaned forward from his seat on the sofa. His grimace was unsettling. Ivy shifted nervously.

"Mikey's not asking, Ivy. He knows you're upset. He said he's sorry for walking off the visit and all that. Won't happen again, but he wants to see you up there this week. Otherwise, I'll be back. And if I gotta come back, he might not want me to just talk to you. You know how Mikey can get sometimes."

Bam locked eyes with Ivy, his expression unflinching. Then he broke into an unexpected, sinister smile.

"It's good to see you again. Good to know where you are."

He walked out of her house with his cronies in tow. Ivy rushed to shut and lock the door behind him. Then she charged up the stairs to check on her sons with tears pouring down her face. She found them safe in Noah's room on a phone call with their father. Noah handed her the phone, careful to avoid eye contact. It was clear that she was livid.

She snatched the phone. "Mikey! You're a fucking—"

"I'm not gonna tell you again," he said, cutting her off. "Get up here. I'm not playing with you, Ivy. Don't make me hurt you."

The phone line went dead, and she glared at her sons. In a rage, she threw Noah's cell phone across the room, sending it crashing into the wall. Both boys looked on in horror.

"Your father doesn't own me! He doesn't control my life anymore!"

She was yelling at them, but the words were more for her own reassurance. She stormed out of the room and into her own, slamming the door shut. She wanted to throw herself down on the bed and cry. Instead, she called her family back in Brooklyn. Michael wasn't the only one who knew some goons. The time had come to fight fire with fire. She snatched her cell phone and frantically dialed.

"It's Ivy!" she shouted into the phone. "I need some help out here in Staten Island."

Sharpshooter

Coco watched with a grin as Ziggy lit a row of candles on a table at the far end of the very large living room. They were in East Hampton at his home, a beautiful place with spacious rooms and the warmest, calmest vibes Coco had shared with a man in a very long time. They were enjoying a mini paradise far away from the madness of the city.

They had spent the day together on his sister's yacht, followed by dinner at a lovely restaurant in the heart of town. Ziggy knew everyone, of course, which guaranteed that they were treated like royalty wherever they went. Coco, never one to shy away from VIP treatment, was in her element here with him.

He returned to his seat beside her on the couch and pulled her back into his arms. She wasn't usually this affectionate with the men she dated, but Ziggy was nothing like the men she had been with before him. He was vocal, passionate—seemingly in every way. When he laughed, he did it big with his mouth wide and his eyes dancing. Always dancing, those eyes. When he took her to bed, he did it with equal fervor. It seemed as if every molecule in his body, every brain cell, every taste bud, was focused on her alone. He was opinionated and boisterous at times, quiet and romantic at others. Ziggy was quite a man.

She couldn't help comparing him to Derek from time to time. After all, Derek had been the man she'd spent most of her adult life with. By now, his attempts to contact her were less frequent. She assumed that he had given up on reigniting the flame between them. She didn't care, though. Now, Ziggy had her full attention. He listened to her when she talked. He asked her questions, really paid attention to her answers, and seemed to genuinely appreciate the depth of who she was.

Coco wasn't kidding herself. She kept in mind that neither of them had seen the worst of each other yet. She had been honest with Ziggy about her family dynamics and had opened up to him somewhat, but she held back part of herself still, hesitant to let herself freefall with a man so unlike herself.

However, there was a connection between them that couldn't be denied. Ziggy seemed to really *see* her. The real her. It hadn't been lost on her that he never called her by her nickname. She wasn't "Coco" to him. It was "*Cara*" that he whispered desperately in her ear in the throes of their passion, and it turned her on to be seen that way. To be called by her name. To have her body, her mind, and her deep-brown skin appreciated so openly and unapologetically. She could tell that Ziggy truly found her beautiful. It didn't matter that she was Black, and he was white. They were feeling each other. And he didn't care who knew it.

Coco settled into his arms and felt his facial hair prickly against her skin as he nuzzled into her. He inhaled her scent and kissed her softly on the cheek.

"You really do smell like cocoa butter. It's not just a stereotype." He was laughing as he said it.

Coco sat up and swatted him, but she was already laughing,

too. "That's coconut oil you're smelling, not cocoa butter, smart-ass."

He laughed even louder now. "I'm sorry. Such an amateur." He pulled her back into the space she was in before. Closer to him. "Whatever it is, I love it."

She looked at him. Her mind raced for a witty comeback. She opened her mouth to speak, but it didn't matter. Ziggy covered her mouth with his own, kissing her in that deep, erotic way of his. She kissed him back, the fire between them so intense that she wasn't sure how she wound up straddling him. Or how her body and his found themselves locked together again. Even as he reached desperately for a condom and thrust himself into her, and she wound her hips, grinding herself so erotically that he watched her—rapt—she was aware that this was different. This was raw, and from the look on his face, and the strength with which he gripped her waist, Ziggy was loving it.

Coco went over the edge, her orgasm making her throb around him powerfully. She looked him in the eyes, her breath ragged.

He grinned, still hard inside of her. He scooped her up and laid her down on his Persian rug.

Ziggy wore her out that afternoon, sexing her every which way she could imagine until the candles flickered low on their wicks.

"You should come to LA with me next week. I have to do some work out there on a few projects, but I'll have plenty of time to spend with you. You could come to work with me. I would love that. Show you what I do in the studio, and how I work."

Coco smiled. She took a deep breath and kissed him. "I can't just drop everything and go to LA with you."

"Why not?" He waited for her answer.

Coco floundered. She really had no excuse. She could take a few days off, do her job remotely. Truthfully, a trip to the West Coast might be exactly what she needed.

Still, something was gnawing at her, telling her that this was all too good to be true. How could it all be so perfect so fast? There had to be a catch.

"I'm having work done on my apartment," she lied. "Plus, we should probably not . . . I don't know. I don't want to . . ."

He sat up and looked at her. "It's too much? Too soon?"

"No!"

She hadn't meant to yell it. She cleared her throat. Fuck it. She was going for it.

"I just got out of a bad relationship. It wasn't even a relationship, to be honest with you. I let some fool waste my time for years. I let him share my bed and get my hopes up, and he let me down. I don't want to be let down again. So, really, I just want to take it slow so that I don't get in too deep. I don't want to rush right in, expecting the world . . . just to be disappointed again."

Ziggy listened to every word. He pondered it sincerely for quite some time—so much so that to Coco, it felt like forever before he finally spoke.

"I understand how you feel, but I'm not him, and I'm not going to disappoint you."

He kissed her softly on her forehead, then tilted her head toward him.

"I know how you feel. I told you when we met that I had someone that I cared for. And I let her go. She left, married someone else, moved on. That was two years ago. Now, I've met you, and I haven't felt like this in a very long time. And this time, I'm not going to blow it."

He took her face in his hands and kissed her, deeper this time.

"I won't disappoint you."

Coco had never believed anything so deeply in all her life, and for that night at least, he kept his word. He didn't disappoint her one bit.

Deja tried her best not to roll her eyes. She had been watching her sister flirt feverishly with their waiter for the past ten minutes. The poor, scrawny bastard was clearly no older than twenty-five and had probably agreed to cover everybody's shift for the rest of the summer just so that he could have the privilege to serve this table tonight. Nikki fluttered her eyelashes, flashed him her sexiest grin, and leaned forward over her menu with her breasts laid out like a feast before him. Finally, she looked up at him and placed her damn order.

"Umm . . . I guess you can bring me the blackened salmon. You said it's good. So, I'll trust you."

The young man smiled like a maniac, all thirty-two of his teeth visible at the same time. Deja groaned audibly, feeling sorry for the pathetic young man. He didn't stand a chance with Nikki unless he owned the place.

Without being asked, Deja said, "You can bring me the Cajun pasta."

She handed him the menu and shooed him away rudely. He didn't seem to notice, barely taking his eyes off Nikki as he assured them that he would be right back with their drinks. Deja finally gave in and rolled her eyes the moment he turned his back.

"Do you have to do that shit everywhere we go?" Deja shook her head, irritated after only twenty minutes in her sister's presence.

"Do what shit?" Nikki asked innocently.

"Flirt, put your titties in the boy's face, sway your hips extra hard. You don't have to sell sex *all* the time, Nikki."

Nikki waved her hand dismissively. "Relax. You should try it. You would get a lot more free shit if you learned to smile a little more." She shook her head. "Flirting ain't never killed nobody."

"You ain't getting nothing free in here," Deja mumbled. "Trust me."

As if on cue, their young waiter returned bearing their drinks. He set them down on the table and smiled at Nikki. He gestured toward two servers following closely behind him, both male and both smiling at Nikki maniacally.

"These are some complimentary appetizers," he said. The two other servers set two platters down on the table as Nikki gasped.

"Thank you!" she sang. She clapped her hands excitedly and shot a glance at her sister. "See?" she said. "Free!" She winked at Deja and dug into the calamari.

Deja was pissed. "Is Ramon here tonight?" She name-dropped the restaurant's manager. He was a friend of hers, or so she had thought. Deja had helped Ramon find an apartment in SoHo for his mother. And despite that assistance, she had never gotten any free appetizers when she came in here before.

The waiter glanced at her briefly. "Ramon is out of town. He's back next week." He returned his attention to Nikki. "Can I take a picture with you?"

Nikki happily obliged. Deja watched, feeling dismissed. She chewed her calamari and looked on silently. The waiter left, visibly overjoyed by his encounter with the vixen.

Nikki laughed at her.

Deja piled her plate high with the free appetizers Nikki's fans had brought them. She figured she might as well enjoy the shit.

Nikki watched her. "Why do you always have to be so bitchy toward me?"

Deja waved her manicured hand dismissively. "I just think

you're better than *this.*" She gestured at Nikki's skintight dress. "You might as well be shucking and jiving out there the way that you carry on sometimes."

Nikki laughed.

"I'm serious," Deja said. "You have this platform now. I'll give you that. Everywhere you go, everybody's sweating you. So now what? You wanna sing? Rap? You wanna act? What's the next move? 'Cause popping your pussy every five minutes and being loud is gonna get old real quick."

Nikki shrugged. "I don't have to do shit but stay cute and keep getting this money."

Deja grimaced and looked away like her point was proven.

"You're wasting the spot," Deja said. "Somebody else could take what you have and show the world something new, not just recycling the same old stereotypes for money."

"I'm doing what I want, on my own terms. I don't see the problem."

"And that's why I worry about the time you spend with Bree."

Nikki was crushed. She loved her little niece. She set her fork down.

"You're stupid. You think I'm a bad influence on your daughter. Meanwhile, I'm the only one that girl talks to. Did you know that she's the only one of her friends that isn't fucking yet?"

Deja's jaw dropped.

"Exactly! I'm the one encouraging her to keep it tight. I'm trying to teach her how to outmaneuver these boys instead of falling victim and selling her soul for a man the way you did."

Deja felt tears forming in the corners of her eyes and fought them back. The truth in Nikki's words had hit its mark.

When she spoke again, her voice was lower, softer. "You're right."

Nikki frowned, assuming she had heard wrong.

"I've been acting like a bitch lately," she admitted. "It's not that I think I'm better than you, or that I'm ashamed of you. I just . . . I feel like something's missing. In my own life. And I've been taking it out on you."

"*You're* missing," Nikki offered. "The old you. Before you got married to Bobby, you were a different person. You were fun and lighthearted, smart and vibrant. You cut yourself off from your whole world just so that you could fit into his. You're so committed to this role you're playing that our own mother hardly hears from you. I wouldn't hear from you, either, if I didn't force my way into your life."

"Seriously?" Deja dabbed at her eyes, feeling like Nikki was beating up on her now.

Nikki didn't back down. What her sister needed was some tough love. And she was about to give it to her.

"Yeah," Nikki said. "You complain that I pop up unannounced. Well, I do that shit more for Bree's benefit than for you. She can't relate to you and Bobby. Y'all are too polished. Too neat and clean, and that's not who we are. You're just at the point where you're finally tired of pretending."

Deja looked at her sister. "You're right," she admitted at last. "I'm bored with my life . . . with everything. I've been feeling like this for a while now. And until Rashid came back on the scene, I wasn't sure what was missing. But now that he's back, I know what it is. I've just been going through the motions for years. Telling myself that I have everything I wanted, and I should be happy. But I'm not happy. That's the bottom line."

She took a long deep breath. Nikki watched her in silence, hoping she would continue. They were finally getting somewhere.

"I loved him," Deja said. "I loved Rashid more than anybody. When Mommy almost lost the house, he came through for us.

He took care of me, took care of all of us. And then when he needed me most, I couldn't stand the heat. I didn't want to spend my life going upstate for jail visits, accepting collect calls and all of that. And part of me was mad at him for leaving me out here by myself. I felt like he was the only person who truly listened to me, understood me. Then he was gone. So, to get back at him, I disappeared, too."

A few tears fell then. She wiped her eyes with her napkin.

"Then I got as far away from that life as I could and never looked back. None of it was intentional. I didn't even realize that was my motivation until now. Seeing Rashid again, talking about things I wouldn't let myself think about all these years . . . I felt like I'm revisiting a side of myself I buried a long time ago. I miss that part of me. But I feel guilty about it because with Bobby, I have everything I ever wanted. So, what reason do I have to be so miserable?"

Nikki shook her head. "You don't have everything you want. You have everything you *think* you should want. But it's not what really makes you happy, Deja. And that's okay."

Deja was torn. She loved her husband, loved the family they had built together, the sense of security she enjoyed as Bobby's wife. He was, no doubt, the safer choice; the life she had chosen to live was one with few variables. Rashid's reappearance in her world had shaken it at its very foundation.

Nikki sipped her drink then set the glass back down. "So, seeing Rashid again got your panties in a bunch, huh?"

Deja laughed. "He definitely made me realize that I was living a lie. He said that the Deja he knew had joy that was contagious. I'm not sure when I lost it. But I want to get that joy back."

"Do you still love Rashid?" Nikki asked.

Deja shrugged. "I don't know. I feel like there's still so much left for us to say. I've been calling him and sneaking off to see him from time to time. But it feels wrong to creep around and see him behind Bobby's back. I wouldn't want him doing that to me."

"You should tell Bobby that seeing Rashid again made you remember who you are. And see if he can handle that."

Deja shook her head. "I did. And he's been walking around the house not speaking to me ever since. I think I'm about to ruin everything just because I'm having some type of midlife crisis." She chuckled a bit.

Nikki didn't laugh. "You're bugging. Bobby married you knowing your past. He knew who Bree's father was. He just believed that Rashid was never coming home, so he never thought about how that would affect everything. Obviously, you thought the same thing. But now y'all have to face it. Figure out how to move forward."

Deja shrugged. She wasn't sure how that would be possible.

"I'm sorry for the way I've been acting toward you. I've been taking my frustrations out on the wrong people."

Nikki agreed. "Yes, you have, bitch, but I forgive you."

She winked at her sister, clinking glasses with her, and they both drank to that.

Ivy League

Ivy watched her son dunk the ball right in the face of a player on the opposing team. The crowd jumped to their feet, cheering and screaming. Ivy's voice was the loudest of them all.

"THAT'S MY BABY!"

She felt a wave of excitement pulse through her body. Amid her euphoria, she could hear some nearby fans chanting King's name, and it made her smile.

From his seat beside her on the bleachers, James cheered, too. He had popcorn in his lap and spilled a little of it in his excitement. Ivy had invited him to Kingston's game today for two reasons. The first reason was she wanted to have their first "date" on neutral turf. She thought it would lessen the awkwardness of being out with a man for the first time in more than fifteen years—longer, if she considered she hadn't been out with a man besides Mikey in over twenty years.

The second reason for inviting James here was to send Michael a message. He was furious that she hadn't visited him despite his threats. She had installed a sophisticated alarm system to keep Mikey's goons at bay, and she had laid into Noah and

Kingston so bad that an awkward silence had descended on the house ever since. They knew now that if they let anyone into their home without her permission, the wrath of God would rain down on them like never before. She let them know that she alone was the head of her household and that Michael was no longer in control.

Two weeks had passed since Mikey's goons had shown up. Her cousins Keith and Tommy from Brooklyn had rushed out to Staten Island the moment they got her frantic call. They found her still trembling from her encounter with Bam and his henchmen. Her cousins had listened in silence as she described the situation. She told them about her last visit with Mikey, how he'd walked off and she had made up her mind to move on with her life. She told them about his menacing calls and letters since then and how she ultimately came home to find his men in her home. Tommy had looked Ivy squarely in the eyes and leveled with her.

"This is the point where shit can get ugly. I know Mikey and Bam and them niggas. This ain't a joke. That shit was a power move. Him sending them over here was your final warning to get in line. So, I'm gonna ask you this. Think about it before you answer. Are you a hundred percent sure that you want to leave him?"

Tommy had been more serious than she had ever seen him.

"Because if you're not sure, you're probably better off just putting your pride aside and going back up there to see the man."

Ivy had insisted that she was sure.

"I want out of this shit, Tommy. I want Mikey to leave me alone so I can move on with my life. I don't want to see him get hurt, but I'm not gonna let him hold me hostage anymore."

Tommy kept it real with her. "In a perfect world, he would hear what you're saying and let you walk away in peace. But this world is far from perfect. Niggas like Mikey don't like to lose.

It might come down to him getting hurt, Ivy. Better him than you."

Tommy pulled out a .45-caliber Smith & Wesson and held it out to her. She took it gingerly and felt the weight of it in her hands. She looked at her cousin anxiously.

"Is it loaded?" she asked.

Tommy shook his head. Her cousin Keith pulled a box of bullets out of the deep pocket of his hoodie and gave her a lesson on how to load and unload it, hold it, aim, and shoot.

"Your alarm system is your first defense," Tommy said. "You hear that go off, you call me. I'll be on my way with the quickness. The alarm system you got should scare them niggas off before I get here. But if not, you got this right here to protect you. Don't be afraid to use it."

Since then, Ivy felt a bit safer. Still, she found herself looking over her shoulder constantly. Always on alert in case Mikey sent someone after her.

Despite her fear over what Michael might do to regain control, Ivy was determined to get a new lease on life.

She hoped to see how James interacted with her boys today. In the few weeks since she had met him, Ivy had spoken to him on the phone occasionally. Their conversations so far had been lighthearted and easy. They talked about their respective careers, their kids, and their common interests. She had tested the waters to see how Noah and Kingston felt about her dating. As expected, neither of them was happy about her ending her relationship with their father—even if the only "relationship" they had ever seen between their parents was one surrounded by prison bars.

Rather than sit with them today, Noah sat at the other end of their row of bleachers alone. From the moment James had arrived, Noah's energy had shifted. He made an excuse to disappear, saying he was going to get snacks at the concession stand. Now he sat pouting like a brat while Kingston scored a three-pointer and widened his team's lead. Ivy looked at him and shook her head.

"King is killing 'em out there!" James said, visibly impressed.

Ivy proudly looked on as Kingston jogged down the court, his large Afro distinguishing him from all the other players.

"He loves the game. Always has. Since he was a kid, I've never seen him without a basketball in his hand unless he's sick. Even then, he's watching it on TV."

James watched her eyes light up as she spoke about her son. Over the past few days, she had shared a lot about herself during their conversations. He knew that her man was locked up and that the boys were reluctant to see her move on from him.

"Did their father play ball, too?" James asked.

She shook her head. Mikey had always been focused exclusively on the drug game.

"No. Neither did Noah. But for some reason, King just had a natural love for it. Being tall helped, but he loves the game so much that I believe he'd be playing even if he was five feet tall."

James watched him play, impressed by the skill and restraint the kid displayed.

"I was the same way," he said. "Loved the game. After I left high school, though, life got real for me. I got sidetracked. You got Kingston on the right track. Long as he stays there, the sky is the limit for him."

She nodded. "That's what I keep telling him. It's the reason I stay on his case all the time. I need him to stay focused on his future. No distractions."

James nodded. "It's hard to keep them focused nowadays. I have three sons, and they're all grown. But they still need my guidance."

"Do you see them a lot now that they're all grown up?"

He shrugged. "Not as often as I wish I did, but things change the older they get. One of them just got married. One is working for Transit and the youngest is in his last year of college. So, they're busier than they used to be." He looked at her. "It's bittersweet. When they were little, I always had to live my life around their schedule. Now they're grown up, I'm divorced, and for a while, I wasn't sure what to do with myself. It's funny. When kids grow up, it forces the parents to figure out who they are aside from being a mother or father. I spent the last four or five years learning what I like to do and who I am as a man."

Ivy thought about who she was as she listened to him. She wasn't sure if she knew her true identity outside of being Mikey's wife, Noah and Kingston's mother.

She sipped her soda and watched the score climb in the Warriors' favor. King eventually led his team to victory.

After the game, Ivy and James stood outside the gym, waiting for King to finish making his rounds. Ivy leaned on a wall, watching parents and students milling around. She was grateful for the diversity in this school. This looked more like the New York City she knew and loved. She saw Black people of all shades, white people, Muslim girls with their hair covered, and kids who looked like they were from a variety of different backgrounds. She chuckled to herself thinking about how angry the president and his legion of supporters on Staten Island's South Shore would be if they witnessed this group of students laughing and talking together.

James and Kingston's coach were in a spirited conversation about Kingston's best moves during the game. Ivy half-listened while looking around for Noah. He had disappeared right before the end of the fourth quarter, and she hadn't seen him since.

Finally, she spotted him and Kingston exiting the gym together. James saw him, too. He and the coach wrapped up their conversation and made their way through the crowd until they reached Noah and Kingston.

Kingston was talking animatedly to one of his teammates, and it was clear that he was still on an adrenaline high after his game. He greeted several of his friends with loud handshakes and hearty pats on the back as they congratulated him on a great game. Ivy noticed that Noah had conveniently busied himself in a conversation with a girl standing nearby.

Ivy looked at James apologetically.

He waved her off. "It's all good. He's a star. Gotta talk to his fans."

She smiled, glad he understood.

"When I drove Noah and King home that night, they said that y'all ain't had a decent meal since you moved out here." James shook his head as if the thought of that deeply troubled him. "I can't have that."

Ivy laughed.

"Not when my brother is a professional chef," James explained. "His name is Patrick. He lives with his wife and their baby not too far from here. If you want, we can stop by there when King—"

"YO! I'm STARVING!" Kingston's voice boomed as he barreled over to Ivy and Noah.

He looked at his mother and grinned. Experience had taught him that she dreaded his sweaty, musty, post-game hugs. He flashed her a smile and gave her a fist bump instead.

"Hey, Ma."

Kingston seemed to notice James for the first time standing a few feet away. He offered him a half-hearted smile.

James stepped closer and gave Kingston a congratulatory handshake.

"Good game, young man!"

"Thank you," Kingston offered weakly.

"What's he doing here?" Noah cut right to the chase, nodding his head in James's direction. Noah's facial expression made his disapproval quite clear.

Ivy looked at James apologetically. Until now, she thought her sons' overprotectiveness was kind of cute. They loved her, loved their father, and were reluctant to see her move on. But now they were being downright rude. She felt like slapping the shit out of both of them.

James rolled with it, though. He didn't flinch. "I love basketball. Came to see the game."

Noah scoffed. "And to see my mother, too?"

James smirked.

Ivy wasn't amused.

"Noah, please don't make me embarrass you out here."

She closed her eyes and shook her head slowly, imploring him to heed the warning.

James laughed and tried to break the ice.

"I was telling your mother that my brother Patrick is a cook. I thought y'all might be hungry, so we could stop by there and get something to eat if you want. But I'll warn you now. You gotta bring your appetite anytime you roll up on Patrick."

Noah and King exchanged glances. Ivy watched them. Knowing her sons as well as she did, she read them like a book. Kingston wanted to say yes. She had never known him to turn down a good meal in his life. But seeing the look in Noah's eyes, Kingston shook his head.

"Nah," he said. "No, thank you, I mean. We're gonna go get something to eat with a few of my friends."

Ivy's eyes narrowed.

"Yeah," Noah agreed. "We're good."

James nodded.

Kingston ignored his grumbling belly and looked at his mother. "You should come with us, Ma."

Ivy laughed. "Y'all are funny," she said. "Go 'head and eat at Wendy's with your friends. I'm gonna go with James and get something to eat. I'll see y'all when I get home."

Noah started to protest, but it was too late. Ivy had sauntered off through the thinning crowd. James looked at both young men and grinned.

"Good game, King. Good seeing you again, Noah. Y'all be safe."

He followed Ivy and left them standing there together.

Noah looked at his brother. "What's the deal with that nigga?"

Kingston shrugged, staring after his mother and James. "I don't know, but I hope she brings us home a plate."

Ivy and James walked to the parking lot and headed toward her car. James was grateful that she was a few paces ahead, giving him a good view of her full figure as she strutted along.

"So, I guess I'll follow you?" Ivy turned to him as she asked. She adjusted her sweater, hoping her gut wasn't poking out. Then she chided herself for caring. James was nobody, she reasoned. She was just doing this to defy her sons and show them who was boss. It had nothing to do with how cute he was, or how long it had been since she had a man's attention this way.

He nodded. "My brother doesn't live far."

He walked off toward his car, and Ivy climbed into hers. She exhaled once inside and started the vehicle. She checked her reflection in the mirror, then followed James as he pulled out of the parking lot. She admired the car that James was driving, a pretty black two-door Jaguar. Her sons would be impressed by it, too. If only they weren't currently acting like assholes.

She knew that their resistance to James had little to do with him personally. In fact, they'd liked him until he'd showed interest in her. It was her decision to move on from her relationship with their father that was really bothering them. They wanted her to continue playing the role of dutiful and long-suffering wife while everyone else lived life to the fullest.

Before Michael had gone to jail, their home was full of music, laughter, and fun. People came over all the time for card games and dinners. The two of them went on dates alone, leaving Noah with family while they enjoyed nights on the town then came home and fucked like teenagers.

Nearly two decades had passed since then. She felt desperate to get her life back.

Ivy steered her SUV through the streets of Staten Island, following closely behind James as he maneuvered through some sketchy-looking neighborhoods. She stopped behind James at a red light and looked around, noting the street signs. They were at the corner of Broad and Hill Streets. Looking around, this felt more like Brooklyn than any part of the borough she had seen so far. Bodegas and discount stores dotted the block on one side, housing projects on the other. She glanced at a couple of roughnecks talking loudly to each other.

One of them walked into the street and made a beeline for James's car as he sat idling at the red light.

Ivy's heart raced, wondering if she was about to see James get jacked. But to her surprise—and relief—the man smiled as he approached. James lowered his window and extended his hand in greeting. They had a brief conversation before the light turned green and James waved farewell, continuing the trip to his brother's house.

"James got some interesting friends," she muttered to herself.

At last, he turned up a narrow block on a steep hill and Ivy followed him toward a street lined with old Victorian houses. She saw that James was looking for parking, so she did the same. She found a spot near the corner and slid into it easily, activating the emergency brake for good measure to keep the car from sliding down the hill.

James was waiting for her curbside. He led her toward his brother's house.

"I think you'll like Patrick," he said. "I know you'll like his food."

Ivy laughed.

Patrick's house was a large multilevel dwelling on what looked like a nice suburban street. She noticed a police squad car driving slowly up the street, seemingly in search of crimes in progress. She hadn't seen many police cars patrolling her part of the island. Still, she felt much more comfortable here among her own people than she did at home. She climbed the porch steps behind James.

"I was worried about you back there for a minute," she said. "I saw that guy walk up to your car at the red light and I thought it was about to be a situation!"

James laughed.

"That's the Stapleton Projects. I grew up out there. My brother and his wife had a restaurant over there on Broad Street a few years ago, but the building got sold to a new owner and he had to close. We still get love from the people in the neighborhood. Stapleton is like one big, dysfunctional family." He laughed. "Some people raised generations in the neighborhood. Kids all grew up together and now it's deeper than just being neighbors."

Ivy liked the sound of that. It reminded her of the way Brooklyn used to feel before it got gentrified.

The door opened and a man who resembled James very closely stood smiling back at them.

"Hey, come on in!"

Patrick greeted his brother then looked at Ivy and smiled even wider.

"What's up, y'all?"

James stepped inside, and Ivy followed suit. They were immediately joined by a lovely woman with a *fierce* short haircut that Ivy immediately noted. She wondered where she got her hair done and decided to find out before the night was over.

James set about introducing everyone. "This is Ivy." He gestured toward the couple. "Ivy, I'd like you to meet my brother Patrick and his wife, Cheryl."

As James was talking, a toddler barreled into the room, running in his direction. He laughed and scooped the kid up with one hand. "And this is Joshua. He's got a lot of energy, so let me apologize in advance."

They all shared a laugh as Patrick and Cheryl led them into the dining room. Ivy's eyes widened when she saw the dining room table laid out with all the food she loved. Steak, macaroni and cheese, cornbread, mashed potatoes, rice, greens, and candied yams. It looked like Thanksgiving!

Patrick saw her expression and smiled. "Don't be shy around here." He gestured toward one platter in particular. "Those are my famous mashed potatoes over there. I put bacon in 'em and cheese. Get you some."

Ivy was nearly drooling as she looked around at all of it.

Cheryl laughed. "Come, let me show you where the bathroom is so you can wash your hands."

Ivy thanked her and followed her down a short hallway.

Patrick looked at his brother.

"She's fine!"

James laughed. "I told you. Soon as she stepped in my shop, I knew I had to ask her out. Her kids ain't feeling it, though."

"How many she got?" Patrick asked.

"Two boys. One of them is grown. The other one is in high school. We just came from his basketball game."

"Is he good?"

James nodded. "He's real good. Star player. Both of them seem like good kids. They're just not trying to see their mother with no man besides their father."

Patrick was intrigued. "What's his story?"

Ivy and Cheryl emerged from the bathroom, chattering about hairstyles, and James plastered on a smile.

"I'll tell you later," he mumbled to his brother.

"My baby can *cook*!" Cheryl was saying. She winked at her man and handed Ivy a plate. "Get on over there before James eats it all himself."

James laughed. "She ain't lying. I come over here every chance I get to eat up Patrick's leftovers."

Ivy thanked Patrick and Cheryl for their hospitality and headed toward the food. There was no need to worry that it might run out, though. Patrick had made enough food for a small army. As they sat down at the table to eat, Ivy looked at him in amazement.

"You cook like this all the time?"

Patrick nodded. "All the time," he repeated. "It's what I love to do. I cater, make deliveries, and do church functions and all that. I'm cooking constantly, seven days a week. And I love it. It don't feel like work to me at all."

He smiled, and Ivy thought he looked like the happiest man she had ever seen.

"Cheryl is an accountant. So, she keeps me on my toes, especially now that she went into business for herself. She's home a lot more now since she ain't working no nine-to-five. And that means she's over my shoulder every day making sure I don't give away more than I sell." He laughed.

Cheryl nodded. "Because he'll do that if I let him. He's got a heart as big as the planet. He'll give away free food, work for less than he deserves, or overextend himself if I don't stay on his case. And that's cool because I'm a beast when it comes to that. I don't play. God gave him a gift, and he uses it for good. But sometimes in our community, it's hard to stay afloat because everybody's looking for a handout."

Ivy nodded. "I know what you mean. I do hair. So, you can imagine all the sob stories I hear." She shook her head. "You have to stay on top of your business. God wants us to prosper, too."

Cheryl agreed. "Girl, preach!"

Ivy laughed.

"So, James tells me that you just moved out here from Brooklyn. How you like it so far?" Patrick asked. He bit into an ear of corn.

Ivy shrugged. "It's . . . really different from Brooklyn," she said. "Over where I live now, there's not a lot of Black folk. My neighbors are Russian, Italian, or Irish. One family is from India. We're the only Black people in the area who ain't on staff."

Cheryl laughed at that. "Yeah, I know what you mean. I moved out to Staten Island from Forest Hills, Queens, back in the nineties. Believe it or not, this place is actually a lot better with the racial tension now than it was back then. Most of the people out here have been here all their lives. Their families go back generations, which means their racism and ignorance goes back that far, too. The brown folks are mostly on this side. Over where you are is the white side. So, I can imagine the types of looks you must be getting."

Ivy agreed.

"We're not what they're used to, but they're just gonna have to get over that. I lived in Brooklyn all my life and watched it go from an urban oasis to a yuppie paradise. All in the blink of an eye! Before I knew it, the neighborhood I grew up in was unrecognizable. And now the gangs are taking over the area where I raised my boys. My oldest son went away to college and I was worried sick about the younger one out there on his own every day coming home from school in that crazy atmosphere. So, I moved out here, hoping to find a better life. And we ain't going nowhere no time soon."

Cheryl high-fived Ivy across the table. "I know that's right."

"This is the first time I'm getting to know Staten Islanders besides my friend Deja. I appreciate you inviting me here. Feels good to meet new people."

Cheryl bounced the baby on her lap.

"How are your boys liking school so far?" Patrick asked, chewing. He was working on a piece of steak now.

"My older son, Noah, is on a break from college right now. His major is dentistry, so during his time off, he got a little part-time job working at a dentist's office on Hylan Boulevard. My younger son, King, is a junior at Curtis High School."

She sipped her wine.

Patrick sized her up, smirking. "So, you keep saying that you're from Brooklyn, huh?"

He was eyeing Ivy suspiciously. She nodded, wondering what he was thinking.

Patrick stroked his goatee as if deep in thought. "Hmm."

He looked at Cheryl and winked. She chuckled, knowing where her man was heading.

He turned his attention to Ivy again. "People from Brooklyn think they can play spades. Are you one of those people?"

Ivy laughed. "*Of course,* I play spades!" Her voice had risen several octaves and she was sitting forward in her seat now.

James was grinning widely. "Cool! You can be my partner, Ivy."

She looked at him sidelong. "You sure about that? If we lose, I'll never forgive you."

He balked. "If we lose, how do you know it's gonna be my fault?"

She shook her head. "'Cause I'm undefeated. Spades is not a game to me. It's war."

He laughed and extended his hand. "Challenge accepted. If we lose, it's all on me."

Ivy shook his hand just as Cheryl produced a deck of cards from a nearby drawer.

She laughed excitedly. "It's on!"

Pledge of Allegiance

Patsy watched her brother closely. He seemed distracted, distant even, as he sat just a couple of feet across from her at the visiting table.

Michael held his hands clasped together in front of him as he sat listening to Kingston talking about his recent basketball game. It had been two weeks since that game, but the way Kingston spoke about it demonstrated the passion the kid had for the sport. He sounded as excited about it as if it had happened yesterday.

"I know I'm going to the NBA, Dad. I can feel it. I'm gonna make you proud."

Kingston nodded as he said it, a smirk on his face.

Michael smiled.

"I'm already proud of you. I'm proud of both of you."

He looked at his sons. Noah had grown into a man without him being there to guide him. Kingston was in the process of doing the same. It broke his heart to think of all the milestones he had missed with them. Learning how to ride a bike, how to drive, how to survive. It was clear that Ivy had done a remarkable job in his absence. He both loved and resented her for it.

"I wasn't at King's game," Patsy said. "Me and my kids went to a wedding that weekend, so we couldn't be there."

Patsy was always a staple at her nephew's games, cheering just as loudly as his own mother. Her kids and Michael's were close in age and spent a lot of time together. In Patsy's opinion, Ivy went out of her way to distance her boys from their cousins. True, Patsy's sons were young fathers, in and out of jail, and trying to find their way in life. One was an aspiring rapper, the other was becoming a habitual baby daddy. But they were good boys in Patsy's biased opinion. Ivy was a stuck-up former trap queen who was starting to forget where she came from.

"I heard Ivy brought a guest to the game," Patsy said, smugly.

Noah winced a little, instantly regretting he had shared that information with his aunt on the way up there.

Michael's jaw clenched. He looked at his sons and neither of them seemed eager to make eye contact. He felt anger bubbling up inside him without explanation. Somewhere deep inside, he already knew what his sister was alluding to.

"What's she talking about?" he asked.

Noah cleared his throat, glanced sidelong at his brother, and they locked eyes for a second. As close as they were, he could tell from even that brief exchange that Kingston felt as conflicted about this as he did.

"Mom invited somebody . . ."

"A man?" Michael cut to the chase.

Noah and Kingston both nodded reluctantly.

Noah looked at his father, trying to gauge his level of fury. "Dad, it's a long story."

Michael huffed and sat back. "I got time, Noah."

Noah sighed. "Me and King were driving some of his friends home one night."

"The night Ivy was at that party with Coco and Deja and all of them," Patsy added for emphasis.

Noah shook his head and looked at her pleadingly. Patsy ignored him and fluttered her hand as a signal for him to continue his story.

Reluctantly, he did so. "My car broke down. We stopped at a gas station and they had like a small mechanic shop in the back. The guy that worked there said he could look at it in the morning. We were gonna get a cab home, but he offered us a ride. Cabs are expensive in Staten Island," Noah explained.

"That's because Ivy moved them out to the whitest part of the borough she could find. All the Black kids they hang with live miles away from them."

Patsy shook her head in disapproval of how Ivy was maneuvering these days.

Kingston decided to take responsibility for his part in the saga.

"Me and the guy started talking about basketball. He used to go to my school. Played basketball there, and he said he knew my coach. We had a long conversation about the team and he dropped us off at home."

Michael was incensed. "What's this nigga's name?"

"James," Kingston said.

"James WHAT?" Michael asked.

The boys looked at each other and shrugged. Michael sucked his teeth in frustration and disappointment. Clearly, he had taught his sons nothing about life. So far, he learned that they had allowed a stranger to drive them home without knowing anything about him besides his supposed first name.

Kingston tried to recall the name he had asked his coach about.

"Marshall, I think. Or Martin. I can't remember."

Noah continued the story, eager to get it over with. "We went back the next day to get the car, and Mom came with us. They started talking and the next thing I knew, the guy was asking for her phone number."

Michael closed his eyes, inhaled deeply, and then exhaled. He opened his eyes again and looked at his sons.

"And what were you two doing while this nigga was standing in front of you disrespecting our family?"

Michael's voice was considerably louder than usual.

Kingston was quick to defend himself. "We stepped up! Both of us did. We were like, 'Nah, she's good.' But she got all mad and sent us to the car, told us to stay out of grown folks' business."

Patsy shook her head again. "She gave that nigga her number, and, apparently, they been chopping it up for weeks now. Meanwhile, she's too busy to come up here and see you."

Michael took a moment to let it all sink in. "So, she brought this James nigga to your game?"

His focus was on Kingston who nodded.

"For what?"

The question was rhetorical. But Patsy answered anyway.

"That's what we're all trying to understand, Mikey. What the fuck is going on with Ivy lately? I know that Noah and King are probably pissed off at me for bringing this up, but I felt like you needed to know. First, she left Brooklyn, then she decided that coming to see you was too much. Now she got a man coming around your sons. Noah left out the part about her going out to eat with him and leaving them to fend for themselves after King's game."

Kingston protested. "It wasn't like that," he said, side-eyeing Patsy. "She invited me and Noah to go with them. She thought we would want to sit down and get to know him or whatever. Talk about basketball . . . I don't know. But me and Noah said no."

"And she left with that nigga." Patsy sat back, pleased with herself for letting her brother know what time it was with his wife, the woman he had put on a pedestal for years that Patsy never felt she deserved.

Michael wanted to explode, but he knew that was pointless. The subject of his rage was Ivy, and she was not there. Hadn't been there in over a month. For the first time, he began to face the possibility that she might not be coming back.

"You know . . ." He shook his head, laughed a little, then looked at his sons. "As heated as I am right now, I'm not gonna disrespect your mother. Ivy's a good woman. Smart." He nodded, thinking back on all the times he had consulted with her over the years. Both in the streets and in business. She had always given him sound advice, always seemed loyal. Until now.

"But I'll be honest with you. I didn't see this shit coming. Not from her. I expected Ivy to ride it out with me all the way. Thought she was solid enough to hold it down, but I guess I was wrong."

Kingston and Noah stared at him, both aware that this was their father expressing hurt in the only way that he knew how. They watched him closely, hanging on his every word.

"She's human. You know what I'm saying." He shrugged. "It is what it is."

He forced a smile that none of them found convincing.

"Y'all go over there and get me some of them chicken wings I like. Put them shits in the microwave till they get piping hot. I don't care who gets mad about how long it takes." He looked around at the other visitors lined up by the vending area. "Tell them to come see me if they got some shit to say."

Noah and Kingston stood and walked over toward the vending machine like they were told. Patsy inched closer to her brother.

"I know you're upset, Mikey. Not just about this new nigga, either. I could tell from the second you sat down that something got you feeling some type of way. You know it, too."

He nodded. Patsy could always see right through his poker face.

"You always follow your gut instinct. That's what you told me, and I know your gut gotta be telling you that Ivy done switched up. She's gone, Mikey. She left you. Just like Deja did to Rashid."

Michael looked at her, anger pulsing through every vein.

"If you ask me, she's the reason Ivy has this new attitude all of a sudden."

Michael frowned. "Who's the reason for it? Deja?"

Patsy nodded. "Yup. Think about it. All these years, Ivy's been by your side, ride or die. Meanwhile her good friend Deja married a cop, moved out to Staten Island, got her kid in some fancy private school, living the American Dream and shit. Ivy probably wants that same thing. Now she's living on Staten Island just like Deja, drifting away from you." She shrugged. "I think they all done lost their minds," she added. "Coco, too. She was supposed to come with me today."

Michael nodded. "Yeah. What happened with that?"

"Our little sister—chocolate, ebony princess of the family—is fucking with some white man."

Michael groaned.

"She said she likes him, too. Been spending all her time with him. This weekend, she went out to the Hamptons with him to meet his sister. Shit is moving too fast if you ask me, but the problem is nobody asks me."

Michael's mind was reeling. His wife had abandoned him and

was seeing another man, inviting that man into the presence of their children. His little sister was fucking with a white guy, which was disappointing in itself. But hearing that it was hindering her from keeping her promise to visit her incarcerated brother was even worse. Michael had been a provider and a protector for the family for his entire life, and the only ally he seemed to have left was his sister Patsy. As grateful as he was for her loyalty, he knew that she was limited in ways that she could help him under the current circumstances.

He sat back, glanced across the room at his sons, and shook his head.

"Ivy must be out of her mind to think I'm gonna just let this shit ride."

By the end of the visit, Michael was barely able to contain his rage. He did his best to enjoy his time with Patsy and his boys, but all he could think about was Ivy's refusal to come and see him. About the control he felt slipping from his grasp as he faced the rest of his life behind bars without her.

He called her when he got back to his dorm. She didn't answer. He called again and again, his fury building each time she declined his call. A corrections officer noticed him hogging the phone and spoke up.

"Norris! Time's up."

Michael ignored him. He dialed Ivy's number again, got her voicemail, and hung up. He picked up the receiver and dialed again.

The CO started walking toward him. Michael turned to face him and held his hand up.

"I'm almost finished."

"You're finished NOW, Norris. Back to your cell."

Michael finally complied, sulking reluctantly away. Inexplicable rage had taken over him and he looked around for a way to express it. It didn't take long for him to find what he was looking for.

A Puerto Rican kid owed him money for some drugs. Or at least he owed Michael the equivalent of money in jail. They bartered with cigarettes, food, and other items as payment. And this guy owed Michael something. He laid eyes on him and decided that it was time to pay up.

"Yo, Reyes! Where my cigarettes at?" Michael barked across the day room.

The other inmate looked like a deer caught in headlights. "I . . . I got a visit tomorrow. I think I'll have it then."

Michael wasn't satisfied.

"You said that shit a week ago!" He rushed toward the smaller inmate and began pounding on him mercilessly. Other inmates crowded around, shouting and egging on the fight. Finally finding an outlet for his pent-up frustrations, Michael reached inside his sock and pulled out a shank he had made from metal he stole from the kitchen. He began jabbing it in the other inmate's midsection, puncturing him relentlessly.

One of the COs rushed toward the commotion. Michael released his bloody victim and turned, meeting the CO with equal furor. They fought viciously with punches connecting and inmates hollering. An alarm went off somewhere and Michael could hear it as he dominated the officer, straddling him and punching him with all his power. Blood spilled from the officer's face, and before Michael knew what happened, he was being pulled backward by an army of guards. They beat him, stomped him, kicked him, and pummeled him until he passed out on the cold prison floor.

Part Three

Second Chances

"So, Deja told me that you tried to get me in trouble with the cops the other day."

Rashid looked at his daughter as he said it with a slight smirk on his face.

"You lied on me. Said I canceled on you and your little boyfriend had to come and pick you up."

Bree averted her gaze, embarrassed. She nodded. "I just wanted an excuse to hang out with him."

Rashid grinned, sitting back in the booth at the diner. "So, you and King like each other, huh?"

He wondered if Mikey knew that their kids were a potential couple.

She shrugged. "Well, *I* like *him*. I think he likes me, too, but I'm not sure. That's what I was trying to see. But then I got in trouble."

He laughed. "I hear good things about King. Everybody says he's a good kid with a mean jump shot."

Bree smiled. "We talk about you a lot," she said. "About you and about his dad. I know you two were friends."

Rashid nodded. "King's dad is my friend for life. Me and Mikey went through a lot together."

Bree stared at her father as she sipped her smoothie, a million unanswered questions swirling through her mind.

Rashid seemed to sense that. "What you wanna know?"

She hesitated briefly, then forged ahead full throttle. "Did you do it? I know you said you didn't, but everybody says that. I just want to know the truth."

He looked her in the eyes and spoke clearly. "I didn't do it," he said. "I wasn't there that night. I was nowhere near there. I was with your mother in Prospect Park at this tree she likes. I was innocent of what they sent me to jail for, but I was guilty of other things. I wasn't a saint by any means. When I was hustling, I hurt a lot of people. Whether I meant to or not. Even if I was innocent of that particular crime, I paid a hefty price for the shit I did. And now my conscience is clear."

Bree thought about that. "Did you know the man? The victim?"

Rashid resisted the urge to laugh. The guy that Mikey had gunned down in 2003 was no victim. In fact, Marlon was a thief and a liar who had set Mikey up to be robbed. If Marlon's plan had succeeded, Mikey and Ivy would probably be dead. But he decided not to tell Bree those details.

"I knew *of* him. On some street shit. I didn't know him personally, but I don't expect you to understand that. That's a world you don't operate in. And that's a good thing. Your mother did a good job making sure that you stay away from all that."

In many ways, Rashid felt that Deja had gone too far in her quest to shield their child from the life that had nearly consumed them. Keeping Bree away from him entirely, marrying a cop. But he chose not to say that to Bree, opting not to speak ill of her mother.

"What you need to know is that I wasn't some ruthless killer like the newspapers described. I was just young and dumb enough to get involved in the streets. Everybody that gets involved in that world pays a price. It cost me a lot of valuable time with you. Time with my mother and the rest of my family. So, now I'm just trying to make up for that lost time. I want to get to know you and I want you to know that you can trust me. You can tell me anything."

Bree nodded.

He grinned again. "You can start with telling me about you and King," he said. "What's up with that?"

Bree giggled shyly. "I told you already. I like him. I think he's cute. And he's smart, too. But there's another girl who likes him, too. She goes to his school. So, I was trying to get his attention by having him pick me up from dance class that day."

Rashid chewed his food and nodded. "Did it work?"

"Yeah. He asked me to go with him to this awards dinner his team is having. I was happy and excited. Until I got home."

Rashid watched her expressions as she spoke, saw so much of himself in her.

"They were arguing when I got there. I could tell," she said. "Mommy was giving me that fake 'everything is all right' smile that she does whenever he's on one of his rants."

Rashid tried not to react outwardly to what he was hearing. He wanted Bree to feel comfortable sharing with him the details of what was going on at home.

"He goes on rants a lot?" he asked gently.

Bree shook her head.

"Not usually, but lately, he's been really irritated. Starting arguments all the time over nothing. Mommy called him out on it that day. He was all pissed off because King dropped me off. He said he didn't like the idea of me getting involved with him.

Mommy said that you were the real reason why he's acting all strange lately. He got mad and left. So, she sat me down and talked to me about it. She said that it had nothing to do with me and King. She thinks that he's acting out his frustrations over you coming back. Me and King are just his focus right now because he can't say what's really on his mind."

Rashid chewed his food, listening. To him, it sounded like Deja's carefully constructed glass house was shattering around her.

"Has he been acting the same toward you since I came back, or has he changed?"

Bree thought about it.

"Honestly, it's like he's more overprotective than he was before. I mean . . . he's a cop. So, I've always known that there were eyes on me all the time. That I can't get away with anything without him finding out. But over the past few weeks, he definitely keeps a closer eye on me. And he seems really dead set against me and King going to my friend Jennifer's Sweet Sixteen party together. I mentioned it last night and he said no. But I already invited King and I don't want to go without him. We're supposed to talk about it again tonight."

Rashid nodded. "What you gonna wear?"

Bree's eyes widened at the thought and she smiled. "I don't know," she said. "It gotta be something *nice*!"

Rashid laughed and wiped his mouth with his napkin. "All right then. Let's go shopping."

Two hours later, Rashid drove his Cadillac up to the driveway of Deja's house and looked over at his daughter in the passenger seat.

"Thank you," she said, beaming. "I always have so much fun with you. And I like talking to you."

He smiled. "You're welcome, baby girl. You deserve it. Remember what I told you. Nobody is gonna come between us from now on. You're a big girl now. With or without your mother's permission or that nigga RoboCop's permission, we have a bond now. Nobody can break that. You're my daughter. I'm your father. That's all there is to it."

Bree leaned over and hugged him tightly. Rashid hugged her back, peering over her shoulder at Deja as she exited the house and walked down the driveway in their direction. He sighed, wishing she would leave them alone for once.

Rashid and Bree exited the car as Deja approached.

"Hey," Deja said. She hugged Bree and looked eagerly at Rashid.

He waved at her half-heartedly.

"I just wanted to find out if you're coming to Bree's dance recital next month," Deja said. "We have to request the number of tickets we want so . . . I wasn't sure if you and your mother want to come."

Bree looked at him excitedly. "You should come!"

Rashid nodded. "When is it?"

Deja gave him the details and he made a mental note of it. His gaze was focused now on the doorway of Deja's house as Bobby emerged and started walking toward them. Rashid was amused and annoyed by his presence and smirked as he approached.

Deja turned and saw him, frowning immediately.

"What's wrong?" she asked.

Bobby shook his head.

"Nothing," he said. "Just came to see what all the conversation is about. That's all."

Rashid laughed. This guy was a clown.

"Bobby, go back in the house," Deja pleaded. "We're just talking about Bree's recital."

"Okay, so let's talk about it," Bobby said. "What's up?"

Deja scowled at him, furious.

Bree moved closer to her stepfather. "Mommy just wanted to know how many tickets she needs to get. That's all."

Bobby looked at Rashid. "You planning on coming?"

Rashid, still smirking, nodded. "Wouldn't miss that shit."

"Bobby, go back in the house," Deja said again.

"No," Bobby said. "Why don't you and Bree go in the house? Let me and Rashid have a conversation. I think it's overdue."

Rashid nodded in agreement.

Deja shook her head. "Let's all go inside." She took Bree by the hand and nudged her husband toward the house.

Bobby didn't budge. "What's in the bag?" He gestured at the large garment bag Bree carried.

Rashid answered for her. "I took her shopping. Bought her a dress for her date with King to her friend's Sweet Sixteen. Looks real pretty on her."

He watched the muscles in Bobby's face tighten and his shoulders tense. Rashid smiled, pleased.

"Well, you can take that dress back," Bobby said. "You should have talked to us about it first. Bree's not going to that party with King."

Rashid stepped forward. "Yes, she is. Because I said she can go. If you got a problem with that, we can settle that shit. Right now."

Bobby rushed forward, and Deja and Bree held both men back as best they could.

"Daddy, please!" Bree pleaded, pushing Rashid toward his car. "Just go."

Rashid moved to shove Bree aside but caught himself. This was his baby. He took a deep breath and stepped back, his chest heaving with rage.

"Don't fight," Bree pleaded. "You'll get in trouble. And you remember what we said. Nothing can come between us from now on. Right?"

Rashid nodded, hugging his daughter tightly. "That's right."

He kissed her on the forehead, and then turned and walked back to his car.

"Fucking coward!" Bobby yelled out after him.

Bobby looked down at Deja, who was yelling loudly for him to cut it the fuck out. He watched Bree slowly coax her father to walk back to his car, although it was clear that Rashid wanted to fight him.

Several of the neighbors spilled out of their homes, shamelessly watching the drama unfolding. Bobby came to his senses and calmed down. He stormed back toward his house with Deja in hot pursuit.

The second they were inside, Deja lit into him.

"That's it. I want you out of here tonight."

Bobby scoffed. "I'm not leaving. You're out of your mind."

"Either you leave, or Bree and I are leaving, but that's it. I'm done with this shit."

Bree rushed up the stairs to her room in tears, tightly gripping the garment bag with her dress in it.

"Deja, what the fuck is wrong with you lately?"

Deja balked. "You're the one walking around here acting like a dictator all of a sudden! Since Rashid came back, all you do is walk around here trying to keep tabs on me and Bree, monitoring every move. You think we don't notice? You're hovering everywhere, watching, listening, inserting yourself in conversations and situations that don't involve you."

"Just say it, Deja. Since he came back, you don't see me as Bree's father anymore. Neither does she. Now that her real father is back on the scene, I don't count now. My opinion doesn't matter. I raised that little girl. From the time she was a year old, I've been the only father she ever knew. But now I'm inserting myself in her life. In yours. Is that right?"

Deja shook her head, but Bobby wasn't finished.

"Met you when you were struggling to figure out your life after that nigga left you with a baby and no lifeline while he went to jail for killing somebody!"

"Keep your voice down, Bobby!"

"Why? She should know that her father is a fucking killer! That he's not the best example of what a real man is. So, maybe he's not the one who should decide who she dates. Maybe he likes King because King is like him—a fuckin' thug wannabe whose life is headed nowhere. And instead of seeing it clearly like the Deja I know—the Deja I fell in love with—you're so busy trying to suck up to this criminal that you're gonna wind up right back where you were when I met you. Lost and alone because you were stupid enough to run behind some thug instead of living the life you really deserve."

"Get out, Bobby."

Bobby looked her up and down in disdain. Then he walked off, leaving her standing alone in the middle of the room. She listened quietly as he packed his things, piled up his car, and left their home. He didn't tell her where he was going, and Deja didn't bother to ask.

She could hear Bree crying softly in her room but didn't bother to knock on her door. She didn't have the right words to say to her daughter. Didn't have the right words to even encourage herself.

Rashid sat in his car and watched Deja's husband as he walked into the 120th Precinct on Staten Island's North Shore. He had followed him here after watching him storm out of his house.

Rashid assumed that Bobby was on his way to the precinct to see if he could find some reason to lock Rashid up again. Bobby wore plain clothes as he climbed the steps and walked through the doors, but in Rashid's opinion, everything about the guy screamed POLICE. His tight, stiff walk; his corny outfit; his fucked-up hairline. Rashid shook his head again at the thought of Deja marrying a man like this.

It had taken every ounce of self-control he possessed not to kick Bobby's ass earlier. There were several clear reasons why he had restrained himself. Bree was, of course, the most important factor. Another was the fact that Rashid knew it would land him back in jail. Bobby was a cop, after all. There was no way that any run-in with him would end in a positive way for Rashid. He couldn't risk his freedom over Deja's husband's clear insecurities.

He thought about the conversation he'd had recently with Patsy. Mikey's sister had reached out to him with a message from her brother. He wanted Rashid to find out everything he could about some dude Ivy was involved with.

Rashid had done his friend the favor. He put his ear to the street and gave Patsy the rundown on who James Marshall was. James—"J-Roc" as he had been known back in the day—was a local Staten Island guy who'd played ball in high school, just as Kingston had said, but what Ivy might not have known was that his hoop dreams had gotten sidetracked when he did an eight-year bid up north for armed robbery. He had come home from jail in 2010 and seemed to be on the straight and narrow ever since.

Patsy brought that information back to her brother and Mikey had sent another message for Rashid. He wanted Rashid to give James a warning that he should stay away from Ivy and her sons for his own good. Mikey wanted that message sent to James in a very clear fashion, involving violence and intimidation.

Rashid had been struggling with the choice ever since, wondering if he would honor his friend's request or draw the line here. But his conversation with Bree today had put things into perspective for him. After serving fifteen years in prison, Rashid realized that it was time to change his way of thinking.

He thought about the feelings that had coursed through him earlier when he'd almost come to blows with Bobby. For a moment, he'd felt like the old Rashid. The one capable of doing anything to protect his pride and reputation. In a flash, he had been sucked back into the darkness of that rage that existed within him, but hearing his daughter's pleading voice had brought him back, reminded him that he had buried that old version of himself. And he had walked away.

He knew now that he had made his decision. He was going to turn down Mikey's request to confront James on his behalf. Rashid decided that his days as a gangster were over. Even as he watched the doors of the precinct, waiting for Bobby to emerge, he knew that he was no longer the same man he once was. The old Rashid would have been consumed by the need to let Bobby know who he was fucking with. To make him understand that he wasn't going to back down at all. Ever. No matter what a confrontation of that sort might cost him.

He gripped the steering wheel, reminding himself that he had a curfew. That the last place he needed to be right now was parked across the street from a police station in Staten Island worrying about some cornball Deja got herself entangled with. He put his car in drive and headed home, more determined than ever to turn over that new leaf he and Bree had discussed.

Soul Food

On a Sunday afternoon while her shop was closed, Ivy met up with Deja, Nikki, and Coco for their regular hangout. They chose a different restaurant or spa to experience every time they hung out this way. Today, they were meeting at an Ethiopian restaurant in Brooklyn. Each woman arrived looking fresh faced, fabulous, and giddy, eager to share the details of the new events in their lives.

They ordered food, each of them bantering with the server. It was clear to everyone seated around them that these women had come to have a good time.

"Wait a damn minute!" Nikki shouted. "I went to LA for two weeks and all this shit happened?"

Coco had just finished telling the ladies about her blossoming relationship with Ziggy. She looked more alive than she had in ages. She sat forward in her seat with her spine gracefully curved like a cat's. She giggled a little.

"I had my doubts at first. When you introduced me to Ziggy, I thought you were playing some type of joke on me."

"Please, bitch! At first, you thought I was hooking you up

with Mr. Edwards. Panic was written all over your face." Nikki laughed. "You know I wouldn't do you like that. But don't knock old-ass Mr. Edwards. I'd be his side piece any day. Nigga owns most of Brooklyn!"

Coco and Ivy laughed. Deja discreetly rolled her eyes.

"I didn't know *what* to expect. You told me I was meeting some guy named Ziggy, and that's all you said. Never in my wildest dreams did I expect *him*."

"Ziggy is the coolest white guy I know," Nikki said.

Coco agreed. "So far, I really like him. I wasn't expecting that. To be honest, I think I was trying to sabotage it at first. I was real matter-of-fact when I told him about Mikey's situation. Like a part of me wanted to scare him off. But it didn't work. He wasn't repelled by it. If anything, he found it interesting and appreciated my honesty. I think he might dispel a bunch of myths I had about white men. He's the first one I've ever dated."

Deja froze with her fork in midair. "You've never been with a white guy before?"

Coco shook her head. "Nope. Not white, Hispanic, Asian, Indian. I've only dated Black men my whole life."

Deja frowned. "What? I tried out all types of guys before I married Bobby." She shook her head and looked at Coco in amazement. "You're not serious, right?"

Coco nodded. "Dead serious. My whole life, every man I've ever been with was Black."

Ivy thought about it. "I had a Puerto Rican boyfriend in high school before I got with Mikey. Does that count?"

"No," Deja said. "They're Black, too."

Nikki waved her hand. "Lord knows I don't discriminate."

Deja seemed genuinely surprised by Coco's revelation.

"So, what is it? You're saying that you're only physically attracted to Black men?"

Coco thought about it. "I find men of other races attractive," she explained. "I just never imagined myself being sexual, being in a relationship, being in love with anyone other than a Black man."

Deja chewed her food and considered that. "How has that worked out for you?"

"Not so well," Coco admitted. "I fucked around with Derek all these years, holding out hope that he would get his shit together and love me right. Instead, he has a baby on the way with someone else."

Nikki nodded. "I'm glad to see you giving a white guy a chance, Coco. I bet he treats you better than Derek ever did. Plus, you're successful, pretty, you got your shit together. It's time to level up. These so-called brothers out here sell out and get somebody light, bright, or white the second they make it."

"Not all of them do," Deja interjected.

Nikki sucked her teeth. "*Most* of them do. Basketball players, rappers, shit . . . the fuckin' suit-and-tie Wall Street niggas get them a Becky as soon as that salary hits higher than six figures. Meanwhile, successful bitches like us are sitting around expressing loyalty to the Black man like he's some type of fuckin' prize. Half them muthafuckas got so much baggage they need Iyanla to help them unpack it."

Coco and Ivy laughed at Nikki's monologue, but Deja was less impressed.

"I think you're grouping all Black men together. That's not fair."

"They ain't all bad," Nikki allowed. "Every now and then you find a good one. But most of the time, there's no upside to being devoted to niggas when niggas don't give that same energy back to us."

"So, you haven't been seeing Derek?" Ivy asked skeptically.

Coco looked a little guilty then. "I haven't seen him, but I've been talking to him on the phone. He's going through a lot."

Ivy frowned. "A lot of shit that he did to himself. That man broke your heart and got another woman pregnant, and you're still giving him the time of day?" She shook her head.

Coco's face fell. "Well, damn. Now I feel bad."

"You should," Ivy said. "And you need to figure out why you're attracted to emotionally unavailable men. Ziggy has been doing everything right. He's everything you said you wanted. So, you shouldn't be wasting your time with Derek at all."

Coco nodded.

"You're right. Derek doesn't deserve my time. I think being Mikey's sister has a lot to do with it. Being a part of the family I grew up in, I saw Black men as strong and powerful, but I also saw them struggle to be vulnerable and I watched them repress their feelings. So, that's the type of man I'm used to. Being around Ziggy has been blowing my mind. He's different. He listens to me and he's honest with me in return. I really like him so far."

She did a little shimmy in her seat.

Ivy eyed her friend suspiciously. "You slept with him already, didn't you?"

Coco giggled again, and Nikki laughed, slapping her friend a congratulatory high five.

"Mmm!" Ivy faked outrage, all the while grinning happily for her friend. "So, how was it?"

"Shit!" Deja said. "From the looks of it, he blew her mind."

Coco nodded. "He was so romantic. Patient and tender and sweet. He had me crawling up the walls. It was nothing like I imagined. And I mean that in the best possible way."

"What were you expecting?" Deja was all ears.

Coco shrugged. "I thought it would be awkward, you know?

Like he wouldn't be the one to take control. I was prepared to ride him till the wheels fell off."

Laughter peppered the table.

"But he grabbed me by the waist and pulled me close to him. Then he kissed me like I have *never* been kissed before."

The captivated expressions on her friends' faces almost made her stop and laugh. But the memory of that kiss was nothing to laugh at.

"He bit me softly; sucked my lips, my tongue, my neck, each and every one of my fingers . . ."

"Damn!"

Deja fanned herself at the thought. She hadn't been kissed like that in years. She felt herself growing angry at Bobby the more she thought about it.

"Then he picked me up and laid me on the couch and took me over. I mean . . . it was incredible."

Coco shoveled a forkful of rice into her mouth and chewed.

Ivy threw her head back in mock ecstasy. "Girl!"

"I'm telling you, he took his time, and he made me feel so beautiful." Coco was beaming. "He was amazing. And I ain't mad at his size down there. He's got some girth!"

Nikki shook her head in complete amazement. "This turned out better than I ever thought it would." She laughed. "I was hoping you two would hit it off. But this is way more than I imagined." She clinked glasses with Coco.

"He's not what I expected," Coco admitted. "Even when we're not in bed. He's thoughtful and fun to be with. I'm not going to rush anything. But I'll tell you right now that I'm feeling him."

Deja was thrilled for her. "When are you going to see him again?"

Coco gave a shy smirk. "He's at my place right now, waiting for me."

"Oooooh!" Deja, Nikki, and Ivy cooed at the same time.

Coco could barely contain her joy. She was grateful for this lunch date with her friends. She had spent weeks keeping Ziggy at a distance. Now that they were moving forward, she was eager for their feedback.

"Wow." Deja sat back in her seat. "That news is going to be hard to top." She looked at Ivy. "What's your story?"

Ivy laughed. "Well, damn! It ain't as good as Coco's!"

Coco laughed.

Ivy took a breath and spilled the beans. "I met a man, too."

Coco, Nikki, and Deja gasped so audibly that nearby diners glanced in their direction. A butter knife clanked as it fell to the floor.

Ivy laughed hard at her friends' reactions. Clearly, it had been too long.

"Noah and Kingston introduced me to a guy named James."

"Wait! The *boys* set you up?" Coco was shocked. She had been so preoccupied with Ziggy that she missed a lot. "Who is he? Where did they meet him? Spill it!"

Ivy held a hand up. "Hold on, I'm going to tell you."

Deja chewed her food in silence. She was so excited by the sound of this. Ivy had met a man! That alone was a reason to go to church and praise the Lord on Sunday morning. Without hearing another word, Deja was already sold. She sipped her wine.

"Noah's car broke down at a mechanic shop the night of Nikki's party."

Deja thought back to the house party the boys had at Ivy's house that night and winced a little.

"The man who works there helped them out and gave them

a ride home. He and King hit it off because it turns out he used to play basketball at King's high school."

Ivy took a breath. This was a lot to process, even for her.

"Anyway, we started talking on the phone. Nothing serious at first. But lately, things are heating up. We went out for dinner after King's basketball game."

"He went to King's basketball game?" Coco could barely stand the suspense. She tried to remember the last time she had spoken to her brother, or to Patsy for that matter. Apparently, she had missed a lot.

"I invited him," Ivy said. "I thought since he hit it off with King, we could all hang out and see if James was worth getting to know. But the boys acted like the nigga was trying to stick me up."

Deja chuckled. She had seen how protective Ivy's sons were of her, especially considering their father was away from home.

"At first, I thought it was cute. They were just looking out for me, trying to make sure that I don't get played. Which was cool in the beginning. I wasn't really gung ho about going out with this man anyway. You know I've been devoted to Mikey for my whole life."

Coco nodded. She knew better than anybody.

"In the beginning, I was just flirting with him to test the waters, see if I still had my old touch." She grinned. "But when I started getting to know James, I started liking what I was seeing and hearing. He's a good man and I enjoy being with him. So, I've really been trying to get Noah and King to give him a chance. But that ain't happening. Noah's been at Patsy's house more than ever, and King basically stays in his room if he's not out with his friends. Like they're mad at me for wanting to have a life of my own for the first time."

Ivy shook her head. "Anyway, after talking to him for a while,

I invited him to King's basketball game. Afterward, everybody was hungry. James invited us to dinner with his brother, who's a chef."

"So, you met his family?" Coco interrupted again.

"They were very nice." Ivy decided to plunge forward since her friends weren't giving her the chance to spill the fine details. "His brother is married to a nice lady named Cheryl. So, that's the best part. I finally made some new friends for the first time since my move."

Deja smiled. That was a relief. She knew that Ivy was beginning to second-guess her move to the island. Now that she was making new friends, she hoped the situation would improve.

Coco sipped her drink. "Does Mikey know?"

Ivy nodded. "Noah and King went up north with Patsy to visit him. They ratted me out."

Nikki sucked her teeth. "Damn! And they say bitches gossip!"

Deja laughed.

Ivy looked at Coco sadly. "He went berserk after the visit. Got in a fight with another inmate and a CO. They sent him to the box for six months."

"What?" Coco was shocked, her heart racing at the thought of her brother locked down in solitary confinement for twenty-three hours a day for six months. "Why didn't anybody tell me?"

"I thought Patsy would fill you in after she went to see him. She told Michael everything. About me and James, about the basketball game." She looked at Coco. "I didn't tell you that a few weeks ago Mikey sent Bam and his crew over to my house to threaten me."

Coco shook her head. "No, he didn't, Ivy. Please don't tell me that."

"He did," Ivy said. "I came home and Bam was in my house

telling me that Mikey expected to see me on a visit. And if I didn't go, something was supposed to happen to me."

Coco felt secondhand embarrassment for her brother. "I'm sorry, Ivy. He's losing it, obviously. Threatening you . . . he doesn't mean it."

Ivy shrugged. "After Bam issued the warning, and Patsy went up there and told him about James, Mikey kept calling me. I wouldn't answer so he wrote me a letter. Cursed me all the way the fuck OUT. Do you hear me?"

Ivy shook her head at the thought.

"Called me everything in the book. A bad mother, a fucked-up wife, ungrateful, disrespectful, nasty, grimy. Noah and Kingston accept the charges when he calls their phones. When he calls me, I don't bother answering. No sense in paying to get verbally abused."

She looked at Coco.

"After he got in the fight, they beat him up pretty bad. Sent him to the box at a different prison even farther up north than before. I'm sure Patsy will tell you all about it when you talk to her. She thinks it's all my fault. She told Noah and King that if I'd been a better wife, Mikey wouldn't have gone off like that. So, right now, things are tense between me and the boys. Kind of a standoff. They want me to bend and do what Michael wants, and I'm determined to live my life on my terms, regardless of how many temper tantrums Mikey throws."

Coco sighed. She made a mental note to call Patsy later. She wanted to know where Mikey was housed now and how he was doing. Coco knew her brother well, and it sounded like he was coming unhinged. Losing control had sent him into a tailspin.

"Mikey loves you, Ivy, no matter what bullshit he said to you when he called. He's hurt. He doesn't want to lose you. But I've been telling him for years that the position he expects you to play is unfair. No love, no romance, no real chance to live a full life. He thinks that because he supported you financially that you owe him blind loyalty for the rest of your life."

"I do owe him something," Ivy said. "That's what I told myself all these years. I loved him. He took care of me. I thought I owed him my devotion forever. Part of me still feels like I owe him that. But it's been sixteen years. I asked for a break and Mikey walked out on me. I dipped a toe in the dating pool and he spoke to me like a dog. I don't deserve that. Not after all the shit I put up with. I saw Rashid a few weeks ago. He came to deliver a message from Mikey as well."

Deja perked up at the mention of Rashid's name. "What did he say?"

"He told me that he was on Staten Island to see Bree, and he decided to drop by and tell me that Mikey loves me. And that I've been riding with him for so long that I might as well continue." She chuckled. "I told Rashid to let Mikey know that I won't be back. And he can keep his love if it means that I have to do what I'm told. I told Rashid that he should stop fighting Mikey's battles for him. And I hope he takes my advice."

Nikki's mind was reeling from so much information. "Okay, so this James guy. You like him so far?"

Ivy nodded. "I do. We have a lot in common. He used to hustle. Did some time in prison and then came home and changed his life. He mentors teenage boys. I think Noah and King will like him when they stop acting stupid and give him a chance."

"So, he's a mechanic?" Deja asked.

Ivy nodded. "Yup." She sighed. "I'm trying not to get too caught up in that."

"The money?" Coco clarified. She knew that Ivy was accustomed to being with a man who provided completely.

Ivy nodded. "I know I must make more than him. But most of the brothers in my tax bracket ain't interested in a sister like me. They want a Becky. So, I might have to get over the fact that I make more than most of the men I'm attracted to."

"Black women have been dealing with that reality for years," Coco agreed.

"And which neighborhood does he live in?" Deja wanted more.

"He rents a place over in Stapleton. Lives alone. He has three sons. All grown and away at college like Noah should be." Ivy rolled her eyes, reminding herself to nag Noah about that when she got home. She wanted to make sure that his one semester off didn't turn into an extended stay.

"I'm looking forward to living like that. King is on his way to college in another year or two. Hopefully, Noah will go back to school soon. And I can't wait to have the house all to myself."

Coco sucked her teeth. "Please! You know you're going to miss those boys. Probably be driving up to their schools every chance you get."

Deja and Nikki laughed.

"Nope! You know I've never lived alone? Think about that! Michael and I got together in high school and I became a mother soon after. I want to see how the other half lives."

"Mmm-hmm," Nikki said. "Especially now that you met James!"

"You're really not bothered by the income gap?" Deja couldn't hold back the question any longer.

Ivy smiled. "I'm not. So far, at least. I really enjoy James's company. And I'm okay with the idea of dating a man who rents his home and makes less money than me. For now."

Deja nodded. "I hear that. Fingers crossed for James."

Ivy grinned again. "I learned that he's not afraid of a challenge. He was bold enough to step up and volunteer to be my spades partner at his brother's house."

Both Deja and Coco gasped. They had seen firsthand how seriously Ivy took a spades game when she'd cursed out one of Deja's guests for "reneging" at a family barbecue years ago.

Ivy laughed. She was aware that she held a notorious reputation for ruthlessness in the game.

"We won!"

Now the ladies applauded, both knowing that James had passed a very crucial test whether he knew it or not.

"Until now, we always see each other at his brother's house. We meet there every now and then. Eat, play cards, sip sum'n. It's cool because there's four of us. No pressure. But I'm going out with him one-on-one this weekend. Kinda nervous about that."

Ivy took a long sip of her drink after that.

"Don't be nervous," Deja said. "There's still no pressure. If you like him, you like him. if you don't, you don't. Just relax and go with the flow."

Ivy nodded and smiled, although to her that sounded easier said than done.

"Hmm!" Nikki mumbled loudly. "I thought my life was exciting, but y'all bitches been busy over the past few weeks." She shook her head. "Did Deja tell y'all that her and Bobby are separated?"

Ivy nearly spat her drink out. Coco's jaw dropped.

"NO!" they both yelled.

"Bitch, I just did your hair on Thursday. You didn't say a word!" Ivy was pissed.

Deja looked embarrassed. "Nikki is being dramatic. It's not official. Me and Bobby are just spending a little time apart. That's all."

"Nah," Coco said. "Don't downplay it. Who moved out? When did it happen? What caused it? COUGH IT UP!"

Deja glared at her sister. "I was gonna tell you about it. But Big Mouth beat me to it."

She sighed and looked at Coco and Ivy apologetically.

"Everything happened so fast. Rashid came back in the picture, and Bobby started getting territorial. Over me, Bree, and especially over Bree's relationship with Rashid. He started making stupid demands."

"Like what?" Ivy pressed.

"Like demanding that Bree stay away from King," Nikki said it flat out. She was sick of Deja sugarcoating the hard facts.

Ivy looked offended. "Okay . . . what?"

Deja sighed. "Bree has a crush on King. She's been doing regular teenage-girl shit to get his attention. Bobby got wind of it, and he . . . he doesn't approve."

"He wants Bree to be with one of the prep school boys over on the South Shore," Nikki added. "King is too Black for Bobby."

Deja sucked her teeth and started to protest, but Nikki wasn't finished.

"I think he's taking his frustrations out on King when the one he's really mad at is Rashid. He can't take a stand and say that Rashid can't come around and see Bree. So, he's taking a stand on King instead."

Ivy felt her blood boiling at the thought of Bobby—or anyone else—deeming her son unworthy of their daughter. Kingston was a good kid with a promising future. Ivy had done everything she could to ensure that society did *not* see her sons as a threat or a stereotype. And here Bobby was doing just that.

"That's bullshit," was all she managed to say.

Deja nodded, agreeing. "He's bugging out, Ivy. And it has nothing to do with King whatsoever. Nikki is right for once."

Nikki shot her sister a glare. Deja continued.

"So, we had a big fight. We both said a bunch of things we probably didn't mean. And Bobby left. He's been staying at one of the rental properties we own. He still comes by every day. He's NYPD, so I'm sure he's keeping tabs on us. But he's giving me and Bree space. Right now, it's a good thing. I think all of us need to take a break."

Nikki looked at her sister. "Did you tell Rashid yet?"

Deja nodded. "He keeps warning me that this could get ugly. The timing is bad. Rashid doesn't want Bobby to do something desperate because he feels like he's losing his family."

Deja looked at Ivy.

"That's what Michael is doing. So, Rashid has a point. Men like Bobby and Michael want to be perceived as powerful. They want the world to think they have it all. You and I played along for a while and now we're not. But if my marriage falls apart, it's because of the way I handled things. The way I ran away from shit that I needed to stay and face. Now it's all coming back to haunt me. But you stayed, Ivy. You didn't run. You made sure your sons have a relationship with their father, and you were loyal to Mikey. Don't doubt yourself. Moving on with your life doesn't erase the years you rode it out with your man. It just clears the path for you to ride it out for yourself from now on."

Ivy smiled at her friend, truly grateful for those words.

Nikki raised her glass high. "It's our turn, ladies. In the words of Lil' Kim: 'Fuck niggas, get money!'"

Takeoff

Ivy couldn't understand her nervousness. Her hands hadn't stopped trembling since she'd slid into her cutest bra and panties in preparation for the evening. Tonight would be her first real date with James.

She was having second thoughts. She considered making an excuse and backing out of it altogether. She didn't owe anything to James. She could stay home, order food, and watch Netflix.

But she pushed herself to go. She reminded herself that he was fun and easy to talk to. That she was playing an active role in taking her life back from Michael. Staying home would make this just like any other Saturday night, home alone letting her best years slip by.

During their many conversations, Ivy learned that James was a hardworking man. Apparently, he was an honest one, too. He had shared the details of his past with her, even the ugliest parts. She admired the way he'd turned his life around after his incarceration, and how he seemed determined never to go back to prison again. When he and Ivy talked, their conversations were full of discussions about their work, their parenting, and whatever recent craziness was going on in politics or pop culture. Ivy had started to look forward to their interactions each day. They were a breath of fresh air after so much time spent by herself. Until now, she hadn't realized how much she missed having a man's attention. She thought about the way her heart roared in her chest when James stood close to her. He towered over her when they stood side by side. As a tall, big-boned sister, it wasn't every day that she met a man she could look up to. She had to admit that James turned her on.

Noah and Kingston had plans of their own for the evening. Noah was spending the weekend at his aunt Patsy's house in Brooklyn. He had tried, unsuccessfully, to persuade his brother to come, too. But Kingston had his heart set on seeing some movie with his friends that night. Bree was among them. Ivy had been keeping an eye on the budding relationship between the two of them. Ever since Deja revealed that Bobby wasn't happy about Kingston being Bree's potential boyfriend, Ivy had been nursing a bruised ego. She liked Bree and thought she and Kingston were cute together. So, she didn't protest when she noticed her coming around more often. *Fuck Bobby,* she thought.

James arrived right on time. Ivy wasn't sure if her outfit was too much or too little for the occasion since he hadn't told her where they were going. She wore a pair of jeans and a sexy black blouse she had been eager to wear for the longest time. She was tall enough as it was, so she opted for a pair of flat Gucci slides for both the fashion and comfort they gave her. She hoped that this look would fit the evening no matter where James was taking her.

When she opened the door, he was already smiling. That smile had once irritated her, but now it was a welcome sight. She smiled, too, and felt her nervousness quickly subside now that they were face to face. She welcomed him into the foyer and watched him look around, in awe of the place.

"Wow. What a beautiful home." James had seen it from the outside the night he'd dropped off Noah and Kingston after their car broke down. But seeing it now on the inside, he was even more impressed by how much Ivy had managed to accomplish singlehandedly. It had been clear from the start that Ivy ran a tight ship. She kept her boys under her constant care and scrutiny. Looking around now as Ivy ushered him into her living room, he could tell that she was the kind of woman who led by example.

She thanked him and offered him a drink. He declined.

"I'm driving. Gotta make sure I bring you back home without a scratch. Otherwise, your sons will kick my ass."

Ivy laughed. "Whatever!" She grabbed her purse and led him out the door. "Let's go."

James escorted Ivy to his car. She had to admit it was a beauty. The black leather interior seemed to sparkle in the moonlight, and she looked around for the source of the citrus aroma that filled the car. It looked and smelled so fresh and so clean. James slid into the driver's seat and looked at her.

"Where are we going?" she asked.

He smiled. "We have so much fun beating my brother at spades all the time, so I wanna take you to the casino out in Queens. See if you're good at blackjack, too."

Ivy grinned. That sounded like a great idea. She had plenty of money to burn, and she loved the thought of blackjack and booze. Plus, it would give them a chance to get more comfortable with each other on the ride.

"Let's go. I got a pocket full of cash."

James laughed. "Oh, yeah?"

He started the car. He had no plans of letting her spend a

penny. He wanted to show her a good time tonight. So far, he liked everything about her—including her reluctance to open up right away. It showed that she was selective, which made him feel special for having the privilege of her company. He was looking forward to getting to know Ivy on a much deeper level.

"I got some money to burn, too," he said. "Let's see if we can flip what we got and come back rich."

Ivy laughed and rubbed her hands together in anticipation. All nervousness subsided as they spent the ride listening to old-school hip-hop and R & B. James even sang along a couple of times. Badly. But Ivy pretended not to notice and even joined in, harmonizing with him.

Their conversation flowed easily. Both had bold personalities and appreciated each other's brutal honesty.

"So," she said, looking at him with a smirk on her face. "You did eight years upstate for armed robbery?"

He glanced at her sidelong, trying to gauge her reaction.

"I'm not proud of it. I had everything going for me at the time. I was at the top of my basketball career. College scouts were checking me out. I was on my way. But the niggas I was hanging out with . . . they had nothing going for them. Most of them sold crack, robbed, that sort of thing. Most of them didn't go to school. I thought keeping them around was a sign that I wasn't forgetting where I came from. I let them influence me to do stupid shit. Like running up in stores and robbing the register, sticking up the hustlers in other neighborhoods. I had no business doing any of that shit. Unlike the rest of them, I had a promising future. We got caught doing a stickup, and they sent every one of us away. I lost everything and had to start from scratch to get back on my feet."

He shrugged.

"That's what I keep trying to drill into my sons' heads. The system was too happy to lock up a bunch of teenage boys for years. It didn't matter to them how much potential we had. They didn't care. And the world still doesn't care. Black men can have their whole future ahead of them and see that shit snatched away from them in the blink of an eye. They can never afford to be off point. As Black men, they gotta see the world differently. Whether they want to or not. The friends they hang around, the girls they date, all that matters in the end."

Ivy nodded.

He glanced at her for a moment.

"I got a visit from your husband."

Ivy snapped her head in his direction. "What?"

"Mikey Norris, right? Locked up north in Elmira for murder. Well, from what I understand, they sent him to Southport now. He's in solitary confinement for stabbing a nigga and fighting a CO, right?"

Her heart sank. The elation she had been feeling a few moments ago subsided. She nodded.

"He sent some of his friends to see me down at the mechanic shop where I work. I wasn't there, but they insisted on waiting for me. My coworker told them I was gone for the day. But they must not have believed him. They spent the whole afternoon taking up space in the shop. Four of them, he said. Stayed till closing time."

James chuckled at the boldness of these Brooklyn niggas trying to strong-arm him.

"My coworker was calling me to let me know what was happening. But I was with you. And when I'm with you I put my phone on silent. So, while we were at my brother's house watching a movie and getting to know each other, your ex had his enforcers out looking for me."

"James, I'm so sorry."

"You don't have nothing to be sorry for, Ivy. You told me

what time it was when I met you. I could see how your sons look out for you. I knew that being with you meant having to prove myself to a few people. What I didn't know was that your husband—"

"He's not my husband."

"He thinks he is."

She sighed.

"I didn't know that he's been holding you hostage for years. You didn't explain it to me like that. When you described your relationship with him all these years, it sounded like you stayed because you loved him. But a dude that operates the way your ex does . . . he's a dictator. Probably took you years to realize that a woman as strong as you could be dominated by a man. But that's what dictators do. They dominate. You say you're leaving him, moving on with your life. He sends his boys to make sure you know that's not an option. That's not love."

Ivy's eyes welled with tears and she looked out the passenger window to hide it. James was hitting the nail on the head with his assessment of her relationship with Michael.

"He's trying to scare me off. Make me think it's better to avoid problems by walking away. I thought about it. But I like you. I like the way I feel when I'm around you. And I think I make you feel good, too. We have fun together. We see eye to eye. Your ex is smart. He knows he lost a good woman. I can understand somewhat why he's acting so crazy. But that's his loss. I want to get to know you better. And I'm willing to deal with his bullshit as long as you are."

She looked at him and smiled.

James sighed. "My coworker said that they roughed him up a little before they left."

Ivy gasped.

"It's okay. He's fine. It was nothing serious. They just pushed him around a little, called him names and shit like that. When he closed up the shop, they watched from the parking lot, trying to intimidate him some more. So far, they haven't been back. But if they do come, I'm gonna be ready. It might get heated. I just thought you should know in case that happens."

She was relieved that Michael hadn't succeeded in scaring James off, but part of her wondered why he was willing to risk it all for her.

"Why? Why you wanna involve yourself in some shit this messy?"

James smiled at her. "Because you're fine! And I like you. And you deserve to have a solid man by your side. I think I could be that man."

Ivy agreed.

By the time they arrived at Resorts World Casino, they were laughing like old friends. When James reached for her hand, Ivy gave it to him gladly. It felt like a perfect fit.

Deja sat in her living room, clutching a glass of wine in one hand and her cell phone in the other. Bree was out at the movies with Kingston and his friends. She was home alone with nagging thoughts of Rashid dancing through her head.

She dialed his number. With her eyes shut, she waited as the phone rang. Rashid picked up on the second ring.

"Yo."

She hesitated, her eyes wide open now. "Rashid?" Her voice quivered as she said it, and she hated herself for it. She cleared her throat. "It's Deja."

He didn't respond right away. For a moment, Deja wondered if the call dropped. His voice came through the phone just as she was about to call his name.

"What's up? Is Bree all right?"

"Yeah. She's fine. She's at the movies with her friends to-night."

Rashid waited for her to go on. "You good?"

She thought about that question. The answer was no. "I want to see you."

That was all she said, but Rashid felt the intensity of her words through the phone. "When?"

She smiled, relieved. "I can come there now. To your place, if that's cool."

He thought about it. He had been keeping her on a long leash for weeks. But the truth was he wouldn't mind her company right now.

"Yeah. That's cool. Come through."

Two hours later, she was at his door. She knocked and waited with her heart in her throat for him to answer.

He opened the door and stood looking at her. He gave her a faint smile and stepped aside, welcoming her in. Her eyes scanned the room as she entered. It was a modest one-bedroom apartment with hardwood floors and a pretty impressive kitchen for NYC.

"Nice place," she said.

He thanked her. "You do real estate. So, you would know."

She sat down on the leather couch.

"You want something to drink?" he asked, still standing, still not seeming especially happy to see her.

She nodded. "Can I get something strong?"

He looked at her, his curiosity tugging at him. Then he went to the kitchen and poured them each a glass of Hennessy on the rocks. He returned and handed her one.

"You said strong. Let's see if you can hang with this."

She smiled, took a sniff, and recoiled a little. "Fuck it," she said, grimacing. "I'm gonna need it." Then she sipped it.

Rashid sat down next to her. "What you got to say, Deja?"

She took a deep breath and plunged in.

"Since you came home, I've been off balance. I thought I was on the right track. I was doing what I thought was best for Bree at the time. And for me. And I thought Bobby was the safe bet. He loved me, loved her, and we had a good life together."

Rashid listened, noting her speaking of that "good life" in the past tense.

"I told you all that before. But the part I didn't tell you was that it never felt right to me. Even when I was saying my vows, when we closed on our first house and the stock portfolio started getting thicker. None of it felt right."

She took a deep breath. Admitting this to herself and to Rashid was the hardest truth she had ever told.

"I was trying to fix what we fucked up. Without the crack game, you could have owned a company, I could have gone to college, and things might have been different. Instead, you wound up a felon and I was a single mother. It felt like the wrong life for Bree. Being with Bobby gave me a way out of that. And I jumped at the chance."

Rashid nodded. "Good. So, you should be happy with yourself."

"I'm not, though. And I haven't been happy for a while. Nikki noticed it. My mother, my friends. Everybody except me. Until you came back. Then I realized how true it was. I've been unhappy for a while."

He looked at her. "That's why you and RoboCop broke up?"

Deja chuckled a little. Rashid was consistent with calling Bobby by that name.

"We didn't break up. We're just . . ."

"Broken up," Rashid finished for her. "It's all good. Shit sounds like it was doomed from the start. All he was for you was a safety net. You got what you wanted. Now you're ready to bounce. Just like you did to me."

Deja felt the blow of his words. She shook her head. "It's not like that. I'm not the cold-hearted bitch you think I am, Rashid."

"Who are you then?"

"Just Deja. The same girl you used to love."

She closed the distance between them without thinking, leaned in, and kissed him softly on his lips with two soft pecks. He let her but didn't budge.

She sat back afterward and looked at him expectantly. He stared back at her in silence.

"I wanted to do that since you showed up at my door that day," she said honestly.

He nodded. "I know."

Deja's energy had given her away long before she'd found the courage to step up verbally.

His matter-of-fact reply disappointed her. "You didn't want it, too?"

Rashid cupped her face in his hand, her skin soft against his strong palm. He could have crushed her in half for all the torment she had put him through when she'd abandoned him. Instead, he stroked her cheek gently and shook his head.

"I never said that."

He kissed her, though his kiss was not as tender as hers. Rashid devoured her with a passion and an intensity that she didn't expect. He grabbed her hair, pulled her head back, and kissed her neck, biting and sucking it so hard that a moan escaped her lips.

"Rashid!"

He scooped her up, laid her on the floor, and unleashed all the frustration he had been holding inside for years.

Breakdown

Tonight was cool." Bree was looking at him with a sexy little smirk on her face. "I had fun with you, King."

She certainly had. Tonight, she and King had gotten closer than ever before. They'd spent the early part of the night kissing and snuggling up with each other in the dark and quiet corner of the movie theater, and then even more at Kevin's house afterward. She was supposed to be home by midnight, though. So, reluctantly the lovebirds had cut their little make-out session short.

He grinned. "I'm glad you had fun. We should hang out more often."

Kingston was trying to play it cool, but he really liked Bree. Since the day she let him know she had a crush on him, he started seeing her in a new light. Their date tonight had only confirmed it for him. Bree was the girl who had his attention.

She looked at him regretfully. "I wish I didn't have this stupid curfew."

King shrugged. "It's all good. I'll just have to come scoop you up tomorrow so we can pick up where we left off."

He was glad to see her face light up at the sound of that. He hated to end the night now. But it was already twenty minutes after midnight, and both needed to get home before they incurred the wrath of their mothers.

"Sounds good," Bree said.

He got off the highway at Arthur Kill Road and Huguenot Avenue and pulled up to the red traffic light. While they sat idling, he leaned over and kissed her softly on her pillowy lips.

The car started sputtering, interrupting their sweet moment. They both sat back, looking confused.

"The engine sounds funny," Bree said.

King remembered that sound. The car sounded the same way it had the night it broke down the first time. Sure enough, the engine sputtered some more, then shut off.

He groaned. He turned the key and started the ignition again. He saw the "Check Engine" light come on and started mumbling to himself immediately.

"Nah, come on! Not now, please!"

The car sputtered again. This time, King gunned the engine as the light turned green. He made it to the next intersection before he was forced to stop for another red light. As he sat idling for several seconds, the car shut off again. This time, it wouldn't restart.

"Shit!" Bree said.

Kingston pounded on the steering wheel. The last thing either one of them needed was to be even later getting home than they were now. He tried the ignition once more and his heart raced when the car roared to life. He put the car in drive, and the engine made a series of noises as it tried to do its job. He pressed the gas, and the car accelerated slightly. But soon, the engine sputtered once again. He managed to steer the car to the side of the road, but it shut off almost immediately. The car came to rest at an odd angle, barely avoidable by the handful of passing cars.

"Don't worry," Bree said. "I'll call my mom to come and get us."

She pulled out her cell phone and dialed Deja's number. It went to voicemail, and Bree frowned. She dialed again. Same result.

For the next several minutes, King tried to restart the car to no avail. Finally, he pressed the button to pop the hood and climbed out of the car to see if anything looked strange. He had no training as a mechanic, but he was desperate. Maybe something was clearly out of place and needed a quick adjustment. He found nothing.

"FUCK!"

King felt like a fool for borrowing Noah's car tonight. He could've taken an Uber like he usually did. But he wanted to flex for Bree, show her that he could handle a car and her, too. Noah and Ivy had both warned him that the car was still not functioning at one hundred percent, and he'd ignored them. He had smoked a little weed at Kevin's house and the high was completely worn off now. Realizing that he was still about half a mile from Bree's house and a mile away from his own, he held his hands above his head in frustration.

A curtain parted in the window of a house nearby. Kingston and Bree didn't notice, too preoccupied with their car trouble. The man in the window was watching from the safety of his darkened bedroom, watching the tall Black guy in the middle of the street pacing back and forth, then circling a car parked at the curb.

The man in the window groaned and muttered under his

breath. He thought about the conversation he'd had earlier at his friend's retirement party. Crime was up in their borough. In the darkness of his bedroom, the man watched the unfamiliar Black male circle the car, cursing loudly. A bunch of different scenarios played out in his mind. This guy could be high. He could be violent. He decided that he looked menacing. Possibly a car thief.

Kingston stood with his hands on his head, dread washing over him. He wondered how he would explain this to his mother because if he had to walk home, he would definitely be late getting there. Even if she were having the time of her life with James, she wasn't the type to stay out all night. He was now in a race against time to beat his mother home and avoid her wrath.

He pounded the hood of the car angrily.

Bree leaned out of the passenger window and called out to him.

"My mom's not answering. I'm calling my dad now."

Kingston nodded. He peered off down Huguenot Avenue, a quiet, tree-lined strip of road that suddenly seemed endless. It was dark, with few streetlights to illuminate the way. They could walk home, but it would be one hell of a walk.

He shook his head and walked back around to the driver's-side door. Bree was on the phone with Bobby, and Kingston could hear her end of the conversation.

"Kingston's car broke down and we're stuck on the corner of—what? Because Mommy said I could go out with him tonight. Yes, I tried to call her but she's not picking up."

Bree looked exasperated as she explained their predicament to her father.

Frustrated, Kingston resigned himself to making the long walk the rest of the way home. He spat on the ground and vowed that when he got home tonight, he was going to call Noah and tell him what a piece of shit his car was.

He leaned into the car and spoke to Bree. "I think we should walk. I know your Pops don't like me. I heard my mother talking about it with Aunt Coco on the phone the other day. Plus, it's gonna take him a while to get here. If we start walking now, I might be able to beat my mother home from her little date."

Bree sighed. "I think we should wait, King. These white folks out here ain't used to seeing Black people walking through these neighborhoods in the middle of the night."

He sucked his teeth. "I'm more afraid of my mother than these crackas out here."

Bree laughed. "I'm gonna call my mom again. Hopefully, she answers this time."

Deja's phone had been on vibrate. So, she had missed Bree's two earlier calls. She was surprised by how comfortable she felt in Rashid's place. It was definitely beneath the standards of the real estate she sold. But now, lying in the afterglow of the steamy sex they had just enjoyed, she felt more relaxed than she had in years. She heard her iPhone buzzing on his bedside table. Glancing at the clock, she saw that it was past midnight. She frowned when she saw Bree's name on her phone screen.

"Bree? What's the matter?"

Rashid sat up when he heard their daughter's name. He had assumed it was RoboCop calling Deja at such a late hour. The frown on Deja's face gave him a reason to be concerned.

"His car broke down? Okay . . . yeah. I'm on my way."

She hung up and looked at Rashid. "Bree and King had some car trouble. His car broke down a few blocks from my house. I'm gonna go pick them up."

She climbed out of his bed reluctantly and started searching the room for her clothes. They had been scattered in various places during sex. She wished she could call what she and Rashid had just done lovemaking. But the truth was, it had been more animalistic passion than love that they had just expressed for each other.

She began to get dressed slowly, wishing Rashid would say something to her. But he sat silently in the dark and watched her without a word.

Kingston began to walk toward the front of the car to check under the hood again, but he was interrupted by a voice in the dark.

"PUT YOUR HANDS UP!"

His adrenaline surged instantly, and he spun around with his heart racing, searching in the dark for the source of that voice, those words. The "Brooklyn" in him put his instincts on high alert. This could be a robbery.

He quickly scanned the scene and settled finally on an older white man dressed in a black tracksuit standing in the street a few feet behind him. The man's silver hair glinted in the moonlight, slicked back as if to emphasize the scowl he wore. He was standing close to an SUV that was parked near the spot where Noah's car had come to rest.

Kingston's eyes narrowed. For a moment this old man seemed harmless.

"You heard me, nigger. Put your fucking hands up!"

Too stunned to speak, Kingston froze, staring at the man. All he saw in his eyes was hatred. It was the first time he had heard the N-word hurled at him by a white person. Let alone an old white man three times his age.

Bree heard it, too. She frantically dialed her mother's number again.

Fully dressed now, Deja looked at Rashid. "So, what happens now?"

He looked confused. "You mean with us?"

She nodded.

He shrugged. "Deja, you're married. What you think happens now?"

She didn't know what she expected, but she hoped that this represented some turning point in their relationship. That it had been more to him than just a physical thing.

"I—"

Deja's phone buzzed again, and she frowned.

She answered quickly this time. "Bree—WHAT? OH MY GOD! OKAY . . . CALM DOWN!"

Rashid was out of bed now and throwing on his clothes. Fuck a curfew. His baby girl was in obvious trouble.

"What happened?" he asked Deja anxiously.

She held up her hand as she listened intently to what Bree was saying. "Okay. Listen, Bree. It's okay. We're on our way!"

Deja looked at Rashid. "We gotta get to Staten Island right the fuck now!"

The white man kept his gaze locked on Kingston.

"What the fuck are you doing over here? This ain't your neighborhood. You out here looking for cars to steal? Looking for a house to rob? Get the fuck outta here!"

Kingston laughed uneasily. This guy had to be kidding. If not, he was crazy.

The man took a step toward him now. "I said get the fuck outta here before I call the cops. They should lock all of you's up and throw away the key!"

Bree was out of the car now, standing timidly on the passenger side of Noah's BMW.

"Our car just broke down. We're just trying to get home," she explained.

The man ignored her, his focus on Kingston. "Fucking

degenerates and drug addicts over here bothering hardworking people!"

His face was set in the most hateful scowl Bree had ever seen.

Something deep inside Kingston began to register that this was not a joke. He felt no fear but was surprised by the balls of this man. His initial shock gave way to pure fury.

"Yo, FUCK YOU!" Kingston's voice echoed down the block.

Bree scrambled for her cell phone and desperately dialed Bobby again.

"Dad, please hurry up!" In a flood of words, she tried her best to explain the desperate situation they were in. "This man is crazy. He's calling us niggers."

Kingston took one step in the man's direction, his hands fisted and ready to fight. He was prepared to kick this old man's ass. Kingston moving in his direction seemed to startle the man, and Kingston saw the instant flash of fear in his eyes. It was the last thing he saw before he heard the crack of the gunshot that pierced the stillness of the night.

In that split second, Kingston braced himself to feel the pain of a gunshot wound. The man, too, seemed to be waiting for the desired effect. Finally, Kingston felt the heat of the bullet, which had pierced his upper left arm. He reacted instinctively then.

In a blind fury, he rushed the man, sending him barreling backward.

"King!" Bree got out of the car, crying frantically.

Caught off guard, the man recovered quickly. He lifted his arm to fire again, but in a flash, Kingston was on him, punching him in the face with all his might. That punch was followed by another. King was on top of him, struggling for the gun, punching him in what felt like a frenzy to both of them. The man fought back, using all his skills as a boxer and an army veteran to fend off the blows. He tried to get the gun angled toward King so that he could fire again, but King was straddling him, overpowering him easily. He finally wrested the gun out of the older man's hands.

Still crying and screaming near the passenger side of Noah's car, Bree stood frozen. Her cell phone's ringing snapped her out of the hysteria momentarily and she anxiously reached for it.

"DAD! OH MY GOD! PLEASE GET HERE! KING'S CAR BROKE DOWN AND THIS MAN JUST SHOT HIM!"

King was raining down blows on the old man with the gun he now held in his own hand. Pure rage overtook him as he pummeled the man who had dared to call him a nigger and suggest that he was a thief; this coward who had ambushed and shot him. This white man had him fucked up.

"AAAAHHHH!"

His voice was hoarse and deep, echoing down the tree-lined block. He hadn't realized that he had been screaming the whole time, taken over by a fear he hadn't known existed within him until now. The pain in his left arm was impossible to ignore at this point. He relented, finally realizing how close he had come to being killed, how lucky he was to be alive. He stopped hitting his assailant, and his gaze fell down that same street he had looked down moments earlier. The road home seemed like an impossible journey now.

"KING!" Bree yelled out again. "King, stop! Please!"

Kingston hovered over his now helpless assailant, but he was aware that some of the neighbors had spilled out of their homes during the encounter. He stood quickly, still holding the gun, and stepped away from the bleeding old man sprawled across the concrete beneath him. The man who had just tried to kill him.

"Call 911," King said to Bree, his voice raspy and hoarse from yelling.

His hands were also shaking. He was in shock, although he didn't know it. Slowly, he began to emerge from the mental fog he had been in. He set the gun down slowly on the pavement. His arm hurt like hell, and he felt dazed, slowly becoming aware that chaos had ensued around them. Suddenly, the whole neighborhood seemed to be outside. He could hear voices shouting now, panicked and loud. He blinked, and his eyes felt heavy. It felt like he might pass out. The mixture of pain, adrenaline, fear, and rage was a toxic cocktail for his young body. He wanted to cry but decided that was a waste of his energy.

Bree was at his side now, asking him if he was all right.

"He shot you," she said, dazed. "Oh, my God, King. We gotta get you to the hospital."

Kingston's senses were all operating in slow motion. He heard police sirens blaring as they pulled up. Feet were rushing toward him now. Lights shined in his face. People were talking to him, shouting at him, but he couldn't respond. Couldn't really make out the words that they were saying to him and to each other.

One of the cops rushed toward them and grabbed Bree roughly by the arm, yanking her away.

Kingston felt his knees buckle slightly, and all he could think about was how much trouble he was in.

"He shot me!" he yelled. "He shot me!"

His mouth wasn't moving as he wanted it to. He had a busted lip and his mouth was bleeding from the fight with the old man. He put his right hand up and opened his mouth to tell them again that he was shot. But by then, all he saw was the rush of feet running in his direction. He felt the blow of fists as the police descended on him. He could hear Bree screaming in the background. She was begging the officers to stop, telling them that they were hurting him, pleading with them to listen. But there was no reasoning with the cops. They beat him with their sticks until the pain became too much. Kingston winced, his eyes closed, and the whole scene faded to black.

Black and Blue

Ivy sat in the passenger seat of James's car as they exited the highway, laughing at his impression of her.

"You had that blackjack dealer *shook*! Talking 'bout, '*You better not throw another hard hand over here. I know that!*'" James cracked up. "You're no joke."

Ivy looked at him, grinning. "I'm glad you know!"

She had won big at the casino and already had plans for the money. She wanted to get Noah a nice watch for his upcoming birthday. Now she wouldn't need to dip into her savings to pay for it.

"I think I might like you, James. You're lucky for me."

She patted her purse for good measure. As she did that, she felt her cell phone vibrate inside. She had turned the ringer off hours ago while they were at the tables. She reached inside to answer it. To her surprise, she saw Deja's number on the screen.

"Hello?"

James turned down the volume on the radio.

"Ivy!" Deja's voice was dripping with angst.

"What's wrong?" Ivy could tell instantly that something wasn't right.

"Bree just called me. She told me King's car broke down near my house. Some neighbor came out and confronted King and they got in a fight. Bree said that the man shot King."

Ivy's heart dropped. Instantly, she felt her pulse racing with the worst thoughts.

"Deja!" she yelled. "Oh my God!"

She glanced at James, panic written all over her face.

"He's all right, Ivy! Bree said King fought the man and got the gun away from him. Then she hung up. Now I'm calling and she's not answering. Me and Rashid are on our way there now. You gotta meet me there."

Ivy was barely aware of the tears streaming down her face as she listened to Deja rattle off the details of where Bree said the car had broken down. Ivy looked at James, shaking her head, unable to speak. James looked back at her, concerned. It was clear that something was terribly wrong.

"Deja, what are you saying to me? Somebody shot my son?" she demanded.

Deja was suddenly crying, too. "I don't know, Ivy. Bree won't answer her phone anymore. But I'm on my way there. I'm just a few minutes away."

Ivy hung the phone up and looked eagerly at James. "Something happened to King. I gotta get to Huguenot Avenue."

Without a word, James floored the gas and sped in that direction. He gripped her hand, giving it a reassuring squeeze.

"Please, God," Ivy prayed out loud. "Please let my baby be all right."

Bobby arrived at the scene and rushed anxiously toward the melee. He pulled out his shield and identified himself as an

NYPD sergeant. The officers on location parted and let him through.

The scene was partly roped off now to keep neighbors from interfering. He saw an older white man being wheeled away on a stretcher, his neck in a brace. Then his eyes rested on a sight that stopped him in his tracks.

He saw sixteen-year-old Kingston, lying in a bloody heap on the ground. He was unconscious and bruised, with paramedics tending to an ugly wound on his left arm. Kingston's feet were shackled as he lay sprawled across the pavement.

Bobby found himself and rushed forward. As he grew closer, an officer charged in his direction with equal eagerness. They met each other halfway.

"Can I help you?" the officer asked Bobby.

Bobby had already determined that this guy was a captain, evidenced by the insignia he wore. Aware that the man outranked him, he politely identified himself.

"Hi, Captain. I'm Bobby Maddox, sergeant with the community affairs bureau and—"

"Thank you, Sergeant. This scene is still active. So, I'm gonna need you to step over there and I'll send one of the officers to speak with you in a minute."

"Daddy!" Bree called out.

He turned and found her standing among a huddle of officers a few feet away from where Kingston lay motionless on the ground.

Bobby rushed forward toward her. Bree ran and hugged him tightly, starting to cry.

"The man shot him," she said. "King didn't do anything wrong. He was just trying to figure out why the car broke down and the man came out of nowhere and started calling King a nigger and threatening him."

Bree's words rushed forth like a flood. Bobby did his best to keep up. He held her close to him and assured her that she was fine now. That she was safe.

"You stay here," he said. "I'm gonna find out what I can about King. Then I'll go with you to give your statement. I got you, baby girl. It's gonna be all right."

Deja turned the corner and her heart seized in her chest. All she saw before her was a road lit up with flashing lights. Police cars and an ambulance were on the scene of what looked like a horrible accident. The street was flooded with cops and paramedics.

"We gotta get out," Rashid said. "Park the car."

A uniformed officer approached her car on the driver's side and stated the obvious.

"You can't go this way, ma'am. There's an incident up ahead."

Deja spotted the back of Noah's car, the rear of it peeking out at an unusual angle as if it had been involved in a crash. She knew the car by the vanity license plates, "NOAHDON" on the back of his BMW. Deja threw the car in park and hopped out with Rashid right behind her.

Bobby got Bree comfortable in the back of one of the squad cars and turned to walk back toward where Kingston was still lying on the cold pavement. But he froze when he spotted Deja emerging from her car across the street. He waited expectantly. Then his heart sank as Rashid emerged from the passenger seat. Bobby's fists clenched as he stared furiously in their direction.

The officer stopped Deja. "Ma'am, I just told you that you can't go this way."

Deja pushed back at the officer, determined. "That's my daughter in that car!" she yelled. "Was there an accident?"

The officer shook her head. "The scene is under investigation. I need you to stay back."

Deja didn't listen. She rushed toward Noah's car but was quickly blocked by the officer.

"I'm not gonna tell you again. GET BACK!" she barked in Deja's face.

Deja stared at her, wanting to curse her manly ass out. Rashid touched her gently on her arm. He gestured with his head across the street where Bobby stood, staring back at them.

The expression on Bobby's face was indescribable. Too many emotions were present at once. Concern for Bree mixed with rage and heartbreak at the sight of Deja and Rashid emerging together from her car.

"Go talk to him," Rashid suggested. "I'll wait here and see if I can get any information on Bree and King."

Deja nodded and slowly walked across the street. She got to Bobby's side and looked at him, guilt written all over her face. She still had the scent and taste of Rashid all over her. But none of that mattered much now. Bree and King were in trouble and she needed Bobby's help.

"Bree called me frantic. She said that King's car broke down—"

"I told you not to let her go out with him."

Deja ignored him. That wasn't important at the moment. "Some neighbor came out and confronted him and pulled a gun on King." Deja got choked up just saying the words. "Now she's not answering my calls and—"

"She's fine. I just spoke to her."

Deja's eyes went wide. "Where is she? I need to see her."

Bobby looked at her coldly. "It's an active crime scene. They won't let you in."

Deja frowned. Bobby loved to flaunt his clout within the

NYPD. Now suddenly he was acting like he had to follow protocol to the letter.

"She's my daughter, Bobby. Get me in there."

He looked past her at Rashid. "You were with him tonight?" His gaze shifted to Deja accusingly. "While Bree was out with a thug, so were you."

Deja glared at him. She spoke to him through clenched teeth. "Bobby, this is not the time. I need to see Bree. Now." She choked back tears. "My daughter called me crying because her friend just got shot. Fuck your feelings right now. I need to see my child."

He scoffed and stared at her in disgust.

Rashid, frustrated that he was getting nowhere with the cops, walked over and joined them. His attempts to remain calm were failing. He approached Deja and Bobby, his expression serious.

"Excuse me," Rashid said, looking directly at Bobby. "No disrespect, but I need to see Bree. Check on King. I know you have some pull with these people. So, all of our problems aside, I'm asking you to let me see my daughter."

Bobby smirked at him, enjoying watching Rashid grovel.

"No disrespect," he repeated Rashid's words. "All you've been doing is disrespecting my family since you came back. Now you need my help?"

Rashid took a deep breath as Bobby continued.

"You keep calling Bree *your* daughter. But who did she call when she was in trouble tonight? Did she call you?"

Rashid stepped forward. "Where the fuck is my daughter?"

Bobby stepped forward, too. "Bree is fine. I told Deja that. She's with me. When I find out more, I'll let Deja know. You should get home. I know it's past your curfew."

Rashid saw the sneer in Bobby's eyes and wanted to beat the

shit out of him. He knew that if it wasn't for that badge and gun, Bobby would never have the heart to speak to him this way.

Their face-off was interrupted by a commotion behind them. Ivy had just arrived and was trying to fight her way past a group of cops who were holding her at a safe distance. She was shouting, flailing her arms and giving the officers hell.

Deja and Bobby rushed in her direction. "IVY!" Deja called out. "Ivy, calm down."

Ivy was having none of that. She charged in Bobby's direction, her expression desperate, tears falling with each step.

"Where is he? What happened?" she demanded all at once.

"Kingston is under arrest. He's hurt. That's all I—"

"WHAT . . . HAPPENED, BOBBY?"

Ivy shouted, her fists balled up in anger. If he didn't tell her something soon, she was prepared to whoop *his* ass out of pure frustration.

"Ivy, it's an active crime scene. They're not letting me get in there yet."

"What do you mean they're not letting you in? You're a fucking sergeant!"

"You gotta calm down."

"Don't tell me to fucking calm down! I need to know what happened to my son."

Bobby sighed and walked back toward the scene. Ivy was hot on Bobby's heels. As they grew closer, she saw Noah's car, saw Kingston lying on the ground. His mouth was gaping open, his eyes were half-closed, and dried blood clung to his ebony skin. Ivy took off running in his direction.

"KING!" she called out. "KING, OH MY GOD! WHAT HAPPENED?"

Her wails echoed down the block. Cops held her back, and she fought them with everything she had.

Bobby walked over to the captain and explained the situation. The captain followed him back over where Ivy stood, and Bobby introduced them.

"This is his mother," Bobby said. "She just got here, and she wants to know what's going on."

"Hello. Ma'am, if you calm down, I can tell you what's happening with your son," he said. His tone was flat and condescending.

Ivy could barely contain her rage, but she knew that she would have to be still for this son of a bitch to talk to her. And she desperately needed answers, needed to be allowed to get to her son. She stopped straining against the cops who held her back and stood reluctantly still. Rashid stood at her side, hoping to offer support. Ivy found none. She only wanted answers.

The captain addressed her at last.

"We're still getting all of the details. But, apparently, your son Kingston Donovan was caught breaking into a car, and a neighbor confronted him."

There was a pause. Ivy waited breathlessly for him to say more.

"Can you tell me how old your son is, ma'am?"

"Not until you tell me what happened to him. Why is he unconscious? Why is there blood all over him? *What the fuck happened to my son?*"

Ivy was tense. She felt her body physically quaking under the pressure.

The captain spoke again. "As I explained, he was confronted by a neighbor. We received a call at around twelve o'clock this morning and our officers responded to the report of a shooting. When they arrived, the officer discovered that a man had been pistol-whipped and left near death outside of his home. Our officers encountered your son here at the scene and found him standing next to the weapon—a Taurus 9mm handgun. I'm told that he resisted arrest."

"Resisted arrest?" Deja said the words like they tasted bad in her mouth. "King would never do that."

The captain seemed less convinced. "He fought our officers, and they had to use force to subdue him."

Ivy burst into tears, and Rashid did his best to comfort her. She wept loudly. Her knees felt weak, and her mind was racing. Her heart was beating so fast that she breathed deeper to avoid a heart attack.

"Why did they have to beat him like that?" Ivy asked. "He's sixteen years old. He's a kid!"

The captain glanced at Kingston's tall, imposing frame and wondered how a kid so young could look like that.

"The injuries you see are not just the result of the arrest. EMTs are treating him for a gunshot wound to his left arm," the captain said.

"Who shot him?" Deja demanded.

The captain looked at her, annoyance written all over his face.

"We're still investigating. The scene is still active. The detectives aren't even here yet. We don't know everything."

Bobby sighed. He looked at Ivy and tried to explain the procedure to her.

"When the detectives get here, they'll pull the camera footage from every house that has them. They'll interview all the neighbors and mark all the shell casings and voucher the car as evidence."

Ivy looked the captain in his icy blue eyes.

"My son is sixteen. He's lying over there on the ground SHOT! I need to see him."

All of them were distracted by the frenzy of the paramedics

loading Kingston into a waiting ambulance. Again, Ivy tried to rush to his side. Again, she was held back.

"You can meet us at Staten Island Hospital," the captain said. "By the time we get there, I should know more."

He turned and walked away, leaving Ivy trembling with rage and anxiety. She looked at Bobby, tears streaming steadily down her face.

"You've known my son since he was a little boy. And you're just standing there letting them keep me away from him. You're not even trying to help. I need to see my son! I need to know who did this to him. Can you help me or not?"

Ivy's chest heaved with fury.

Bobby looked at her, then he looked at Deja and Rashid and shook his head.

"Probably not," he said flatly. "King is in a lot of trouble. He should get a lawyer as soon as possible."

He looked at Deja. "I'm going to check on Bree. They're gonna take her in for questioning. I'll call you when we get to the station."

He shot a glance at Rashid, then turned and walked away, leaving all of them standing there helplessly.

Ivy locked eyes with James. "I need to get to the hospital."

James nodded. "Let's go."

Battle Lines

Ivy's face was streaked with mascara as she rushed into the hospital. James was right by her side.

A cop in plain clothes greeted them as they entered. He extended his hand to James. "Detective Paul Cunningham."

James shook the man's hand without enthusiasm.

"Are you the young man's father?"

James shook his head.

"I'm Kingston's mother," she said angrily. "I want to see my son!"

Detective Cunningham introduced himself to Ivy and offered her some weak words of comfort as he led them into a small room near the visitors' waiting room.

"Where is my son?" Ivy repeated.

"Kingston is in custody. He's under arrest for felonious assault and he's having emergency surgery right now."

Ivy collapsed into a seat nearby, weakened by the weight of all of this.

"Our detectives are on the scene right now conducting an

investigation. I'm here to speak with you to see if you can give us a little background on your son."

James looked at the detective. "Exactly what happened tonight?"

"Police were called to the scene of an apparent attempted robbery near the corner of Arthur Kill Road and Huguenot Avenue. From what we've been able to gather so far, a neighbor became suspicious about what looked like a car theft in progress. He encountered the suspected robber—your son Kingston. An altercation ensued, and Kingston produced a firearm and beat the man until he was unconscious."

Ivy closed her eyes, breathed deeply, and willed her heart rate to slow down. "My son doesn't have a gun."

"He had one tonight, ma'am."

Ivy glared at him. She didn't know what the fuck was going on, but none of it made sense.

"What kind of car was it?" James asked.

Detective Cunningham consulted his notes. "Black BMW."

"That's my son Noah's car. King's older brother." Ivy's voice was flat, but her anger was palpable. "So, King wasn't breaking into nobody's car."

The detective scribbled something on a sheet of paper. He cleared his throat.

"Our officers arrived on the scene, and your son resisted arrest. He was subdued with force."

"Did the cops shoot my son?"

"No. It appears at this point that prior to our officers arriving on the scene, there was a struggle of some sort between your son and a local homeowner. During that struggle, it seems that your son was shot. We're still in the early stage of our investigation, obviously. But we've spoken with some witnesses who gave us their account of what they saw."

"What is King's condition now?" Ivy demanded.

"In addition to the gunshot wound, your son suffered some lacerations to the head and torso during his fight with the victim. The doctors will tell you more about his condition when they finish—"

"I want to see my son right now." Ivy's tone was even as she spoke. She looked the detective in the eye unflinchingly.

"We'll let you see him as soon as possible, ma'am. He's sixteen, so as his mother, you'll be allowed to visit with him briefly after his surgery. It's pretty serious, so I think it's best that you let them do what they can to save your son."

The detective's tone was soothing, but the words still cut like a knife.

Ivy looked at James desperately. "Ivy, I know he's gonna be okay," James said.

Ivy stared at him in silence for several moments. Her eyes closed slowly, her breathing sped up, and her chest heaved. Tears flowed forth from her eyes like rain, but no sound escaped her mouth. She felt like the world had stopped spinning. Like life couldn't possibly be going on around them while her son's was hanging in the balance. She doubled over in pain, both physical and emotional, and cried from the depths of her soul.

The detective gave them space to digest the situation, moving quietly to the corner as James did his best to console Ivy. A nurse entered and gave them water and a blanket for her as Ivy sat trembling in the chair. James stood close to her, muttering comforting words that did little to ease the pain.

"He's alive. He's gonna be okay. King is strong."

Suddenly, Ivy seemed to summon strength from deep within herself. She glared through her tear-filled eyes at the detective who was watching them from across the room and addressed him.

"Who did this? Who confronted my son? Was it some white man?"

The question hung in the air like a noose.

Detective Cunningham cleared his throat. "Yes, ma'am. The victim is white. As I said, he's in surgery right now. He hasn't regained consciousness at all."

Ivy seethed. "You keep calling the white man a victim. But you say that my son is in police custody. If neither one of them has been conscious for very long, how did you come to these fucking conclusions of yours so fast? Huh? My SON is the victim! My son was shot and he's sixteen years old. HE'S THE FUCKIN' VICTIM!"

Ivy's voice boomed down the corridor.

"Mrs. Donovan, we're still trying to sort out what happened. We're relying on the testimony of several eyewitnesses right now. I didn't mean to be insensitive." He stepped forward a little. "Is it possible for us to ask you a few questions?"

The detective sat across from her, and Ivy stared at him impatiently.

"Did Kingston have permission to drive his brother's car?"

"Yes!" Ivy hissed.

"Do you know where Kingston was tonight? Where he was coming from or where he might have been going?"

Ivy gripped the towel in her hand so tightly that her hands ached. "He was out with his friends. He borrowed his brother's car for the night. He was probably on his way home." Her voice got softer. "I told him to be home by twelve thirty."

The detective was scribbling again. He continued his narrative.

"The nine-one-one dispatch received a call, and police were

on their way to the scene. In the meantime, a neighbor encountered your son. Asked him what he was doing. Apparently, they exchanged words. Witnesses state that your son produced a weapon, attacked the man, and that a fight ensued. They're saying that Mr. Currado fired the weapon at your son in self-defense."

Ivy shook her head. "That didn't happen. I know my son. He wouldn't attack anybody for no reason. And King doesn't have a gun. He's not that kind of kid."

Ivy glared at him, her blood pressure rising.

"That man attacked my son, and I want him arrested," she shouted angrily. "King would never break into a car. His brother let him drive his car while he was away this weekend. We live on Wycliff Lane. The car must have broken down while he was on his way home."

Ivy was seething. She stood and loomed over Detective Cunningham.

"This white man saw *my Black son* standing next to his own car and he made up his mind that he was up to no good. Right? And he approached him? Is that the story?" She laughed at the madness she was witnessing. "He shot my son, and now y'all have my son under arrest even though you've beaten him unconscious. Am I getting this right?"

She looked around the room at everyone in disbelief.

"My son wasn't stealing no damn car! And if he beat somebody half to death, it was in self-defense. If my son is under arrest, then I want the muthafucka who shot him arrested, too!"

Her voice echoed off the walls.

"Ma'am, I understand that you're upset. But please, have a seat. Let's talk for a minute, and maybe you can help me piece this thing together. I'm here to find out what happened."

Ivy felt like she was living in the Twilight Zone. It was clear as day what had happened. Her son was hurt, and she wanted justice by any means necessary. Reluctantly, she took a seat and exhaled. She wanted to fight. She wanted to finish off the man who had confronted her son. Wanted to hit this detective sitting calmly before her right now. Wanted to go to war with every racist cracker she had encountered since moving to this godforsaken borough.

"I *live* in the neighborhood. My son was probably just trying to get home. How can it be self-defense when my son is sixteen years old? How old is this man that shot him?"

Detective Cunningham stared back at her. "Like I said, I understand you're upset."

"You don't understand a damn thing about me. You don't know what it's like to get a call in the middle of the night that your son is in police custody, and I can't see him. To find out that some grown man shot your sixteen-year-old son . . . you don't understand shit."

Silence hung between them for a while. The door swung open, and a doctor entered, a South Asian man with a clean-shaven face who looked exhausted and triumphant at the same time. Ivy's heart rate surged.

He bowed his head in Ivy's direction. "My name is Dr. Golshan. Are you Kingston's mother?"

Ivy nodded wordlessly, her pulse racing.

"I've treated Kingston since he was brought into the ER. He is in stable condition."

Ivy sighed, relieved.

The doctor continued. "He has suffered a gunshot wound to the upper left arm. The bullet exited the body and doesn't appear to have caused any significant damage. He also suffered several blows to the head and there are bruises over his body. I'm afraid he has a few broken ribs and perhaps a concussion. But overall, I believe he will be fine. He also suffered some aftereffects from the force of the Taser, which we'll examine further once he's awake."

Ivy looked at James. "When did they mention using a Taser on my son?"

James shook his head. This was the first he was hearing about this, too.

The doctor continued.

"We've stabilized him, but he was in a lot of pain. We have given him some sedatives and medication to relieve the pain. But each time he has spoken to us, he has asked for you. Your son is a very strong and athletic young man. That will work in his favor as he recovers."

Ivy listened to the doctor describe Kingston's injuries. She was grateful that this seemingly kind and gentle man had been the one to care for her baby so far while being furious her son was suffering such horror.

"Thank you," she said, tears cascading down her face. "Can I see him, please?"

The doctor nodded, but the detective cleared his throat.

"Mrs. Donovan, I'll be happy to bring you to your son as soon as I ask you just a few more questions."

Ivy glared at him. She wanted to protest, but she suddenly felt weak, as if she might collapse at any moment. She had little strength left to fight.

"To your knowledge, is your son in any gangs, or has he had any recent run-ins with your neighbors?"

Ivy had to hold herself back from launching at him across the short distance between them.

"No."

James spoke up again. "King is a good kid."

"When did you move to the neighborhood?" Detective Cunningham pressed.

"Last year. In August." Ivy's fists clenched.

"And where did you move from?"

"Brooklyn."

"What was the reason for the move? Was your son in any trouble?"

"WHERE THE FUCK IS MY SON?" Ivy's booming voice echoed throughout the small room. "I'm not going to ask y'all again!"

Detective Cunningham stood at last. He apologized to Ivy, who was so angry now that it was taking great effort to calm her down. James rubbed her back, steadying her.

Dr. Golshan led Ivy and James out the door and down the long, cold hallway. Detective Cunningham followed at a reasonable distance. Ivy shivered as she walked, aware that James was still holding on to her. He hadn't really let go all night.

They followed the doctor down a seemingly endless hallway to a room at the end of the emergency wing. Detective Cunningham stopped them there.

"Kingston is under arrest. So, only his mother is allowed to see him at this time."

James nodded. Dr. Golshan looked at Ivy.

"Your visit with him will be brief," Detective Cunningham asserted. "One of our officers will remain in the room with you the whole time. I know that seems insensitive, but we have to follow procedure."

The detective and his officers wanted to make sure that no contraband was passed between the prisoner and his mother. They would be watching Ivy like a hawk the entire time.

James waited with Detective Cunningham as the doctor led Ivy to Kingston's room.

"As I said, Kingston has been given sedatives. So, he may not be awake for very long," the doctor explained.

Ivy nodded, stepped into the doorway, and peered inside. She paused, staring at the tall figure lying still on a gurney covered by crisp, white sheets that were stained with blood.

Kingston was sprawled on top of the hospital bed hooked up to an IV with blood everywhere. His right arm was shackled to the bed while his left arm was wrapped in a thick bandage. His left eye was red and swollen, and his nose was bloody. His mouth, too, was caked with dried blood. He was breathing on his own but unconscious.

"King!"

Ivy called out his name, hoping that he would turn to her and respond. Silence greeted her. Her hands flew up to cover her mouth. Her eyes searched his face and body, which was swollen and bruised. She thought about the life coursing through his young veins and reminded herself that he was strong. The reality of it all hit her with tremendous force as she neared his side.

His big Afro was fanned out beneath him like a halo. She stared at him and all his familiar details. His facial hair, his skin, his mouth. He lay silently before her, his body longer than the bed. Her eyes settled on the handcuffs that secured his right arm to the bed. They had her baby shackled like a slave. She felt the fury rise inside her again.

She looked at the lifeless expression on her son's face. She imagined the fear he must have felt in those fateful moments. Thought of how long it had taken her to get there. How alone he had been during that time. She tried to recall the very last thing he had said to her. Wondered how long it might be before he woke up again. All these thoughts flooded her mind as she stood crying at Kingston's side. Her body shook with the force of her sobs. But there was no sound. No words. Only silence.

Finally, Ivy closed her eyes, gripping Kingston's hand in hers, and prayed hard. She was so grateful that he was alive. But she was also mad as hell. She finished praying and looked down at her son.

"They won't get away with this," she whispered. "I swear."

Bree was in tears after being interrogated for hours at the police station. Rashid had agreed to join Ivy and James at the hospital where everyone was awaiting word on King's condition. Deja had finally gotten access to Bree without Bobby's help. Bree was a minor, and Deja was her mother. So, despite his insistence that Deja wasn't allowed into the crime scene, once they'd arrived at the precinct she had been by Bree's side without budging.

They left the interrogation room and found Bobby waiting for them in the hallway. Ignoring Deja, he looked at Bree.

"Are you okay?"

She nodded, although she felt far from okay. "Do you know anything about King? Is he all right?"

Bobby shook his head. "Last I heard he was in surgery."

"I want to go to the hospital," Bree said. "I want to be there when he wakes up."

Bobby sighed. "Bree, you need to get some rest."

Deja groaned. She sent Bree to get something to drink at a nearby vending machine. When they were alone, she looked at Bobby.

"I know you're pissed at me. Pissed at Rashid. But Ivy and King have nothing to do with this."

"I don't have a problem with Ivy and King," Bobby said. "My concern is about Bree. Always has been."

Deja shook her head.

"You stood there and did nothing while those cops kept King lying in the street like an animal. You told Ivy that the only help you can offer her is the advice to hire a lawyer. You're acting like you don't know King at all. Like he's just another one of those '*savages*' you and your other cops lock up every day."

Bobby laughed. "I do know King. I know who his father is, and what his future is probably gonna look like."

"Because you caught him having one house party?" Deja laughed, too, at the absurdity of it. "Now he's a criminal? The kid didn't resist arrest, Bobby, and you know that. They used excessive force on him. Bree saw it with her own eyes. The neighbor that confronted him was a racist. He called King a nigger and accused him of trying to steal a car. You could help clear all of this up. You brag all the time about all the power you have, but you're so mad at me that you'd rather let King suffer. And watching him suffer is making Bree suffer, too. But you're too selfish to care."

Bobby shook his head. "Don't talk to me about being selfish, bitch. You let me fall in love with you and your daughter. Build a life with you. And then you took it away from me. All of it. You, our daughter, our marriage. The second he came back, you changed. You don't give a fuck about me. So, why should I give a fuck about your friends?"

Bree joined them again with a Snapple iced tea in hand. Bobby smiled at her sympathetically.

"Get some rest, baby girl. Everything is gonna be all right."

He looked at Deja. "I'll be by later in the week to get the rest of my things. Tell Ivy I said good luck."

As he walked away this time, Deja felt the last of the love she felt for him fade away. She grabbed her daughter's hand, squeezed it tight, and led her out of the police station.

"I got you, Bree," she said. "Let's go see about King."

Coco was in bed with Ziggy, nestled in the curve of his arm. His morning woody pressed against her invitingly. She started to grind in his direction but was interrupted by her cell phone ringing. She reached forward and answered Ivy's call.

"Hey, girl."

Ziggy pulled her back into his embrace.

Ivy's voice was low and solemn as she spoke. "Coco, there's been a . . . situation. I'm at the hospital. Kingston is under arrest. And he's been shot." It pained Ivy to say it out loud.

Coco abruptly pulled away from Ziggy. "What? What happened?"

She was out of bed now, her hand over her mouth, all air sucked out of her lungs in an instant.

"A man . . ." Ivy continued. "A neighbor thought King was breaking into a car. They had some type of confrontation. Somehow, King got shot. King then beat the man unconscious. Then the police came, and they beat King up really badly. They claim that he was resisting arrest. We're all at the hospital right now with him."

"My God!" Coco cried, fumbling the phone. She recovered it quickly, locking eyes with Ziggy. Her expression was one of pure horror. She wondered instantly whether this neighbor was one of the white racists Ivy had spoken of. Looking at Ziggy, she didn't feel comfortable asking the question. He looked at her and scrambled to the edge of the bed, concerned.

"Ivy, is anybody with you?" Coco's heart was pounding in her chest.

Ivy felt a headache setting in. "Yes. James is here. Deja and Rashid and Bree. Patsy's on her way. Can you get here? I really need you right now."

Coco was nodding, though it occurred to her that Ivy couldn't see that. "Yes. I'm coming. I'll be there soon."

They hung up and Coco locked eyes with Ziggy.

"Ivy . . . my nephew was arrested last night. He's been shot."

Ziggy was on his feet, frowning. "What?"

Coco rushed for her bag and ran into the bathroom to get dressed. She called out to him, telling him everything that Ivy had just told her. Her words came pouring forth quickly. He stared after her, then sprang into action. He asked for the name of the hospital and got busy. By the time Coco emerged from the bathroom, Ziggy was dressed and ready to go.

"Driver just pulled up." He pulled her close, hugging her tightly.

Coco cried, all the emotions she was feeling falling with her tears. She imagined the pain that Ivy must be feeling right now.

Ziggy held her, comforting her softly. And then together, they rushed to Staten Island.

Public Enemy

Noah stood against the wall in the hospital waiting room. The room was full of people, yet silent except for Aunt Patsy sobbing softly beside him.

"This ain't right," she kept saying over and over again between sobs. "They don't get to do this shit to him!"

Noah couldn't agree more, although he didn't respond. He wished that he could make it all go away. Suddenly, he felt like the man of the family, even more than he had his whole life in his father's absence. He had always felt a responsibility to set a good example for his little brother. To keep his head on straight so that King would do the same. Now, with King lying handcuffed to a gurney with a gunshot wound, Noah felt a responsibility toward his mother this time. To protect her and shield her from the pain she was suffering.

His two cousins, Brandon and Dashawn, stood near the door. A lady who had introduced herself as some hospital administrator and the doctor who had cared for Kingston when he'd arrived by ambulance were in an adjacent room speaking to Ivy in soft voices. Noah had heard them discussing insurance and ridiculous shit that seemed unimportant while his brother was handcuffed to a hospital bed with bruises all over his body. Noah was enraged, needed to yell at someone, to vent his frustration. For now, there were no words at all. Only his aunt's cries and the stir of the hospital staff and police hustling about.

Soon, even that was inaudible to Noah, replaced by a ringing in his ears. Tears flooded his eyes and his heart felt like it was figuratively *and* physically broken. A dull ache had taken residence in the center of his chest, and he felt weak because of it. But he kept standing there, unable to make any sense of anything. This couldn't be happening. Not to King. No way.

Noah's fists clenched involuntarily as rage built up inside him. Finally, the tears that had pooled in his eyes began to cascade down his cheeks. Overcome with sadness, hurt, and fury, Noah wept.

Patsy comforted him until his tears subsided. Noah sighed and turned to his cousins who were standing near the door.

"What breaks my heart is knowing that he almost made it home." He shook his head in disbelief. "He was right near our house. Like three or four blocks away!"

His voice cracked, pained by how close Kingston had come to making it home safely. He cried silently, then abruptly wiped his tears, sniffling back his pain.

Bree spoke softly.

"King didn't do anything wrong. I don't care what the cops say. I saw the whole thing. All he did was get out of the car to see if he could fix it. He was frustrated. Not acting crazy the way these so-called witnesses described. That man was a racist. And the only thing we were guilty of was driving a BMW and being Black in a white neighborhood."

Deja closed her eyes, exhausted both physically and emotionally. She rubbed Bree's back comfortingly. Rashid sat on the other side of their daughter, holding her hand.

While Bree was being interrogated earlier at the police station, Rashid had been on the phone with his parole officer. He wanted to get ahead of the situation since Bobby had mentioned it last night. He explained that he had been out past his curfew due to a family emergency. He called his job and told them that he wouldn't be at work for a couple of days while he made sure that his daughter was okay. He had gotten everything situated so that he could focus on the person most important to him. He squeezed Bree's hand and smiled at her. She laid her head on his shoulder and he held her close.

Detective Cunningham was back again. Patsy rolled her eyes at the sight of him. He introduced himself to Noah, explained that he was working on the investigation, and that he had a few questions for him.

"The man Kingston encountered tonight is named Vincent Currado. Do you know him? Ever run into him around the neighborhood?"

Noah shook his head. "I don't know too many of our neighbors."

"What about Kingston? Is it possible that he had a prior encounter with this man? Maybe there's some history between them?"

Noah shrugged, still hesitant to trust this man. The police were the reason his brother was hurt.

"Well, he owns a home in the vicinity of where he encountered your brother. His wife claims that they saw Kingston acting erratically in the street near the vehicle. That they watched him trying to pry the windows and doors open. And apparently when Mr. Currado confronted him, Kingston charged at him."

Noah stared the detective down.

"To your knowledge, was he involved with any gangs? Either when you lived in Brooklyn or since he moved to Staten Island?" Cunningham asked.

Noah exhaled deeply and looked at his aunt incredulously. "You hear this shit?"

Patsy shook her head, frowning, and glared at the detective. "So, let me guess. Now you're gonna try and make my nephew out to be the bad guy?"

Cunningham shook his head. "Not at all. These are questions that I have to a–"

"Is Vincent Currado in any gangs, Detective?" Patsy asked. "Is he in the mafia? Huh? Did you ask his wife that? Is he handcuffed to his hospital bed like this? That muthafucka is the one you need to be arresting. Not my nephew. King is the victim, you son of a bitch!"

She stared hatefully at Cunningham. Noah's glare was equally as menacing.

"If this Currado guy recovers, will he be arrested, too?"

The detective shrugged. "It depends on what we uncover during our investigation." He looked at Patsy compassionately. "I realize that this is a very difficult time for you and your family, but I assure you that we're doing a very thorough investigation."

Cunningham looked around to make sure that he had spoken to everyone present and established their relationship to Kingston. He looked at James.

"What is your name, sir?"

"James Marshall."

"And your relationship to Kingston?" Cunningham asked.

James shrugged. "I'm just a friend of the family. I met them not too long ago. A few weeks maybe. But I can tell you that King is a good kid. Not the kind to be breaking into cars or attacking some homeowner at random. King plays basketball, goes to school, and stays out of trouble."

Detective Cunningham nodded. "But, by your own admission, you haven't known him very long, right?" He jotted down something in his notepad.

Patsy sucked her teeth. "Well, I've known him since the day he was born," she said. "My nephew ain't no damn criminal. He's a good kid who would never do nothing crazy."

"You are Ms. Donovan's sister?" Cunningham asked.

"No," Patsy retorted sharply. "I'm his father's sister."

"And where is his father?" Cunningham stopped scribbling and looked at her expectantly.

"He's locked up."

Detective Cunningham was scribbling again. "I'm sorry, ma'am."

Patsy shook her head. "Y'all *are* sorry. This family has been through so much already. Now this!" She shook her head again. "It's too much."

Detective Cunningham finally left the room. Patsy sucked her teeth and watched him go.

James slowly walked out of the room and into the hallway. He needed a moment to collect himself and he felt like he should give the family a little space.

Rashid followed him out. "'Scuse me, brother. Can I talk to you for a minute?"

James stopped walking and turned to face Rashid. He hadn't seen the guy before, but he could tell that he was familiar to Ivy.

Rashid caught up to him and extended his hand in greeting. James shook it.

"I'm Rashid. Family friend."

James nodded. "Me, too. My name is James."

"J-Roc, right?"

James's smile faded. He looked at Rashid questioningly, then nodded slowly. "We met before?"

Rashid shook his head. "Nah. I just know who you are. That's all."

James's mind was in overdrive. He looked Rashid up and down, waiting for him to say more. Rashid stood there quietly.

"Okay. So, what's up?" James asked.

Rashid smirked. "Ivy's your lady?"

James wasn't sure how to answer that. Still trying to add this up, he tilted his head. "Who's asking?"

"Her husband is a friend of mine. He's asking."

James let that sink in. "Ivy and I just met not too long ago," he said. "We're still getting to know each other."

"What you wanna know?"

James didn't appreciate being interrogated this way. He knew that every word he said to Rashid would get back to Ivy's supposed ex. He could tell from the way Rashid was talking, standing, and looking him in the eye that he was from the streets. He knew enough about Ivy's past to discern that Rashid had already done his homework on him. Already knew his reputation and his movements. James knew that Rashid had an unfair advantage.

"If your friend has questions about what's going on, he should ask Ivy," he said.

"I'm asking you."

Both men stood face to face with their shoulders squared.

"This ain't the time for us to have this conversation," James said. "But I respect you delivering the message from Michael. You can tell him I heard it loud and clear."

Rashid smirked again. "I'll let Ivy know that you had to go. I'm sure she'll understand."

James stood there for a few more seconds, tempted to walk

back into the waiting room and stand his ground. But then he reminded himself that he had been seeing Ivy for just a few weeks. As much as he liked her, if she came with this much baggage, maybe it was best to walk away.

He stuck his hands in his pockets and walked down the hospital corridor toward the elevator bank. Something didn't feel right about leaving. He wasn't sure if it was his pride bothering him, telling him that he had just allowed Rashid to punk him. Or maybe it was the nagging voice in his head telling him that he shouldn't leave Ivy's side. He turned around and saw Rashid still standing there, watching.

Rashid waved at him sarcastically. James turned back around and walked on.

Weary

Nikki arrived to a chaotic scene at the hospital. Ivy was somewhere speaking with authorities while the rest of her family paced the floor of the waiting room, raising all kinds of understandable hell. Nikki spotted Deja and Bree sitting on cushioned chairs in a corner of the room, locked in what looked like a deep and serious conversation. Nikki walked over and joined them.

Bree stood up and hugged her aunt tightly.

"I got here as soon as I could. Are you okay?"

Nikki pulled Bree away from her and looked her over from head to toe, her eyes scanning her body for any scars or bruises.

Bree nodded. "I'm fine. King is the one who got hurt."

Nikki hugged her again. "Tell me everything that happened."

They sat together as Bree recounted the events. She was an emotional wreck, and Nikki and Deja did their best to soothe her as she spoke of the way the cops had beaten Kingston. Bree had always considered herself woke, but now she was closer to the fire than she had ever been before. Wearing a Black Lives

Matter T-shirt was one thing. But when the victim was someone you knew, it hit differently.

"He's gonna be okay," Nikki reassured her. "King is a strong boy. He kicked that man's ass because that man tried to kill him. If the cops do their job, he'll be off the hook in no time. All we need to focus on now is making sure he makes a full recovery."

She squeezed Bree's hand, lacing her fingers through her own. "You'll see."

Bree laid her head on her aunt's shoulder and cried softly. "Now I understand why some people hate the cops. The way they beat King . . . he didn't deserve that."

"No, he didn't," Nikki agreed. "Cops can be heroes sometimes. But they can be terrorists, too. They get on the force just so they can walk around with a gun and harass niggas. They hide behind their badges and bully us. Those are the kind of cops that beat King like that. Fuckin' animals!"

She glared at her sister. "Where the fuck is Bobby? Is he telling you anything?"

Deja shook her head. "When Bree called me last night, I was with Rashid."

Deja looked at her sister suggestively, and Nikki's eyes widened.

"*Okay,*" Nikki said.

"We rushed there together, and Bobby was right at the scene when we got there."

Nikki looked around for Rashid. Deja noticed.

"He went to get everybody something to eat."

Nikki nodded.

Deja continued. "Anyway, Bobby was upset."

Nikki's eyes widened. "I bet he was."

"He's not being very helpful." Deja's tone made it clear that was an understatement.

Nikki and Deja locked eyes, not wanting to say too much in front of Bree. Nikki shook her head.

"He's an asshole for that."

Deja groaned, gesturing at Bree.

"Fuck that!" Nikki said. "She's old enough to know what's going on. She's not dumb. Bobby's mad that Rashid is back. Fine. But he's known King his whole life. He's known Ivy for years. His beloved police department beat that boy senseless just because he was Black, and he kicked a white man's ass. Bobby's bitch ass should be bending over backward to help right now."

Bree agreed. "Every one of those cops that beat him should be arrested for what they did to him."

Nikki's eyes narrowed. "But that's not gonna happen. Don't even get your hopes up about that shit. Every time they attack one of us, kill us, or terrorize us, they get away with it. This time won't be any different. Watch!" She shook her head sadly.

Deja looked at her daughter. "Bree, don't you let their hate and their racism make you stop being who you are."

Bree nodded. Nikki smoothed her hair.

"I don't apologize for my Blackness," Nikki said. "Neither does somebody like King. Wearing that big Afro, being as big as he is, taking up space—that shit is intentional. And it's brave because it pisses white people off. It puts his Blackness right up under their noses where they can't ignore it. It makes them uncomfortable. '*How could this big Black guy have a car this nice?*' They don't like seeing us move into neighborhoods that they don't think we should be able to afford. They don't like to see Black kids like you going to private school with their kids, dancing ballet on the same stages as their kids. Subtly, there's a constant reminder to 'stay in our place.'"

Nikki looked at Bree seriously.

"I want you to make sure that you're constantly out of place. Make money they don't think you deserve; live in places they don't want you to be. Wear designer labels they don't think you should be able to afford. Succeed, live your life, and do it while being one hundred percent yourself."

Bree took in all of Nikki's wisdom, digesting it slowly as she sat there.

Nikki hugged Bree close to her, and her niece rested her head on her shoulder again. Nikki glanced sadly in her sister's direction. She knew that Deja hadn't lived her life on her terms. That she had spent the past several years trying to keep her voice down, trying to turn down the volume of her Blackness, to forget who she was. She hoped that her sister would find the nerve to take back her power, too. In whatever form that might take.

Ivy finally finished talking to the police and providing her insurance for Kingston's care. She couldn't believe they still wanted her to pay after all that her family was enduring at the hands of a racist neighbor and an overzealous police department. She walked into the waiting room toward her friends and family, looking drained and moving slowly.

To Deja, she looked like she had seen a ghost. She got up and rushed toward Ivy, her arms outstretched.

Ivy fell into her friend's embrace. "Don't worry, Ivy. He's gonna wake up soon asking about the playoff game. Watch."

Ivy managed a chuckle, though she felt no levity. She thought of her son's love of sports and wondered if he would ever be well enough to play again.

Dr. Golshan returned, searching for Ivy. When he found her, he looked at her with optimism in his eyes for the first time since they met.

"Your son has started regaining consciousness, Mrs. Donovan. I spoke with the police and they said that you can see him briefly. I think it will be good for him to see your face when he wakes up."

The whole room erupted in applause and Ivy smiled for the first time in hours. Eagerly, she followed the doctor down the hall to King's room.

She stepped into it, nodding a greeting at the cop stationed inside. She told herself that this cop was just doing his job, and if she wanted to see her son, she knew that she had to play nice with them as much as possible.

Ivy set her bag down on a table near her son's bed and began gently fluffing the flimsy pillow beneath his head. She pulled the sheet up to his waist, careful not to put pressure on his weakened body. She felt a lump in her throat as she eyed a bandage on his stomach where a little blood had begun to seep through. She rubbed his legs and massaged his feet, hoping to get a reaction out of him. But Kingston just lay there, still. Finally, she sat down beside him and sighed.

She tugged at his ear, something that always got a reaction out of him when he was alert. Usually, when she did it, he reacted by tilting his head in that direction, tickled by the sensation of his earlobe being yanked on. She did it impulsively, in that way that only a mother knew about her child. Knew what made them respond. It didn't disappoint.

Kingston's body twitched, his head tilting toward his right, where his mother tugged again at his ear. He groaned, the shock of any movement sending pain coursing through his body. His eyes slowly fluttered open, and Ivy cried tears of joy.

"King! It's me, Mama! I'm here, baby. You're okay."

Kingston's vision was blurry, but he managed to make out the teary-eyed, smiling face of his mother. He fought to smile despite the pain. The result was a grimace that made Ivy wince as well.

Kingston's hands clenched, and he turned toward the IV in his arm, then at his shackled right arm, confused. He tried to sit up, but the pain sent him backward against his hospital bed. Groaning, he looked at his mother helplessly.

"Ma. What happened?"

She shook her head. "You tell me," she whispered anxiously. "Deja called me. She told me the cops arrested you. They said that you were breaking into a car and some man—"

"He called me a nigger."

Kingston tried to fill in the blanks. The memory of it all came flooding back to him now. Standing by his brother's car, angry. Bree in the passenger seat. The voice in the dark, calling him that vile word. The struggle for the gun.

Beating that man . . . the flash of the police lights . . . the rush of adrenaline and the pain of their sticks and Tasers.

He looked at his hand again. It wasn't making sense. "Why they got me 'cuffed up?"

His speech was slurred, his lips swollen after the beating he had endured. His words came out slowly because of the medication.

Ivy shook her head. "Tell me what happened, King."

"He called me a nigger, and then he pulled a gun out on me. He pulled the trigger."

Ivy closed her eyes against the pain of that.

"He shot me. But I went into survival mode. I started fighting him."

Ivy listened anxiously, hanging on his every word, every groan, as he retold the story. She tried to imagine it as he spoke, horrified by what her son had endured and survived.

Kingston groaned again, determined now to lie still to avoid feeling the stabbing pain of several cracked ribs.

"He tried to fight me back, but I fucked him up. 'Scuse me, Ma. I'm sorry . . ."

Ivy laughed. "That's okay. Keep going." She was grateful that Kingston had fought for his life and won.

"Tell me what happened when the police came."

Kingston tried to remember. "The neighbors . . . they started coming outside. They said they called the cops on me. I was still holding the gun."

He shook his head and looked at his mother. In his eyes, Ivy saw the innocence of a child who had been faced with a very adult situation.

"I put the gun down. And I was talking to Bree. She was saying that her parents would be there soon. I was in a lot of pain from the gunshot. Them cops jumped on me. Started kicking me, punching me."

Ivy glanced at the cop in the corner and knew that King needed to watch what he said.

"Okay," she said. "That's all—"

"I tried to explain what happened, but they just jumped on me. They . . ." He looked at his hand again. "They arrested me?"

His mother nodded with tears in her eyes. "Yeah," Ivy managed. "The man is in a coma."

Kingston shook his head again. "Nah. He tried to kill me for no reason. I was just pissed off because the car broke down. That man had no reason to come outside his house."

He winced again, pain coursing through his body.

"That's enough for now, King. Relax." Ivy stroked his dark brown skin, ran her fingers through his hair.

"You think I could go to jail for this, Ma?" Kingston's voice was small and childlike as he asked the question.

Ivy shook her head, defiant. "Over my dead body."

Ivy returned from King's room and gave everyone an update. She sat in the waiting room surrounded by her friends and family.

James walked into the waiting room and saw that everyone was still there. He smiled.

"Good," he said. "I know y'all must be hungry."

Ivy looked up and smiled at the sight of James and his brother Patrick standing with arms full. They carried bags filled with food Patrick had cooked and brought over for Ivy and her family.

Rashid, seated nearby talking to Nikki, looked up and made eye contact with James. He frowned, but James offered him a smile in return and focused his attention on Ivy once again. He walked over to her and handed her a plate he had prepared especially for her.

"I know you don't eat pork, so I made sure this one don't got none on there."

She took it and thanked him. He sat down next to her and she hugged him, ignoring the glances of her family and friends.

"Thank you, James. I appreciate this."

"Don't thank me. I wish I could do more. How's King?"

"He's awake, thank God. Dr. Golshan said he's gonna be in pain for a while, but he'll be fine. Now we just gotta worry about getting the charges against him dropped."

James nodded. "That'll happen soon, hopefully."

He noticed Rashid eyeing him from across the room. He looked away and saw Noah glaring at him also from where he stood.

"I'm not gonna stay," James said, looking at Ivy again. "You need to be with your family right now. But I'll be back in the morning with some more of Patrick's cooking. And Cheryl's sister works here. She's a nurse in the cardiac unit, so you give us a call if King needs anything. I just want you to know you're not by yourself."

She wanted to kiss him. Would have, if they had been alone. Instead, she took his hand and squeezed it tightly.

"Thank you, James. For real." She laughed. "I know you must be thinking this is a lot. You just met me, and our first date ends with my son getting shot."

Ivy was laughing, but she wanted to cry. This was exactly the type of situation she had been working her ass off to avoid. Moving her sons out of Brooklyn was supposed to be a good thing. Buying a home on a tree-lined cul-de-sac and driving luxury cars was supposed to be the stuff dreams were made of. Instead, she was living a nightmare.

He grinned. "I just met you, but I feel like I know you well enough at this point to say that you're an amazing woman. You have two great kids who love you. And this ain't your fault. It ain't King's fault."

He kissed her hand.

"And when all this is said and done, we'll get a do-over on our date."

Ivy smiled. "That's a deal."

He stood to leave, then turned back to her once again. "Call me if you need to talk. See you in the morning."

Ivy watched James and Patrick leave. She thought about Mikey and how she would have a lot of explaining to do when they spoke again.

"Jesus," she whispered under her breath. "Give me strength."

Rashid followed James out of the waiting room. This time,

James was standing there, anticipating his arrival. Patrick waited by the elevators.

"Surprised to see you back here," Rashid said.

James smiled. "I went and did some research on you, too. Since you know so much about me, I figured I should know about you. I found out you just came home a few months back. You did fifteen."

"Sixteen total," Rashid clarified.

James nodded. "You got your daughter. Lost a lot of time with her. So, I'm sure you understand how valuable time is."

Rashid nodded.

"Your friend is away. From what I understand, there's a good chance he's not coming home anytime soon. Meanwhile, Ivy's out here with two sons on her own. Trying to keep them alive and on track. For years, she's been doing it by herself. And she's tired of it. She's human. She wants to live her life and find love again. Have a family, travel. All that shit we dreamed of when we were locked up north."

Rashid stared back at him.

"I started to walk away after our conversation earlier. Leave Ivy alone, let her figure it out with her sons on her own. But then when I left, it didn't sit right with me. So, I want you to give your friend a message for me. Tell him that I really like Ivy. I'm not trying to waste her time. I'm definitely not trying to be a father to his kids. I got three sons of my own. But since you ran my credentials, I'm sure you know about me. I don't play games. I put in work. And I would make sure that Ivy and her sons are okay. That she's happy." James nodded. "You tell Michael I said that."

Rashid stared at him, expressionless. He thought about the things Mikey had asked him to do to this nigga when he found him. He understood the desperation his friend felt at the thought of losing his family. But, as he stood listening to James, Rashid realized that this guy might not be bad for Ivy. It was obvious that he cared for her. And for her sons.

"Respect," Rashid said. "I'll give him the message."

James walked away, and this time, he didn't bother looking back.

Coco and Ziggy arrived at the hospital and rushed toward the wing Ivy had described to them on the phone. Ziggy squeezed her hand tightly, his mind racing.

Deja spotted them as she emerged from the restroom and rushed down the hall in their direction. The friends embraced, and Deja greeted Ziggy. Coco locked eyes with her.

"How's Bree?"

"She's okay. They didn't hurt her. But the cops beat King up pretty bad."

In a hushed voice, she explained to Coco what had taken place.

In her retelling of the chaotic events, she mentioned the fact that the neighbor was white. Coco glanced at Ziggy sidelong, wondering if he realized the significance of that particular detail.

"Ivy's been really strong," Deja said.

"James—the guy Ivy was telling us about at lunch—he's been so good to her this whole time. He's really nice. His brother is a chef and brought food for everybody. And the brother's wife—her name is Cheryl—she has a sister who's a nurse here. So, she's been filling Ivy in on what's happening behind the scenes. What the police and doctors are saying behind closed doors. We found out that the guy who King had the altercation with is admitted here, too. They brought them both to the same hospital."

Coco nodded, digesting the information. She glanced around anxiously.

"Where is everybody now?"

"In the waiting room."

Deja led the way in that direction. Ziggy followed closely behind them. They entered the waiting room and Nikki greeted them first.

"Ziggy!" She hugged him. "It's good to see you even if it's under fucked up circumstances."

She left him standing there as she sat down nearby to eat her food.

Coco made the rounds to everyone and hugged Ivy tightly. Next she greeted Noah and pulled him into a warm embrace.

"You okay?" she asked gently.

He nodded. He hadn't stopped staring at Ziggy since the moment they had walked in.

"Who is this? King's lawyer?"

Coco shook her head. "No," she said. "This is Ziggy. He's my friend."

Ziggy smiled weakly and said hello.

Noah nodded at him, watching him with suspicion now. Ziggy stood there, feeling out of place. Being here, he suddenly realized how serious the situation was. He had seen the police and the swarm of detectives in the lobby. Now, being the only white person in the room, he felt like he should go. He was grateful when Coco looked in his direction and excused herself from the activity for a moment. She approached Ziggy with a blank expression on her face.

"You should go," she whispered, as if reading his mind.

She hoped that she didn't need to explain any further. Her friend and her family were in distress.

"I'm going to stay with Ivy. Maybe for a few days if I have to. I'm sure she's . . ." Coco was at a loss for words.

Ziggy nodded quickly. "I understand. Just, please let me know what I can do. Anything you need."

Coco kissed his cheek, thanked him, and watched him leave.

On his way to the door, he encountered Patsy. She had just come back from a trip to the bathroom and nearly knocked him down as he approached the doorway.

"Who are you? Another detective?"

Deja and Coco both rushed over at the same time.

"He's with me," Coco explained.

Patsy looked him up and down suspiciously. "Oh. *This* is your little friend, huh?" She scoffed. "Well, this is a family gathering. I don't think you should be here right now."

Coco opened her mouth to speak, but Ziggy beat her to it.

"I was just leaving." He walked out the door without another word, leaving Patsy scowling after him.

She directed her glare at Coco next.

"You a fool, little sister! Them crackers want to fuck around with us and all that. But they'll gun your sons and brothers down without question." Patsy's glare was cold and hard.

Coco rolled her eyes and walked away.

Deja glowered at Patsy. "You know I'm half white, right?"

Patsy sucked her teeth. She had never particularly cared for Ivy's prissy little friend.

"*Half,* bitch! That's what you need to remember. Your mama's Black. At the end of the day, you a nigga to them, too."

Patsy scoffed and walked away toward her sons, still mumbling to herself. "'Half white.' Like that's something to be proud of!"

Patsy looked at Ivy. "They're running a smear campaign against y'all. They're not trying to give King a fair trial. One of your neighbors was on the news saying that y'all never tried to fit in. They said you're not friendly and that y'all always come through with your music blasting in your cars. They said that King was always coming around with large groups of boys that looked like a gang."

Noah balked. "King ain't in no gang."

Patsy continued her rant. "They got pictures from his Instagram."

She looked at her sister-in-law regretfully. Patsy and Ivy were both tough mothers. It was one of the few things they had in common. So, knowing that, Patsy knew full well that what she was about to say would set Ivy off. She sighed.

"They got pictures of him smoking weed out of a bong with a few of his friends, and a picture of him with a beer bottle in his hand."

Ivy frowned. She had never thought to follow her sons' social media accounts. She thought she hovered over them enough physically, so she didn't need to do it virtually, too. Now she felt stupid, hearing that King's wild teenage antics were being twisted to paint him as a problem child. She looked at Noah helplessly.

"Ma . . . I don't have no pictures like that on *my* Instagram page."

"What about Facebook?" Patsy pressed.

Noah side-eyed his aunt.

Ivy felt a lump in her throat and a sense of intense doom. It felt like the walls were closing in on them. Now, she dreaded the results of the toxicology tests the doctors had performed on King immediately following the altercation.

Patsy had her hands on her hips and a frown on her face.

"Let's stop fronting. These white people out here don't want to tell the truth, so they're starting to spread a bunch of lies. That man saw King out there. All tall and Black with his Afro. Out there with that nice car in that nice neighborhood. He made up his mind that he was a fuckin' thug, and he went out there and tried to hunt him down. He thought he'd shoot some nigga and get away with it. And, instead, that nigga beat his ass!"

"Patsy—" Coco closed her eyes as she said it, suddenly feeling a headache coming on. She was sick of her sister's loud mouth.

"No, 'Patsy,' my ass. It ain't no fun when the rabbit gets the gun. King defended himself, and unfortunately, the man got fucked up. Now they trying to make it seem like he's a bad kid, and that's bullshit!"

Patsy was sick of beating around the bush.

"I'm not trying to tell you what to do, Ivy. But if King was my son, I would kill somebody before I let them railroad my baby. Dead ass."

Patsy walked away before Ivy could respond. It didn't matter. Ivy had no words left, anyway.

It was late in the evening. Patsy and her sons had gone back to Brooklyn. Noah had gone home to take a shower. Rashid had to get back to adhere to his curfew. Bree was curled up asleep in one of the waiting room chairs.

Alone now, Ivy, Deja, Coco, and Nikki sat in silence for a while until finally, Ivy looked up at them and spoke, her voice hoarse from hours of yelling and crying.

"I don't know how to just . . . how can anybody expect life to go back to normal ever again after all of this? Even if everything gets cleared up and they let King go? Am I supposed to just act like nothing happened? Somebody tried to kill my son. And when he wasn't successful, the cops came and tried to finish the job."

Deja's eyes filled with tears as she imagined the worst.

Ivy continued.

"Just because he was Black. Just because they decided that my son didn't belong in such a nice neighborhood. That if he was touching a fancy car, that he must have been trying to steal it. As hard as I work! As tough as I am on my kids to do the right thing. Some grown old-ass man approached my teenage son and called him a nigger. Then he pulled out a gun and tried to shoot and kill my child."

That truth hung in the air like a thick, heavy fog. Nikki locked eyes with Ivy and felt the pain she saw there.

Tears fell from Ivy's eyes, and she shook her head, looking away.

"When I moved out here, I was looking for my little piece of the American Dream. That's what we all want. Right?"

It was a rhetorical question, but Ivy looked at her friends expectantly nonetheless. Each of them nodded.

"I work hard. I pay my taxes. I keep my sons out of trouble. I handle my business, and I'm out here raising young men who have respect. And even though I go to work every day and mind my business, somebody shot my son because his car broke down in a white neighborhood. IN NEW YORK CITY! Not some backwoods Southern town. They've been staring at us like we're exhibits at the zoo since the day we moved in. And I tried to just shrug it off. Tried to pretend like it wasn't happening. Because that shit is just another part of life for Black people." Ivy was yelling now.

Deja futilely tried to calm her with gentle whispers of reassurance, but it was no use. All the rage that Ivy had been feeling for the past several hours was boiling over.

"I used to sit in that big-ass house I bought and read the local newspaper. *The Staten Island Advance.* And I noticed the difference in how they report the stories. The white boys who crash their cars into a pole while they're high out of their minds on opioids—that's on page sixteen. And they don't release his name because he's a minor. But a Black kid the same age from the projects who got caught with an ounce of weed—he's on page one. His full name, picture, and everything."

Ivy's eyes were wide with amazement and disgust as she

spoke. Deja, Nikki, and Coco sat enraptured, hanging on her every word.

"And I told myself that I was overreacting," she continued. "That I was just being too sensitive. It was probably just part of getting used to a new neighborhood. This was supposed to be my new normal. I warned my sons about how different things are out here compared to Brooklyn. Told them to keep their eyes open and stay on point. And we all just went on with life. I kept working, kept grinding, even tried to go out and find a little romance after all these years."

She laughed maniacally.

"I fooled myself into believing that I could have it all. As a Black woman in this country! That I could have success in my career, commas in my bank account, a nice house and car, maybe even find love. Be happy. But that shit is never really possible for us. That American Dream shit is an illusion that I allowed myself to believe in. Now my son is lying in here on a fuckin' gurney with his ribs broken and his head cracked open. And I feel responsible for it."

"NO!" Coco yelled it louder than she meant to. "No, Ivy, I'm not gonna let you do that to yourself. This is not your fault."

She was pointing at Ivy, her expression serious.

Deja agreed. When she spoke, her voice was barely audible.

"Ivy, if anybody's to blame, it's me. I'm the one who convinced you to move out here. I sold you that house. And from the second you got here, it's been one situation after another with your neighbors."

Deja dabbed at her tears, weighed down by her guilt. It wasn't just the fact that she had encouraged Ivy to move here. It was the secrets she had kept from her as a friend. Like Kingston's party when the neighbors had called the police. Deja wondered now whether keeping Noah and King's secret had been the smartest move.

"A few weeks ago, me and Bobby caught Noah and King having a house party with a bunch of their friends. It was the night of Nikki's party. We went by there to pick up Bree after we left the party. And when we got there, the house was full of kids. Music blasting, alcohol, weed. Some of the neighbors called the cops."

Ivy frowned.

"Of course," Nikki said dryly.

"Bobby showed them his shield and squashed the whole thing. I promised the boys that I wouldn't tell you. I chalked it up to typical kid shit. But you're right. We don't have the luxury of our kids doing typical teenage shit like having house parties, getting high, or underage drinking. For white kids, that's a 'mistake.' For our kids, it can be a death sentence." She looked at Ivy apologetically. "I'm sorry."

Coco stared at her, dumbfounded. "Don't you start blaming yourself, either." Coco felt like she was stuck in a nightmare she couldn't awaken from. "How is it possible that this . . . racist son of a bitch . . . tries to kill Kingston and we sit here and find ways to blame *ourselves*?"

She looked at Ivy. "You need to think positive. King would be so upset to hear you speak like this. This boy loves you with all his heart. He wouldn't want you finding reasons to blame yourself for wanting a better life for you and your children. *That's* why you moved out here. King is thriving out here. He likes his school. He's making friends. Him and Noah had a party. So fuckin' what? If it was any other house on the block, those neighbors would have ignored it. They know what happens when they call the cops on Black people. I'm just glad that Bobby was there."

Ivy nodded. "I am, too." She looked at Deja. "Thank you."

"Don't thank me yet. Bobby stopped taking my calls now, so we might have lost our NYPD insider. Ever since he saw me and Rashid together, he's on his Blue Lives Matter bullshit."

Ivy frowned. She had noticed that Rashid was around all day and that Bobby was absent. But she had been too preoccupied with other things to comment on it.

"Are you two breaking up?"

Deja shrugged. "I don't know what happens next. Right now I'm not sure if I care."

Everyone's eyes widened hearing her say that. Deja's marriage had been as much a part of her identity as her pretentiousness for years.

"I love the life we built with Bree. But I don't love Bobby anymore. I had to admit that I've been miserable for a long time. I thought having the picture-perfect life would make everything fall into place. For a while, it did. I thought I was happy. Then Rashid came back on the scene, reminded me of who I used to be. The things I wanted out of life."

"Things like what?" Coco asked.

"Like real love," Deja said. "Back when I was with Rashid, he excited me. Seeing him walk into a room got me hot. Hearing his voice—all of that excited me. He wasn't predictable, though. I could never really get too comfortable with him. There was always the threat of some rival drug dealer, the cops, other girls who wanted his attention. Being with him kept me on my toes. Then he got sent away and I decided not to gamble like that again. I chose the sure thing. Bobby lives his life inside the boundaries. He loves me way more than I love him. I was able to get comfortable with him. But the downside is that I haven't been excited in years. He doesn't give me that feeling of being swept off my feet. He never did."

Nikki smirked. None of this, of course, was news to her. "So, you think you want to be with Rashid now?"

"No," Deja said. "Not really. I don't even think it's about Rashid. It's about me settling for a mediocre life and then being bitter watching you live an amazing one."

Nikki smiled. "Sounds like you've been doing some self-reflection, Deja."

Deja grinned. She looked at Ivy.

"I thought the way to achieve the life I wanted was to conjugate my verbs in standard English and rub elbows with the right people. I thought all of us were immune to bullshit like this because we'd 'arrived.' But none of us are immune. Black men, Black women, Black kids, Black cops . . . to them we're 'still nigger,' like JAY-Z said."

Ivy nodded.

Coco sighed.

"It has me wondering if a white guy like Ziggy could ever really understand how it is for us. When I got the call about what happened to King, he was so supportive. We rushed here and found out all the details from Deja. And then the shit got uncomfortable. His whiteness stuck out in this situation. Patsy said it, but everybody in the room was thinking it. When I told him that he should go home, I could sense how relieved he was. So, is that what it's gonna be like? When some racial shit goes down, we run from it?"

Ivy thought about it. "To be fair, you just started seeing him. This is a heavy situation to deal with in the early stages of a relationship."

She thought about James, pleasantly surprised by the fact that this hadn't scared him off. At least not yet.

Deja agreed.

"What's the alternative? You go back to dealing with emotionally unavailable Black men who waste years of your life stringing you along the way Derek did? Do I go back to dealing with a Black man who has a felony on his rap sheet because he's the kind of guy I'm most attracted to? Does Ivy go back to being lonely and single just so she can keep an eye on her sons twenty-four/seven? Why the hell do Black women have to make choices like that?"

Nikki clapped her hands. "Preach, sis!"

"Seriously, Ivy," Deja said. "What's the next step? What happens now?"

Ivy sighed. "The lawyer is gonna call me in the morning. I'll find out then."

"What about your house?" Coco asked. "You think you'll sell it and move someplace else?"

"Part of me wants to do that. The other part feels like that's letting them win. Should I leave the house of my dreams because my neighbors are a nightmare?"

"I don't think you should leave, Ivy," Deja said.

"She can't keep living over there in that fuckin' fishbowl with her sons," Nikki pointed out. "She needs to move. The tension in her neighborhood was already thick. Now the white people on this fuckin' island are gonna be coming after Ivy and her sons with pitchforks and tiki torches."

"But if she leaves, they win. They get their neighborhood back and the message goes out that Black people aren't welcome there. Nothing changes. If you stay, you shake things up."

Coco nodded.

"I agree with Deja. If you leave, you give them what they

want. They don't get to decide who lives where. You worked hard all these years to give your boys the best life possible. And you're doing a great job. I know you're upset, but don't make any big decisions right now."

Coco rubbed her friend's hand reassuringly. "Everything is going to be all right. You'll see."

Ivy nodded, wishing she felt as certain.

Flip Side

When Deja and Bree got home, they noticed Bobby's car in the driveway. Both groaned inwardly at the sight.

They went inside, and Bree went quickly to her room. After the events of the past twenty-four hours, all she wanted was a hot shower and her own bed.

Deja found Bobby in the kitchen. He was leaning on the counter sipping a cup of coffee. Their eyes met as she entered.

"She okay?" he asked.

Deja was tempted to curse him out. Hours had passed since the shooting and Bobby hadn't called or texted either of them. For all he knew, Bree could have been in a padded room losing her mind after all she had been through. But Deja didn't curse or yell. She was past that.

"She's fine," she said.

Bobby cleared his throat. "A detective friend of mine got assigned to the case. Glover."

Deja looked at him eagerly, hoping he found out something she could share with Ivy.

"They're running ballistics on the gun and going door-to-door pulling camera footage across a four- or five-block radius. They're trying to create a time line of events. They'll see if they can spot the car as it got to the scene, see how it all went down minute by minute. So far, they got a bunch of footage to work with. The good news is that most of the homes have surveillance systems. It might take them a while to review all of it and piece it together. But if everything happened the way Bree said it did, this will all be over soon."

Deja closed her eyes and let out a deep sigh. She was exhausted physically, mentally, and emotionally. Spent.

"I can't forgive you, Deja. So, I don't know where we go from here."

Deja opened her eyes.

Bobby continued.

"I know you fucked him. Rashid. Even if you didn't, I know you want to. And that has nothing to do with him being Bree's biological father. That's all about you and your unresolved feelings for him."

She looked at him.

Bobby stared back at her. "So, you want to tell me the truth?"

Deja nodded. "Yeah. I do." They sat down at the table and she began. "I haven't been happy with you for a while. I wasn't happy with this marriage."

She looked him in the eye.

"I did fuck Rashid. And he's not the first man I cheated on you with. I cheated with one of my clients months ago. I've been lying to you, living a double life. Publicly, I was your doting wife. But behind your back, I was doing my own thing."

She could tell that he was furious as he listened. She didn't care. What he had done to King was unforgivable. The man she'd thought she loved once was dead to her.

"When Rashid came back, I think I rediscovered myself. I feel more like myself when I'm with him than I've felt in years. I don't have to fake it or pretend. And I like myself more. Bree and I have gotten closer. I think this marriage has run its course."

Bobby had pain etched all over his face. "So, you want to be with some guy that just spent sixteen years in prison because he makes you feel like the old Deja?"

"I didn't say that I want to be with him. I don't think this has anything to do with him, honestly."

Bobby agreed. "You're right. It has more to do with your sister than anything else."

"It's not about Nikki, either."

"Yeah, it is. I can't understand why, but it's obvious that you're jealous of her life."

She shrugged. "You know what? You're almost right. I'm jealous of her *happiness.*"

The look on Bobby's face was one of pure disgust and disbelief.

"You sound like a fool, Deja. What reason could you possibly have to be jealous of your sister? What? You want to be a reality show stereotype?"

"Is that what you think she is? Or is she a woman who's not afraid to be herself? She's out there living her dreams on her own terms."

"And you're jealous of that? All these years you haven't been living your dreams, too?"

Deja felt like she was talking to a wall.

"Bobby, no, I wasn't. My life sucks. You married me because I fit the part. The damsel in distress you could swoop in and save. We had a tidy little life together. But you don't even know who I am! Or what I'm really like. Because I didn't know until recently. It's like you're not hearing me."

"So, you think the grass is greener over there with Nikki and Rashid." He shook his head. "I can't believe the shit you're saying right now. You're fascinated by a drug dealer who just came home from jail. Infatuated by the nigga he used to be. A fuckin' criminal. And by your sister. An Instagram ho with thousands of followers. You sound crazy, Deja. We're not kids anymore."

She laughed. This conversation was only illuminating the ways her husband misunderstood her.

"After Rashid got locked up and I went on with my life, I wanted to get as far away from danger as I could. I wanted something guaranteed, no variables. And that's how our relationship is. You don't take risks, never break the law. You see everything in black and white, no gray areas. Safe. I didn't realize it, Bobby, but I don't even like you. The sellout with blue blood flowing through his veins that I saw out there in the field is not a man I want to be married to. And you don't want to be married to me, either. Not this version of me. So, that's enough. I want out."

Bobby's rage boiled over then.

"You're a fucking fraud, Deja. I thought I married a smart, driven, passionate woman who wanted a good life. You acted the part, too. Convinced me you were nothing like your hood-rat sister."

Deja was seething. "Watch your mouth, Bobby."

"But you're just like her. Money hungry. That's why you married me, right? Good credit score, solid family man. Safe bet. That's what you said. Had me thinking I had a wife when all I really had was a concubine."

"Fuck you!"

"Nah. Fuck YOU, Deja. With your phony ass. Go run back

to Rashid. You know he's never gonna forget that you left him? He's never gonna look at you the same. All he wanted to do was prove that he could still fuck you. That you were still his, like a piece of property. And your stupid ass fell for it."

"This is not about Rashid. That's what I keep trying to tell you."

"It was about him the other night when you showed up with him. Asking me to get you two past the crime scene to see Bree. You know how fuckin' cruel that was, Deja? To come to me with her 'new' father and ask me to help you. After you just fucked him?"

Deja couldn't look at Bobby. She fixed her gaze on a spot on the table as her eyes flooded with tears.

"You're a filthy bitch. An ungrateful, miserable bitch. All these years with you, I begged you to have a baby with me. Fifteen years, and you gave me one excuse after another. The timing wasn't right; your career was just taking off. It was never the right time. But since Rashid came back on the scene, I see you for what you are now. You never had any intention of being my wife or being a mother to *our* children. It was always about you. And it's still about you. Poor Rashid has no idea what he's in for."

Bobby shook his head, smiling sadly.

"I want a divorce," he said. "I'm filing the papers today. So, you can have your convict boyfriend back. Go run after your sister and be happy. I'll let you go. All I want is to keep a relationship with Bree. I'm still her father, no matter how hard you try to replace me."

Bobby looked at her long and hard, trying to make sense of what happened with them. They had built an amazing life together. Now that was all erased and their marriage was in pieces. He shook his head, stood, and walked out of the house.

Deja didn't try to stop him.

• • •

The police were a constant presence, as was the press now that the story had broken. It was the top headline across the borough. An elderly man's life hung in the balance—parallel to a young Black male's fate. Ivy returned home reluctantly after King's arrest. He was still in the hospital, recovering from his injuries. She had only been allowed to visit with him twice. The last time, she had sat at King's bedside while he slept.

As she'd sat there, she read the local newspaper on her cell phone, marveling at how the island had divided itself along color lines as the story broke. The Black community—and the city at large—was outraged at the shooting of an unarmed Black teenager by what was being described as a "concerned neighbor." A picture was being painted through carefully selected photographs and sweet testaments from friends and family of a frail old man who confronted a would-be thief, only to be beaten within an inch of his life. King, in contrast, had been labeled an "aggressive teen." The man's wife was giving interviews, painting Kingston as a thug who attacked her husband after he came outside to look after his own property that he thought was being burglarized. She cited her husband's record as a war veteran and called on the police to charge Kingston with attempted murder.

As Ivy scrolled to the end of the story, she did something she knew she shouldn't. Against her better judgment, she clicked on the "Comments" section of the news site. Her heart sank. She had read these kinds of vicious and evil remarks before during other sensational cases involving Black youth. But this time, they were talking about *her* baby. King was innocent. But they spoke about him as if they knew him personally, as if he were a total waste of life. Each sentence she read felt like a slap in the face.

If it was self-defense, why did he resist arrest?

These fatherless bastards should all be locked up!

They should stay over in the projects where they belong. They come over to our side of the island stealing cars and attacking people. Because there's nothing to do on the North Shore besides smoke pot, use crack, and cash their government checks.

Have you seen this "kid"? He's a seven-foot-tall athlete. And Mr. Currado was supposed to know he was sixteen? Of course he brought his gun outside to face King Kong!

They wanted to lock Kingston up and throw away the key, even though he was the one who had been attacked. King's attorney, Maury, had already warned Ivy to expect King to be formally booked when he was released from the hospital. Ivy was prepared to post bail, determined that her son would not spend a single night in jail for this. Each time Detective Cunningham and his partner, Detective Glover, stopped by, Ivy got a sinking feeling in her gut. Something told her that the walls were closing in on her son.

Detective Glover promised Ivy that he would be honest with her throughout every step of the investigation and that King would get a fair shake. Ivy wasn't sure if she believed him. It was hard to trust the same police department that had brutally beaten and arrested her son.

Ivy now sat in her favorite seat near her kitchen window, gazing out at the neighborhood. She knew they were all talking about her, discussing her sons and the case that had the whole city abuzz. She wanted to hide. Not from embarrassment, but from a deep desire to fade from the glare of public scrutiny. Her parenting was being called into question by people who knew nothing about her besides the things the press reported.

Kingston's social media posts had been picked apart by the local newspaper. Suggestions were made about possible gang affiliations, drug use, and criminal activity. Ivy just wanted it all to go away.

She did a double take as she spotted her neighbor Teresa approaching her driveway.

"Shit!" Ivy cursed. She got up and walked to the door just as Teresa rang the bell.

"Hi," Ivy said flatly as she opened the door. "I wasn't expecting company."

"So good to see you home, Ivy. I heard the news. I just wanted to come by and tell you that I'm so sorry. I know what a good mom you are and how hard you work."

Ivy nodded, wishing Teresa would go away. She didn't.

"For the record, we're not all the same around here. Some of us are actually capable of thinking for ourselves. We see that you're a hardworking mother raising her two sons and doing the best she can. What happened with Kingston was unfortunate, but I know he's not the guy they're trying to make him out to be."

Ivy waited for her to continue, listening intently for signs of bullshit.

"I moved here from Queens in 2008. My husband and I didn't fit in at first. Everybody out here knows each other. So, they were suspicious of us. We were the new family on the block just like you and your boys are now. That's why I come over all the time bringing you tea and selling you Girl Scout cookies. I'm just trying to do the things I wished the new neighbors had done for me when I first moved in here."

Ivy felt her heart soften a little, a tiny pang of guilt pulling at its strings.

"I know I'm a pain. My daughter Michaela tells me all the time to lay off. But I wanted you to know that not everybody out here is an asshole."

Teresa left out the part about how some of the neighbors were already circulating a condolence envelope complete with a sympathy card and a lot of cash for the Currado family. They were outraged that some newcomers had moved in and disrupted the peace and tranquility of their lives.

"I don't know Kingston very well. But, from what I've seen, he's just an average teenage kid. He doesn't get into any more trouble than the other kids around here. So, I don't know why everybody's acting like he's a monster all of a sudden."

"It's because we're Black," Ivy deadpanned. "So, if he has a drink or smokes some weed, then he *must* be a car thief and a monster who goes around looking for old white people to attack."

Her tone was heavy with sarcasm and pain.

"I hate to say it, but you're right." Teresa seemed genuinely sad to admit it.

"It's an old story. Nothing new," Ivy said. "My son isn't the first Black boy to be vilified. He won't be the last."

"Well, no matter what they try to say about your sons, I see them all the time. I know they're good kids, regular kids just like all the rest of the kids around here. The way I see it, your son defended himself. The rest is just a sad turn of events. You guys don't deserve all of this."

Ivy forced a smile and thanked her.

"Listen," Teresa said. "I know I get on your nerves a lot when I come over jabbering all the time." She chuckled at herself. "I can't help it. It's just the type of person I am. I just wanted to make sure you felt welcome here. Not everybody around here likes to meet new people, you know what I mean?"

Ivy nodded. She knew exactly what Teresa was saying.

"But I want you to know that I'm here if you ever need anything. I know what it's like to move to a new place and try to fit in. It can make you feel alone, isolated and all that. As long as I'm around, you should know that you have a friend in the neighborhood."

Teresa smiled. To Ivy, she seemed sincere, which surprised her.

"Having said that, I want to tell you that I hope you're not planning on selling your house and moving away for good when this is all over. That's not what you should do, if you ask me."

Ivy hadn't asked her. Still, she was surprised to hear Teresa say this.

"Why not?" she asked, intrigued.

Truth was she had already been house hunting. A few of her clients had offered her help in finding a new home in a place less resistant to change than Staten Island was.

"Because you belong here. You, your sons, and your family and friends belong here. You moved here, started a new life here, and you deserve to be happy here. You guys didn't do anything wrong. So, why should you run away and let these people have what they wanted all along? Stay and show them that you're not afraid of them. I've got your back."

Ivy saw the serious expression on her neighbor's face and knew she meant what she was saying. She smiled, and this time it was for real.

"Thank you, Teresa. You do get on my nerves sometimes," she admitted. "But I appreciate the way you've welcomed me and my sons into the neighborhood. You crossed the line in the sand and came over to offer your friendship to me. That means a lot. Not too many people around here have been very nice to us."

"I know," Teresa said. "And screw 'em! You don't owe them anything. At the end of the day, you have to do what's best for you and your boys. But just consider the option of staying. If you do, I think it'll send a powerful message to Staten Island that's been long overdue."

And with that, Teresa winked, waved, and walked back to her house across the street while Ivy watched her go.

Coco was glad to be back to the comfort and familiarity of her own bed, her own shower, and her own raw emotions. Truthfully, she wanted to be alone, but Ziggy had called and texted her so much that she had finally agreed to let him come over tonight.

Everything looked and felt different when viewed through the lens of Black versus white. She had been living in such a blissful bubble with Ziggy that she had convinced herself that racism wasn't as prevalent anymore. That ignorant Southern hillbillies and Trump supporters were the only ones they had to worry about as an interracial couple. Kingston's encounter with his neighbor out in Staten Island had shown her that nothing could be further from the truth. Racism was still very much alive and thriving in America.

She lingered in the steam of the hot shower for longer than usual, trying to wash away the ugliness of what her family was going through. To wash away the ugliness of what Coco, herself, had done.

Coco had spent the past several days deep in thought about where she and Ziggy stood. She knew for certain that Ziggy was unlike any man she had ever been with. He made her feel happy and understood, and he listened to her. But, in the wake of King's arrest and the racial divide that had resulted from it, Coco was longing for familiarity—so much so that when Derek called, she found herself answering.

Derek—the same guy who had been stringing her along as a friend with occasional benefits—had heard about what had happened to Ivy's youngest son. He'd called, concerned, knowing that Coco adored her nephews. Their conversation had been cordial and innocent at first. They'd discussed the dramatic events, the status of the case, and how Ivy was holding up. Then Derek had asked if Coco wanted company. After a moment's thought, Coco had said yes, and an hour later, she had been back in bed with the man who had broken her heart.

The sex had been good, but definitely not worth the dirty, empty feeling that lingered afterward. Nothing had changed. Derek was still expecting his first child with another woman. Still an asshole. Ten minutes after their mutual orgasm, Coco had thrown Derek out, telling him to lose her phone number. She had spent the rest of that night watching a Dave Chappelle comedy special while downing a half gallon of Breyers vanilla ice cream. She laughed until her laughter turned to tears over what she had just done, over what was happening to Kingston, over all the shit that was dragging her down.

She had been beating herself up about sleeping with Derek ever since. Choosing not to move forward with Ziggy was one thing. But going back to a loser like Derek was a whole different level of dysfunction. She knew she was better than that. She hated that she had allowed Derek back into her bed again. It wasn't lost on her that she had been ignoring a romantic, passionate, emotionally and physically available man because their races were different. Meanwhile, she had availed herself to a morally bankrupt, uncommitted, and inconsistent cheater just because he understood her Blackness. It was enough to make her question whether what happened to Kingston had sent her into a psychological tailspin.

She changed into a pair of shorts and a T-shirt before texting Ziggy, telling him that he could come over. She made herself something to eat in the meantime and listened to her favorite playlist while she got her thoughts together. She told herself that she wasn't disappointed when her doorman rang and told her that Ziggy was on his way up. Surely, it was simply fatigue. The events of the past several days had been emotionally and physically exhausting. She hoped Ziggy would understand that all she needed right now was his arms to hold her and make her believe that it would be all right.

He arrived with flowers, fruit, and wine in hand.

"I've been missing you." He said it softly but with an undeniable intensity.

Coco gave him a kiss before retreating to the kitchen to get some plates and glasses. She came back to the living room and found that he had turned on the TV and gotten comfortable on the couch. She smiled and tried not to be annoyed that he had turned off her music. She had been in the zone before he came. But she shrugged it off and took a seat beside Ziggy on the couch and sighed.

He sat up and used the corkscrew to open the wine he had brought. He looked at Coco affectionately.

"This has been tough for you, I know."

She nodded. "Yes, it has. It's even worse for Ivy. This whole situation is crazy."

She accepted the glass of wine he offered her and took a long swig. Afterward, she looked at him.

"Kingston is a good kid. He plays ball, chases girls, normal teenage shit. He was minding his business. On his way home from a date. His car broke down. And some . . . man confronted him with a gun and tried to kill him. King defended himself and now he's under arrest for that. It's hard for me to try and make sense of this shit."

She took another sip.

Ziggy sat back with his glass in hand and watched her. "You've been a great support for your family these past few days. I know you must be tired, Cara."

She nodded her eyes downcast.

Pulling her into his arms, he reclined into the crux of the sofa and cradled her.

Coco exhaled. She needed this. Being wrapped in his arms this way felt safe in a society that had gone completely insane.

"How is all of this making you feel?" Ziggy asked.

She rolled her eyes. "How do you think?" she snapped. "I'm pissed off."

She sat up and faced him. Now that he was here, she needed to be sure she wasn't wasting her time.

She reversed the question on him. "How do you feel about it? As a white guy, can you understand what this is like?"

He didn't respond right away, giving his reply some thought. Then he shook his head.

"No," he answered honestly. "As a white guy, I can probably never fully understand what this is like for you. For Ivy and her sons. I can only imagine that it must be infuriating to watch someone you love literally fighting for their life because they're Black. I imagine that Ivy must worry all the time about her kids. That you probably find yourself having second thoughts about us because I'm a white guy who may never fully understand it."

She sipped her wine. All of that was true.

"I understand," he said.

"I think that's why I never dated outside of my race before. The men in my life were always Black, so there was always the shared experience of being discriminated against. This is the first time I'm in situation where I have to question whether the man in my life can identify with how I feel as a Black woman."

"Is it?" he asked. "You felt understood by the men you were with before?"

She thought about Derek and shook her head.

"I'm talking specifically about race," she explained. "At the hospital the other day, I could tell you felt uncomfortable," she said. "So did I. The whole situation is disgusting. But when shit gets uncomfortable, can you handle it? Are you built for that?"

"Cara, I won't lie to you. I've never had to face anything like this firsthand. I've seen other cases in the news. I was outraged each time. This is the first time I've been this close to a situation like this. It's new for me. But I'm not scared to try. Knowing that we live in a world where some people are ignorant doesn't scare me off from wanting to be with you."

Coco sat back, relaxing as much as she could at the moment.

"What if we get serious and end up having kids together? Would you tell our son that he needed to humble himself and answer any white stranger who approaches him and asks where he's going and what he's doing?"

Ziggy looked wounded by her words, but she pressed on.

"What if we had a daughter and her skin was as brown as mine? And she came to you complaining that *all* the boys—even the ones who were just as dark as her or *darker* even—say that she's ugly because she's got dark skin? Huh? How would you handle that?"

Ziggy could sense her agitation. It was clear to him that Coco was experiencing a wide range of emotions and was having a hard time processing everything that had happened recently.

"I know it won't be easy," he said. "If we get serious, wind up getting married and having kids . . . the reality is those kids will be just like Ivy's kids. And each time they step outside, we'll worry about them. There will be people like Ivy's neighbors and her sister-in-law Patsy who hate to see an interracial couple together. But none of that deters me. I like you, Cara. I like the way I feel when I'm with you. And I want to keep moving forward with you. One step at a time."

She leaned over and kissed him then, softly on his lips. She smiled at him after.

"Thank you," she said. "I needed to hear that. Keep being patient with me."

She got cozy in his arms again. He kissed her sweetly on her forehead as she drifted off to sleep.

"I will," he whispered.

Raindrops

A heavy rain began to fall as James and Ivy arrived back at her house after a very long day. Ivy had gone to visit King in the hospital. He was making a good recovery, and his doctors were optimistic that he would be released by the end of the week. Kingston's attorney had requested a bail hearing and managed to ensure that he would be out on bond until his case went to trial. All he had to do was stay out of trouble in the meantime. Ivy planned to make sure he did exactly that.

Things were looking up on all fronts. Even the man who had shot her son was expected to make a full recovery. The Currado family continued to vilify Kingston publicly, but Ivy was doing her best to ignore them. What mattered was that she and her sons were okay. Noah had returned to work and the whole family was under the guidance of a counselor. Things were starting to return to some semblance of normalcy for the first time in days.

After her brief visit with Kingston at the hospital, James had picked Ivy up and whisked her away to his brother's house for some good food and company. Noah was staying at his aunt Patsy's for the night, and Ivy had the house to herself.

They stepped into her foyer and dropped their wet things on the floor. Ivy reached to turn on the light switch, but James caught her hand in midair.

He looked down at her. "I was thinking about what your neighbor said to you the other day. That you should stay here instead of moving somewhere else."

She nodded, enjoying the way her hand felt in his.

"I think she's right. If I had my way, you would stick around."

Ivy looked at him, smiling. "Oh, yeah?"

"Yeah," he said, nodding. "That way you can be close to me any time I need to see you."

She raised an eyebrow. "*Need* to see me, huh?"

"That's what I said."

Their faces were inches apart, and James went for it. He kissed her, slowly and sweetly, there in the darkness of her home. Rain battered the windows as they kissed, both holding on for dear life.

Ivy wasn't sure when it happened. Lost in his kiss, she didn't notice how they got to the living room, or when their clothes came off and they sank to the floor with the raindrops playing a sensual melody in the background. She came to her senses when their skin made contact with each other and a moan escaped her lips. James was on top of her, inside of her, and Ivy was clinging to him and calling his name. He made love to every inch of her, consuming her with a passion he had kept hidden until now. They lay together afterward, breathless and entwined on her living room rug.

After a few moments, James broke the silence.

"Staten Island isn't like the other parts of the city. The racism is even worse here. Eric Garner got killed out here. The white people in this borough supported the cop who killed him. They raised money for him, held rallies for him, wrote letters. They hung blue ribbons on the trees in front of their houses to support the police. They don't care when they kill us. But if we kill one of them—even in self-defense—it's a different story."

Ivy shook her head. "If I had known it was like this out here, I never would have moved here."

He shrugged. "Then you wouldn't have met me."

She looked at him. When their eyes met, he smiled. She did, too, nodding slowly.

"Okay. That's true."

"Maybe you moved out here so that things would change," James said. "People out here are stuck in a time capsule. They want to keep things the old, familiar way they used to be. Black people over there. Whites over here. And when a few of us did move over here, they weren't like you. Powerfully Black. Real Black. Seeing you and your sons was a wake-up call for your neighbors over there on the South Shore. It's a new day, and they gotta get used to a new normal."

She smiled. Talking to James reassured her.

"Your sons are lucky that they have you to talk to," she said. "Somebody who understands what they're dealing with."

He nodded. "You can talk to me, too, you know? I'm versatile like that."

She smiled wider. "Thank you so much. Seriously. For everything. For driving me to my son's bedside when I got the call. For showing up with food and a shoulder to cry on every time I turned around."

He laughed.

"No, seriously," she repeated. "Thank you."

He sighed. "You don't have to thank me. I like you. You have a tough outer layer, but I can tell you have a heart of gold."

Ivy blushed a little.

"You're a great mother. A good friend. A real woman. And your sons are great, too. They want to see you happy. You deserve that. And you should be able to live your life wherever you see fit. I hate that this shit happened to y'all. I'm only doing what I can to make it a little easier on you. That's all."

She could feel herself falling for him. And she didn't fight it.

"You have made it easier," she said softly. "I know I haven't been easy to get to know, especially under these circumstances. But you keep hanging in there. I need that right now, James. I appreciate you being in my corner."

He leaned in and kissed her tenderly. He gazed into her eyes afterward. "If you stay, you won't be facing all these people by yourself. I'll be with you. We can take it slow. I know you have your sons to think about, and that you've been doing everything yourself for years. But you don't gotta be by yourself anymore."

Ivy touched his face, her mind made up for sure now. "I ain't going nowhere."

Hours later, Kingston's lawyer, Maury, called with the bombshell.

"Are you sitting down?"

Ivy clutched the phone in a vise grip as she slumped on her sofa.

"Yes," she muttered.

She waited expectantly, listening to Kingston's lawyer on speakerphone. She glanced at James, hopeful.

"I got good news," Maury said. "The DA's office called to tell me that they decided to drop the charges against Kingston!"

Ivy and James both cheered. Ivy raised her arms in the air victoriously, jumped off the sofa, and paced the room. With her eyes cast skyward, she thanked God for the news.

"Surveillance cameras from the neighboring homes showed the real story. Kingston and Bree were telling the truth. Vincent Currado was the aggressor and it was a clear case of self-defense.

Kingston didn't see the gun because Currado had it tucked behind his back when he first approached him. Currado said something to your son. Then Currado fired a shot. That's all that I know so far. I haven't seen what happened with Kingston and Currado after that. But the part I have seen already puts holes in Mrs. Currado's 'eyewitness' claim that her husband fired in self-defense."

Ivy was elated.

"I'm still waiting to see all of the evidence in discovery. From what I'm told, it could show proof of police misconduct. Kingston had clearly dropped the weapon and backed away from it *before* the officers attacked him. If the video shows that, Kingston will have a very strong case against the NYPD."

"Oh my God. Maury, thank you!" Ivy cried tears of joy as a wave of relief washed over her. "Thank you so much."

"It's my pleasure, Ivy. Now, listen. The Currado family is probably not going to go away quietly. I'm sure they plan on continuing to slander your family in the press. Just be prepared for that. But the worst is over. Kingston is a free young man."

James hugged Ivy, squeezing her tightly. It felt good to hear some positive news for once.

Ivy called her friends and family one by one to deliver the good news. Kingston would be a free man when he was released from the hospital. The nightmare was over.

Days later, on the steps of Staten Island's borough hall, Ivy and her sons stood behind Roy Freeman, a representative from the National Action Network, as he gave an impassioned speech about the evils of brutality against young Black men in America. He was speaking so vehemently that beads of sweat flew off him as he gestured wildly at the lectern as if delivering the most important speech of his career.

King and Noah watched him, rapt, while the crowd cheered loudly, applauding Roy's words and echoing his indignation. It was a large crowd, filled with people who were collectively outraged by Kingston's arrest and the police department's overall handling of the case so far. Roy Freeman and his network had organized this rally, busing in supporters from other boroughs and from out of town. James had been instrumental, too, using his connections in the Stapleton area to bring Staten Island's Black community out en masse.

Now that video of the incident had made its rounds on the news and online, anger had spread across the city like a wave, sparking a mass student walkout on this last day of classes. Those students mingled now in the dense crowd at their feet.

Ivy had watched the surveillance video with tears in her eyes. It showed Kingston circling his car, visibly frustrated, then the man in the dark approaching Kingston as he was walking away. She watched their exchange, wishing there was clearer audio of what was being said between them. Unfortunately, the audio was of poor quality. For Ivy, it was enough. Proof that Kingston had visibly reacted to something the man said to him and had taken a fateful step forward that nearly cost him his life. He had not charged. And despite Currado's claims to the contrary, the gun had not been visible during their entire encounter. Instead, it was clear to Ivy that her son had encountered a bold racist who was confronting him with a verbal attack while tucking a concealed weapon behind his back. Kingston had no idea of the danger he had been in. The thought of that still sent chills up her spine.

Finally, Roy concluded his remarks, turned to Kingston, and pulled him closer to the lectern. Roy turned to the microphone and spoke again, his voice steadier now.

"I want you to hear from Kingston Donovan himself. The

media tried to portray him as a thug, a gangbanger, and a menace. But the video that came out recently tells a very different story. It shows a boy who was racially profiled, attacked verbally and physically, and who fought to defend himself."

The crowd cheered wildly. Roy turned to King and stepped back from the lectern, gesturing for him to step forward. Kingston reluctantly did so, waiting for the applause to die down and praying that the jitters in his gut would go away. His lawyer and his mom had helped him put together a speech for this occasion, and his hands trembled slightly as he gripped it now.

He stood for moments that seemed to go on forever before he finally found his voice and spoke into the microphone as the crowd grew silent.

"I've heard a lot of things on the news over the past few days about who I'm supposed to be. I'm not a thief. I don't belong to any gangs. I go to school and play basketball. I hang out with my friends. That's what I was doing on the night of June ninth. I was out with my friends having fun, watching a movie. I had a curfew, and I was trying to beat my mother home so that I wouldn't get in trouble."

He heard a few snickers from the crowd, which helped him relax a little. He settled into his speech and started making eye contact with some people in the audience.

"My car broke down and I was racially profiled when I got out of the car to try and figure out the problem. I was upset, like anybody else would be if their car broke down on their way home. I was approached by Vincent Currado, who racially profiled me. He called me a nigger and asked what I was doing around there. He accused me of trying to steal a car. He pulled a gun on me, and he pulled the trigger. I realized that I was shot, and I blacked out at that moment. All I knew was that I had to defend myself."

Some people in the crowd shouted words of encouragement. He took a breath and kept going.

"I didn't go out to hurt that man. I didn't want to have any problem with him at all that night. All I was trying to do was get home. I heard that man call me a nigger. I saw the gun, heard the shot go off, felt the bullet, and I realized that I had to fight for my life. So, that's what I did.

"When the police came, they attacked me without listening to me while I tried to explain what happened. My friend Bree was there, and she begged them to stop, but they ignored her. They weren't interested in hearing our side of the story. They beat me, Tased me, cracked my ribs, busted my lip open, and put me in the hospital. I'm grateful that they didn't kill me."

King thought about that last sentence as he read it, realizing the weight of those words. He hadn't truly realized how closely he had danced with death twice that night. He took a deep breath and looked out at the crowd full of young Black and brown faces just like his own.

"I fought back. I got the gun away from him and I fought for my life. And I won."

The crowd cheered.

"Finally!" someone yelled out.

Many of those who stood cheering shared the sentiment. *Finally* someone Black had fought back and won. At last, there was no grieving Black mother. Instead, Ivy stood proudly and watched as King found his voice.

"And I'm gonna keep fighting," King said. "For justice against the NYPD."

He stepped away from the lectern to applause. Ivy hugged her son, smiling. She had never been prouder of him.

Can I Live

Michael walked into the booth in the visiting room at the new facility and sat down. No hugs or kisses, no hand-holding this time. He was in solitary confinement now and subjected to a booth visit. Plexiglass separated them, and they had to communicate by phone. He picked up the receiver and just stared at Ivy for a while.

"I thought you weren't coming back here," he finally said.

"I wasn't," she said. "After you walked out and left me sitting there last time, I swore I wasn't coming back. But a lot has happened since then. I felt like we needed to talk about it in person."

Her drive here today had been a reflective one. Ivy had left home in the early morning while it was still dark outside, climbed into her car, and made the five-hour journey up north. During the long drive alone, she had done a lot of thinking. Now she had her thoughts all lined up and knew what she wanted to say.

"How's King?" he asked.

"He's doing a lot better. Physically and mentally. School is out, so he's enjoying the start of the summer. Him and Bree have been spending a lot of time together."

"So have you and J-Roc," Mikey said.

Ivy stared back at him. She wasn't surprised anymore by the things Michael knew about her. Even in jail, Michael had a lot of friends who kept an eye on things for him. She shook her head and looked away.

"Noah was here a week ago with Patsy and her boys. Seems like the only visits I get these days are from Patsy and Noah. You and Coco done forgot about a nigga."

Ivy glared at him. "I had a lot going on these past few months, Mikey. In case you haven't noticed."

He shook his head. "None of that shit would have happened if you stayed in Brooklyn."

"That wasn't an option."

"Why not?" Michael really wanted to understand what had caused Ivy to disrupt their lives the way she had.

She looked at him.

"You spend so much time feeling sorry for yourself and looking at your own situation that I wonder if you ever put yourself in my shoes, Mikey. The day you got sentenced, I lost my soulmate. Lost my partner. Now I was a single mother raising two sons in the heart of Brooklyn. I felt like giving up. But somehow, I managed to keep coming up here to see you, keep Noah and King from going off track, keep everything afloat on my own. Eventually, I got a rhythm going and it worked for a while. My career was taking off, the boys were growing up, you had everything you needed in here. Then I looked around and realized that while I was flying around the country doing hair, Noah and King were still two Black boys growing up in

Brooklyn. When I was out of town, they stayed with Patsy. And I love your sister and your nephews, but that's not the life I want for Noah and King."

Michael didn't disagree. Patsy was more of a friend and peer to her kids than she was a parent.

"The neighborhood started changing. Gangs everywhere. Noah and King are in that age group. I was losing sleep. Buying that house on Staten Island felt like the Promised Land to me. Suburbs. Tree-lined streets. White picket fences. I thought it was the perfect move for us."

She shook her head at how naive she had been.

"But this whole situation with King has taught me a hard lesson. You can run as far away from Brooklyn as you want. Use your talents, move to the suburbs, get that white picket fence and all of that. And they will still try to gun you down in the street if they think you don't belong there. You can put a basketball in your kid's hand or a computer. They will still pump bullets into them, and call it justified."

Ivy felt defeated in so many ways.

"I used to warn them about how to handle themselves when they deal with the cops. Keep your hands where they can see them. Don't talk back. Don't make any sudden moves. I taught them that. But no matter where we go or how they behave, they're Black men. And that makes them a target. All I was trying to do was give them—and myself—a better life. A real chance to not become a statistic."

"Like me?"

Michael had listened to everything she said and it all boiled down to this. He sighed.

"I spoke to Rashid the other day," he said. "I called him, and we talked about a lot of shit. He was telling me about being home and getting back in touch with Deja and his daughter. He told me that he had a lot of hate in his heart for Deja over the years. The way she left him was fucked up and he had a right to be mad. But he said that when he came home and saw how it is now, how life went on without us . . . it changed his mind."

Ivy was all ears.

"When you come in here, everything about your life stops on that day you go to jail. At least that's how it feels to you. Everybody out there keeps moving, but we're still stuck at who we were on the day we came to jail. When we think about the world outside of here, we picture it the way it was when we left. But Rashid said that he didn't realize how it must have been for Deja. For you. Sixteen years ago, y'all had to figure it out on your own. He said he realized that there's no right or wrong way to do that. Deja chose to cut him off and make a family for her daughter somewhere else. You chose to stick around with me, and I don't think I ever really thought about how unselfish that was."

Ivy hadn't realized how long she had been waiting for Michael to notice her sacrifices. Hearing him now brought forth a flood of tears.

"In here, you can't be afraid. Everybody is, but nobody admits it. Even me. As big and bad as I am, when I heard the judge give me that sentence, I got scared. *Fifteen years,* Ivy. The only way I could face it was knowing that I had you and that you had my back, and my sons would still know me."

Michael was trying not to cry himself. He felt emotional saying all of this out loud for the very first time. He sniffed and continued.

"I was hard on you. Demanding. Visits every other week, phone calls constantly, letters, packages, money on my books. That was a lot for me to expect from you. When I talked to Rashid, he told me that he got three visits a year for fifteen years. And the only person who came to see him was his mother. And here I am having a fit because my biweekly visits from you were slowing down. Meanwhile, I'm getting visits from my sisters, my niggas." He shook his head in shame. "I put too much on you."

She nodded. He had.

"But I let you," she said. "I wanted to help you carry the burden because I love you. And I knew that you were out there doing what you were doing for us. To give us a good life. And you did, Mikey. You took care of us. All of us. I wanted to repay you for that. Show you that I appreciated your love. I came up here every two weeks with pride to be your wife. I'm still proud of you."

He felt that in his heart and smiled. "Rashid told me that he talked to this guy James. He said that from what he can tell, James seems like a good man. He seems to really care about you."

Michael's smile was gone now. The thought of Ivy with another man still made him want to self-destruct. The idea of a man around his sons playing stepdad sent him into a rage. But he looked at Ivy and tried his best to do the noble thing.

"Rashid said that he found a way to forgive Deja for what she did. He said he can sympathize with her even if he doesn't agree with what she did. I think I should be able to do that, too. Especially since you didn't run like she did. You've been here with me all these years. And when you got tired, you didn't hide like a coward. You came and told me. I just wasn't man enough to hear you. But I hear you now. I understand. If you like this guy, you have my blessing."

Ivy wiped her tears away. "I'll always love you, Mikey. No matter what."

He looked at her, his broken heart and wounded pride tormenting him inside. But he plastered on a smile and nodded.

"I know."

• • •

Weeks went by and the first weekend in August was upon them. Ivy was back at her hair salon, back to the everyday routines that had been in place before her life had turned on its ear.

Coco and Deja showed up unexpectedly after she finished one of the few clients she had booked for the day. It was a Friday afternoon, and the shop was packed. But Ivy had scaled back her personal appointment schedule to accommodate just a few VIPs this week. She didn't want to overexert herself, aware of the fact that she was still easing back into some sense of normalcy in her life. She hadn't booked any clients on the West Coast over the past few weeks, still cautious about leaving her sons alone in Staten Island for any length of time.

So, when Coco and Deja arrived with wine bottles in hand and told her to pack her shit up for the rest of the afternoon, it made her smile. It was a welcome surprise as she went about the task of getting back to life.

"We're going on a picnic, bitch. Just the three of us." Coco smiled triumphantly.

"Nikki flew back to LA yesterday," Deja explained. "Filming the new season of 'Sex & Hip-Hop.' Otherwise, she would be here, too."

"Okay . . . wow . . . A picnic?" Ivy asked, frowning. She looked outside at the lovely weather and tried to recall the last time she had been on a picnic.

"Yes," Deja said excitedly. "It was my idea. We'll go to Coney Island, grab some towels, lay out there, and talk."

Coco held up the bags full of wine she was carrying. "And drink!"

Ivy laughed. She was tempted to protest but knew it would be pointless. Her assistant and all the stylists in the salon formed a chorus of encouragement, telling her how cool it sounded and urging her to go. She narrowed her eyes at all of them and pretended to be annoyed.

"Y'all just want me to get out of here for the rest of the day," she teased. But she knew it wasn't true. She looked at Coco. "What kind of wine?"

Coco laughed. "All your favorites! Let's go!"

Twenty minutes later, they were at their destination. They spread their towels out and put on their sunglasses. While Deja slathered on sunscreen, Coco uncorked wine bottles and handed each lady a gift.

"What are these?" Ivy asked, staring at the odd contraption. "It looks like a wineglass trapped inside a plastic bottle."

Coco smiled. "It's a wine sippy cup," she said. "We won't get arrested out here as long as we drink out of these." She clinked her cup against Ivy's. "Cheers!"

Deja laughed, checking hers out. "Thanks!"

"Only you," Ivy said, laughing. "Classy and ratchet at the same time."

They got comfortable and settled in for an afternoon of sun and relaxation.

"How are things with Ziggy?" Ivy asked.

"Things are good," Coco said. "We just booked a trip to Jamaica for two weeks. That's a big step for me. I've never been on vacation with a man before. Let alone a white man. I wanna see what he looks like with a tan."

Deja laughed.

"Nikki keeps predicting that y'all are gonna get married. She said she already started planning the wedding and she swears she's gonna be the maid of honor." She put her sunglasses on and sat back in her beach chair. "I told her that the church would get struck by lightning the second her foot hit the aisle."

Coco laughed. "You better leave my girl Nikki alone."

Deja laughed, too. Things between the sisters had gotten much better. Now that Bobby was out of the picture and Deja was reacquainting herself with the woman she truly was, they were finally beginning to like each other.

"Ivy, what's going on with you and James?" Coco asked, grinning. "Every time I call you lately, you're over at his place. Y'all getting serious?"

Ivy smiled at the mention of his name. James was everything she had been missing in her life.

"I like him a lot," she said. "He's a good man."

She thought about everything she had been through lately and how he had been there for her every step of the way.

"I didn't realize how much I missed being with a man. Feeling his hand on my waist, being kissed, him holding my hand. It feels like some schoolgirl shit."

Deja smiled. "That's good. Maybe saving yourself all these years helps you appreciate how good it feels to be with someone again."

"Have the boys changed their minds about him?" Coco asked.

Ivy nodded. "Now that their father gave them permission, they're starting to open up to the idea. He comes by the house sometimes and they'll talk to him about sports. He'll bring food over from his brother's house and he'll sit down and eat with us. Baby steps."

"That's wonderful, Ivy," Deja said. "I'm happy for you."

"I'm happy for you, too. You have a whole new lease on life lately."

Deja laughed.

"I do," she acknowledged. "I feel like a whole new me. I've been spending more time one-on-one with Bree, listening to her more. We've gotten a lot closer since King's incident. I think she's finally started to trust me and now she talks to me all the time about her feelings and what's going on with her in school." Deja's face lit up as she spoke about her stronger bond with her daughter. It was the thing she was happiest about lately.

"What about Rashid?" Coco asked. "You still spreadin' it wide for him?"

Ivy laughed so hard she nearly spat out her wine.

"You're a fool," she said to Coco.

"Seriously," Deja agreed, giggling. "And *yes*!" she answered. "Every chance I get."

The three friends laughed.

"But it's just sex. Rashid will never let me anywhere close to his heart again, and I deserve that."

"What about you and Bobby?" Ivy asked. "Are you guys talking, at least?"

Deja nodded. "Barely, but we're able to have a conversation now without it turning into an argument. It was rough for a while. Both of us had a lot of anger toward each other. He was mad at me for what happened with Rashid, mad that Bree's father was replacing him in her life. I was mad that he'd abandoned us when Bree and King got in trouble. We could have really used his support then. But he let his feelings get in the way. So, both of us had a lot to get over. Now we're at a place where we're starting to let shit go. For Bree's sake."

"Good," Coco said. "I think it's dope for Bree to have two dads. Whether you and Bobby are together or not, he was still her father for sixteen years. If it's possible, y'all should do everything you can to make it work."

"Right!" Ivy agreed.

Deja sipped from her cup.

"How about you and Nikki?" Ivy asked. "You two seem like best friends lately. I see you doing a lot more traveling with her and you two are out at parties together. I never thought I would see the day!"

"Yes, we're getting along much better now. I realize that I was the problem. I was being a bitch because I wasn't happy. Now we're good. My mother is thrilled."

"What's up with you and Bree wearing your hair natural now?" Ivy smiled. "While I was on set last week, Tee Tee told me that you brought Bree in to get a twist-out. I love it!"

Deja beamed with pride and patted her head full of curls proudly.

"I love it, too. I just had an epiphany one morning. I run one of the top Black real estate firms in the country; having a dialogue with my child about her Blackness being beautiful, and meanwhile, I was coming in every week—sometimes twice a week—to get my hair as straight as possible; that's hypocrisy at its best."

Ivy thought about that and nodded. Jokingly she said, "Well, let's hope all of my clients don't have that epiphany. I make a whole lot of money doing relaxers, wigs, and weaves."

Deja and Coco laughed.

"Anyway, once I decided to go natural, Bree followed suit. We started going to therapy together, just to help Bree process everything that happened and to sort through some of our own problems as Black women. It's been really helpful."

"That's cool," Coco said, smiling. She was liking this "new" Deja, too.

"After what happened with King, I started to get scared off from Ziggy. The whole situation made me wonder if I could be with a white man for real. Like . . . could we be happy together while being so different? I thought about breaking up with him, honestly. I thought it would be smarter to get out now before I get my feelings in it. But we had a conversation about race, and his answers to a lot of things surprised me. In a good way. Since then, we talk about it all the time. And we're honest. Sometimes, the conversations get heated. We both have strong opinions. But when it gets too intense, we step back and remind each other that it's all superficial. Skin color is just a shell casing."

Deja giggled at that.

"My mother would love to hear you say that. When we talk about my father, she always reminds me that he was the love of her life, even though they had nothing in common as far as their background. He had grown up wealthy and white and she grew up in the projects and Black. But love is love."

She looked at Ivy.

"I know that what happened with King is horrible. But just be careful not to paint all the white people in Staten Island with the same brush. There's a race problem out there. That's a fact. But there are some good people out there, too."

Ivy nodded. "Okay, Iyanla, I see you've been doing your work."

Coco and Deja laughed.

They continued to sit sipping wine and catching up on each other's lives until the sun started going down. As they left the beach with all their belongings, Ivy stopped them.

"I love y'all," she said. "I know we don't say it all the time. Not until something terrible happens. But now, I'm gonna start saying it more."

Coco was grateful for her sunglasses as her eyes welled up with tears.

"I love you, too," Deja said, gripping her friends' hands. "Y'all are my family. The only family I've got, really. So, you're special to me. Just know that."

Ivy looked out at the ocean and smiled. "When King was in

the hospital, do you remember that conversation we had in the waiting room about being Black women in America and how hard it is?"

Coco and Deja nodded.

"Ever since then, I've been realizing how strong we are. How resilient. How fuckin' fabulous we are! And I know this much. We can survive anything. As long as we have each other."

The three friends embraced against the backdrop of the sun setting over Brooklyn.

Acknowledgments

Monique Patterson, I can never thank you enough. You push me to the limit in the best possible way, never accepting less than my best. Working with you is an honor and a privilege. You are awesome!

Sara Camilli, the Literary Lioness, thank you so much for your patience, your tenacity, and your guidance. Your confidence in me gives me wings. Thank you from the bottom of my heart.

My children, Ashley, Quaviel, and Justin, thank you for putting up with endless conversations about my story lines and characters. You are my heartbeats.

Leah Llano, you are a beautiful person inside and out. Your spirit is loving and your heart is golden. Working with you is a joy, and I am grateful for all that you do to keep me on track. Your future is so bright that I'm blinded by the light.

Ashley Williams

TRACY BROWN is the *Essence* bestselling author of *Boss, White Lines III: All Falls Down, White Lines II: Sunny, Aftermath, Snapped, Twisted, White Lines, Criminal Minded, Black: A Street Tale,* and *Dime Piece*. She lives in Staten Island, New York.